Gitane Marie

*Through the Eye of the Black
Madonna*

Linda Oxley Milligan

Library of Congress Control Number: 2018904494

Beak Star Books, Powell, OH

ISBN: 1-944724-01-X

Beak Star Books
Powell, Ohio 43065
www.beakstarbooks.com
Cover Design by Andy Bennett
www.B3NN3TT.com

To Christabel

Chapter 1

Dream

Barry Short's eyes opened to his own reflection in the window glass of the train compartment he was riding in. He looked drawn, slightly older than the face he had seen that morning in the mirror in his dwelling in France. "Coffee, that'll pick me up," he muttered almost inaudibly.

The trip had been made long by the circuitous route he had chosen, flying from Paris to Athens and on to Alexandria to avoid the airport in Cairo where he most certainly would have been seen. He would take the train south into Upper Egypt from Alexandria he had thought. "No such luck," the ticket agent said in his best colloquial English. "All trains lead to Cairo."

"What did I expect?" he muttered to his own image in the mirrored glass. He passed his hand across his forehead as if its touch would magically remove the creases time and sun had etched into his brow. He longed for a soft bed. His eyes closed. His head bounced rhythmically against the train compartment window until a hard vibration pummeled him back into wide-eyed consciousness, revealing a pair of startled blue orbs set in a handsome face that in November retained its summer tan.

His eyelids dropped, their weight having won the battle long enough for him to be overtaken by the beginning of a dream. A figure appeared, the sight of which jolted him back into wakefulness. It was a golden statue of a man with the head of an Ibis, the ancient Egyptian god Thoth. Try as he might, he couldn't shake the image. He tried to force himself to keep awake, but his lids dropped as if they were lead. The statue began to say something he was not sure he wanted to hear.

It was the likeness of the very statue he had returned to its dark hiding place eight months earlier after he had learned it was the key to the tomb of the ancient priest and architect of the first pyramids, Imhotep. Thousands of years ago Imhotep had taken his secrets with him into his tomb, secrets that the wise architect believed might doom humanity if they fell into the wrong hands. Barry, also a wise man if not as learned, likewise knew the world to be full of fools and knaves and determined those secrets along with the statue must remain concealed. He thought he had put it all to rest when he returned Thoth to his hiding place, yet the statue was speaking to him now for reasons he could not fathom. A student of dreams, Barry knew the only way to silence him was to listen. So he fell back into sleep and allowed the dream to run its course.

Thoth reappeared, glimmering as he sat undisturbed in his dark burial place in a shaft of a seldom-noticed alcove submerged below the Great Pyramid of Giza. The statue seemed to move forward out of the shaft or perhaps Barry's dreaming mind moved inward. It was hard to discern, even for him. Thoth grew larger until its navel widened, drawing Barry's mind into a black pit that lightened to gray as he wandered forward into the cave opening. He could make out an image of a woman in that twilight, all dark and smooth as if she were carved from fine black basalt. Her head was adorned with a crown, more disc than crown, he observed. He saw she held a child as he drew nearer, but this was no ordinary child. Like Thoth, its head was that of a bird. The bird child lifted itself out of its mother's arms and flew into her eye, which opened wide and emitted an intense white light. Barry saw the child disappear, and then he saw the figure of a man follow it. As his mind drew nearer, he could see that the man was himself. With that recognition he was transported through the whiteness of the eye into a field of white, bell-shaped flowers. He recognized their scent just as the train screeched to a halt jolting him out of his sleep. He awoke, thinking, *Lilium candidum*, the Madonna lily. Before he left his seat to enter the Cairo train station, he pulled his journal from his backpack and wrote down the details of the dream lest he forget.

The scent was still with him when he stepped off the train into the new morning light. He roused himself with an energetic stretch as the sun poured over him as if to cleanse and refresh. He needed coffee, he thought. He also needed not to be seen.

Chapter 2

Cairo

Barry feared that if he were to be recognized, he ran the risk of ending up like Hans Bueller or worse. A club on the head had forced old Bueller into an unexpected retirement some months back, putting him in the monastery where Barry was now headed. To avoid such an outcome, he had taken certain precautions to minimize the risk. He had chosen a circuitous route; and before he left France, he had phoned a friend, a Washington, D.C. investigator interested in the smuggling trade in and around Egypt. "If I go missing," he had said to Stuart, "you know where to look."

He checked the departure time and track number for the train to Aswan before he entered the station. It wouldn't leave for sixty minutes. He spotted a few inconspicuous benches to the rear of a large waiting area. Head down, he bought a cup of coffee and a copy of the *Cairo Tribune*, passed the seated crowd, and sat down on one of the back benches with the paper propped up and opened wide. He attempted to occupy his mind with scant news stories of important meetings and trade agreements, but he couldn't stop thinking about the letter.

Bueller had sent it to Barry's bungalow situated on a half acre near the Olentangy River in Delaware County, Ohio, inconveniently located halfway between Chicago, where Barry's institute is located, and Meadowcroft Rockshelter, primary site of his new archeological research. It could have lain in his mailbox for up to two weeks. Paul, Barry's informally adopted eleven year old nephew, found it on one of his visits to Barry's house to collect mostly junk mail and remove any advertising flyers strewn around the front door. The boy conscientiously forwarded the letter to Barry; but since the time Hans Bueller mailed it from his monastic retreat near the Red Sea, its arrival in Barry's small town mailbox, and subsequent forwarding to France, two months had lapsed. Unable to phone Bueller at the monastery to explain his tardiness, Barry

3

was eager to get there since he knew that Hans would not have summoned him if it were not important.

He recalled Bueller's image the last time he had seen him. He lay wounded in a bed at the Old Cataract Hotel in Aswan with his physician, Doctor Shabaka standing nearby. "Omar Shabaka! Why didn't I think to call him?" he said, slapping his hand hard on his knee. He knew why. For the same reason he had not double-checked the train routing that had unexpectedly taken him to Cairo. This trip was too hastily planned. Would the monastery be that far south, he wondered as he reconsidered his destination?

He tossed the paper down on the bench, returned to the vendor to buy a long distance phone card before being directed to a public phone near the street entrance to the train station. He was determined to talk to Omar Shabaka before he boarded. It was perhaps this single minded purpose coupled with his exhaustion that might have explained his recklessness, for he made no effort to conceal his face as he walked through the most crowded part of the train station toward the public phone.

In his past life Barry had been a well-known figure in the Cairo archeological community. He had the rare capacity to see both sides of most situations in a contentious field, thus often found himself cast into the role of intermediary between Egyptian, American, and European archeologists; between traditionalist researchers and cutting edge pioneers; between treasure hunters and true archeologists. He knew them all. He was so remarkably good at the nearly impossible task of arbitration that he had become very well liked, his personality having made a greater mark on the progress of Egyptology than his research, which he suddenly, and from the point of view of his colleagues, rather inexplicably cut short about eight months earlier when he bulldozed his dig sites, sold his jeep, and left the country.

He had told them he had accepted an assignment that would take him back to the States, that he was homesick. No one believed him for a moment. His colleagues knew that if anyone was born for Egypt it was Barry Short. If they had not known him so well, they would have been inclined to credit the rumors that claimed he left the country taking with him an ancient artifact of great consequence. His closest associates

4

denounced the rumor, proclaiming the obvious truth that Dr. Barry Short was no smuggler. But even his staunchest supporters couldn't entirely quell the speculation, particularly since it was known that shortly before his departure he had been seen associating with Hans Bueller, who had an unsavory reputation regarding the handling of Egyptian archeological treasure. Dr. Bueller was the only Egyptologist besides Barry to know the truth of the matter. Given his reputation, had he declared that truth no one would have believed him. The plain fact is that Hans Bueller had and still has a credibility problem.

Bueller had come into possession of an ancient artifact that had a bit of magic to it. Beyond its beauty, antiquity, and value in gold, it was also the key to unlock the sought after tomb of the great Imhotep, a tomb that both Bueller and Barry believed must remain forever concealed from smugglers and scholars alike in a world not wise enough for its momentous contents. Bueller hadn't always been of that opinion. When he stole the artifact he was not so wise himself and was fully prepared to exploit the object for all that it was worth, but possession of the golden statue had changed him from the fool that he had been into an almost virtuous man.

Few believe in that kind of magic, and no one except those who were directly involved in the event would have imagined it possible for Hans Bueller to have undergone such a transformation. He did though, and when it happened he sought the help of a man he knew he could trust to do the right thing. Barry's brief involvement had condemned him to become the target of unsavory artifact thieves, the very people who had first spun the rumors about him.

"Omar," Barry said into the phone, entirely unaware of the set of eyes that rested upon him as if their bearer were taking notes. "Yes, it's me. I'm in Egypt at the train station in Cairo. I've come to see Hans. Look, I've bought a ticket to Aswan, but I was not sure—Oh, I just assumed— Right! I should get off in Luxor and you will drive me. Thank you, thank you very much."

Chapter 3

Insurance

Natalie ordered a glass of Pinot Grigio as she sat waiting in a velvet booth at the Old Ebbitt Grill for Stuart who as usual was late. In spite of a stuffed Walrus head hanging on the wall, this long established restaurant is as romantic as it gets in notoriously unromantic Washington, D.C. Perhaps it is the gas lamps that soften the mood, she thought. She knew why Stuart was happy to adopt this place once she suggested that it might make a good end of the week haunt. The regularity of their dinners there had relieved him of the ceremony of asking her out on dates and relieved her of the anxiety of waiting for his call. Their meetings were more like quasi-dates, a kind of Friday after work ritual, which this thirty-year-old bachelorette and thirty-five year old bachelor found less committal.

She observed the host pointing Stuart to her booth. He pulled off his suit jacket and tie as he walked over and tossed them unceremoniously into a rumpled heap at the back of the booth and slid in next to them. Before saying a word, he caught the waiter's attention and pointed to Natalie's glass of Pinot Grigio.

She studied his appearance for those few seconds. His looks were in sharp contrast with the formality of the restaurant's patrons: the lobbyists, politicians, and political aides, who like Natalie sat comfortably in dark suits and white shirts that had become the fashion in an ever more stately D.C. Stuart's longer than respectable blonde hair looked like he had just come in from sailing, which of course he had not. It was clear by his looks that it was an effort of will for him to fit into the beltway culture. Natalie, on the other hand, was made to wear suits, silk blouses, and pearls. Yet she was not offended by his appearance. In spite of his fashion failings, he was the most handsome man in the room.

They rarely talked about work, politics, or the local gossip that passed for news in Washington. Instead they talked about films they had seen or would like to see. Often they would recount their adventure in Egypt last February when the two of them coincidentally met in Cairo and Stuart subsequently joined Natalie and her family on their cruise down the Nile. And they always talked about her family, who Stuart had gotten to know quite well on that trip. Tonight was no exception. Just before leaving work she had gotten a disturbing phone call from her mother that she recounted in the hope that he could relieve her anxiety.

Anxiety was a contagious condition that mother and daughter had passed back and forth for many years now. The cure was quiet assurances from someone whose opinion they both trusted, someone like Stuart who worked for the State Department.

"Mom had one of her dreams last night," she said.

"Yeah," Stuart said, only marginally interested.

"It must have been a really bad one for her to call me at work. She almost never calls me at work."

"I have bad dreams all the time," he said. "We all do. But they're only dreams. They don't mean anything."

"Tell that to my mom. She's a dream expert. She studies them."

"Okay, what was it about?"

"That is what's so odd. She doesn't remember. Mom always remembers her dreams. She even records them. She said she lay in bed nearly paralyzed and unable to reach her notebook and pen she keeps by her bedside. She said she floated in and out of consciousness for some time before the paralysis left her, but by then the dream had faded. Still, she said she was left with a very bad feeling that stayed with her all day."

"It sounds like your mother had a nightmare. We've all had them. When I was a kid I had them so bad I would sometimes have to sleep in my parents' room."

"I know, I had nightmares too when I was a kid. But Mom's not a kid. You have to admit that."

"Of course she isn't. I was only...."

"And she has a track record! Mom's dreams are like premonitions."

"Oh, come on Natalie. Give me a break."

"In Egypt she knew something was up with Dr. Bueller."

"We all knew something was up with the old coot! You didn't have to have a dream to know that. We just didn't know what that something

7

was. At any rate, if she can't remember the dream, how can you call it a premonition?"

"Well, you're probably right. She's just upset that Barry has gone off to Europe and never writes. She's feeling separation anxiety. That's what I told her."

"Barry! I thought you said she didn't remember the dream."

"She doesn't, but she said she woke up with a really bad feeling about Barry, so she presumes it was about him."

"That's odd. I got a call from him I think it was on Tuesday or maybe Wednesday."

"Barry called you from Europe?"

"Yeah, I think he was buying insurance."

"When did you start selling insurance?"

"Not that kind. He wanted me to know where he was going if something should happen to him."

"What?"

"Yeah. He was about to leave for Egypt. He had a letter from Hans Bueller asking him to come right away, so he was trying to arrange to fly there. He told me he planned to fly to Alexandria and take a train south so that he could bypass Cairo. He was afraid that someone would recognize him if he went through the airport in Cairo."

"And you let him go?" she nearly shouted.

"Well, I could hardly stop him!" he shouted back.

The waiter eyed them from across the room. The customers in the booth opposite them glanced their way. They lowered their voices.

"Now, I'm really worried," she whispered.

"I am too," he said. "I've been a little worried ever since he called."

"There's something else, which probably contributed to my mom's state of mind, but now that you've told me this," she paused without elaborating on the nature of the something else she had referred to.

"What?" he said, feeling like a cat swatting at a sardine being dangled slightly out of reach.

"It probably isn't anything," she said.

"Let me be the judge."

"My brother has sent Barry several emails telling him he and Rosalind are coming to Europe. He was hoping to get an invitation to visit, but

8

Barry hasn't answered."

"Maybe he's too busy for company."

"You know better than that. Besides, if he was too busy, he would say so unless he's so busy he hasn't read his email, which is what I'm beginning to think."

"When are they going over?"

"Tomorrow. They're flying to Amsterdam to visit Rosalind's sister. Their plan is to rent a car and drive through France and visit Barry there. Do you know how long he was planning to be gone?"

"He didn't say."

She forgot herself and raised her voice. "You didn't ask?"

"Didn't think to until now."

"Maybe you could use your contacts to find out what's going on, if he's all right and everything."

"I'd better look into the situation myself." He raised his hand at the waiter signaling that he wanted the check while Natalie quickly drained the half filled glass of wine that remained. The waiter, fearing that the two of them might soon cause a scene, was happy to oblige. In no time they were out on 15th Street flagging down a taxi that took them to Stuart's apartment near Dupont Circle before it carried Natalie home to her condo in Alexandria, Virginia.

He kissed her goodbye through the cab's open window. "I will call you when I learn something."

"Before then if it takes a while. I'll be worried until I hear from you," she said, thinking she would probably be worried after she hears from him, but hoped not as much.

Sophie sat on the cat stand that stood in front of the ninth floor living room window that looked out towards Washington. She seemed not at all surprised to see Natalie come through the door as if she had observed her roommate's entire trip along Washington's fast moving expressway. Natalie popped frozen lasagna into her microwave, offered Sophie some treats and dangled a stuffed mouse for the cat to swat.

She resisted the temptation to call her mother thinking it better to wait until Stuart had more news. She hoped it would be reassuring and that Barry's situation was really okay. Why upset Mom further, she thought, her conversation with Stuart having put her in the grip of

9

anxiety. Why spread the contagion? So instead, she poured a glass of wine and spent the rest of the evening glancing at unread magazines that had begun to pile up.

The phone rang at ten the next morning while Natalie and Sophie still lay in bed. Stuart had learned that Barry had entered Egypt at the airport in Alexandria the night before. He presumed that by now he was en route to Dr. Bueller's monastic retreat. He told her he had just booked a flight to Egypt that would leave Dulles International in a few hours. "Just in case Barry needs my help," he said.

"Maybe I should come too," she offered. "What can they do to me at work beyond firing me?"

"That's enough, isn't it?" he replied in his most rational tone. "You really can't do much to help anyway. It would just make my job more difficult. I would have to look out for you too. It's bad enough that Barry got the boneheaded idea to sneak back into Egypt, but if you're there too, and I'm trying to get him out unnoticed...."

"Okay, okay, but I thought it was Hans Bueller's boneheaded idea."

"It was, but you get my point. Just because Bueller made a request didn't mean Barry had to agree to it. He could have written him and explained it was too dangerous. Hans knows that anyway."

"So why did he ask him?"

"I don't know. Maybe when folks get old," he said, honing in on the fact that Bueller was approaching ninety and Barry was sixty, "they throw caution to the wind."

She smiled. "I don't think Hans would have asked Barry if he hadn't thought it was really important for him to come. Barry probably knows that, which is why he's taking the risk. As for me, you're right. I should stay put. I would just be a liability."

That was how they left it. She reluctantly told her mother the whole story. Instead of fueling her mother's anxiety, as Natalie had feared it would, the news brought Madeline some relief. She already knew Barry was in danger, and she was comforted by the knowledge that Stuart would be there to help him.

After Natalie got off the phone she checked her email and found a note from her brother with Summer's Dutch phone number and email address. *"It's too late to give the information to Stuart now,"* she replied to John. *"He's already left. I will pass it along when he phones me, which he will surely do."*

Chapter 4

El Quseir

Leaning against his gray van, Omar Shabaka looked in the sandy haze like a pillar of polished granite pressed against a temple ruin. Upon closer inspection, his white linen suit brought out the depths of his brown eyes and bronzed skin, revealing a youthful face in an otherwise antique appearance. He, like his father, is a physician. Unlike his father he had been privileged to train at the Cairo Medical College after having learned the traditional arts passed down through generations of his family. Doctor Shabaka thus practiced his art on both Egyptians and tourists alike, which is how he had come to know Barry Short.

The February before he had been called in to look after Dr. Hans Bueller at the Old Cataract Hotel in Aswan. He nursed Bueller back to health after thieves had struck the old man on the head. It was not the head wound for which Shabaka's remarkable medical skill became evident, it was his treatment of a festering wound to the soul that had eaten away at Bueller for most of his long life. Hans Bueller at 86 had been made a new man by his treatments and had embarked on a fresh life, tucked safely away in one of Egypt's ancient Christian monasteries near the Red Sea.

The train whistle blew in the distance. Shabaka walked toward the platform as passengers emptied out of cars and scrambled towards the entrance to the station, among them a man dressed in jeans and a corduroy jacket with a backpack slung over his shoulder. He recognized him right away but noted that he looked different than he had before. It is his dress, he thought, and his posture. Barry had looked like a man in charge when Doctor Shabaka had first met him months earlier. Now, well, it was hard to say. He looked like a man with something to hide.

"It's so good to see you Omar," Barry said, grateful that the doctor had put aside his work to drive all the way to Luxor to escort him to Bueller's hiding place.

Shabaka, detecting Barry's gratitude in his intonation answered, "Oh, no trouble at all! I am pleased to see you but so surprised. I thought you had left Egypt for good."

Barry fumbled through his backpack. "Well, that was the plan, but I got this letter from Hans. He asked me to come at once, and he sent it more than two months ago, so I'm a little late."

"It will not take us long to get there," Shabaka said. He led Barry off of the platform and through the station.

"I realized while waiting for the train in Cairo that I didn't know exactly where Hans is. That's when I thought of you," Barry said as if to explain his last minute imposition on the young doctor's time. "I'm sure I could have found him, but that would have wasted time. I'm sorry to have called you at the last minute and with so little notice but..."

"Do not worry yourself. I'm looking forward to spending time with the two of you. I saw Hans only a few weeks ago in Aswan. He looked quite well. He drove in with the abbot who had a few days of business there. Hans used those days to make sketches for the children's book he is writing. I think I wrote to you about that."

"Yes, you did, and you told me about the other books he's writing too. But it's not his health that concerns me now. He indicates in this letter that he has something important for me to see and that it can't wait."

Doctor Shabaka looked quizzical now that his own curiosity was piqued. "Have you eaten?" he asked. "There's a very good restaurant nearby."

"Thank you for asking," Barry said while furtively looking around the train station. "I'm not comfortable going out in public in Luxor. Too many of my former colleagues live here. I'm trying to get in and out of the country without even my friends seeing me. You know how people talk."

Shabaka heard his words and read his looks and ushered him quickly into his van as two rather innocuous appearing businessmen looked on unnoticed.

"Of course," Shabaka said after considering the situation further. "It will take us a few hours to drive across the desert to El Quseir, and from there we will have to drive several more hours north along the Red Sea to reach the monastery. Our arrival would not be welcomed in the middle of the night so I suggest that we stay at a hotel in El Quseir, have dinner and relax. We can drive on to the monastery in the morning. I doubt that you will see any colleagues in El Quseir unless you surprise me and tell me your friends are scuba divers."

"You're right about that," Barry laughed. "My friends are more likely to be underground than underwater." Barry thought a moment about what he had earlier said and added, "I didn't mean to imply that you are not my friend Omar. You are a friend in a different category, a trusted friend."

"I knew what you meant."

The drive across the desert to El Quseir was quicker than expected in spite of there being quite a few cars and vans along the route and an occasional bus carrying tourists to or from Luxor and the Red Sea. With all of this coming and going, it was no wonder that neither Barry nor Omar suspected they were being followed.

Barry pulled his backpack out of the rear of the van once they arrived at the hotel, but instead of entering the lobby, he walked towards the sea. "Oh, this is beautiful."

"That's Aquarius above us," Omar pointed. He stood silent for a few moments and then whispered as if at the end of a prayer, "May the heavenly waters pour forth."

"There, over there!" Barry said as he pointed north. "Isn't that the Great Square of Pegasus, the winged horse?"

"Yes, and there at its corner is Andromeda, the chained princess."

"I miss this," Barry said. "I've never seen the stars anywhere so bright as they are in Egypt."

Omar agreed, believing Barry must be right, although he himself had never been outside his country.

The sea air invigorated the men. Barry looked back towards the hotel. "They have a patio."

"We can eat under the stars if you like," Omar said. "We should check-in first."

Twenty minutes later they were seated on the hotel patio waiting for freshly caught grilled fish. The remaining guests had already finished their dinners and were eating desserts or drinking coffee. They were fortunate that the cook had not refused their order, proclaiming the kitchen closed and demanding that they satisfy their hunger with a cold sandwich. But this was a resort of the highest order and a new one at that. The cooks, waiters, and other hotel staff had already adjusted to their guests keeping unreasonable hours. That's why people come to these places, the management had said.

Doctor Shabaka thought it an appropriate time and place to bring up the subject that had sparked his curiosity earlier at the train station. "You said that Hans has something for you to see. What do you think that could be?"

"I have no idea, but it must be significant or he wouldn't have summoned me here. You mentioned in your letter that Hans is working in the library at the monastery."

"Yes, it's the ideal job for him if he must labor at all. No heavy work. He sorts and dusts the books, that's all. For a man like him such work would be more interesting than laborious."

"Hmm," Barry muttered. "I'm sure you're right about that. Tell me, what kinds of books are in this library?"

"It is a very old monastery. I imagine there are many very old texts, perhaps some Coptic codices."

"Or even Egyptian papyrus scrolls?" Barry asked.

"That's possible, very possible indeed," Omar said, realizing that he may have answered his own question. "Maybe he found something of great value while he sorted and dusted his way through the library."

The two men ate their dinners quickly not wanting to trouble the hotel staff any longer than they already had since it was now well past midnight. Within an hour they had retired to their respective rooms. They were comfortable, airy rooms with large patio doors opening to the outside. Before he retired, Barry sat on the little private patio outside his room to take a final look at the constellations. The sea air was perfumed with fragrances from flowers that still bloomed in the hotel gardens. Hoping to fill his lungs and soul with as much of the sea and the sky as he could that night, Barry went to bed with his patio door left open. His mind fully at rest, he fell fast asleep.

Chapter 5

Club on the Head

Barry's was not the only door left open that night. The blissful quiet that had enveloped the gardens ceased when late night revelers at the resort's disco pushed open its doors to let in the fresh, cool sea air. Thump, da da, thump, da da, thump reverberated across the resort grounds. Barry grew restless under the sheets. Thump, da da, thump, da da, thump. He rolled over turning away from the opened patio door. His body grew still again as if he had settled back into sleep. Thump, da da, thump, da da, thump. What dreams could such loud rhythmic sounds have generated in his sleeping mind? Did he find himself in a war zone under heavy artillery fire? Was he transported to jungles that rang dangerously with the steady rhythm of drums? Whatever he was dreaming, he was unaware of a real threat drawing near that had nothing to do with dance music or dreams.

Two men climbed over the low railing onto Barry Short's patio. They were the same two men who had gone unnoticed at the train station and had watched as Barry and Omar left together in Omar's van. They were the same two who had followed them to the resort and had watched as Barry and Omar stood near the sea gazing at the stars and ate their late night dinner on the hotel terrace. They had watched as Barry and Omar reentered the hotel and room lights came on that marked their locations. They had waited as Barry Short relaxed for a few minutes on his not-so-private patio before retiring. After they were through watching and waiting, the thieves broke into Omar Shabaka's van searching for anything of interest or value; and then believing that Barry was surely asleep, they slowly closed in on his room.

The music grew louder, jolting him out of his dreams. He climbed out of bed, went to the patio door, and slammed it shut just as two men dressed in business suits were about to enter his room. He and one of those men stared at each other for what seemed like an eternity from opposite sides of the glass as if assessing the other's determination. Barry quickly locked the door latch before either man could pry it open. He grabbed the phone and rang the desk. "Say, two men just tried to enter my room through the patio. If I hadn't just woken up, I could have been robbed or worse. Could you notify my friend, Doctor Shabaka?" he said as he watched the men disappear over the patio railing.

Dressed only in his pajama bottoms, he lunged through the patio door, over the railing, and out into the garden. He looked at the riotous crowd who had spilled outside of the disco and realized it was their voices that had mercifully awakened him. Two figures dressed in business attire charged through the crowd and headed towards the parking lot. He followed until he felt a knock on his head and fell unconscious to the ground.

When he opened his eyes he was back in his room with Omar Shabaka standing over him. His head hurt. A stranger was seated at the small table near the patio door looking studiously at the two of them.

Omar bent down and pressed a towel with a soothing ointment to his scalp wound. "Ouch!" Barry said.

"I'm sorry. It should feel cool."

"It's cool to the skin, but the pressure is killing me."

"Be still. You need this ointment to prevent infection. There," he said as he dabbed the rest of it on.

"I feel like I've been hit over the head with a hammer."

"You were! They broke into my van and took all of my tools. Fortunately, I had taken my medical case into my room."

The man who had been seated walked over to the bed, stood over Barry, and introduced himself.

"How do you do? I am Mr. Diab. You phoned me earlier when you called the front desk for help."

"I'm afraid I'm not doing too well," Barry said. "Thank you very much. You were very prompt, but perhaps not prompt enough." He winced as his head continued to throb.

"If you had not pursued them," Mr. Diab scolded, "you would not have been injured."

"I know, I know."

"Did they take anything from you?" Mr. Diab asked. "Would you like me to telephone the police?"

"No, nothing, only my tools," Omar said. "Petty theft, nothing to bother about. Does the hotel have seltzer water and lemons?"

"Of course, in the kitchen."

"Would it be too much to ask you to bring them to me?"

"No trouble at all." He walked to the door, relieved that the guests did not want him to fetch the police. It was a new hotel, and he didn't want that kind of publicity. He was already fielding complaints from the local residents about the noise. If they thought the hotel had become a magnet for crime too, well, then his troubles would quadruple.

"Very nice man," Barry said after Mr. Diab left the room.

"A little officious."

"Were they only petty thieves like you said? Did I get this rather large lump on my head defending your toolbox?"

"What do you believe?"

"I don't know what to think. They were about to enter my room just as I shut the patio door right in their faces. If it hadn't been for all that noise waking me up, maybe you would be nursing more than a simple head wound. I don't know."

"So you got a look at them?"

"One, maybe. I looked him right in the eyes, angry eyes. Probably because I shut him out. I don't know what to say about them. They didn't look like thieves; they looked like businessmen."

"Maybe they are businessmen."

"Well, what would they come into my room for? If they were common thieves, the answer would be money, a watch maybe. But why would two well dressed businessmen try to enter my room in the middle of the night?"

"It was late. Maybe they thought it was their room."

"Why then would they have run away? And why would they have clubbed me like this? And why would they have stolen your tools if they were only businessmen who lost their way?"

"Very good questions. They probably took the tools to pry open your door not imagining that you had left it open. You say no one knows you are here in Egypt?"

"No one that I know of except Stuart, my investigator friend from

17

Washington. I let him know where I was going just in case something should happen to me."

"I don't believe I had the pleasure of meeting him, but I do remember you telling me about him. Wasn't he the fellow who tried to capture Hans Bueller's assailants?"

"Yes, that's the one."

"Didn't you tell me he failed? Women weren't they?" Omar asked in a rather snide tone for such a well-mannered man.

"They got away into Sudan. He lacked the papers to legally enter that country. He had no choice but to let them go."

"Oh, yes Sudan," Omar said. Realizing he was ruffling Barry Short's feathers, he shifted the conversation back to the more pertinent issue facing them. "Yes, I could see that would be a problem. Sudan is not friendly with Americans, particularly American government investigators. You say no one saw you arrive at the airport and no one saw you at the train station?"

"I flew into Alexandria very late at night to avoid the Cairo Airport. No one was about, and no one knows me in Alexandria anyhow. I slept for a little while at the train station; it was all but deserted. Then I had a layover at the train station in Cairo. That's when I phoned you."

"You weren't recognized in Cairo?" Omar asked, now quite sure that he must have been.

"Well, I can't be sure, but I didn't know it if I was."

"Someone knew you were at this hotel. They knew which vehicle in the parking lot you were traveling in. They must have followed us from Luxor. They were looking for more than tools," he said before revealing a new fact. "They had pulled everything out of the glove compartment and the console."

"Hmm, perhaps I wasn't as careful at the train station as I had thought. I kept a newspaper in front of my face. Oh crap! I must have let my guard down after I got the idea to phone you. No wonder those two didn't look like common thieves. Artifact smugglers, thieves of a higher order: businessmen thieves. That's what they are. I can't believe this. I tried to be careful, but it sounds like a report of my return went out on the rumor pipeline."

"Rumor pipeline?"

"Oh, you've got to be in the business to know about it. It's how these antiquity thieves communicate."

"Well, they are gone now," Omar said as he daubed more cooling ointment on the wound. "Maybe being clubbed over the head was fortuitous."

"Fortuitous!" Barry shouted, his head and shoulders rising from the pillow.

"Fortuitous," Omar insisted. "You left Egypt because you were afraid of getting clubbed over the head like Hans had been. Well, now you've been clubbed. There is nothing left to fear. Besides that, you were clubbed in the company of a very fine physician. I would call that fortuitous."

"I see your point," Barry agreed as he rubbed his head. "But I'm not so confident the threat has passed. These men may have fled, but oh, how these types talk. By tomorrow dozens more like them will know that I'm here."

"By then we will have left this hotel," Omar counseled, "and we will be safely tucked away behind monastic walls."

There was a light tap at the door before it opened. In came Mr. Diab carrying a tray with a bottle of fizzy water, a glass, and two lemons. "Will this do?" he asked.

"Yes," Omar answered. "This will do nicely."

"Will there be anything else?"

"No, there won't be. Thank you for your assistance," Omar said as he escorted Mr. Diab to the door, which he locked securely with a dead bolt and chain after Mr. Diab's departure.

Doctor Shabaka opened his medical valise and pulled out a surgical knife, which he used to cut the lemons in half. He squeezed the juice of both lemons into a glass. Then he pulled a large amber vile from his bag and poured quite a bit of the honey into the lemon juice. He added the fizzy water, stirred the mixture with his knife, and ordered his patient to drink.

"This will ease the pain and let you sleep," he said soothingly as Barry Short took his medicine.

"Will you stay here tonight?" the shaken patient asked.

"Yes, of course."

Barry drifted off to sleep before Omar could push a chest of drawers in front of the locked patio door. To his relief he found an extra pillow and blanket in the closet, making it unnecessary to request anything more from Mr. Diab. He made a bed for himself on the floor and fell into a sound sleep.

Chapter 6

Amsterdam

Morning light slipped through a crevice in the glass patio door, falling upon the chest of drawers that blocked it shut. Later, as the light intensified, it crept through the narrow opening in the center of the window drapes, sending a golden sliver across the room where Barry and Omar slept. Faint voices and laughter rippled through the sea air as hotel guests gathered on the terrace for their breakfast buffet. But the inhabitants of this room remained quiet, removed from the activity into the place their dreams had taken them.

***

Passengers arrived at Schiphol suffering the effects of sleep deprivation after their long flight from the U.S. The airport agents were sympathetic as they passed John, Rosalind, and their little dog through customs. A taxi took them quickly to Summer's address on Bloemgracht Street, a street composed of two small lanes on either side of a canal.

"Bloem" is the Dutch word for flower and "gracht" means canal, a fitting name for a canal street whose residents filled the tiny yards of their pitched roof flats with as many fall flowers as they could pack in. A Heron swept down from a light pole, flew over a small arched bridge where early morning risers walked, and landed on a steep slate rooftop as if it had come to see the visitors. Summer greeted them at the door that was marked with a painted chessboard to denote the chess club that was located on the first floor of the building where she lived. She helped carry the luggage up two flights to her third floor combination office and apartment.

Her accommodation was a perk provided by her employer, a New

York City record label who had made significant inroads into the European music market. Summer had parlayed her position as manager of her college radio station into a record label management job in New York City, which had led to this new assignment, vice president of European operations.

The living room comfortably held a couch, TV, and several chairs on one side and two desks and bookshelves filled with hundreds of CDs on the other. There were cartons more of CDs in a spidery storage room in the basement that she, being a bit arachnophobic, was afraid to enter. That assignment she left to her assistant. A small, modern kitchen opened into the living area separated by a table for meals. To the rear was a bath and two bedrooms, one leading out to a rooftop patio. The most spectacular feature of the apartment was its magnificent views seen from a row of large living room windows.

The gracht flowed below the windows carrying silent canal boats while birds and bicyclists went singing past weaving around large bare trees that in the summer had shaded the cobbled lanes and colored the glassy water green. Rising above the rooftops and to the right was the grand tower of the Westerkerk, a beautiful old church whose carillon bells played melodies on the hour. To the left and across the canal stood the Anne Frank House, a solemn reminder of a grimmer time. Cafes serving homemade soups, cheeses, salads, and beer were situated around the arched bridge. Only a short bike ride away was a little British establishment that made the best blueberry muffins ever baked, which Summer offered to her guests upon their arrival.

"This place agrees with you," Rosalind said after observing how physically fit her sister had become. It must be all the bicycling, she surmised. Her skin and blue eyes were clear; her dark blond hair had turned golden under the sun.

"Christabel!" Summer exclaimed in a high-pitched voice meant for a small dog. Delighted, the little pup broke into a full smile and leaped up and down at her knee begging to be picked up. She obliged, taking the white furry animal up into her arms. Christabel licked her face.

"Yes, this is great," John said, looking about at the peach colored accent wall, the red couch, and blue chair.

"Thanks. You should have seen it when I got here," she said looking quite pleased with herself as she held the now calm dog in her arms. "It was a mess. Beer stains all over the carpet and walls, and the kitchen was filthy. I had to scrub and paint everything and replace the carpet."

"It looks spotless now," Rosalind said.

"I keep my shoes off inside to keep it clean," she said looking at their feet.

The visitors took off their shoes, and Summer showed them where to store them in the hallway just outside her apartment door.

"How did the place get so dirty?" Rosalind asked.

"The record label let the bands stay here while they toured Europe. They can't stay here anymore," she asserted with assurance, as if this point had been well argued and won.

"You've civilized the place," Rosalind laughed, knowing well her sister's capacity to organize people, places, and activities to her liking.

"Um, this muffin is really good," John said. "Hey, I gave your phone number and email address to a friend of ours who is over here. I told you about him, Barry Short, the archeologist who is working in France. Has he called yet?"

"Oh, that's the one you want us to visit while you're here. No, he hasn't phoned. Give me a minute and I'll check my email." She went over to one of the desks, opened her laptop and typed in her account. "No, nothing new here."

"Could I use your computer to check my account?" John asked.

"Sure," she said as she gave up her chair and desk to John.

"Will you be able to come with us when we drive south into France?" Rosalind asked.

"Of course I'm going," she insisted.

"I only asked because I wasn't sure you would be able..."

"Jos will be here," Summer interrupted.

"Who?"

"Jos, my assistant. While I was trying to untangle Dutch tax law I found out that we can't legally operate over here unless we employ a Dutch person, which is a real break for me," she said smiling. "They never would have let me hire him otherwise. I'll take my phone with me in case something comes up that he can't handle, but things are quiet now that the jazz festival season is over and I've turned our accounting over to the tax lawyers. All Jos needs to do is fill requests for CDs and keep the books."

"Nothing here from Barry," John said from across the room. "But Natalie wrote. Oh, wow! She sent this Saturday morning. She says she had dinner with Stuart Friday night. He heard from Barry earlier last week. Barry was going to try to sneak into Egypt to visit Dr. Bueller. Stuart is alarmed, she writes. He phoned her Saturday morning just before he flew to Egypt to track Barry down before anything happens to him."

"Barry's in Egypt?" Rosalind said.

"That's what she says. If Stuart flew there yesterday, he's in Egypt by now too."

"This certainly complicates things."

"Well, Natalie writes here that she is sorry she hadn't read my email until after Stuart had gone, but she will be sure to give him our phone number here when he phones her."

"If he phones her."

"The question is when not if," John retorted.

"What shall we do? Should we cancel the trip to France?" Rosalind asked.

"No way! I want to go to France," Summer said.

"I'm not sure," John said. "We need to talk to Barry first. We still don't know where he lives."

"Didn't you say he lives in a cave somewhere north of Carcassonne?" Rosalind said.

"A cave!" Summer said. "I thought he was researching prehistoric men; I didn't think he was one."

"Ha, ha!" Rosalind said. "He's a very sophisticated man. He's looking for evidence of a link between ancient inhabitants of France and the Americas."

"Apparently there are a lot of these troglodyte caves in France. I suppose he found himself a furnished one to get into the spirit of his research," John said with a grin. "All that I know is that he lives in some remote area of Languedoc."

"I thought he was in the South of France," Summer said.

"He is," John answered. "Just not the South of France you're

24

thinking of."

"Oh! You thought we were going to Provence," Rosalind said.

"And Cannes and Monte Carlo."

"Languedoc is west of all that," John explained. "It's not so touristy."

"Provence is touristy for a reason," Summer said. "It's beautiful. Cezanne and van Gogh painted there. I've seen pictures of fields of lavender and sunflowers. And the Riviera is the most sophisticated travel destination on Earth. You can actually see real aristocrats in Monte Carlo."

"Didn't Barry say he lives across from a winery that has a wild boar's head on the wall?" Rosalind said.

"I think he did say that. I know he said there are plenty of wild boar around there."

"Don't you guys even have an address?" Summer asked.

"That's the problem," Rosalind said. "All of our communication has been by email so we never thought to get his address until right before we left, and he hasn't answered any of it. So no, we don't have an address. I sure hope he's all right."

"We'll hear something soon enough now that Stuart's in Egypt," John said. "He's not going to mess around for long down there."

"If not, I guess we will be hanging around here longer than we anticipated."

"I was really looking forward to going to France," Summer said. "I thought we would visit the chateaus in the Loire Valley, and you know, that place where Leonardo da Vinci lived."

"Amboise," her sister said. "Maybe we will. I just hate to leave until we've heard from them." She rose from her chair and stretched. "I really need to get some rest." She made her way into the guest bedroom and curled up on the mattress with Christabel, who nestled into the small bend of her knees.

Chapter 7

The Monastery

S unlight crept in through the edges of the drapes rousing Omar Shabaka from his slumber and to his patient's side. "The wound looks good," he whispered. "You must get up now; it's late. We should leave before any more larcenists arrive."

"What time is it?" Barry asked, looking around the room and seeing no clock.

"It's past noon. Let me help you into the shower," he said as he pulled Barry up and out of his bed.

"That's okay. I can do it. What wonder drug did you give me last night?"

"Honey."

"Oh, honey!" Barry snorted, deeply amused as he headed into the bath to shower and dress.

Mr. Diab was no longer on duty at the hotel desk when they checked out, and his replacement appeared to know nothing about what had transpired the night before. The two men paid their bill and slipped quietly out of the hotel. They drove about fifty miles north along the Red Sea when Omar turned west on the most inconspicuous of roads, if one could call it a road. It felt more like a camel trail as the van bounced along its rocky course. Nothing appeared to lie ahead except stretches of sandy desert and craggy hills. But once they arrived on the other side of the first hill, they could see a large edifice that appeared to protrude from the side of a mountain.

"This must be it," Omar said.

"You've never been here?" Barry said quite taken aback with this admission since it was Omar who had recommended the monastery as a retreat for Dr. Bueller.

"My father has several times when he was younger and more able to travel," he said, his eyes fixed on the edifice that lay ahead of them. He turned to Barry. "I would never have sent Hans here if I was not absolutely sure that it was the right place for him."

Barry nodded, knowing that was true. He had never known a man more trustworthy than Omar Shabaka, certainly not Hans Bueller, who in the past had been quite devious and unpredictable. That was in the past, he thought to himself. Bueller had a miraculous change of heart. He knew that.

The building loomed over a high stone wall that enclosed its entrance. It blended so inconspicuously into the mountainside that the two were nearly indistinguishable. "This structure definitely isn't Pharaonic," Barry said. "It doesn't look Roman or Greek either. How old is it?"

"No one knows. It seems always to have been here. My father says there are no records surrounding its construction."

"Has anyone examined the building techniques?"

"The stones are of the same material as the surrounding mountains, but the central core of the building appears to have been carved out of rock. Blocks of stone were used to construct the wings. My father thinks those wings are later additions and the original building is the carved core."

"Yes, I can see that. The central part of the building looks more chiseled than anything else, as if the side of the mountain had been hollowed out."

The two men pulled up to a gated entrance. Omar tugged the chord of a bell that announced them. The gate opened, and they drove in and parked.

The large interior courtyard was lavish in its own way with a huge, round gurgling fountain in its center that drew water from a deep well. Finely made channels shot out from the root of the fountain like spokes, irrigating all manner of vegetable plants, fruit trees, palm trees, and flowers. A circular path had been constructed that along with the channels would have given an airborne traveler the impression of looking down through a kaleidoscope. On the ground the sojourner could cross the channels without dampening a shoe thanks to slabs of rough granite that acted as little walking bridges, allowing the walker to make his way unimpeded round and round the spiral path. It was not clear to Barry whether the path was used to gain access to the plants or for the purpose of meditation.

A man greeted them who recognized Doctor Shabaka right away for he was the abbot who Omar had met less than a month ago in Aswan. Barry would not have taken him to be an abbot by his dress. He donned no robes but wore loose, gray pants and a white, collarless shirt with three quarter length sleeves. The style was so peculiar that Barry rightly surmised the clothing was designed and made on the premises less to designate a religious order and more for comfort and utilitarian convenience.

"I would say I'm surprised to see you but in all good conscience I cannot," said the abbot as he put one hand on Omar's shoulder and extended the other in a warm handshake. "I knew you would visit us soon."

"Father Paul, it's good to see you again, but I must admit that my arrival was unplanned. I brought this man to see our mutual friend Hans Bueller. Father Paul, let me present Dr. Barry Short, a long time friend and colleague of Dr. Bueller."

"I'm very pleased to meet you. If you are half as interesting as your colleague, I'm sure you will be delightful company."

"I'm happy to meet you too, and I hope you will not find my company too tedious because I must acknowledge that my life has been not nearly so interesting as Hans Bueller's."

"Well, you're quite young yet. You have plenty of time to dress it up." He winked.

Barry paused, pleased this man considered him young. As he looked at Father Paul more closely he was struck by how youthful this octogenarian looked in spite of his creased skin, aged by time and sun. It was his eyes, he thought, his gait, and his lithe body. All but for age, he was the spitting image of another Paul he knew. He thought of young Paul at home in Ohio keeping his lawn mowed and checking his mailbox.

"I apologize for staring," Barry said, "but you remind me of someone. His name is Paul too, only he is about seventy years your junior."

Father Paul smiled broadly, revealing beautiful white teeth and a hearty personality. "May God help this young lad then," he said as he ushered the men inside the monastery.

The entrance hall was large and open with unadorned stone walls and a domed ceiling with a large round opening at the top to let in the natural light. The room's interest lay in the floor that was tiled in a herringbone pattern of black and white polished stones. The effect was to draw the eye downward as one felt challenged to try to connect the zigzag lines that were formed and then broken by the pattern.

Father Paul asked the two visitors to seat themselves on a plain but pleasantly wide wooden bench while he searched for Hans Bueller. Apparently Bueller was not hard to find because minutes later he entered the vestibule. He beamed as he pulled the double doors wide open and walked towards the two men who now stood up.

"Barry, you've come! I nearly gave up on you," exclaimed the slight man who embraced him with the fondness of a child who hugs his father after a long separation. "Omar!" he cried, "I'm so fortunate to see you again and so soon."

"I'm sorry I took so long Hans. I only got your letter less than a week ago," Barry said and pulled back, obviously a little embarrassed and surprised at Bueller's excessive show of affection, excessive at least by the standards of their earlier long standing and often contentious relationship. Bueller had become a changed person, he reminded himself, although he looked much the same as he always had: thin, white, and veiny. And he must get lonely living out here surrounded by miles and miles of desert and sea. With those thoughts in mind Barry returned the hug of the very elderly man.

Father Paul poked his head through the double doors, clearly delighted at the joyous meeting. "I've asked that two more places be set for dinner," he said. "It will be served in an hour. If you will be so kind as to stay with us for a few days, I will have rooms made up for you."

"Of course z'ey will stay with us," Bueller said, and then looked at Barry and Omar and in a more timid voice asked, "Won't you?"

Barry looked to Omar for he was unsure of the doctor's schedule and thought it rude, once he considered it, that he had not already asked the busy man about his appointments.

"We can stay for a few days," Omar replied. "I have nothing until Wednesday when I must be back in Luxor."

"Very good, very good!" the excited little man said. "Z'at will give me z'e time I need to explain every'zing."

"Your letter sounded urgent. I can't imagine..."

"No, you never would have imagined, I don't z'ink. Neither did I, but I will show you. First I will show you z'e library, and z'en we will have dinner. Z'en tonight I will begin."

Bueller led them through double doors into a large central hallway and up a spiral stairway into the library. Their eyes were drawn to a great wall of windows that flooded the room with natural light, the primary source of luminescence on which the library patrons depended. Nearby stood five long rickety tables with benches as well as a few worn but comfortable looking chairs. Books lined the shelves of the three high walls that made up the rest of the room, broken only by the double door they had just entered and a single door located across from the bank of windows. That door, Bueller told them, led into a room that housed their most precious antiquities that must be protected from the sunlight.

"How do you read them in there?" Omar asked once Bueller opened the door into the pitch-black space.

"My oil lamp, of course."

Father Paul made another appearance, this time poking his head into the library and motioning Hans Bueller over to him. The two men spoke quietly for a few minutes, and then Hans turned to Barry and Omar. "It's nearly time for us to go z'e refectory for dinner. Would you please wash up first? Father Paul will take you to your rooms. I'm afraid I must see to another guest," he said before he scurried off.

"Are we that dirty?" Barry said looking at his hands and down at his shirt.

"I think you will like your rooms. They're not large, but they're very comfortable," Father Paul said.

He escorted the two men out of the library and down the spiral stairway into a hallway that led into one of the new wings of the building, if you can call a structure that was probably several hundred years old new. They arrived at two rooms located across the hall from one another. Father Paul opened both doors and bid them enter.

"You will find fresh water, soap, and towels. I will be back for you soon." He smiled and walked down the hall until he disappeared into another stairwell.

The space was tiny and sparsely furnished with a twin bed and a dresser with a pitcher of water next to a washbowl, towels, and soap. Barry noticed a pot protruding from under the bed. He wondered if the entire monastery was without indoor plumbing or only the sleeping quarters. What the room lacked in plumbing the bed made up for in comfort. He collapsed on the soft French blue comforter pulled over crisp, white sheets. His head sunk into two fluffy pillows, and he instantly dozed off. He was still quite tired from all of his travel and from the injury he had suffered the night before. Then this place, he realized, the quiet of it, he thought as he dozed off. In what seemed like only seconds he heard a knock on the door.

"Are you ready?" a voice asked. He recognized the hospitable voice of Father Paul.

"I must have fallen asleep. Please give me a few minutes."

He roused himself, splashed cool water on his face, and scrubbed the grit that had accumulated under his fingernails with the fine soap that had been provided. He combed his hair back, tucked in his shirt, and looked respectable enough to join a group of monks for their evening meal. Father Paul and Omar Shabaka were happily engaged in conversation in the hall outside his door when he opened it, obviously not minding the wait since it gave them a little time to become better acquainted.

"Sorry to interrupt," Barry grinned.

"Don't you look nice," Omar smiled, having by now become comfortable enough with Barry to crack a joke or two. "Even your wound looks good," he said after inspecting it closely.

"I had been curious about that," Father Paul said now that the subject came up. "I didn't want to pry."

"Oh, it's nothing," Barry said. "It could have been a lot worse. Just a club on the head from would be thieves."

Father Paul looked concerned.

"It happened at our hotel in El Quseir," Omar explained. "Two thieves tried to break into Barry's room."

"I did not know they were having those kinds of problems down there. It must be a consequence of the new tourism."

"I don't think the problem is in El Quseir," Barry said. "We believe the men spotted me at the train station in Luxor and followed me there."

Father Paul looked decidedly disturbed but was too polite to ask Barry for further explanation. It was clear by his expression, however, that he was no longer sure he welcomed their visit. He quietly led them into the refectory.

The refectory was located below the library in the original part of the building. There were rows of wooden tables with oil lamps and benches and chairs full of men of varying ages and sizes who smiled at Barry and Omar as they entered the room. The monks had been waiting patiently for their arrival. Barry was embarrassed that the dinner had been held up by his nap, but Father Paul told him not to worry as he led them to a table in the rear of the hall where Hans Bueller sat with a newly arrived guest.

Barry was flabbergasted. To the right of Bueller sat a rather scruffy looking Stuart. Breaking decorum and ignoring the chair Father Paul had pulled out for him on Bueller's left side, Barry grabbed the empty chair next to Stuart. He did not mean to be rude. In fact, he hardly noticed Father Paul, the chair, or anything else. He was entirely absorbed in one burning question. What brought Stuart across the Atlantic to Hans Bueller's table? Hans, looking a little confused but not at all upset, graciously welcomed Omar Shabaka, who having nowhere else to sit, allowed Father Paul to seat him in lieu of Barry. An amused Father Paul then walked to another table across the room and sat down.

"What the blazes! Where did you come from?" Barry asked.

"I'm happy to see you too," Stuart said sarcastically.

"I'm sorry," Barry replied apologetically as he passed the plates of food that were circulating around the table. "Of course it's good to see you, but I didn't expect you. I have no idea why you are here or how you got here."

"I flew into Cairo yesterday on Egypt Air. Flew from Cairo over to Suez, got a rental which I drove down the coast, and here I am," Stuart answered rather glibly as he pushed the vegetables into his rice and lamb mixing it into a kind of stew.

"You know what I mean," Barry rejoined. "What are you doing here? How did you find me?"

"The United States government can find just about anyone," Stuart answered slyly, rather enjoying seeing Barry Short in such a dither, particularly since from Stuart's point of view, Barry had ruined his Friday night dinner date with Natalie.

Returning the sarcasm Barry said, "Are they after me for something?" He turned his full attention to his dinner as if to say, I've had enough of this game.

Stuart dropped his knife and fork to the table, and in a more serious tone replied, "You left without telling anyone but me where you were going, and you never really explained what was so important that you would risk returning to Egypt. You made me responsible for you. Isn't that why you told me, for insurance?"

"I didn't think of it that way," Barry said looking down at the white cotton napkin on his lap. I thought someone should know in case..."

"In case anything should happen to you! I'm here at the behest of Natalie and Madeleine to make sure nothing does."

"I intentionally tried not to worry Madeleine. Did you tell them I was here?"

"No, they told me! Sort of. You entirely wrecked my Friday night. Do you know that?"

"What?" Barry said, not at all understanding what Stuart could be talking about.

"Madeleine phoned Natalie at work Friday afternoon because she had some kind of bad dream with you in it. She thought you were in trouble, and that made Natalie upset because her mother was upset. So when I told her you had called me earlier in the week and you were going to sneak into Egypt, she freaked. That was it; our date was over. I told Natalie that I would see what I could do to get you back. So here I am."

Barry sat quietly for a few moments. A young man swept by and lifted up his dinner plate followed by another who left dessert in its place. It occurred to him as the rice pudding was being served, he had been so distracted that he had eaten his entire meal without tasting it. He would relish his pudding, he thought. Before he did, he turned back to Stuart both humbled and embarrassed. "I should have known better. I was never going to get away with this deception," he sighed. "At any rate, I'm happy you're here," he said rubbing his head. "I think I might need a little insurance."

"I thought as much."

Hans Bueller proposed a toast to his friends who had come to visit him, some from a great distance. "Here! Here!" answered the large gathering of monks who held up their glasses of rich, sweet wine.

Chapter 8

Esoteric Manuscript

Fire flickered before exploding into a flame that stayed safely contained within the globe of Bueller's oil lamp. Lit in shadow and light, his face took on neither the aspect of an angel nor its opposite. Rather, the flame brought out the features of a complicated mortal with deep furrowed brows, intense eyes, aquiline nose, and the sweetest of mouths.

"Come z'is way," Bueller said as he motioned Barry, Omar, and Stuart into his library. He unlocked the door of the room that housed the library's collection of ancient books and manuscripts, pushed the door open, and led them inside.

The room was larger than Barry had expected, quite large for a room with no windows. Books and black leather cases lined the shelves and gathered dust in stacked piles. Barry caught a glimpse of what appeared to be a stairwell in the rear of the room nearly hidden by great piles of books and boxes. A single table stood in the middle of the disorder on which Bueller placed a black box.

"Do any of you have a wipe?" he asked.

Omar Shabaka pulled a cotton handkerchief from his pocket and handed it over to Bueller who removed a light coating of dust from the case before opening it. "Here," he said as he lifted a curled manuscript with brittle edges from the case. He placed it on the table and carefully spread it out by securing its corners with four flat stones.

"I found z'is papyrus as I was sorting through z'ese boxes and categorizing z'ere contents so z'at I might organize z'is rare and ancient material for future research and scholarship. You can see z'at has never been done before," he said as he looked about at the disheveled piles. "A terrible shame. If it had been known z'at all of z'ese riches were here, z'ey would have been invaluable research assets. I can see already z'at some of z'is material will lead to z'e rez'inking of many established ideas.

But I don't have z'e time for all of z'at. Instead, I have made it my goal to catalogue all of z'is, put it in some kind of physical order so z'at various items can be easily found, and z'en publish my catalogue for future researchers."

"It's very noble of you to serve knowledge," Omar said to the elderly man. "Most men would hoard it for themselves."

"Z'ank you," was all that Hans Bueller said, knowing that for most of his life Omar's description of "most men" would have fit him perfectly.

"Z'en I came upon z'is," Bueller said as he gazed upon the manuscript that lay spread out on the table. "It is so curious and perhaps so important z'at I could not put it aside. So I wrote you and asked you to come right away," he said to Barry.

"I cannot read hieroglyphics, Hans. You know that. You've often commented that it's my biggest failing as an archeologist," Barry said, looking quite embarrassed to have to admit his shortcoming.

"Yes, it is. But you have other gifts, greater gifts perhaps." He paused a few moments before he spoke again. "I can trust you, and I know you will pursue z'is mightily. Besides, I've already translated it for you and made you a copy of z'e translation."

Omar, who could read hieroglyphics as well if not better than Bueller asked, "May I read this?" Bueller nodded. "This looks old, very old. The hieroglyphic style is predynastic," Omar said as he perused the manuscript. Bueller nodded his head in agreement. "It is written to or about a lady. That's curious. A goddess maybe, but I'm not sure. A lady with a looking glass. She reflects upon herself. She is perhaps very vain."

"Nothing new about that," Stuart remarked, his laughter indicating the pleasure he took in his own wit. The other men did not laugh.

"These lines suggest something more," Omar continued and then paused.

"Go on man! What do they say?" Barry demanded.

"It's rather hard to translate these symbols into text line for line. I would be curious to see your translation Hans," he said looking up at the old man who stood over him as he studied the text.

"I would like to hear you translate to see if our interpretations match," Bueller said.

36

"Give it a shot, Omar," Barry urged, nearly beside himself in anticipation.

"All right, it reads, 'She looks upon herself who is not there. But sees instead before her all the world. Whatever was, whatever will be is in her care. For she is the maker of the world.'"

Hans nodded his head in agreement.

"Why, I've never heard mention of this lady before." Omar said. "Do you know where this papyrus was found?"

The elderly Dr. Bueller, his face ablaze from the lamp answered, "No, I do not. Z'at is part of z'e mystery."

"Will you continue to read?" an enormously curious Barry demanded.

"Within her face are all faces, all time, the cosmic burst of creation."

"It must be Isis," Barry said.

"No! No!" Omar exclaimed. "Isis is the giver of life. This lady came before. She envisioned the life Isis gave. 'And holds the mirror of world.'"

"I thought you said you were not sure if she was a goddess?" Stuart said, only mildly interested in what the other three men considered a tremendous find.

"She seems more than a goddess," Omar replied.

"Yes, you see z'e gods and goddesses of z'e Egyptian pantheon, like the Greek and the Roman pantheons, have z'eir domain. But z'is lady's domain is everyz'ing!" Bueller nearly shouted.

"God is a woman?" Barry smiled as he examined the crumbling document. "How old do you think this is?"

"Z'at is another mystery. I am sure it is very old."

"The technique used to make the papyrus attests to that," Omar said.

"I have more to show you tomorrow," Bueller said, his face suddenly showing signs of fatigue. "Z'ere is a statue, and z'ere are oz'er z'ings I found with z'is z'at were defaced. I cannot go on tonight. It must wait for tomorrow."

Putting his arm around the old man, Omar walked Bueller through the door into the library. "Yes, yes, you must get some rest. If I can get some hot water, I will make you some of my special tea."

"Z'at would be wonderful! I have missed your teas very much," Bueller said, recalling the zesty lemon and honey brews Omar Shabaka had made for him nearly a year ago when he nursed him back to health.

"I will leave the recipe with you this time," Omar said as he helped him out of the library.

Barry locked the door to the manuscript room and placed the key and oil lamp upon Hans Bueller's desk. "Do you have a room?" he asked Stuart.

Stuart looked puzzled.

"Did they give you a room? The abbot? Did he give you a room?"

"Oh, no. I told him I would be staying elsewhere, a hotel someplace."

"You can room with me tonight. The closest hotel is more than fifty miles from here in El Quseir."

"That's very kind of you."

"Don't think anything of it. I may be needing a bodyguard more than ever now."

Stuart was surprised that Barry had made the offer when he discovered how small the room was and how small was the twin bed that took up most of the space. An argument ensued over who would get the floor. Stuart said he would sleep on the floor in deference to Barry's greater age. Barry argued that he was not that much older than Stuart and that Stuart had flown all-night and driven all day and therefore deserved the comfort of a mattress. Stuart won the argument, pointing out that he was at least twenty-five years Barry's junior, a point that Barry didn't like being reminded of.

Barry pulled the thick blue comforter and one of the pillows off the bed and handed them to Stuart. "There, it won't be so bad."

The two men stripped down to their underwear. Barry crawled between the clean white sheets of the bed. Stuart turned out the oil lamp before rolling himself into the comforter that he spread on the floor.

"Are you all right down there?"

"A hotel might have been better. But I couldn't have made that fifty-mile drive tonight. I'm worn out," Stuart replied and began to doze.

"It's a very nice hotel too," Barry agreed. "I was very pleased with it until I got clubbed."

"What!" Stuart sat up.

"Oh, I forgot I hadn't told you yet. Yes, last night. Some thieves followed us all the way from Luxor. They must have recognized me at the train station there. They tried to break into my room. I went after them, and they walloped me. I was out cold."

"You've got to get out of here," Stuart said, fumbling to find the matches to light the lamp.

"Hold on! They don't know where I am. They took off after the incident, and no one followed us here this morning."

"Hey, you were the first to tell me about the trajectory of rumors among thieves in this country. By now anyone interested in knowing has learned you are in Egypt. The word probably traveled up the Nile to Cairo riding a big wave."

"What a nice image," Barry muttered as he snuggled into his sheets. "A wave gently rolling along, undulating all the way to Cairo. How would they find me?"

"I found you didn't I! Some of them have probably kept tabs on Bueller since he's been here, and they will find you just like I did."

"Not tonight," Barry said, barely able to utter another word.

"Well, you're probably right about that, but we're getting out of here tomorrow. Tomorrow, right?" Stuart said urgently. The only reply was a deep, resonant snore.

Chapter 9

Synchronism

Barry was rolling on a soft wave towards Cairo when a rough tug on his shoulder threatened to overturn his felucca.

"Get up!" a voice shouted. "We've got to get outta here."

"What? Where?" Barry muttered in a sleepy voice. He opened his eyes to dim morning light and saw Stuart standing at the washbasin drying his face. "That's my towel!" he complained.

"Sorry. I hadn't washed my face since leaving D.C. I hope you don't mind too much."

"Oh, that's okay I guess. What time is it?"

"It's six. Get up and get dressed. We've gotta go."

"Hold on just a minute! I can't go until I've said goodbye to Hans and Omar, and Hans will want to show me whatever he brought me down here to see."

"The longer we hang around here, the deeper the trouble," Stuart scolded.

"Trouble, what trouble? There's no trouble here."

"There will be if we don't get outta here soon."

"Ah, don't worry so much. We will go after breakfast, after I have made my goodbyes. I didn't come all the way here just to turn around and leave."

"Okay, after breakfast. Right now get dressed and go with me outside so we can phone Natalie. I can't get a signal inside this mountain. See, no signal at all," he said as he attempted to make a connection.

The two men left the room and made their way to the central hallway that leads to the vestibule and out into the garden. They saw no one on the way.

"I hope we're not locked inside this place," Stuart said, now worried that the monks had not yet awakened and opened the building.

"Oh, they're up. Smell," Barry said while filling his nostrils with the scent of baking bread. "Most of them are probably at their morning prayers, that's all."

"You're probably right," Stuart said as he pulled open the unlocked door leading to the outside. "I'd better learn where the other exits are. You never want to be trapped in a building with only one way out."

"Right," Barry agreed, although in truth he thought Stuart's concerns were a little paranoid.

The two men wandered along the spiral path looking for a place to sit. They passed a variety of flowers and herbs and walked over several footbridges that crossed the irrigation streams coming from the well. Failing to see any benches, they settled on a comfortable spot on the ground under a tall palm tree and next to the stream.

"Remarkable place, isn't it," Barry said to Stuart who was punching in Natalie's phone number.

"I've never seen any place like it," Stuart said while he waited for a connection. "There, I've got one, but it's weak. We had better make this fast. It's ringing," he said, looking relieved. "I told her I would call her as soon as I made contact with you. Here, you take the phone and surprise her."

"Natalie, is that you? I can barely hear you. Yes, it's me, Barry. He's here with me. Yes, we're in Egypt. We're going to try to leave today. How is your mother? Tell her not to worry. Oh, they are!"

Barry turned to Stuart, "John is in Europe. He's trying to reach me."

"Get a phone number."

"Stuart asks if you have a phone number. I'll wait." He turned to Stuart. "It's past midnight there. She had to get out of bed to get the number. Okay Natalie, go ahead. I'll repeat it: 31.20.420.3658. Got it." He handed the phone back to Stuart.

"Isn't that Holland's country code?" Stuart said. "Natalie? Natalie? The phone went dead."

"Sorry you didn't get a chance to talk to her."

"Well, at least she knows I'm here, and you're all right; that is what's important." Looking around he added, "We were lucky we got through at all out here in no man's land."

"Should we phone John?"

"It can wait until we're someplace where we can get a better connection."

"This no man's land is very beautiful," Barry said. He slipped off his shoes and socks and soaked his feet in the little irrigation stream. "Feels good. Join me." Stuart followed suit. "I feel bad that I caused so much worry. They weren't supposed to know I came here. Did you say that Madeleine had some kind of dream?"

"Yeah, yeah. That's what Natalie told me. I don't believe in that dream stuff myself."

"You should never discount the importance of dreams," Barry said. "Why, this morning when you woke me up I had been dreaming that I was lounging in a felucca that was bobbing along the waves as it sailed to Cairo. I know where that dream came from. You suggested that wonderful image last night. 'Riding a big wave,' I believe I'm quoting you correctly."

"I said something like that."

"It's funny how those things affect the mind. I found it restful, so voila, like magic my subconscious incorporated it into my dreams."

"I didn't say it to soothe you. I meant it as a warning."

"No matter. It's what my subconscious heard that's important. There are all kinds of dreams, you know. There is a whole body of literature that supports the belief that some are prophetic." Barry stared for a moment at a white lily that floated atop the irrigation stream. "Speaking of dreams, I had a very interesting one on my way down here, so interesting that I wrote it down in my journal. We should go back in now. I need to talk to Hans."

"Remember, we're leaving after breakfast."

"Yes, yes."

A half dozen monks busied themselves bringing food out from the kitchen into the refectory whose doors were now wide open. Others began taking their places at the tables.

"You go on in," Barry said. "Save me a seat. I have to go to my room to get something."

Standing in the hallway in front of his door were Omar Shabaka and Hans Bueller. "Z'ere you are. I was about to go get a key since you did not answer," Bueller said as Barry approached.

"I was out in the garden with Stuart."

"Is Stuart still here?" Omar asked. "He told me he had a hotel room somewhere."

"He was too tired to drive all the way to El Quseir. He's in the refectory right now. They're getting ready to serve breakfast. Since you're here, could you stay a few minutes? I've something to show you."

He rifled through his bag in search of his diary. "I had a dream when I took the train from Alexandria to Cairo. It was compelling enough that I wrote it down so I wouldn't forget the details. Stuart and I were just discussing dreams out in the garden and it came to me. I thought it important in light of what you showed us last night. Here it is. *November 30, Cairo: I just had a remarkable dream,*" he read aloud. "*I saw Thoth, not in person but in likeness. The statue looked just like the one I rescued earlier this year with the body of a man and the head of an Ibis. I seemed to be walking towards the statue when its navel became very large and I entered it, like entering a cave. Inside there was a woman who looked like she had been carved out of black basalt; but she wasn't a statue, she was a sentient being, wearing a crown and tenderly holding a child. When I got nearer, I could see that like Thoth the child had the head of a bird. As soon as I could make that out, the child lifted himself from his mother's arms and flew into her eye, which shone brightly. I saw a man follow the bird-child into the beautiful woman's eye, and the man looked like me. Suddenly I found myself transported into a field of white lilies, Madonna lilies. The dream was so powerful I could smell them.*" He finished and sat silent for a few seconds while looking at the two men before either would speak.

"Z'is is fascinating. Do you remember anyz'ing else?"

"No, that was it. The train put on its breaks, and the jolt woke me up. I don't think there would have been anything else. It felt complete. Did I tell you the beautiful woman wore a crown, not so much a crown but a disk?"

"The crown of the sun!" Omar said.

"And you had z'is dream on your way to see me?"

"Yes, while en route."

"You were chosen by powers greater z'an me for z'is adventure I'm sending you on, which is why I called you here. I want you to research z'is statue z'at I will give you to take. I have z'e name of a monk who is z'e curator of z'e Archeological museum in Narbonne. He is an expert in z'e Black Virgin. Go to z'e Old Palace of z'e Archbishops and ask for him. Begin z'ere and see where it takes you. You will see after I show you oz'er z'ings z'at Europe will be a more fruitful ground for your research z'an Egypt. I feel confident now z'at you will be properly guided."

"Stuart wants me to leave right after breakfast. He says I'm not safe here, and he wants to get me out of the country immediately."

"He is probably right after what happened at the hotel," Omar agreed.

"But we weren't followed here. We were careful of that."

"It's only a matter of time until someone guesses where you are. Your presence here puts this entire monastery at risk," Omar said.

"Well, that's something I hadn't thought about."

Bueller looked distraught. "I will show you after breakfast, and z'en you can leave. But you must stay in touch. I have to know!"

The three men walked down to the refectory and joined Stuart who was dipping his flat bread into his second helping of eggs. Together they plotted the initial steps of Barry Short's departure. He would leave with Stuart since it was assumed that if anyone were watching, they would be looking for Omar's van. Omar would remain at the monastery for several hours after Stuart and Barry's departure to give them a good head start, and then he would make his way back to Luxor where they would meet up.

"I will give you directions to my father's house so you will have somewhere to go where you won't be recognized. My father and I will find a way to get you out of the country unseen," Omar offered.

The plan was set, although Barry still thought it unnecessary. Yet he had to concede that Omar could be right. His presence at the monastery may have put it at risk. He was prepared to leave and leave soon, but first he would have to see whatever Hans Bueller had yet to show him. He thought about his dream, of seeing himself walk into the eye of the Madonna. His intuition told him this is exactly what he was about to do.

Chapter 10

The Goddess Statue

Hans Bueller hoisted a leather box up onto the table next to the oil lamp. The case was larger than the one that held the papyrus the night before, but the windowless room was just as dark. Stuart looked more uncomfortable than he had last night.

"I asked Father Paul to let me know if any strangers come near the place," he said. "Will he know to look for us in this closet?"

"I can take z'is case into z'e main library room, on a table where we can get z'e benefit of z'e light," Bueller said, having noted Stuart's discomfort but misunderstanding its cause. "Can you help me with z'is?"

"Sure." Stuart picked up the case and followed Bueller out of the dark room and into the full light of the library where he deposited the box on one of the long tables near the windows.

"Z'ank you. Is z'is better for you?"

"Do these windows open?" Stuart asked.

Bueller furrowed his brow. "I have not tried them. Z'ey are very old and z'e room stays cool enough."

Barry noticed Bueller's face and guessed at the cause of his worry. "Stuart's not claustrophobic if that's what you're thinking. He told me when we were out in the garden that you never want to be trapped in a building with only one way out. I think that's his concern, isn't it?"

"Sure is," Stuart answered matter-of-factly. "When you're being pursued, you need an exit plan, several if possible."

"Z'ere is no one pursuing you here."

"Stu is in law enforcement," Barry explained. "He plans ahead."

"Oh, if z'at is z'e case, I can tell you z'ere is a wonderful way to escape from here. Z'e staircase in z'e manuscript room goes to a tunnel. Z'e tunnel takes you outside z'e monastic walls."

"What do you use it for?" Stuart asked.

"We use it for noz'ing. Maybe in z'e past z'ey used it for somez'ing.

45

Or maybe like you z'ey built it just in case."

"Do you mind if I inspect it while the rest of you look at these things?"

"Be my guest," Bueller said.

"Can I take this?" Stuart asked holding up the oil lamp.

"Well, of course."

"Barry, you come and get me if Father Paul shows up before I get back."

The three men watched Stuart disappear into the manuscript room and then turned their attention to the case. Bueller opened it and deposited a heavy bundle of damaged texts on the table before them.

"What made me curious about z'ese is z'ey are all damaged in z'e same way. Look here." He showed them example after example of texts with the name scratched out of a cartouche.

"That's not terribly unusual," Barry said. "You see names chipped and hammered out of stone cartouches all over Egypt. Some Pharaoh or another was just engaging in the common practice of trying to destroy the memory or prestige of his predecessor."

"Z'ere is more. I recognized z'at all of z'ese texts had references linking z'em to z'e papyrus manuscript I showed you last night. When z'ey speak of the mirror of creation, z'ey are speaking about her. I wrapped her in velvet. I found her in straw," he said as he removed a smaller box from the case, opened it and began taking off the soft velvet cloth he had packed the figurine in. "Z'e manuscripts are about her," he repeated as the three men cast their eyes on a beautiful woman carved out of black basalt.

Her hair fell all about her face in soft curls that appeared lifted as if by a breeze into feather-like wisps. Her nose was long and regal and her mouth full. Her most outstanding feature were her extraordinarily large eyes, made luminous by the stone having been polished. Perched upon her head like a crown was a shiny round disk.

Bueller held the little statue up to the light, which the crown reflected along with his image. "Her crown is her mirror," he said.

"I see what you mean," Barry said. "It's made from copper. The very material ancient mirrors were made from. Yes, I think you're right."

"Who is she?" Omar asked.

"I do not know her name. Z'ey destroyed it." He gazed at the damaged pages spread out upon the table. "Z'at's what I want Barry to find out. Who is z'is woman who holds z'e mirror of creation? Who is she, and why did z'ey destroy her name?"

"That's quite a task," Barry said, feeling unsure he was up to it. "Can I hold her?"

Barry grasped the statue with his hand. It had more weight than he expected. He turned it slowly so he could examine all its facets.

"It looks very old. I would say it's predynastic. It was well taken care of though to have survived this long intact."

"She was packed in straw when I found her and wrapped in cloth like a mummy. I z'ink she was hidden away for a long, long time."

"That would explain her condition. Look at this pattern on her back; it's nearly worn away. It looks like bird wings!"

"Or fish scales," Bueller said.

"Oh, I see. Wings or scales. What are these marks on the base of her back?"

"Turn her around."

Barry turned the figurine around and saw that the tiny marks he had observed on her back wrapped around the entire bust.

It looks like writing of some sort," Omar said. "But not hieroglyphics, not even the earliest hieroglyphics."

"They almost look like runes," Barry remarked. "I've seen runes similar to these in the caves I've been searching in France."

"Exactly," Bueller said in a business like tone. "Z'ats why you must take her z'ere. I have here everyz'ing you will need to start your investigation. You will take her with you." He took the statue from Barry, wrapped her up in velvet, and deposited her back into her box.

"She must be very valuable," Barry said as he took the box.

"Priceless, and she will be safer where she can return to z'e sunlight. Z'e papyrus manuscript, on z'e oz'er hand, must stay here. Z'e light and air might destroy it if it left its dark home for long. Here is z'e translation I promised you. And here is z'e address of z'e monk I told you about in Narbonne. Show him all of z'is, and he will help you. I know it. Please, please be careful with her."

"Are you sure I should take her? What if something should happen to us?" Barry said as he felt the weight of the figurine in his hand. "She could be lost yet again!"

"She will never be forgotten again." Bueller went over to his desk and returned with his sketchpad. He opened it to a remarkable drawing of the statue, remarkable not only for its likeness but for its spirit he had captured in his careful modulation of shadow and light. "She will be in z'e book I'm having published of lost artifacts. I think she will be on z'e cover."

"Her eyes!" Omar said as he looked at the drawing with admiration. "They are so deep, so wise. I feel as if I'm looking into the very well of creation."

"Am I interrupting anything?" Father Paul asked as he peeked inside the room.

"Oh, no I was just showing z'em some z'ings," Bueller answered.

"Why don't you come in and join us?" Barry said, having already tucked the box inside his shirt. Hans has been showing us these curious ancient manuscripts in which the names have been removed."

"One sees that a lot in Egypt, doesn't one. I only popped in because Stuart—I don't see him here—well, anyway, Stuart had asked me to report any comings and goings around the place. The butcher has made his meat delivery this morning, the postmaster has brought the mail, and there are a group of handymen outside claiming they had been called in from El Quseir for repairs. Do you know anything about that Hans?"

"I have no idea. I don't attend to maintenance."

"I'm not quite sure what to do with them. They've come so far. Maybe I can find a few things for them to do. Could you use a few repairmen in the library? Maybe they could move a few things for you or tighten the legs on some of these rickety tables."

"Repairmen did you say?" Stuart said as he reentered the library from the manuscript room.

"Oh, there you are. I was just reporting to the others since you were not here."

"I was exploring your tunnel. That's quite a dugout."

"Yes, it is. We often try to think of ways we could put it to good use. It seems a shame to waste all the work that was done excavating it. But it is hard to imagine what use we could put it to," Father Paul replied.

"What about these repairmen?" Stuart asked. "What are they here to repair?"

"That's just it," Father Paul repeated. "I do not know; nor do I know who called them. They came all the way from El Quseir so I feel like I should find something for them to do for their trouble."

"I have noz'ing for z'em to do here. As for z'ese tables, z'e only solution for z'em is z'e fire and we build new ones."

"There are many good years left in these tables," Father Paul countered.

"Does this sort of thing happen here very often?" Stuart asked.

"Why, no," answered the father. "We are off the beaten path to say the least. To be quite honest, most of the repairs needed around here we can do for ourselves. Many skilled men live here you see."

"Yes, I'm beginning to see," Stuart said. "If I were you, I would send these men packing."

"I must at least invite them for lunch," Father Paul protested. "It would be impolite to do less," he said as he left the library.

Stuart looked at the three men huddled around the table. "Stay right here until I come back. Don't leave. I'm going to scope things out. Don't go anywhere unless you go into the manuscript room. In fact, that would be a good idea."

"Is he always like z'is?" Bueller asked.

"No, not always," Barry said. "I would say he's a little over excited right now. But maybe we ought to get this stuff out of the sunlight. I can see these texts well enough under the oil lamp."

Chapter 11

Escape

"They look suspicious," Stuart said in complete contradiction to Father Paul's pronouncement. "Are you really going to have them staying here for lunch?"

"Of course I am! And I will give them a little work if I can find it," Father Paul said, determined not to let this ill-mannered American undermine the monastery's long standing tradition of hospitality.

Stuart again peeked through the door of the vestibule where the men were still awaiting Father Paul's return. He had to acknowledge that all four of them looked ordinary enough, dressed, as they were for work in mid-length, gray cotton collarless shirts over loose fitting pants. They looked poor enough too, as if they could use a little money. But the coincidence of their having arrived unexpectedly right at this moment was far too great for him to overlook. He would have to get Barry out of there before lunch and before these men had a chance to do whatever they had come to do. He considered that he could simply go back to the library and spirit Barry through the tunnel he had just explored, but soon realized that would not work. He would have to bring the car around which meant Barry would have to go it alone. The tunnel was in deplorable condition, filthy and dark; and he had not ventured through to the end where it probably gets worse. As far as he knew, it could have collapsed further down, blocking passage to the outside. He had a better idea if he could convince Father Paul.

"I know I've been difficult," Stuart said apologetically after closing the sliver-wide opening of the door to the vestibule. "I know I may be wrong about these men."

"You need not apologize," Father Paul replied, eager to see the best in a man. "You are looking after your friend. I must tell you quite frankly, I've been concerned about his presence here since I learned about his altercation in El Quseir."

"You're quite right to worry. I'm afraid it was more than an altercation. Look, I promised his friends that I would get him out of Egypt safely, and I don't want to take any chances now. So I want to propose a plan that will solve both of our problems. It could provide these men work if they really want it and give Barry and me a clear exit."

Father Paul was quite interested because in truth, he was looking forward to Barry and Stuart's departure. He didn't want any trouble at the monastery, and these two looked like more trouble than the workmen to whom he wanted to offer a little charity. Besides, even if the Father did not want to admit it to himself, he did not like Stuart. He found him brash and was suspicious of his character and motives.

"I was thinking," Stuart continued, "Hans Bueller lacks space and shelving in his manuscript room. These men could build him a few more bookshelves and install them at the bottom of the stairwell near the tunnel."

"Hmm, that's a very good idea. I've been wondering how to make use of that tunnel, at least part of it."

"You might ask them to build a few new wine barrels for you too. That tunnel is the perfect place to store wine."

"That's another very good idea."

Stuart added, "Of course, it's filthy down there. The first thing they would have to do is clean it out."

"Quite right! I'll take them down there right away. I think they were only looking for a day's work and this could take a good week or longer, but I could make it worth their while," the jovial abbot said, his hand already on the door of the vestibule.

"Hold on!" Stuart said, grabbing the abbot's hand. "Could you give me fifteen minutes before you do that? I'll go get Barry right away and take him up to his room to get his things while the men wait in the vestibule. When you take them into the library, we will leave through the vestibule and be on our way."

"Before lunch?" Father Paul replied, apparently not understanding Stuart's full meaning.

"Yes, we must leave now. Don't mention that we've gone, and make sure the men have a nice, long lunch even if they don't want the work."

"That sounds agreeable," Father Paul said, his opinion of Stuart much improved. "I do hope they will want the work though. I've wanted to do something with that space down there. The extra shelves would be a real benefit to Hans." The good father grabbed Stuart's hand and shook it. "So happy to have met you Stuart even if our meeting was a bit short. Since I probably won't have the opportunity to make my goodbyes to Barry, I will ask you to make them for me."

"Of course. Remember, fifteen minutes," Stuart repeated before he scrambled up the stairs to the library.

Inside the manuscript room, Barry, Omar, and Hans were poring over the sheaf of defaced papyrus. They noted the heavily outlined Eye of Horus positioned like quotations marks on either side of the Goddess Nuit whose starry body stretched over the top of each leaf.

"There must be a connection here," Omar said.

Barry agreed. "How unusual to see both the left and right Eye of Horus together like this."

"Protection," Hans said. "Plenty of protection. One eye represents z'e sun, z'e oz'er z'e moon. Later in Egypt z'e connection to z'e moon faded so we usually see only z'e one eye."

"Which supports your thesis that these manuscripts and this lady are very old. But that double dose of protection sure didn't help her much," Barry said as he strained his eyes under the dimming light of the oil lamp to try to find anything left of her identifying hieroglyphics.

"Who knows,' the elderly man said. "Maybe being hidden away here was her protection. Maybe our work will be her awakening. Maybe now is z'e time."

"Maybe," Omar repeated as the three men stood quietly feeling that what had been uncovered was something quite extraordinary.

Their quiet was interrupted with a loud rapping on the door and Stuart's voice, "Come on, we're going!"

Hans Bueller calmly opened the door of the manuscript room and looked rather perplexed. "We are going, you say?"

"Not you! Barry, we've got to get out of here right now. Father Paul is bringing those workmen in here in a few minutes to look at this tunnel."

"My tunnel?" Bueller asked.

"He's going to offer them work cleaning it up and building you some new bookshelves so you'll have more space to put away all of this stuff."

"Shelves for me?"

"Come on Barry. Make your goodbyes so we can go to your room and get your pack and make our escape."

"Escape? I don't understand," Bueller said.

Omar understood Stuart's meaning perfectly. "I will explain it to you later Hans. Have you given Barry everything he needs to take with him?"

"Why yes. I've given him everyz'ing, I z'ink."

Omar scribbled some directions onto a piece of paper and handed it to Barry. "Here is a map to my father's house. I will meet you there when I can leave here without being noticed."

"Thank you my friend," Barry said. He turned to Bueller and hugged him close. "And thank you Hans. I will write you when I learn who our mysterious lady is. I promise."

"But you've only just got here!" Hans said before being interrupted once again by the door to the library opening.

"This is perhaps more work than you had wanted," Father Paul could be heard saying to the men as he led them into the main library room. "I would pay you well, and you could all stay here until it is completed."

"Oh, crap! I told him fifteen minutes," Stuart said. "Barry, I hate to do this to you old pal, but you're gonna have to make your escape through that tunnel. Any more oil lamps in this room Hans?"

"Why yes."

"Good, light one in a hurry," he said as he handed the already lit oil lamp to Barry. "Get going. I'll get your gear and drive around to the opening. If you aren't there when I arrive, I'll come in looking for you. Now, get going. They'll be in here in a few seconds."

Barry stuffed the translation of the manuscript into his large inside jacket pocket together with the statue and directions and followed Stuart down the stairs to the tunnel's entrance.

"It's dirty and dilapidated. I just hope the walls haven't crumbled further down. Get as far as you can, and I'll come after you from the other end."

"I will be fine Stuart. I've been in far worse places than this. By the way, thank you," he said before he disappeared into the dark.

Stuart flew back up the steps and stood with Hans Bueller and Omar Shabaka when Father Paul entered the manuscript room with the men.

"Oh, there you are Hans. I was just showing these men the library shelves and asking them if they could duplicate them for you. I was thinking we might expand your storage area into the lower level near the tunnel opening."

"Z'at would be wonderful! I do need more organized space," he said as he looked about the disheveled piles strewn about the room.

"May we go downstairs?" Father Paul asked.

"Certainly," Hans said. "Let me go with you."

As the workmen, Father Paul, and Bueller made their way down to the site of Barry Short's recent escape, Omar and Stuart reentered the main room of the library.

"I will meet you at my father's house. You need time to get as far away from here as possible before I leave in case they should follow my van."

"Smart," Stuart said. He shook Omar's hand before leaving to go up to Barry's room to collect his things. Minutes later with Barry's backpack in tow Stuart made his way to the vestibule passing the entrance of the refectory along the way. He could smell the steamed rice and lamb as he passed. No lunch for the weary, he thought as he exited the large doors of the vestibule into the fragrant courtyard garden and made his way toward his rented sedan and the gate to the outside.

Chapter 12

The Tunnel

Barry was used to navigating in poorly lit grottos having just spent the better part of the past several months in the caves and caverns of France's southern midsection. It was a good thing too since the oil lamp he held barely lit the tunnel walls he was passing through. He wished he had thought to ask for the fresh lamp.

Voices began to echo from the tunnel's entrance. He turned off his lamp, and as an afterthought he searched his pockets to make sure he had matches to relight it when it was safe to do so. Total darkness lay in front of him. To his rear was a glow coming from the tunnel entrance where the uninvited workmen and Father Paul were assessing the labor involved in refitting the area for additional library storage shelves.

He tied the darkened oil lamp to his belt, stretched out his arms and pressed his hands against tunnel walls for added stability. Feeling relatively secure in his footing, he continued to slowly move forward. The walls were cool and dry and in places the stone was quite flakey. After walking twenty feet or so in this way, a chunk of rock came loose under the pressure of his hand and fell to the floor. He stopped abruptly and looked back. A distant lamp was pointing directly towards him into the deep tunnel. The intruders had heard the noise, he thought. He stood absolutely still for a few moments until the lamp turned away. Not wanting to risk another accident, he carefully made his way through the tunnel without the support of his hands against the walls. The floor felt smooth enough, and the tunnel was straight.

Absolute quiet overtook the dark passageway. He turned around, and as he suspected the glow behind him had disappeared. Father Paul and the men had apparently returned to the library. For caution's sake, he traveled another ten feet in the dark. Convinced the workers would not soon return, he stopped to light the oil lamp. He sighed as he looked ahead. The tunnel that up until then had looked as if it were hand hewn took on the uneven appearance of a natural cave. He ducked his head, as the confines grew lower and narrower. Underground water had seeped inside, making the jagged rocks that protruded from the natural floor treacherous. He again tied the oil lamp to his belt to free up his hands, but when he did the lamp burned out leaving him standing in the pitch black.

"Drat!" he muttered, no longer worried that there was anyone about to hear him. He continued to feel his way along several more feet until he smacked his head against the rock ceiling that had just taken a precipitous drop.

"Ouch!" he cried involuntarily.

"Hello," came a voice from out in front of him.

He paused, unsure of what to do since he was unable to identify it.

"Hello, Barry?" came the voice again.

"Stuart, are you there?"

"Yes, I would estimate I'm about twenty feet in front of you. What can you see from your end?"

"Nothing much. The lamp just burned out, and I hit my head. The tunnel seems to be shrinking."

"You've got little more than a two feet opening at my end," Stuart said. "You're gonna have to get on your hands and knees and snake your way through."

"Oh, good grief," Barry muttered as he unstrapped the oil lamp and placed it on the floor behind him. He compressed his body as much as he could and began to crawl.

"Are you doin' okay?" Stuart asked, feeling like a coach in a spelunking event.

"I'm fine," Barry said in a tone that betrayed he was anything but.

Stuart heard the sound of rock falling followed by a muffled howl.

"Are you okay Barry?"

"My head's not okay. That's the second time I've been walloped while I've been down here."

"I can tell you are closer now, maybe five feet out. Lay down on your back, suck in your gut, and squeeze your way through."

Barry slid along on his buttocks using his feet and elbows to push himself through the narrow opening into the outside.

56

"Can I help?" the coach said as he awkwardly grabbed hold of Barry's ankles as if he were delivering a breach birth.

"No, I think I've got to do this for myself," he answered. He shook his ankles loose and pushed through the tiny opening and sat silent and still for a few moments while gathering himself after a clumsy escape. "This sort of thing was easier to do when I was young," he said as Stuart hoisted him up.

"You did great. I couldn't have done any better. Now, let's get out of here."

***

It was a fine Dutch morning. The air was crisp and brilliant, but far to the west dark skies hugged the horizon. The threesome loaded themselves and their rented bikes up on the ferry just as the bell rang its departure.

"Rain coming?" John asked, hand shading his eyes, as he looked outward.

"I don't think so," Summer said before training her eyes in the direction John was looking. "At least not for a while. Tonight maybe, so don't worry about it."

Another bell rang from inside Summer's backpack. "I've barely left," she complained as she ripped through her bag and grabbed her phone. "Hello Jos, what's up? If one more band gives me grief about their accommodations, or their travel connections, or the food they ate last night, I will scream," she said, reminded of the musician whose call had awakened her the night before. "We're not babysitters Jos," she continued before she paused long enough that he could get in a word. "Oh, she did. Did she leave a number?" Summer looked at John and Rosalind. "Can one of you guys write this phone number down? We got it. Thanks Jos," she said as she clicked off the phone and handed it to John.

"That's Natalie's number," John said. "Is it okay to make an international call?"

"Sure, but keep it short," she said as John punched in the numbers. "Now, wait for it to ring. The service will make the connection and call

57

you back."

"That's interesting," he said as he pondered the little technological wonder in his hand.

"It's cheaper that way," she explained. "Now, answer it."

"Natalie? Is that you? Your voice is a little weak. We just left her apartment a half hour ago on our way to the countryside for a bike ride. Yes, it's very nice. In fact, it's beautiful here. We're on a ferry right now." He looked over at Rosalind and began to repeat the essence of what Natalie was telling him. "Oh, Stuart called, Barry too. They're together, good. Where are they? Egypt, oh, a monastery near the Red Sea. Are they okay? Are you sure? Stuart is going to call us. No, we won't leave Holland until we've heard from them." Summer gave John a glance from which he deduced the meaning. "I had better go now," he said to Natalie. "This is costing. Talk to you after we've heard something."

"So what's going on?" Rosalind asked.

"I'm not sure. You heard most of it."

"What else did she say?"

"They phoned her this morning from the monastery where Hans Bueller lives. The reception was real bad so they didn't speak long. The phone cut off before they were through talking, but she was able to give them Summer's phone number so she expects they will try to call soon. They're going to try to get out of Egypt today and head back to Europe, but she's worried."

"Why?"

"She didn't say, but I could hear it in her voice."

"I wonder if she's talked to your mother."

"That's probably it. She talked to Mom before calling me, and she and Mom worked themselves up."

"Should we head back to Summer's place?"

"I don't think so. She's got her phone, and they're not going to magically appear in Europe today anyway."

"Unless they have a transporter beam," Rosalind laughed.

"Maybe old Bueller built one by now," John chuckled.

"So you should relax and enjoy yourselves!" Summer commanded.

"While we still can," Rosalind said, noting the clouds thickening in the west.

Christabel pushed her head through the zipper opening of the backpack John was carrying her in. Her eyes glistened, her tongue hung out in an excited pant, and her long ears flapped in the sea breeze.

"See, Christabel knows how to relax and enjoy herself," Summer said, and gave her some water.

Chapter 13

Relief

"My throat's dry from breathing in all that cave dirt. Do you have anything to drink?" Barry asked.

Stuart reached around into the back seat and pulled out a bottle of water. "It's warm, but it's all I've got."

"It will do." Barry gulped down half the bottle. "Have you got a towel?"

"No, but here's a dirty t-shirt."

Barry wetted his face and neck with the remaining water and wiped the loose dirt off.

"Do I look any better?"

"Yes, much. Now, duck down in your seat while we exit this road. Just in case."

"Just in case of what?" Barry complained, now quite tired of bending and stooping.

"Just in case those workmen have friends."

"Oh, I see." He scrunched his body close to the sedan's floorboards. The car bounced along the dirt road kicking up dust and stone until it neared the exit to the smooth highway that led south to El Quseir.

"Not yet," Stuart said and pushed hard on Barry's head just as he had begun to raise his tortured body back up on the seat. "Well, lookie here. What'd I tell you? There's a van here parked by the side of the road, and someone's in it."

"What?" Barry said again trying to raise his head.

"Quiet! Stay down!"

Stuart's rental sedan slowed for a stop, made a steady turn onto the highway, and drove away from the van at a moderate speed.

"He's not following us. Wait a few minutes. Then you can get up."

"I'm hurting down here!"

"Okay, you can get up now." Stuart picked up speed. "The driver

60

was probably on the lookout for Shabaka's van. He probably knows its color and license plate number."

"Man, am I hungry!"

"I hope that Shabaka's father has something cooked for you because we're not stopping until I get you safely out of sight."

Surrounded by desert on one side and the sea on the other, they were quite alone until they approached El Quseir. In daylight the town looked like what it was, a fishing village turned resort. Men in shorts and swimming trunks and women in sundresses and slacks strolled up and down the wharf alongside fishermen turned vendors who sold trinkets to tourists. The road from El Quseir to Luxor was another story. It was a busy highway carrying fast moving traffic between the seaport town and the inland hub. They arrived in Luxor in no time.

"Barry, wake up!" He shook the sleeping man's arm. "You've got to help me find this house."

Barry longed for real sleep in a comfortable bed, but more than that he wanted food. Omar Shabaka's father would have food, he thought to himself in his half-awakened mind, which was all the stimulus he needed to rouse himself. "Okay, okay, where are we?"

"We're entering Luxor. Do you have those directions Shabaka gave you?"

"Go to the second major intersection off the highway once you've entered Luxor," he read.

"This must be the first one. Does that one up there look like a major intersection?"

"I would say no. It looks like we intersect with an alley. But that one past it looks to be major. Turn right when you get there. We are looking for number 303."

The van turned into a neighborhood of tightly packed buildings where shopkeepers lived above storefronts. The shops were closed, but upstairs windows were lit. Barry wondered if any of these inviting lights were their destination until he spotted an address on a placard.

"That's only number 56. We've still got a ways to go."

Stuart continued along the road until their sedan drove out of the crowded merchant district and into an area with homes whose tiny courtyards separated one house from the next.

"Here it is," Stuart said.

He slowed the car and saw the address marked on what looked like an unpaved road. He made a turn and drove up to the house of Omar Shabaka's father. Lights illuminated both the gardens and the front double doors, which sprung open when they pulled up. Out marched the elder Doctor Shabaka, looking tall and slender in his long white robe.

"Welcome to my house," the distinguished looking man said.

"You were expecting us?" Barry asked.

"My son phoned me about a half hour ago from El Quseir. He should be along soon. Come in, come in," he said as he ushered them into his home. "Please call me Saadya."

"I'm Barry and this is Stuart." He looked down at the gleaming granite tile they stood upon in the foyer adjacent to the richly colored woven carpets and the arabesque style furniture in the next room. "We should have come in through the servants' entrance," he apologized as he kicked off his shoes in a vain effort to minimize the damage of the mud and sand that was caked on his knees, seat of his pants, the back of his shirt, as well as his shoes.

"The two of you can bathe before dinner?" Saadya said smiling. "Bathe and rest a bit, and by then Omar will have arrived."

Barry's body acquiesced at the thought of real rest, which signaled to him how tired he was. "That would be most agreeable," he said.

Saadya led them to a large guest bedroom with an adjoining bath. "If you leave your clothing and shoes outside the door, I will have them cleaned and laundered. You will find fresh galabayyas in the chest."

"I don't know how to thank you," Barry said, unwilling to go through the pretense of saying he shouldn't impose when his body so longed for a soft bed and his mind for a safe place.

Stuart punched numbers into his satellite phone while Barry soaked in the tub in the other room. "Waxed Disc," a voice said.

"John?"

"Jos," the voice answered. "No John here." The voice paused for a second. "You must be looking for Summer's brother-in-law."

"Yes, I am."

"He will return later tonight."

"Do you know what time?"

"No, but you can call Summer's satellite phone if you like."

He thanked Jos, took down the number, and punched it in.

The bicyclists by then had cruised through hobbit style villages and tourist towns, alongside the great dikes that hold back the North Sea, and past cows that graze the green fields. They had even explored an old windmill that stood next to one of the many bike paths that crisscross the countryside. But when Stuart's phone call came they were dining at a restaurant inside an antique inn wondering if they might have to stay the night as a rainstorm moved in.

The waiter had just brushed crumbs from the white linen tablecloth and dessert was being served when Summer's phone rang. Christabel, who was tucked discretely under the table in her black traveling bag, began to bark. John grabbed her bag and put it on his lap to quiet her.

"This is for you,' Summer said and handed him the phone.

"Hello. Stuart! Where are you?" He got up from the table and walked towards the lobby to take the call and returned in only a few minutes.

"He wants us to meet them in Aix-en-Provence," he said.

"Where are they now?" Rosalind asked.

"They're hiding out in Luxor at the home of Omar Shabaka's father. They're on the run from some men who followed Barry to Hans Bueller's monastery. Stuart thinks they could be the same ones who attacked Barry a few days before at a hotel where he was staying."

"Barry was attacked?" Rosalind blurted out.

"You're kidding!" Summer said. "Sounds exciting!"

The party dining next to them turned and stared daggers, having had enough of barking dogs, phone calls, and raised voices.

"Quiet down," John said. "He's okay," he whispered. "He's got a bit of a knot on his head and a few scrapes from crawling through some cave. I didn't get all the details. Stuart said something about Barry having to sneak out of the monastery unseen. He used some old, decrepit tunnel."

"Cool!" Summer said.

"I would feel better if you had talked to him," Rosalind said.

"He was soaking in a tub when Stu called."

"Hmm. So, when are we supposed to meet them in Aix?"

"Stu said he wasn't sure how long it was going to take them to get out of Egypt, but he didn't think it would be more than a few days."

"Where is Aix?" Summer asked.

"It's in the South for France," Rosalind replied.

"The real South of France?" she asked

"Provence, right, the real South of France," John answered. "Stu said something about thermal bathes in Aix, Barry being in need of one, something like that."

"Yeah!" Summer applauded.

"It's starting to rain," Rosalind said when hard drops pelted the windows. "Maybe we should stay here tonight."

"No, we've got to get back to Amsterdam and prepare to leave," John said.

"There's a local train nearby," Summer said. "They allow bikes on the trains here."

"How far?" John asked.

"Only about two miles."

They braced themselves for the chilly wet ride and were about to pay their bill and leave when Summer's phone rang again. She quickly grabbed it out of her backpack with her eye on the people at the table next to them.

"They probably think we're a bunch of American rubes," she lamented. "It's for you again John."

"Stu? Oh, Barry it's you. I heard you had a bit of an altercation. Yes, that's what Stu said. Are you all right? Well, take it easy. Oh, you are," John said as his face lit up with a broad smile. He turned to Rosalind. "Omar Shabaka's father lives in some pretty nice digs!" He turned back to the phone. "Okay, you want your laptop, camera, and tape recorder. No, no, I don't mind picking them up, but it does mean it will take us a little longer to get to Aix. Isn't your place located near Carcassonne? Oh, it's northwest of Carcassonne, north of Toulouse, near Les-Eyzies-de-Tayac in the Perigord, across the road from the Boar's Head Vineyard. Okay, just a minute. Let me write this down."

John spelled out the word "LES-EYZIES-DE-TAYAC?" with a question mark in his journal and scribbled "Boars Head."

"Does the road have a name?" D 47, he wrote. "I should be able to find it on a map. How will we get in? Oh, the vintner is your landlord. How nice! Okay, we'll meet you in Aix. Take good care of yourself, and thank Stuart for me. Yes, it was really great of him to go over there. Tell Omar hello. We will be talking soon." John clicked off the phone and finished his sentence, "I hope."

"Is he okay?" Rosalind asked.

"Yes, the two of them are very comfortable. They still have to get out of Egypt though." He looked out at the rain and handed the phone back to Summer. "

"You keep it," she said. "I'd rather not be a receptionist."

"Summer!" her sister scolded.

The three pedaled two miles through the downpour and waited ten minutes for the train. They loaded up bikes, wet selves, and a dry dog, who was protected by the safe confines of her bag, and rode back to Amsterdam in the chilly night.

Chapter 14

Riding a Big Wave to Cairo

"**Y**ou may go home now," Saadya said to his servant after the last dish had been placed upon the table. "Thank you for staying late." Omar had arrived only minutes earlier, and the four remaining men now gathered around a table laid out with a sumptuous spread of lamb, rice, spicy potatoes, and fava beans. "Excuse our informality," Saadya said to his guests, "but we are eating much later than either my servant or I are accustomed to."

"No apologies necessary. This is wonderful," Barry said while eating with relish. "How long has it been since I've had fava beans? These are cooked to perfection and spiced perfectly."

"Thank you," Saadya replied.

"The lamb is so tender, mmm. I love the lemon," Barry added. He looked quite comfortable in his white cotton galabayya, as if he had been born to wear it. Stuart, on the other hand, tugged awkwardly at his hem, unsure how to arrange himself on the floor pillow in such an outfit. His black cotton spandex socks looked as out of place as he did.

"Sure is good!" Stuart said. He had mixed the lamb, potatoes, and fava beans, thus robbing each dish of its distinctive flavor except for the rice, which he enjoyed plain.

After the men had eaten, Saadya began to gather up the plates and bowls to carry to the kitchen. Omar protested to his father who refused his help.

"My man will clean the plates tomorrow. I'm clearing the table so we can talk," his father answered.

Talk they did, but not before the elder physician brought out small plates and cups and served slabs of flakey cinnamon pastry and cups of soothing tea. Omar told his father that Hans Bueller had made an exceptional find while sorting and cleaning in the monastery library, and that he had enlisted Barry's help to identify a mysterious goddess, one that none of them had ever heard of. He thought perhaps his father might offer some insight into her identity, although he cannot remember having heard him mention such a woman.

"How do you know this woman is a goddess if you've never heard of her?" Saadya asked.

"We don't know for sure," Omar had to acknowledge. "But I saw the ancient papyrus scroll myself."

"He translated it," Barry added.

"Yes, father, yes I did. It says, 'She looks upon herself who is not there. But sees instead before her all the world. Whatever was, whatever will be is in her care. For she is the maker of the world. Within her face all faces, all time, the cosmic burst of creation. She holds the mirror of world.'"

"I didn't realize you had put it to memory," Barry said, full of admiration for this young man who could not only translate the hieroglyphics on the spot but also instantly memorize the translation.

"She holds the mirror of the world. Very interesting, yes, that is quite remarkable," Saadya said.

"Tell him about the statue," Stuart said. "Maybe he'll recognize it."

If looks could kill, Barry would have slain Stuart.

"You have it with you?" Saadya asked, his eyes betraying his eagerness to see this lady.

"Yes, father. Dr. Bueller asked Barry to take it with him and try to identify her."

"Excuse me," Barry said as he got up from the cushion. "I must get my backpack. I will be right back."

"There were other identifying scrolls that looked by their iconography to be associated with the one I translated," Omar explained. "But the hieroglyphics were scratched out of their cartouches."

"How do you know this statue is associated with these scrolls and with the papyrus you translated?"

Before Omar could answer his father's question, Barry pulled the box from his backpack. He opened it and took the figurine from the soft velvet cloth Hans Bueller had wrapped her in. The lady's copper crown shown brightly even in the low light.

When Saadya took her in his hand to study her closely, he saw his eyes reflected in the round disk of a crown. "I see. What else could she be but a goddess? She reminds me," he began to say as he turned her about in his hand. "I might have said the Goddess Neith who is said to weave the world on her loom, but no, more like another lady, a Yoruban lady, Yemaja."

"Why?" Omar asked, puzzled by his father's remark since the lady in their figurine looked distinctly European, not Egyptian at all, and definitely not at all like any likenesses he had ever seen of either Neith or Yemaja.

"She has fish scales," his father said.

"We thought perhaps they are wings," Barry offered.

"They may be both," Saadya replied. "Yemaja is the mother of fishes. That is to say, the mother of all. She is associated with the sea"

"A mermaid?" Stuart asked with a wry smile.

"Sometimes she is presented as such. But I've never seen her presented with such a crown. The association is unmistakable, and yet she is different."

"Who came first," Barry asked, "this lady or Yemaja?"

"Ah, exactly! That is exactly the question," Saadya replied. "Is this lady a shadow of Yemaja, or is Yemaja a shadow of this lady? I think perhaps the latter."

"Why do you think that?" Barry asked.

"This figurine looks very old. But if the truth is to be spoken, I must admit that I do not know. It is an intuition, not a factual judgment. Her eyes tell me."

Omar turned to Barry. "My father's intuitions are never wrong. I have never known one fail to be true. Never!"

Barry, who did not put as much faith in intuition as Omar, nonetheless was not hostile to the idea that truth might reside in flashes of insight. He had in fact learned to put a great deal of stock in his dreams, not because of faith or superstition, rather because of his own personal experience. When properly interpreted he found his dreams to be invaluable wellsprings of information. Maybe Saadya had learned to rely on his intuition in much the same way; and Omar, never having seen his father's insights fail, had learned to depend on them. Barry would take Saadya's remark quite seriously, but he would need more evidence before he made a final judgment.

"I wasn't going to show her to you for your safety's sake as well as hers," Barry apologized, embarrassed that he had even considered withholding the figurine from his generous host. "Stuart and I must get her out of Egypt undetected. She would be a prize for any thief; and as you might already know, thieves are on my tail."

"I've told my father about your precarious situation, and he believes he can help the two of you reach Cairo undetected."

Stuart's interest was piqued. Not that he hadn't enjoyed the meal they had just finished, he had. But he preferred clams and crab cakes, staples of a Chesapeake Bay diet; and he wanted to get back there as quickly and safely as possible.

"I can get you on a small cargo barge leaving for Cairo tomorrow," Saadya said. "A friend of mine has a shipment of carpets being carried there. The accommodation won't be luxurious, but the two of you can share a cabin. I have here a letter for the captain who will be able to arrange your passage from Cairo on to Europe."

Saadya handed Barry a letter sealed with the blue waxen hieroglyph for water, but before Barry could grasp it, Stuart intercepted the transfer.

"It will do you the most good if you do not open the letter," Saadya urged, looking peeved that Stuart had intruded himself.

"Why so?" Stuart asked as he turned the envelop in his hand, viewing it from every possible angle.

"Because my seal unopened proves the letter's authenticity."

"I'm sorry," Barry said as he took the letter from Stuart. "He's in law enforcement and flew all the way to Egypt to protect me."

Saadya's face lit up with amusement. "Oh yes, I see. That better explains the situation. He seems very unlike you. Not at all an Egyptologist and quite the suspicious type."

"And a very good friend," Barry added. "He helped me leave Egypt once before when my life was at risk from thieves who believed I had a valuable artifact when in fact I had none."

"Now you do," Saadya said, looking from Barry to Stuart. "There is some risk leaving the country with such an object and not just from thieves. This letter is your passage to Europe, but Captain Esam is rather suspicious himself and may doubt that it came from me unless it is carried to him intact. We have our ways here, and you must respect them."

"We will," Barry said as he looked over at Stuart who concurred with a nod of the head. "Thank you for your help and this marvelous meal. Is there not something I can do for you in return?"

"Would you write me when you've solved this mystery and tell me who she is?"

"If I solve it," Barry replied, not feeling up to the task now that waves of exhaustion had begun to drown out what was left of his waking consciousness.

"There is no doubt that you will," Saadya said.

"How do you know that father?" Omar asked.

"From her eyes," was all that he answered before suggesting they retire for the evening.

Barry awoke before the morning light in a soft bed in the home of Saadya Shabaka. The scent of Madonna lilies filled his nostrils. He had been dreaming. He felt both the strangeness of his surroundings as well as the place his dreaming mind had taken him, not feeling quite comfortable in either location. The dream had been vivid. He had stood in a field of the white, undulating flowers while looking out onto a lake before he was transported, as dreams will do, to the edge of its shore. A boat was passing carrying a beautiful woman. He knew her. She had the same face as the woman he had dreamed of on the train to Cairo. This time she beckoned him. He drew back. The water was too cold and she too far away. She glided past him, her eyes piercing into his as if she were planting thoughts in fertile soil. He had just finished recording his dream in his journal when there came a knock at the door. Barry quickly got out of bed to answer it.

"Who's there?"

"I have your clothing," a voice answered.

He opened the door. There stood Saadya's servant, a man of about 45 or so, wearing a long gray robe and holding the now freshly washed and pressed clothing he and Stuart had arrived in along with their now clean and polished shoes.

"Thank you. That was very kind of you," Barry said. He took the clothing and began to close the door.

Using his hand to prop open the door, the servant replied, "You and your friend must dress yourselves. We must leave now."

Barry looked out the window. "It's still dark!"

"I am to take you now before it is light. The boat leaves very early."

Barry felt saddened that he must leave so soon. He longed for the time when he would have been a welcome guest in the home of men like Saadya Shabaka, an interesting man from whom he could learn a great deal. Those days are over, he pined, as he was reminded that he would always remain an unwelcome guest in Egypt, even among friends.

Stuart yawned. Barry, eyes closed, rested his head in the palm of his hand in the back seat of the car before it abruptly stopped at the pier next to the great river, which looked that morning uncharacteristically murky. The two men were roused to alertness by the sudden lack of motion.

"You can sleep all you like in your cabin," the servant said. He directed them towards a boat being loaded with goods and handed them a large box of sandwiches specially prepared for their trip north.

"Thank you, thank you very much," Barry said. He took the box and grabbed his backpack. "Please thank Saadya and Omar for their help. I wish I had seen them this morning to make my goodbyes!"

"It is better for them that you did not," the servant replied, insinuating Saadya's hospitality had put him in a potentially dangerous position that he was doing his best to minimize.

"Yes, you're probably right," Barry agreed. "Tell them that I will write when I can, and I hope to apprise them of the resolution of the mystery we spoke of last night."

At that, Barry and Stuart got out of the car and walked to the boat where they were greeted by a rather jovial merchant who put his arms around the two of them and ushered them onto the barge.

"Forgive me for not telling you my name," the merchant said. "It is better for me if you do not know it. You understand."

"We get it," Stuart replied, not altogether pleased with the situation he found himself in. It wasn't that Stuart didn't appreciate the efforts being made on their behalf by Saadya, his servant, and this congenial merchant, he did. But their behavior brought into broad relief what the circumstances of Barry's return to Egypt had devolved into. The two

71

men were toxic. They were being smuggled out of the country to prevent their being captured by ruthless thieves. But it was not thieves alone that threatened them. If Barry were to be discovered by Egyptian officials trying to leave the country with a valuable artifact, both he and Stuart would be tried, sentenced, and jailed for quite a long time. That reality, more than the other, might explain the obvious desire of their helpers to keep a certain distance.

The merchant brought them to the door of their cabin. "The trip should last no more than three days," he said. "If you will stay in your cabin, it will be better for us all. You understand."

"Of course," Barry said, although he was not certain that he did understand. He had hoped to be out on the deck taking in the sun and sights by day and the stars by night.

The merchant opened the door and the two men entered a windowless cabin. "Do you have a letter for me?" the merchant asked.

"It's for the captain," Stuart replied, uneasy about handing it over to another party.

"I will give it to him personally," the merchant said. Barry pulled it out of his backpack and handed it to him. "The captain will fetch you once you have arrived at your destination."

With that the merchant closed the cabin door and locked it from the outside. Stuart turned the latch hoping to discover the door could be opened from the inside, but it failed. The two men looked at each other and their accommodation. The cabin was comfortable enough. There were two cots and a toilet, but the space was small. And Stuart hated situations where there was only one way out. In this case there was no way out. They were entirely at the mercy of the nameless merchant and the captain.

"Trapped like two rats," Stuart declared.

"Yes," Barry agreed.

"You can't blame him though. He's put himself at risk for two men he doesn't even know."

"From thieves?" Barry questioned in a doubtful tone. "It's not very likely that they would discover our location floating up the Nile even if we were allowed out to take in a little sun."

"Not from thieves, from officials," Stuart said. "The police guards are stationed at every port from here to Cairo, and you are smuggling a valuable artifact out of the country. Anyone who helps you would be considered an accomplice."

Barry sat down on one of the cots. He looked pale. "I hadn't really thought of it that way. I never intended to profit from this lovely figurine." He felt for the box in his backpack.

"No one would believe you. Not with your reputation," Stuart said. "They already think you smuggled other treasure out of the country only a few months ago."

Barry, appearing even paler, looked up at Stuart who had begun pacing back and forth across the small cabin floor, and said, "I hadn't really considered all of that but you're right. Who would believe me?"

"Certainly not the Egyptian officials. Neither would U.S. officials for that matter. We are lucky this merchant agreed to help us at all." He groaned and sat down on the other cot. "I can't wait until we're out of here, out on the open sea on our way to Europe.

Chapter 15

Southward Trek

John looked down at the roadmap. "We're going to have to drive straight through to Brussels and on to Paris. We won't have time for any sights."

"Paris, with all of that traffic! Can't you find another route?" Rosalind said.

"Well, we could go north around Paris and drop down to Versailles."

"I love Versailles! Maybe we could spend the night."

He imagined himself walking in the palace gardens in the tranquil evening after a long day's drive. He traced his finger across the map. "Yep, that would work, and from Versailles we could drive south to Orléans."

"Summer will insist on visiting a castle or two."

"There won't be time unless we spend the second night in Amboise. I guess we could stop there, have a nice meal and drink some Loire Valley red." He traced his finger further south along the map. "From Amboise we will drive south to the Massif Central."

"Where's that?" Rosalind asked, her muffin crumbs dropping on the map.

John traced his finger further south along a road into the Massif. The wide yellow and red highway designation shrunk into a narrow white line.

"How long will the whole trip take?" she asked.

"At least five days." He swallowed the last drops of his tea. "We'd better get moving. I'm going out to rent a car. Be ready when I get back."

Christabel barked and tried to herd him away from the door. Failing in that endeavor, she succeeded in waking up Summer who wandered sleepily into the living room.

"Get dressed and packed," Rosalind said. "We're leaving for France in about an hour."

The highway was smooth and flat. Rosalind searched for windmills and tulips as they passed the flat green terrain spotted with industrial style buildings.

"It's December," Summer said, but that did not assuage Rosalind's disappointment nor explain the lack of the rustic Dutch windmills. "Most of them are up north," Summer explained.

"Not my idea of Holland. The countryside was nicer," Rosalind said

The highway through Belgium and Luxembourg was not much better. But once they entered France and turned off the highway, the landscape looked a bit more, well, French, with thatch and tile roofed cottages dotting the rolling countryside. They were in Champagne country, headed to an inn in Epernay for a night's rest and a quiet dinner after a drive that had proven longer and more tedious than John had expected.

He grew anxious. He tried to call Stuart using the number Stu had phoned him from. He recognized the voice in a recorded message that eventually answered when Stuart did not. John's agitation intensified. He called Natalie at her office in Washington D.C. She had not heard from Stuart in days and was surprised to hear that they were on their way to Aix. John, not wanting to spread the contagion of his own anxiety, quickly ended the conversation.

"They're probably out of range," Rosalind said, trying to calm him.

"He uses a satellite phone. There is no out of range unless they're inside the Great Pyramid with walls so thick they block the signal."

"Maybe he turned it off. Maybe he's asleep."

"At eight o'clock?"

"I'm sure he's fine. Let's have champagne with dinner tonight. We can probably get a good deal since we're in the region."

They drank two bottles, enough to relax all three of them into an early night's rest. The next morning before they left for Versailles, John again tried and failed to reach Stuart and Barry.

***

Christabel sat patiently on John's lap while he picked bits and pieces of dried sycamore leaves from her white fluff. It was late afternoon. He,

75

Rosalind, and the dog sat on a bench outside the Palace of Versailles' famous gardens waiting for Summer who had gone off to shop. The tree they were under would have provided plenty of shade had it still had its leaves and had there been sun to shade them from.

"You would think that her fur contains a magic sticking agent," John observed, as the task of de-leafing the dog seemed futile.

"She needs her brush. It's back in our room," Rosalind sighed as she looked about. "Versailles sure looks different this time of year."

"At least it's not raining," John said.

"The flowers are gone. Why don't you try calling them again?" she urged, hoping that luck or providence would break the spell and bring peace of mind.

"Here." He handed her the leaf-encrusted dog and pulled out Summer's phone. "It's ringing but just barely." After a few moments he clicked off the phone. "I got that damn message again." He looked at the phone. "This thing needs to be charged."

"I'll give it back to Summer," Rosalind said. "Jeeze, I wonder where they are?"

"I don't know, but it's been nearly forty-eight hours since I talked to them. We'd better move out of here first thing in the morning, go pick up Barry's stuff, and get to Aix.

What about Amboise and chateau country?"

"We'll have to skip it. Neither of us is in the mood for touring anyway."

"Summer is."

"Prince Charming will have to wait. Where is she anyway?"

"She's still in one of those shops."

"Let's find her and start thinking about dinner."

"I've got to shampoo Christabel," Rosalind announced as she stood up with the dog in her arms.

Chapter 16

Computer Invasion

Barry's Power Mac had seduced Paul, its monitor being twice the size of his own and fast enough to make his family's computer seem slow and old fashioned. Knights & Swords was ever so much more fun. But after hours of playing, he had grown bored with the game but not the computer he played it on, which is why he was about to open email he believed was sent to him on Barry's personal account.

Weeks earlier Paul had begun to explore the fascinating pages and links Barry had stored on his computer. He liked the archeological sites, particularly the ones with pictures and most particularly the ones about the Indians who had once lived in Pennsylvania and Ohio, maybe right where his house stood, he imagined, as he pictured his neighborhood a field of teepees. Such imaginings were not entirely farfetched. A great Indian mound stood not far from his home, and a giant cavern of stalactites where Indians were thought to have sheltered in harsh Ohio winters was nearby. A number of the articles were interesting enough that the precocious boy had questions. Since Barry wasn't around to answer them, he emailed an author or two or three whose addresses were easily found under "contact information." Over the past few days, Paul had begun a fruitful exchange with one of these scholars who had not yet guessed by either his questions or his prose style that he was only eleven.

Paul believed that Barry would not mind him using his account as long as he didn't "mess with the settings," as Barry had ordered him not to do before he left for France. That declaration had come after Paul had inadvertently substituted the Knights & Swords homepage in place of Barry's. It took Barry a good two hours to figure out how to restore his own. Paul understood Barry's rather emotional outburst as an order to leave all the settings untouched, which explains, in part, why Paul's correspondent thought it was Dr. Barry Short who was generating the storm of email that for several days had been sent from his account. Paul didn't sign his correspondence, having already learned the art of brevity and informality that is the custom in electronic mail. He signed himself as ☺, an emoji he had chosen from the "special characters" selection on the computer. He had not noticed that Barry's automated signature, "Dr. Barry Short" appeared on the bottom of all correspondence just below his happy face.

He pulled his chilly hands from the pockets of his red fleece jacket, rubbed them together to warm them up before he commenced to open an email from an address he was familiar with, AAR, initials for the American Academy of Rome, the location of a friendly Italian scholar he had been communicating with who always typed "From Rosa," in the subject line. What was odd this time is the subject line had been left blank.

A mutual acquaintance has informed me that you have returned to the United States. I have no doubt that you carried something of great interest to me; although I must say, I'm not sure how you were able to return so quickly nor how you got the object past customs without permission and no official declarations. But then you are experienced in these things, are you not? It was not that long ago that another artifact of great interest went missing at the same time you left Egypt, was it not? Do not be so naïve as to believe you can fool me as easily as you have fooled many others. And do not think that you can conceal what you have from me. I have many eyes. I offer you the choice to negotiate an arrangement that will benefit the two of us or risk an accident, an unfortunate break-in, or worse. Sorry to say, I've no control over these matters once I am forced to let out a contract. So don't force me! You may reply to this email with your answer, and I will begin to make proper arrangements, but do not imagine tracing the address will do you any good. It won't. You are caught this time.

"Uh, Oh!" Paul said. The not so veiled threat was enough to alert the boy that Barry was once again in trouble just like he had been last year when he had to leave Egypt. That's why Stuart had to go get him he thought, recalling the conversation he overheard his father having with his grandmother.

He rightly surmised that the evil correspondent had mistaken the boy's email for Barry's and therefore believed Barry had returned to Ohio. He looked about the room then peered through the window into the backyard. Thankfully, no stranger was lurking out there. But when he looked back at the computer and the threatening email that lit up the screen, he imagined a stranger inside the machine gaining access to all of his email. He feared this evildoer might be monitoring the computer right now and knows that it is turned on and the threatening message had been read. He looked out into the street just as a car passed. Could that be him or someone he has sent to do his dirty work? I'd better go home now, he thought. Before he left he looked up Aunt Natalie's information in Barry's computer address book, found her telephone number at the GAO, and punched it into the phone real fast.

"Aunt Natalie!" he cried when she answered.

"Paul! Is everything all right?"

"They think I'm Barry! They said that they might do things to him, take out a contract."

"Who? They? What are you talking about?"

"In the email they sent him."

"You've been reading Barry's email?"

"I didn't know. I thought it was for me."

"Read me what it says."

"Okay." Paul cut to the chase. "And don't think that you can conceal what you have from me. I have many eyes. I offer you the choice to negotiate an arrangement that will benefit the two of us or risk an accident, an unfortunate break-in, or worse!"

"Hmm, sounds bad."

"What should I do?" he said.

"I truly don't know. Here, I'll give you Stu's satellite phone number. No wait! John phoned and said he was having trouble reaching him. Let me give you Aunt Summer's phone number too. Call Uncle John at that number in case Stuart doesn't answer. Can you do that?"

"Sure, if I can use Barry's phone. My parents don't allow me to make international long distance phone calls."

"Are you at Barry's now?"

"Yes, I came over after school."

"That's fine Paul. I'm sure Barry won't mind. He'll know what this is about because I certainly don't," she sighed, realizing trouble was just around the corner. "Just make the phone calls, save the email as unread, and go home after you've talked to someone. Do you hear me Paul? Go home!"

"Okay, Aunt Natalie. Thanks."

He immediately dialed Stuart's satellite phone. A voice answered, but it was a recorded message. Paul left a message of his own. "Hi Stuart, this is Paul. I have to talk to Barry. Tell him it's important. I'm at his house, but I have to go home. I've got Uncle John's number so I will call him now. If you get this message, call Uncle John. Bye."

Summer's freshly recharged phone rang at midnight, just as she was about to fall asleep. "What's up Jos?"

"Aunt Summer! Where's Uncle John?"

"Who is this?"

"It's Paul."

"Oh, hi Paul. He's in another room. I think he's asleep. Is this important? Can he call you tomorrow?"

"I'll be at school. I have to talk to him now!"

"Okay, okay, I'll get him."

Summer wrapped a blanket around herself, made her way down the hall to John's room, tapped on the door, and called out his name.

Christabel barked from the other side of the door. Summer could hear a groggy voice exclaim, "Quit barking!" Then a voice at the door, "Who is it?"

"It's me. You've got a phone call. He says it's an emergency."

"Barry?"

"No, it's Paul."

John opened the door and joined her in the hallway, wondering what the emergency was that could not wait until morning.

"Paul, I thought you were Barry or Stuart."

"No, it's me. They didn't answer the phone so I called you."

"Why? What's up?"

"Aunt Natalie told me I should call you if Stuart didn't answer."

"Why were you trying to call Stuart?"

"To tell Barry that they are going to put a contract out on him."

"To tell him what? Who?"

"I don't know. The man who sent the email."

"What email? Start from the beginning Paul."

"Okay, I sent some emails to people who wrote articles Barry has on his computer. Someone wrote me back, I mean, I thought they wrote me back because it came from the American Academy in Rome, but it was really for Barry, but I didn't know that until I read it."

"Wait, hold on. Why would you be expecting an email from the American Academy in Rome?"

"Because I wrote a lady there who wrote one of these articles, and she is real nice and has written me back before so I thought it was her again."

"Okay, I get it. But it wasn't from her?"

"No, it was someone who doesn't like Barry who says if he doesn't cooperate he will have him hurt."

"That doesn't sound good. You had better read me that email."

"Okay. Here it is. It says, 'A mutual acquaintance has informed me that you have returned to the United States.' Then it says something about Barry bringing something back with him that he is interested in and that if Barry doesn't negotiate an arrangement, he will hire someone to hurt him."

"How is it signed?"

"It isn't. It says Barry should reply back to this email with his answer."

"Who is the author you wrote to at the American Academy?"

"The name is right here," Paul said as he pulled up his earlier correspondence. "Her name is Dr. Palazio."

"Did you tell Dr. Palazio who you are?"

"No."

"And you used Barry's email account?"

"Yes, because he told me not to change any settings."

"Dr. Palazio could have said something to someone, said that she got email from Barry, and word spread maybe to another member of the faculty. I'm not sure what to tell you to do since I don't know what this is all about, but probably you shouldn't answer that email unless Barry tells you to. You probably shouldn't use his email account either. You should go home and stay away from Barry's house until we figure this out."

"Okay," Paul said with some relief, having passed the burden from his shoulders to his uncle's. "I will leave right now."

"Paul, thanks for calling. You did the right thing. Now go home."

"Trouble?' Summer asked.

"Someone is threatening Barry over something that he supposedly brought back to the U.S."

"He's not in the U.S."

"Someone thinks he is, and this someone sounds dangerous."

"Ah, you keep the phone. I've got to get some sleep," she said.

"Me too," John sighed, although he knew sleep probably would not come again easily that night.

"What's going on?" Rosalind asked when he came back into the room.

"I wish I knew. Paul's been messing around on Barry's computer and found a threatening email that may have something to do with whatever the boys have been up to in Egypt."

"Oh lord, what are they doing now?"

"I don't have the foggiest idea, but we'd better get to Aix fast."

Chapter 17

Mende

John did not stop in Rambouillet nor turn off to visit Chartres' famed cathedral. Neither did he veer to the west towards Amboise as originally planned. His goal was to reach Barry's cave by the end of the day, and his pace served that end. He had tried to phone Stuart in the morning before they left Versailles but reached the same recorded greeting. He tried again when they stopped along the highway for lunch, nothing. Each phone call only served to increase his anxiety, which might explain why he raced along the narrow, winding highway at 125 kilometers an hour.

"I'm getting car sick," Summer groaned as the van rounded another switchback in the rugged, heavily wooded Massif Central.

"I know what you mean," John commiserated. "I'm sick of driving."

"Do you want me to take over?" she asked.

"No, I've got the hang of these curves, and it's getting dark," he said as he rounded another bend and was about to go up and around the next. "I don't want us landing in one of these ravines."

"Be careful!" Rosalind said. "It sure is taking longer than we thought."

"It's these switchbacks that are slowing us down."

"This map is deceptive," she said. "It makes the road look straight. If the distances are accurate, we're about to come to a town called Mende."

"What's Mende like?" Summer asked.

"I've never been there," John said. "But that's where we'll spend the night if we can find a place. Otherwise, we'll have to sleep in the car. I can't go any further no matter who drives."

"There's not enough room," she lamented.

"Maybe we can lay down by the side of the road next to a tree," Rosalind taunted.

Minutes later they drove out of the blackened forest and into the darkened town. An inn with a restaurant stood just on the other side of the town center. Cheery light came through the inn's windows lighting a small parking lot. Inside, a raucous crowd of leathery men were gathered round a large bar drinking, smoking, and shouting at one another and to the bartender, a large, dark haired woman, attractive in her own rough way, who presided over the night's entertainment. She glanced at the travelers, said something to the men, smiled, and walked towards them.

"Madame Defarge," John whispered before she was within earshot. "We need two rooms and some dinner," he said in his best French.

The woman answered in a rural dialect. The restaurant was closed for the night, she said, but she had two rooms, and she could direct them to a restaurant in the town that might be open.

The deal was struck. They had their accommodations and exited the inn just as a motorcycle pulled into the parking lot, adding to the large number already parked there. A tanned, unshaven fellow climbed off the bike. He glanced at the Americans, turned away and turned back again, his dark eyes staring at them as if he were sizing them up. Rosalind smiled, hoping to elicit a smile in return, a greeting, something to counter her discomfort. He did not smile. Instead, he turned towards the bar.

"Hasn't that guy ever seen tourists before?" she complained.

"He probably doesn't see many this time of year," John said.

"I doubt they see Americans any time of year," she added.

"How would he know we're Americans?" Summer asked.

"I don't know," Rosalind said. "We probably look different to him. Maybe he was trying to figure out where we came from. I'm trying to figure out exactly where we are. It doesn't seem like France."

"Look at the sky!" Summer shouted. "It's Starry Night!"

"Yes, it does look like the painting," Rosalind agreed. "The color is so rich. I thought van Gogh imagined it."

"He was an expressionist," Summer agreed, "but this color is real enough!"

"At least it is here," Rosalind said.

"That's the place," John said before crossing the narrow, cobbled street to a darkened door. "I'll be right back."

Rosalind and Summer watched the door swing open from across the

84

street. A young girl appeared but only for a few moments before quickly closing it. He crossed back over and delivered the news. "The restaurant stopped serving hours ago."

"This town looks shut down for the night. Let's go back," Rosalind said.

"No, let's keep going."

They searched the dimly lit town looking for somewhere, anywhere to eat, until they stumbled on a small restaurant most of which was taken up by a large pizza oven. A young man dressed in mismatched plaids and checks seated them at one of the few tables in the tiny room. They were as surprised by his appearance as they were to see and hear their hotelier.

"He could have stepped out of a Victor Hugo novel," Rosalind mused. "Been a friend of Esmeralda's in fifteenth century Paris."

After pizza they walked to the town's handsome Cathédrale Notre-Dame-et-Saint-Privas, a large edifice protected by gargoyles jutting from its Gothic facade and the looming statue of Pope Urban V who cast a stern shadow in the soft lights that illuminated the building.

"He sure looks spooky," Summer said.

"The whole place does" John whispered, directing their attention to a couple walking together in the otherwise empty plaza wearing black and red peasant dress, embroidered with golden yellow and green designs. The woman had a black lace shawl over her head, and the man wore his long, dark hair in ponytail.

"This is France?" Rosalind said.

"Occitania," John proclaimed.

"Where?"

"Paris and Versailles were in Gaul, while Occitania was ruled by the Romans. It was a different country. I believe they called it Septimania back then. It didn't become part of France until the thirteenth century. That's when they renamed the region Languedoc."

"That was seven centuries ago."

"I know. I've read there are people who still speak Occitan. I bet some of them live here."

"Roman rule," Rosalind said as she looked about the town with new eyes. "That couple looked Spanish to me."

"They share the same influences.   Occitania sat right next to

Catalonia where Barcelona is. Their languages are so similar that speakers can understand each other. That tells you something," John said.

"What?" Rosalind asked.

"It tells you there was much interaction, shared history and culture. Come on, let's try to get inside."

Except for the glow of prayer candles the cathedral was dark. They sat silent for a few moments, believing they were alone until they saw the silhouette of a man rise up from a kneeling position. He turned and walked towards them wearing the black vestments and the white collar of a priest.

"Bonsoir mon Père," John said.

"I am not the Father of this church if that's what you think," the man answered in British English.

"Excuse me sir," John said, "if you don't mind, who are you then?"

"My name is James Stroud. I'm a tourist. That's all."

"But you're wearing a collar."

"Well, yes, I am an Anglican priest. So you can see, this is not my church."

"I'm sorry. I was hoping you could tell us something about it," John said, embarrassed at having been so presumptuous.

"That depends on what you want to know."

"Is there anything special here that we shouldn't miss seeing?" Rosalind asked.

"There are many things. The Aubusson tapestries are exquisite. I came here to see the Madonna. Here, let me take you over to her."

The curious Madonna's face glistened black, ablaze in candlelight.

"She is very old," the Anglican said. "Legend says the crusaders brought her here from Holy Land one hundred years before this cathedral was built. As for her real age, we will never know."

"She looks pregnant" Summer said, noting her round belly and full breasts protruding from under her carved robe. "I've never seen a Madonna like her before."

"Neither had I," the Anglican replied. "I've seen other Black Virgins but none who are pregnant. That is why I am here."

"She looks entirely different from any representation of the Madonna

86

I've seen," Rosalind said. "Her face looks stern or maybe a little sad, and her posture is erect."

"Her posture is quite traditional. Perhaps the style she is fashioned in is older than you are accustomed to seeing. You are Americans, aren't you?" he said with an affirmative nod of his head. "She is seated upon the thrown of wisdom. What is not traditional is she is without the Christ child."

"At least not sitting on her lap," John said. "I've heard the term 'Black Madonna' before but never knew what it meant. It's literal. She's a black woman. She's the expectant virgin."

"A good choice of words. I've done a study of these representations. Many of them are in France, particularly here in the South, but few like this one."

"What do you think they mean?" John asked.

"I'm not entirely sure. Some believe she is a representation of the Madonna offered to Negroes. One does find evidence of something like her in the Caribbean and Brazil among those of African descent. She does remind me of Yemaja."

"Who?" John asked.

"The goddess Yemaja. She is worshipped in Candomble, a religion most notable in Bahia, a province of Brazil. I visited there once as part of my studies. Candomble weds African deities with Catholic saints. Yemaja is the deity most associated with the Virgin."

"Why would Yemaja be here in the middle of France?" Rosalind asked.

"Oh, no, I didn't mean to imply that. Oh, no. The Black Virgin has her origins on this side of the Atlantic. I only meant to say that in some manifestation she might be everywhere."

"Why is she pregnant?" Summer asked.

"Quite right. I haven't determined that just yet. I can only imagine it has to do with fertility. Perhaps she is a throwback to the early fertility goddesses. The emphasis on her breasts and womb, you see. Or perhaps we are to see her before the birth of the Christ child, while He is still a potential and not a reality."

"Her face looks different," John said. Looking around he added, "Whatever she is the people here certainly do venerate her."

"They believe in her magic and in the magic of dozens more Vierges Noires scattered about Europe. This particular lady is believed to have answered the prayers of the inhabitants of Mende, saving them from Nazi occupation. They consider her a protectress."

"Let me see if I've got this right," John said. "What you are saying is she isn't considered just a statue then; rather, the statue embodies her spirit."

"Exactly. That is what she and all the others are thought to be, an embodiment of spirit."

"I want to light a candle to her," Rosalind said as she deposited seven euros in a slot and lit one of the large candles with the Virgin's picture pasted upon it. She stood before the mysterious lady and made her prayer. "Tell me your story if you will," she whispered softly.

"It is a sight, is it not," the Anglican said breaking the silence of Rosalind's devotion. "If you don't mind, I will be going back to my hotel."

"It was very nice to meet you, very interesting." John said. "We should be getting back too."

"I'm glad I could be of service. I'm always happy to meet fellow travelers who share my interests. Tomorrow I'm off to Le Puy or I would stay and talk longer."

"Why thank you. We've got to get an early start tomorrow too. We're in search of a cave."

"Be sure to avoid La Bête," Stroud said and began to walk away.

Not liking the sound of those words Rosalind called him back, "La Bête?"

"You have not heard of it?" he said smiling. "I thought everyone knew of the Beast of Gévaudan."

"Not us," John replied.

"Legend has it that hundreds of years ago there was a beast, some say a wolf some say a werewolf, who would capture and decapitate its hapless victims who wandered too far off in these isolated parts."

"A werewolf!" Summer cried.

"I did not mean to frighten you," the priest said looking distressed because that is precisely what he had done. "I meant it only as a phrase, a kind of generic way of saying take care of yourselves. Don't stray too far from the path."

"That's good advice," John said, and thanked the priest once again before they made their retreat back to the hotel.

Sleep came quickly but did not last. Rosalind's imagination ran amok with vicious wolves and pregnant African Madonnas, the former carrying off the latter. When she awoke at four from a bad dream, John was sleeping soundly. She guessed that Summer, unlike John, was having a difficult night too, but in the morning Summer reported that she had slept very well, thank you very much.

"Hmm," Rosalind thought, never having imagined herself more impressionable than her sister.

Chapter 18

Dark Forest Road

Rosalind riveted her attention on the handle of the Anglican's umbrella when she saw him standing under a tree outside their hotel. It was beautifully carved and polished in the likeness of a gnarled tree limb. "Hmm, a tree limb carved from a tree limb. Something ironic in that," she said to the others. Her eyes moved from the handle, to the darkening sky, and then back to James Stroud.

"Very glad not to have missed you," Stroud said as he approached. "I was thinking about our conversation while I was out for my morning walk. I believe I was a bit rude last night. You see, I've been on my own little pilgrimage for some time, and each relocation becomes more exhausting than the last. I try to stay at least a month in each place I visit to ease the transition, but I've been in Mende only a few weeks, so I'm really feeling the strain of impending change. My situation is not your fault, and I hoped to find you here so that I might apologize and perhaps help you on your way."

"You needn't apologize. You weren't rude," John said and extended his hand.

"I was not helpful either," he said as he shook it.

"How did you know we would be here?" Rosalind asked.

"Where else would you be? When we parted, you walked in the direction opposite my hotel."

That makes sense, she thought as she looked about and saw no other hotel nearby.

"You said you are in search of a cave. I might be able to help you find it."

John smiled to hide his embarrassment that the good cleric had misconstrued his admittedly vague reference to mean they were in the area to explore one of the many prehistoric cave sites or large caverns opened to the public. "Actually," he said, "the cave I'm looking for is the home of a friend of mine, an archeologist who's been studying the caves you may be thinking of."

"Oh, I see. Where might that be?"

"My directions are a little vague. I'm told it's near Les-Eyzies-de-Tayac, across the road from a vineyard."

"Indeed. Surely you can phone your friend and get better directions. It's easy to get lost in these mountains," he sighed. "Or better yet, perhaps he might meet you at an establishment in Les-Eyzies-de-Tayac and direct you to his home."

"That would be the thing to do if he were there."

Stroud raised his eyebrow in mystification.

"I should explain. My friend asked me to find his home and retrieve some of his things for him. I'm going to see him later in Aix-en-Provence."

"Oh, so that's the situation. In that case the best I can do is offer advice for getting to Les-Eyzies-de-Tayac and suggest that when you arrive you ask after the vineyard. It's not too far from Rocamadour, a place I heartily recommend if you are interested in the Black Virgin. I should be returning there soon myself. Do you have a map?"

John pulled the maps from passenger side of the van.

"These maps can be very deceptive," Stroud said as he studied the various possibilities printed as red, yellow, black, and white lines of varying widths. "If you don't know the area, you might believe you would be saving time by getting off the main road and cutting through a forest or mountains only to find yourself lost."

"I know exactly what you mean," Summer said, recalling the endless turns up winding roads into Mende.

"That's right," Rosalind agreed. "This map made the road to Mende appear straight when it was anything but."

"At least it brought you here," Stroud said. "I have taken roads that later I have wondered why they were ever built. I would suggest the most direct route would be to get on A 75 and take it to Serverac-le-Chateau, and from there take the N 88 to Rodez. From Rodez take the D 911 To Cahors. Then take the A 20 back north to the D 704 to Sarlat, a lovely town by the way. From Sarlat take the D 47 into Les-Eyzies-de-Tayac."

"You consider that direct?" Rosalind said.

"There isn't much habitation between Mende and your destination," Stroud explained.

John took off his glasses, pulled the map up to his nose, and looked at it studiously. "That would take us south. I had thought it would be shorter to drive due west towards Decazeville."

"Deeper into the Massif Central," Stroud said. "No! I'm afraid that would take you adrift in ways you haven't imagined. Look at how small those narrow white lines are. What your map doesn't show is the wilderness you would be driving into. It's very beautiful, but no one lives there. You would be better off driving around the mountains. By following the route I've suggested you will wind yourself out onto the highway in no time. The other route, well—"

"Well, what?" Summer asked, her face pale as if she were anticipating the tightening of her stomach on the winding curves.

"Don't be upset," the Anglican said noting her expression. "You will get there all right. Just follow my instructions."

"I was hoping to pick up what we need at the cave and be off to Aix later today," John said.

"Impossible!"

"But we're in a terrible hurry," Rosalind explained.

"You don't want to be so hurried you lose your way, do you?"

"No, of course not." She thought back to the night before when this strange priest recounted the legend of the Beast of Gévaudan. Don't stray too far from the path, he had warned, a remark that resonated so deeply she dreamed of it. She recalled the image of the wolves carrying off the Black Madonna. "John, did you get the directions?"

"You're the navigator. Did you?"

"I think I did."

The patient cleric carefully went over the route again before they parted. He waved them goodbye; opened his large, black umbrella with the handsomely carved handle; and turned towards the cathedral where he would take one last look at the Vierge Noire before leaving for Le Puy.

A few drops of rain fell on the windshield as they exited Mende. Once they had driven deep into the black woods, deep gorges, and craggy hills of the Gévaudan, it began to pour. Christabel barked as if the pounding raindrops were intruding into her space. Summer let her nuzzle into her jacket to quiet her.

"Why do you think that priest brought up the Beast of Gévaudan?" Summer asked as she surveyed the inhospitable landscape.

"He said he meant it metaphorically," Rosalind replied. "He said he didn't mean to frighten us."

"But it did frighten us, me anyway. A metaphor for what?"

"Well, he said it was a kind of warning not to stray off the path," Rosalind said.

"And then this morning he gave us all of these directions; and when John suggested another route, he was quick to warn him against it."

"So you think what?"

"I don't think it was just a metaphor," Summer speculated. "I think it was a real warning, but I'm not sure what he was warning us against."

"Getting lost!" John chimed in.

"Oh, I get what you are saying Summer," Rosalind said, ignoring John's rationalist interpretation. "Was he talking about something more than a place when he warned where a wrong turn could take us?"

"Precisely,' Summer replied. "I think he meant something more."

A massive bridge, barely discernible through the rain and mist, spanned the two mountains that made up the sides of the jagged valley they were driving through. Thunder shook the earth and the rain became blinding. John inched the car under the bridge.

"We're not going anywhere in this," he said. "I'm going to have to find some gas."

"How much do we have?" Rosalind asked.

"Not much. Can you tell how far we are from the A 75?"

"No, I can't since I don't know where we are." She peered more closely at the map. "The bridge isn't marked here at all, but we can't be far since Mende appears not too far from highway."

"Yeah, but that map doesn't take into account these switchbacks," he said.

"We just passed a sign pointing to a town somewhere up ahead," Summer said. "We can get gas there."

John relaxed a little. He punched Stuart's number into Summer's phone. After a few minutes he put the phone back in his pocket.

Thunder rumbled and the temperature dropped. They covered up with jackets, a thin blanket, anything they could grab from the back of the van without having to climb out and get into their suitcases.

"And this is the safer, populated route," Summer said sarcastically. "There's not a soul about, it's pouring down rain, and we're parked under a bridge that doesn't seem to be carrying any cars across it. I can't imagine what it would be like if we had followed the route you suggested, the one where there aren't supposed to be any people?"

No one wanted to speculate. They were left to the silence of their imaginations.

"Did you hear that?" Summer asked.

"It's just the wind," John said.

"No, it's not. Roll down the window."

"It's raining!"

"Roll it down!"

John started the ignition to power the windows, but instead of lowering his own he lowered windows in the rear seat where Summer sat. She didn't mind that the rain blew in.

"Did you hear that?" she said again.

"It sounds like howling," Rosalind said. "Dogs maybe."

"Or something else."

Christabel dislodged herself from the warmth of Summer's jacket and looked alert. She barked incessantly.

"Can you quiet her down?" John asked and closed the windows.

Summer tried to cuddle the little dog, but she wouldn't have it. She pulled her little body out of Summer's arms and barked. Summer scolded her, but it did no good. The rain, the howling, and the barking continued while the four waited for relief.

94

Chapter 19

Cargo

"We've arrived," the youthful Captain Esam said to the two men sitting in an unventilated cabin of his barge. He pushed the door wide open to let in some fresh air and ushered Barry and Stuart, groggy and sweating, out of the stuffy cabin where they had been hidden for the two and half day crawl up the Nile. "You're fortunate to have such important friends," he said to the still speechless men. "I was able to parlay the contents of Saadya Shabaka's letter for an accommodation to Marseilles. No one would have taken on this risk for less. You must immediately order a taxi to take you to the Cairo railway station, board the next train to Alexandria, and go directly to the port."

Barry and Stuart had revived by the time they arrived at the train station and were just shy of invigorated when they boarded the train. Relieved to be free of the close air of the barge cabin, they chatted cheerfully in their improved conditions. Stuart's phone lay dead in his pocket making it impossible to call Natalie or John to report their progress. He had considered using the public telephone at the train station, but a more cautious Barry warned him off, recalling that was where he had probably been spotted when he had first arrived in Cairo. "Why take chances," he had said. Besides, there was no urgency in making a phone call. They had already directed John to meet them with a car and Barry's equipment in Aix-en-Provence. The only thing they hadn't provided was the name of a hotel. They would find a hotel once they arrive, recharge the phone, and call them.

The thought of being on French soil, particularly in Aix-en-Provence, lifted Barry's spirits as the two men chatted on the train about their mutual friends and not so mutual life experiences. Barry learned more about Stuart than perhaps anyone had as Stuart recounted some of his more adventurous exploits doing undercover work in Brazil and his difficulty readjusting to civilian life after serving in Desert Storm. Barry, in turn, described his most stunning finds and archeological adventures.

"Have you visited Aix before?" Barry asked.

"I can't say that I have."

"It is one of my favorite French towns, the perfect French town if you ask me. The food, wine, ambiance, it has everything; and it's not too big. I want a room at the Aquabella. I really could use a massage and a thermal bath," Barry said before nodding off.

The train made a not so graceful entry into the station at Alexandria jolting the men awake. An hour later, after several cups of coffee, they arrived by taxi at the Port of Alexandria with rather vague instructions. All that Captain Esam had told them was to ask for Mr. Smith, a fictitious name Stuart surmised.

"Where will you go?" the taxi driver asked.

Barry surveyed numerous buildings and what appeared to be multiple piers. "You might as well let us out over there," Barry said, pointing to what looked like the largest of the warehouses. "We'll have to find our way."

Finding their way proved a lot less difficult than they had imagined. Mr. Smith was apparently well known. For when they entered the warehouse and approached a loader asking after the man by name, the loader took them outside and readily pointed the two men to a small building fifty yards away.

"I guess Smith isn't a fictitious name after all," Stuart said.

Inside the small building sat a seedy looking Brit with bushy hair and a matching swollen nose who answered to the name. The Brit sized up the two men quickly. Seeming to know who they were or at least what they were about, he directed them to their ship.

"Walk over to Pier Two and look for the Bristol. When you go on board ask for the captain. Tell him Smith sent you. He'll fix you up."

"How do we get to Pier Two?" Barry asked.

"Just outside the door and to your right," he said, his face contorting into a forced smile. After having made a mile trek to the boat, Stuart and Barry saw the smile for what it concealed, a smirk.

All manner and sizes of ships were docked at the harbor, including military craft, large barges, merchant ships, cruise liners, even small fishing boats. The Bristol looked derelict, unfit to sail. Its faded red paint was adorned with flecks of rust. Even its name, painted white on the ship's hull, was pockmarked with decay. When they drew nearer they saw load after load of cargo being carried on board.

"Apparently this tub is still operational," Stuart said.

"I guess it was asking too much to expect more under the circumstances," Barry replied. "I'm afraid to imagine what these people think we've been up to, needing to be smuggled out of the country and all."

"Is the captain around?" Stuart asked a crewmember who was supervising the loading. He pointed up the gangplank.

The captain, observing, looked down and walked towards them. "So, here's my new cargo," the red faced captain said with a wry smile. "Valuable cargo I've been told. You're going to Marseilles?" he asked, although he obviously knew the answer to that question.

"Yes, Marseilles," Barry answered as he shook the captain's hand.

"I bet you're getting a good price for this cargo?" Stuart said, unable to resist the impulse.

"Aye," the forthright captain answered. "Your friends have paid a tidy sum, assuming you arrive safely at your destination."

Stuart let his guard down. He knew now that the captain could be trusted. "We are in your hands, dear sir," he said and bent over in a mock bow.

The captain, who shared Stuart's sense of humor, returned the bow. "To that end, you will have to put up with a little inconvenience I'm afraid. You will be safer arriving at the next port as cargo. Follow me."

Instead of taking Barry and Stuart up the gangplank, he ushered them through the same loading door his crew was using to haul large containers into the hold.

"You will stay down here for most of the trip," the captain declared. "You can come up for short intervals once we are off shore, but consider this your lodging."

Stuart looked about the dark, musty hold that smelled of diesel fuel. "What are you carrying?"

"Mostly rice, cotton, carpets, nothing that can harm you. I will get you blankets and bring you your meals until it's safe for you to come up."

Barry, who had let his imagination carry him to the thermal baths in Aix-en-Provence under the improved conditions of the train, was not quite prepared for this. "For how long?"

"We leave tonight. We will arrive in Marseilles in two days."

"That's not so long Barry," Stuart said noting his friend's distress.

Likewise observing Barry's distress, the captain said, "Bad case of the collywobbles? Hmm? Don't you worry yourself. I'll bring you up for your breakfast. But tomorrow night as we near our port, you'll have to return for the duration."

Stuart and Barry nodded in agreement. What else could they do? The captain left them in the hold for the remainder of the day, promising to return that evening with their meal.

"Whatever Saadya paid for our passage, at least it included meals," Stuart laughed.

"But not lodging," Barry quipped. "I don't know what I was thinking. I hadn't really considered that Saadya had to pay for us."

"I bet he paid a lot."

"I owe him," Barry said as he sat down on the floor and leaned against a crate.

Chapter 20

Pilgrimage

John backed the van out from underneath the sheltering bridge and turned towards the town that lay ahead. He feared that if he hopped on the A 75 instead they might run out of fuel before they reached a station. As it turned out it was a good ten miles to that nearby town with no gas station in sight. Modernity had failed to invest there, it consisting of only small, unkempt houses swallowed up by murky fog.

"We're really in the boonies now," Rosalind said.

"This was a bad calculation," John agreed. "I hope we have enough gas to reach a station."

"I see something!" Summer said from the backseat. "It looks like a pump anyway."

"You've got sharp eyes," Rosalind said.

A rough looking woman came out of the general store to greet them. "Do you take credit cards?" John asked, knowing that with the high price of gas and the weak dollar a fill-up could cost well over a hundred dollars.

"No credit," the woman answered.

He gave her a twenty-euro bill. She smiled and started the pump.

"This will keep us going until we can find a station that takes credit, but that's it with my cash. I'm going to have to find an ATM when we reach somewhere." He turned to the rear of the van. "Thanks Summer for spotting this place."

"Sorry I don't have any cash on me. I sure would hate to be stuck out here." She opened her door and motioned to the woman. "Y a-t-il une meute de chiens?" she asked.

"Non, pas de chiens," the woman said.

"How do you say wolves?" she said

"Loups," John said.

"Y a-t-il des loups?" she asked. The woman answered with a stony stare, turned away, and returned inside her store. Summer slammed her

99

door shut. "Let's get out of here!"

They found gas, food, and an ATM once they got back on the highway, but time had slipped away. It was noon when they arrived and past one o'clock when they left. The road to Rodez lay in stark contrast to the Gévaudan. Heavy rain and fog gave way to gentle showers that fell on green grazing land that surrounded the medieval town. Cahors lay farther to the west. The road leading there was even lovelier as it was dotted with vineyards spreading out through gentle hills and valleys. Late day sunshine burst through in the west as they turned onto the A 20, the highway that would take them north on the last leg of their journey to Les-Eyzies-de-Tayac.

"Keep your eye out for a hotel," John said.

"But we're almost there," Rosalind said.

"Not soon enough. I'm not sure I could find Barry's cave in the dark."

"You're probably right about that," Rosalind said as she studied the map. "You know, Rocamadour is just a little ways up this road. We could stay the night there and take a look at that Black Virgin Stroud told us about."

"Sounds good to me," Summer said from the back seat. "It sure beats a truck stop."

"Sounds interesting to me too if it's nearby," John said.

"It looks about, well, it looks to be about five or ten miles from the highway. Instead of turning left towards Les-Eyzies-de-Tayac, we turn right on D 673."

"Stroud did make a particularly strong recommendation," John said. "And he was right about staying on the main roads."

The D 673 was hardly more than a paved path, a narrow lane winding through a landscape more rocky and mountainous than anything they had seen since they left the Gévaudan. What appeared to be five or ten miles on the map turned into a far longer stretch on the road.

"Do all roads leading to the Black Madonnas wind around so?" Summer asked after she began to sicken in the backseat.

"It begins to look that way," John said, as he rounded another blind curve. "I'm glad there isn't any traffic coming at us."

"Look up there!" Rosalind said. "There's the town. From here it looks like it might have been carved out of a mountain."

John stopped the van in the middle of the lane and hung out of his window. "It's layered like a great stone wedding cake, the church at the top and in descending order the town's other dwellings and establishments.

"I've got to get a picture of this while the light's still good," Summer said, fully recovered from her upset stomach.

John pulled over, and they all climbed out. Summer began snapping photos.

"How old is it?" Rosalind asked.

"The architecture looks tenth or eleventh century," John said.

"How did they ever build it? It looks as if the cliff could give way and the whole town could tumble down. It's amazing it hasn't," she marveled.

"You can't tell where the mountain ends and the church begins. Like it was chiseled out of the rock," John observed.

The church that had caught his eye he would learn is the Chapelle Notre-Dame, devoted to the Black Virgin of Rocamadour. They drove down into the valley and pulled into a gravel parking lot situated next to a tractor train that carried them up the narrow road to the town's lower level. Here shops, hotels, and restaurants were housed in Rocamadour's ancient structures. They looked about the town for a short time, found a hotel, and checked in before they began their trek up the two hundred and sixteen steps leading to the religious site. Summer leaped ahead of John and Rosalind with the sure-footed agility of a mountain goat.

"It would be a lot worse if we were climbing on our knees," Rosalind said reading from a brochure she had picked up at the hotel. "According to this pamphlet that's exactly what early penitents did."

They stopped a few minutes to catch their breath, and she read aloud. *"Rocamadour has been a major pilgrimage destination since the eleventh century and perhaps earlier. It is the burial site of Zacchaeus of Jericho, the hermit who is said to have been the husband of Saint Veronica who wiped the face of Jesus as he climbed to Calvary. Legend has it that Zacchaeus brought the statue of the Black Virgin with him from the Holy Land."*

Summer slowed her pace. "Is that true?" she asked.

"That's the thing about legends," Rosalind said. "You can't prove them and you can't disprove them either. That's what gives them their power to those who believe."

They stood outside of the Chapelle Notre-Dame alongside a large group of tourists who waited with their tour guide to enter. Eventually, people exited the church and their group was permitted to go inside. The interior looked like a natural grotto at sunset. They joined the others who had sat down on pews of rough wood, expecting, they thought, to overhear the guide give a lecture. Instead, the tourists and their guide began to recite a prayer rather loudly in Polish. "They're pilgrims!" Rosalind whispered. Eventually their prayer turned into song while the trio quietly observed and listened.

The Lady of Rocamadour sat before them on the altar as black as the Vierge Noire at Mende. She was not pregnant but slender under her close fitting robe. The Christ child sat on her lap with the features of a man. The lady, like the Black Virgin at Mende, was not beautiful in the traditional sense, but stately and pensive.

There is more to her than the soft, ivory Madonnas I'm familiar with, Rosalind thought. She lacks the sweet mouth, the veil and blue flowing robes, the eyes full of compassion. Instead, her eyes are full of intelligence. Yet these pilgrims gather here, she observed, asking for her compassion, hoping she will intercede on their behalf and absolve them of their sins, cure them of their ills, or help someone they love.

She studied the miniature boats that hung from the ceiling of the chapel and surmised that the lady is a protectress of the sea and sailors. The boats reminded her of another legend, the story of Mary Magdalene's arrival by boat to Saintes-Maries-de-la-Mer. Some believe she had fled there to escape persecution and brought with her the religion she helped found. Rosalind thought about the legends of Mary Magdalene, Zacchaeus of Jericho, the Black Virgin of Rocamadour, and the Black Madonna of Mende and realized that while the Crusaders had captured then lost the Holy Land, they brought it permanently to France in legend at least.

Chapter 21

Barry's Cave

Rosalind's imagination had not left Rocamadour even as they drove away on the same tight lanes and switchbacks they had arrived on. The rough and craggy landscape looked older and more populated than when she had arrived, as if history had been compressed into a time warp. Old Zacchaeus of Jericho was making his way to what was to become his hermitage, carrying with him a valuable religious object from the Holy Land. Following just behind, but hundreds of years later, were the first of the great processions of penitents come to pray before that object, that Black Madonna who came to be known as the Lady of Rocamadour. Stream after stream of penitents walked the narrow road over centuries of time all with the same purpose, ending finally with the Polish pilgrims whose prayerful worship they had witnessed the evening before.

The spell was broken once they pulled off that winding lane and entered the flow of traffic on the A 20. They traveled only a few miles, and then turned off the highway again into a green and rugged terrain heading west towards Les-Eyzies-de-Tayac. Signs popped up along the road directing visitors to various grottes, some designated as prehistoric.

"I'm going to stop here," John said as he pulled the van into a gravel parking lot of the Grotte Font-de-Gaume. "I have a hunch somebody around here will know Barry."

He parked near a small shop and ticket office and asked the vendor for any information she might have. She pointed to a stone stairway nestled under the trees and directed him to the archeologist on duty who was about to lead a group into the cave. "She can answer your questions if you wish to join them," she said.

"Hey, I would like to go into one of these caves," Summer said.

"Me too," Rosalind said. She put Christabel back inside the van with a few treats, climbed the tall steps that wound up to the cave's entrance, and joined a small group that was gathered around a dark, narrow opening into the mountain.

"Bonjour," the tour leader said. "Vous êtes juste á l'heure."

"Good," John replied.

"You are English?" the leader asked.

"American."

"I will speak in English for you then."

The tour leader was a small, sturdy woman wearing a blue cap and khaki shirt that gave her a look of authority. More impressive than her appearance was her abundant knowledge. She led them back into an eerily quiet cave with a roof so high it was concealed in blackness.

"These works were created by the Magdalenian people some 15,000 years ago," she explained, as she pointed a small flashlight to the many bison and reindeer drawn, painted, and etched into the walls. "The Magdalenians are often referred to as cave people with all the ridiculous associations we attach to the term. They were really very much like ourselves."

"But they did live in caves," John said.

"We find no evidence of that, no remnants of food preparation, for example. The only activity we find evidence for inside these caves was the creation of this art. Observe its sophistication. They used both modeling and perspective, techniques that were lost and rediscovered thousands of years later."

"How could that be? What happened?" Summer asked.

"We don't know," the guide answered. "We could speculate, but we have chosen instead to focus our attention on what can be understood from a careful examination of the evidence. For example, it was once believed that these paintings were associated with hunting, but look at how peaceful these scenes are: no fighting, no wounded, no hostility of any kind. Their purpose, we do not know. Look around, you will find no trees, flowers, sun, or anything else in nature. Just these graceful renderings of animals, often shown in movement as if the artist's entire motivation was to create beauty for beauty's sake."

"They remind me of my buffalo mug," John said.

"Yes, and there's a Native American creation myth at the center of its meaning," Rosalind said. "Excuse me. Is there religious significance?"

she asked.

"You are asking about abstractions," the tour leader replied. "All we know is what we have here. We know the materials they used. We know that they prepared the walls of the cave much like one prepares a canvas. We know that they chose to create their work in the rear of these caves, but we can only speculate why. We know that they chose to paint only these animals, but we can only guess their intentions. What we do know is these Stone Age people were capable of abstract thought. Come here," she said, urging Rosalind to come closer. She shined her lamp on symbols carved into the cave wall. "We have found symbols like these here and in other caves. No one knows their meaning."

"You need another Champollion to unravel this writing," Rosalind said.

"There is no Rosetta Stone here," the tour leader laughed.

"That's too bad," Rosalind said, unable to take her eyes off the symbols until the guide moved her lamp casting them back into darkness.

"I'm fascinated with the symbols," Rosalind whispered to John and Summer.

"They look like runes," Summer said.

"You're right," John agreed. "If we knew what they meant, maybe we could understand all of this."

"Even without understanding, these paintings are beautiful," Summer said as she turned full circle in the tight space to take it all in.

"Here we have another set of symbols," the guide said.

"Look, they all have straight lines in contrast to the curved lines of the animals," John said.

"That one looks like a modified arrow pointed up," Rosalind said. "Almost like the numerical one sitting on top of a straight horizontal line."

The guide did not discourage their speculations in spite of her previous warning against it. Rather, she appeared to delight in them, as if this trained archeologist secretly rebelled against the very restraints she publicly espoused, as if she hoped that someday, somehow, someone would figure this out. And she knew that in all likelihood that would require a degree of speculation.

To better preserve the paintings, she led them back outside after only a short visit. Summer and Rosalind skipped down the long stone staircase to join Christabel while John remained behind so that he might approach the guide on the subject of Barry.

"Do you know an archeologist friend of ours who is working in this area, a Barry Short?"

"Oui! Barry. Oui, I know him very well. You say he is your friend?"

"Yes, that's why we're here. He asked me to pick up some of his equipment at his apartment and meet him in Aix-en-Provence. But I have to find his place first. He said he lives near a vineyard."

"Oui, Barry's cave. It is across the road from the Boars Head Vineyard. If you like, I will take you there. You can follow me."

"If you would, we would really appreciate it."

"I go there for lunch sometimes. Have you had lunch?"

"Why, no we haven't."

"Have lunch with me then."

"I presume if it's a vineyard they have good wine."

"Oui, and cheese and soup. I am Yvette," she said and held out her hand.

John shook it. "John," he said. "And over there near the van is my wife Rosalind and my sister-in-law Summer."

"And your caniche," she laughed, pointing towards Christabel who was barking her head off.

"She doesn't like being left alone," John apologized.

"She can come with us. She's acceptée."

They followed Yvette several miles along a series of roads that led into a forest that eventually opened up to a group of country cottages that formed a small village. Beyond the cottages was a small vineyard marked by a beautifully carved boar's head surrounded by painted vines and grapes that stood in front of a simple stone and wood structure. Inside was a large room with a stone floor, natural light, and rough-hewn interior. A long wine tasting bar stood on one side and several tables filled the other.

"Bonjour," Yvette said to a stout older woman who stood behind the bar. The woman greeted Yvette with a warm smile and chatted before she rushed off into the rear room.

"Sit down," Yvette said directing the group to one of the large picnic style tables. "Aveline has gone to the kitchen to get our lunch. She has mushroom soup today and walnut cake. You will find them delicious."

"Great!" John said, eager to taste some authentic rural cuisine. "Did you tell her what we are here for?"

"Yes, we will go across the road to Barry's after lunch. Aveline was glad to hear he's all right. She has been used to seeing him here daily until recently. What did you say he is he doing in Aix?"

"I didn't. I don't know," John replied. "I presume he's continuing his research."

"There are no Solutrean remains near Aix."

"Maybe he's given up on the Solutreans."

"Hmm, it would be sad if that is true. But I have told him his theory is weak."

"Why do you say that?" Rosalind asked.

"They have no cave art in America like we find here. Just the arrowheads. That's not enough."

John thought again of his buffalo mug but kept it to himself, recognizing that such thoughts are highly speculative. Besides that, the buffalo design was on a mug not in a cave.

Aveline brought out a tray of cheeses, bread, large bowls, plates, silverware, and napkins, which she placed on the table before she scurried back into the kitchen. She returned carrying a large tureen of dark, rich broth loaded with wild mushrooms. Christabel barked. Aveline laughed and patted her on the head before she went over to the bar to get glasses, wine, and a sausage or two.

"I could be wrong," Yvette admitted. "We know the Solutreans were seafaring, and under the right conditions they could have crossed the Atlantic. Maybe he will find the evidence he needs, but he doesn't have it now. It would be a shame if he ended his researches only months after beginning."

"I think something would have had to drive them to take the risk of crossing the Atlantic Ocean," Rosalind said. "Food shortages, war, disease, something that would have propelled them to search out a new land."

"Or maybe they were swept out to sea in a storm," Yvette said. "If that were the case, it was no migration but an accident. That could explain the lack of cave paintings. The boat carried no artist, only seafarers perhaps hunting the walrus. But this is all speculation."

"So you aren't altogether sure you don't believe Barry," John said.

"I need evidence. So far he can't show me much. But it is possible."

Aveline returned carrying a golden brown unfrosted cake that she sliced and served to her guests, and then waited for their reaction.

"This is delicious," Rosalind said. "My compliments to the chef."

"I would love to take some of these walnuts back to Amsterdam," Summer said.

"Aveline gathers and prepares them herself," Yvette said.

"It's perfect. Frosting would ruin it," John said.

"Tu es un hit!" Yvette said to Aveline who smiled with satisfaction, gathered the plates and bowls she had stacked on the bar and carried them into the kitchen.

John stretched. "We'd better get over to Barry's before it gets too late. We have a long drive yet."

The four of them left the table and crossed the road to Barry's cave, which was concealed behind a small grove of trees.

"This isn't a cave; it's a stone house," Summer said.

"It's like a cave," Yvette said as she placed the key in the lock. "Look! This lock is broken! "It's been ransacked!" she said when she stepped inside.

In that faint light all that was visible was a narrow bed, an overturned chest of drawers, a rifled desk, and no evidence of indoor plumbing. Yvette turned on a lamp.

"It doesn't look like the work of a thief," John said as he gathered up the laptop, digital camera, and tape recorder. "His electronic equipment is still here."

"I will ask Aveline if she knows anything about this," Yvette said and rushed outside.

"What do you think?" Rosalind asked.

"My gut tells me Barry's in big trouble," John said.

"Yeah, mine too."

Aveline arrived looking a bit frantic, having been pulled from the kitchen still wearing her apron. She could not control her instinct to begin picking up papers and boxes, close drawers, and tidy up the place all while babbling nonstop to Yvette.

Yvette put her hands on Aveline's arms to try to stop her frantic movements and turned to them. "She knows nothing! As you can see she's quite upset. I told her it was probably the work of children. His valuables are all here, and you recently spoke to him so we know he is certainly all right."

"That's right," Rosalind said hesitantly and looked over at John. "I guess we should be leaving."

"When you see Barry ask him to call Aveline to reassure her. Have him phone me too," she said and scribbled down her phone number.

As they drove away, the trees grew more imposing; and as if to reflect their mood, shrouded the whole forested area in darkness.

Chapter 22

Montauban

The plan was to sleep in Toulouse and take the highway east to Aix-en-Provence the following day. But before they could hope to be on the highway, they first had to navigate the winding rural roads of the Perigord.

"Did I miss a turn back there?" John asked when he found himself in a residential area outside of the town of Sarlat.

"I think you must have," Rosalind said.

"I'll swing back towards the town. Please, keep a lookout for the route markers," he said, not so subtly reminding her that she was the navigator.

"Turn right here," she said. "Here we are."

"I could use a break, and I know the dog needs one," Summer said from the back seat.

They pulled into a public lot in Sarlat's old town district. Christabel scrambled out of the car and pulled Summer over to one of the many trees scattered about the gravel parking lot before the three of them headed toward a nearby cafe.

"I need a beer," John said to a sympathetic waitress. "Maybe several." He turned to Rosalind. "What the hell did Barry get himself into?"

"Maybe you should try phoning him again."

He punched in Stuart's number while sipping a very large draught beer only to hear the recorded message. Exhausted from worry and driving, he threw up his hands after tossing Rosalind the keys.

Soon after they hit the road again, Summer had fallen asleep, slumped over the dog in the rear seat. John had dozed off, leaning against the passenger side window. Rosalind carefully negotiated the traffic circles, one after another after another all the way to the A 20. A tailgater had hovered behind her so close that he had made her quite nervous. She had hoped the offending vehicle would turn the other direction once she had arrived at the highway, but it had not. Instead, it followed her south hugging her bumper. She slowed to fifteen miles below the speed limit hoping it would pass, but it stayed glued to her tail. A sign pointed to Montauban a mile ahead. The situation required some risk taking, she thought. She increased her speed to the max and made a sudden sharp turn onto the exit ramp without signaling the driver behind her. He was gone at last, but Rosalind had no idea where she was.

Rowdy street youths suggested she was in the wrong part of town. Every street she turned down eventually looped around to where she had started. After driving around in circles for more than a half hour, she pulled into a gas station to fill up and get some advice. The attendant directed her back to the highway and suggested she take an alternative route to the upper city, near the river.

"How long have I been asleep?" John asked overhearing the conversation.

"Since we left Sarlat."

"Is this Toulouse?"

"No, Montauban. We were being followed so I shook him, and here we are."

"You shook him?"

"Made a sharp turn off the highway without turning my signal on."

"Is he gone?"

"I hope so."

"It was probably nothing," he said.

In no time they found a gated hotel. Luck, she thought, as she considered how unlucky she had been to take the wrong route in the first place. The gate opened to a secured parking garage. They were safe now.

"We're going to blow the budget here, but it's only for one night," John said returning to the passengers in the car. "I've made a reservation for us at the restaurant in half an hour. They've got a chef."

"Sounds heavenly," Rosalind replied while gathering her luggage, thankful for a comfortable, safe hotel, even if it was expensive.

She was convinced their luck had truly changed when she saw their room. She was certain of it when she feasted on grilled salmon in the hotel dining room. The restaurant was quiet and nearly empty except for a few men here and there discussing business over the remains of their dinner or a bottle of wine and the staff who had begun preparing tables for the morning brunch. All was well.

***

"The breakfast buffet is scrumptious," Rosalind said to Summer who had waited at the table with the dog while she and John had made their selections.

"Sounds good," she said and handed Christabel over in her traveling bag.

Summer studied the buffet table before she made her choices, careful to balance her appetite with her nutritional needs and caloric intake. She scooped up some homemade yogurt, fresh berries, passed on the tempting croissants taking a bagel instead. Her plate full, she stood looking for a place to put it down so that she could pour herself a glass of orange juice.

"Laissez-moi vous aider mademoiselle," a stranger said after observing her dilemma. He grabbed hold of her plate while she awkwardly looked about. In that moment of transition, their eyes met. He was handsome, his dark hair combed back away from deep brown eyes. He smiled.

"Thank you," she said a bit flustered. "I wanted to pour myself a glass of juice, and I wasn't sure where to put my plate."

"I could see that," he said. "Go ahead. Pour your juice now."

Rosalind could not hear the conversation, but she could observe the body language. "Look over at Summer," she said. "Don't be too obvious."

"Who's the guy?"

"I don't know, but she's clearly enjoying herself."

Summer walked towards the table followed by the man still holding her plate. She stopped and pointed towards her travel mates. He looked over and smiled. They returned the smile, which he took as an invitation.

"Mr. de Chevalier, I would like you to meet my sister Rosalind and her husband John."

112

"Please, you may call me Etienne," the handsome man in the dark suit said with a slight bow. "I was just talking with your lovely sister. She said you are American tourists on your way to Aix-en-Provence. I told her I would be in the area and would love you to come to a festive party at Les Baux. It will be tomorrow night. I'm sure you would enjoy yourselves."

Summer looked more pleased than embarrassed by her rapid conquest: She of him or he of her, it was uncertain.

"Here, let me give you an invitation," the man said and pulled a printed card from his inside breast pocket that he handed to John. "Might I see you then?"

John looked at the invitation. "If we can come, we will. Thank you very much."

Etienne put Summer's plate down on the table, smiled at her warmly, bowed slightly, and said, "Until tomorrow." He then left the dining room.

"Wow!" Summer said, letting loose now that Mr. de Chevalier was no longer within earshot.

"How did that happen?" Rosalind asked.

"I don't know!" the delighted girl exclaimed.

"I didn't think France had royalty any longer," John said as he laid the invitation on the table.

"They don't," Rosalind said.

"Then look at this seal. It reads Maison de Bourbon."

Chapter 23

Reunion

Blue sea blended with sky, making one moving canvas that seemed to dance as dappled sunlight bounced across waves. The cliffside opposite was dotted with windmills, sleek, like great gray seagulls. Wind turbines were not a thing of nature, and yet the genius of their design made them look to be, their blades forced to spin by the wind that blew in from the sea. Nature and human technology in harmony, Rosalind thought. Her mental soliloquy on windmills ended abruptly when John tuned the radio to the "Nostalgia" station. *If your baby leaves you, and you've got a tale to tell…*

"'Heartbreak Hotel!' she said. "I can't remember the last time I heard that song on the radio or anywhere else for that matter. And here we are in France, driving along the Mediterranean listening to Elvis Presley."

"I really want to go to this party," Summer said from the backseat. She had been unusually quiet, and her remark made it clear why. She had been ruminating.

"We'll see," Rosalind said. She recalled Summer's childhood fascination with fairytale royalty and her disappointment when she learned from sordid tales of infidelity and betrayal on tabloid TV that real life nobility are not always noble. Despite that early disillusionment, her dreams had persisted as dreams often do in gauzy rebellion against reality. Rosalind knew why her sister had wanted to go to chateau country. To experience the turrets, the velvet curtained beds, the sumptuous gardens, the bridges and moats, the things that for a few moments make the dream seem real. And now there he was, flesh and blood, from the House of Bourbon.

"Once we meet up with Barry and Stuart we will see what they have to say about it," John said.

"I don't see what they have to do with it," Summer said.

"They might want to leave right away."

"They can just wait a day. We've been waiting days for them to call. They can wait for me."

"I'm sure they won't mind," Rosalind said. "They may want to go too. I sure do. How often is one invited to a party given by the House of Bourbon?"

The phone rang. John grabbed it and abruptly slowed down, convinced it was Barry. "I thought I told you not to go over there," he said into the phone. "His computer is gone! Well, it's probably a good thing that you dropped in then. No, I have no idea what's going on; I'm still waiting to hear from him myself. Don't call the police just yet. Okay, I will tell him everything when I talk to him. Maybe he can enlighten us. Don't panic over this. Look, it must be after eight o'clock over there; you'd better go to school. And Paul, keep away from Barry's place. If you feel you must empty his mailbox, grab the mail and take it home. But don't go inside again. Promise? Okay. I'll talk to you later."

John flipped the phone closed. "Barry's cave isn't the only place that's been ransacked."

"Oh jeeze, his house too?" Rosalind said.

"Yep, they took his computer. I'm glad I was able to retrieve his laptop."

"It's a good thing Paul wasn't there when it happened," she said.

"Yep! But he showed up even after I told him not to."

"Kids are like that. At least we know what's going on."

"But we don't know why or who's doing it," John said.

Rosalind turned to look out the rear window. The road was empty. The scene that she had just meditated on had disappeared.

"The good news is that it looks like they don't know where he is," John said.

"We don't either," she sighed.

The phone rang again within minutes of his hanging it up. John was sure it must be Paul calling with something he had forgotten to mention, but it was Barry.

"Where the hell are you anyway?" John said. "We're on our way. We'll be there in about two or three hours. Summer is with us. Can you reserve two more rooms for at least two nights? I will explain later. I've got a lot to tell you, but I can barely hear you. Yes, I picked up your stuff. No, I didn't have any trouble finding it. A friend of yours, Yvette took us there. Yes, she's a pretty nice woman, interesting. Okay, your voice is breaking up. I will head to the old part of Aix and ask someone if I can't find it. Right, I will call you if I get lost. See you soon."

John clicked off the phone and repeated what he had just heard. "They arrived in Marseille early this morning but had to wait to be unloaded before they could get a bus to Aix."

"Unloaded?" Summer said thinking that an odd term for disembarking passengers.

"They were carried as cargo. They crated them."

"They crated them!" Rosalind said, trying to hold back laughter as an absurd image formed in her mind. "Like zoo animals? Monkeys perhaps?"

"They were smuggled out of Egypt as cargo so they crated them," he repeated, this time unleashing a floodgate. There was a certain satisfaction in their laughter, a sense of payback for all the worry and trouble Barry had caused.

"Can you turn that up?" Summer said, hearing the faint sounds of Edit Piaf coming from the car speakers. "They're playing 'La Vie en Rose.'" The radio soon segued into the Louis Armstrong version of the same song.

"Listen to that trumpet," Rosalind said.

They wafted along the highway, picking up speed as they drove. The Nostalgia station played "Georgia On My Mind," "Hold On I'm Coming," "Chain of Fools." The music couldn't have gotten any better. Signs appeared, "Aix-en-Provence 20 km" then "Aix-en-Provence Centre Ville."

"We're looking for a hotel called Aquabella somewhere around here, so keep an eye out," John said.

"Right there!" Summer said pointing to a sign.

He turned into the narrow streets of the old French town, slowed at a sign pointing to the Aquabella, and turned into a cobbled alley that led to what looked like the walls of an ancient fortress. "Thermes Sextius" another sign read. John pulled the van into the hotel entrance drive, took out the phone and called Barry, who promptly appeared along with

Stuart at the door to greet them.

Barry wrapped his burley arms around Rosalind. She pulled back and looked at him closely. "You look a little peaked," she said.

"That's what happens when you spend nearly a week in cargo holds."

"Especially when you're the cargo," John laughed.

"That's enough," Rosalind said now that she had begun to feel sympathetic.

"They only had us crated for a couple of hours while they unloaded," Stuart said, not liking to be the butt of John's joke.

"Incarceration didn't seem to affect you much," Rosalind said.

"He's a younger man," Barry said with a chuckle. "I look a lot better now than I did a few hours ago." Looking over at Stuart he added, "We both do. A thermal bath and a massage can do wonders for you. All that we need now is a good dinner and a comfortable bed, one that's standing on firm ground. Tomorrow we'll be fine."

"I hope so," Summer said, "because we have a very interesting invitation for tomorrow night."

"Have you met Summer?" John asked.

"No, I don't believe I have."

"Barry, Stuart, meet Rosalind's sister Summer."

"Yes, and what's this about an interesting invitation?" Barry asked, looking over at John.

"Summer, you tell him."

"We received an invitation to a party to be held tomorrow evening in Les Baux given by the House of Bourbon!"

Barry raised his eyebrow. "Well, I could see why you might want to attend," he said, amused by the revelation. "Tell me, who do you know in the House of Bourbon?"

"It's some fellow she met at the hotel we stayed at in Montauban," John said. "His name is Etienne de Chevalier."

"We don't know if he's real royalty," Rosalind added.

Barry raised his eyebrow again. "You met him at a hotel?"

Summer blushed. "It wasn't like that," she said. "I met him in the dining room...this morning while we were having brunch. I had mentioned to him that we were on our way to Aix-en-Provence and he offered the invitation when he learned we would be nearby. I'm sure you and Stuart would be welcome to attend with us."

"Well, that was very nice of him," Barry said, secretly thinking that Summer is quite fetching, which probably explains this Etienne fellow's generous invitation. "Are you sure he wouldn't mind us tagging along?"

"Quite sure."

Barry turned to John. "Do you have my laptop?"

"Yes, I've got it here in the van. I'll get it for you."

"Well, let's just search his name and see what we can learn about him, see if he's real royalty. Etienne de Chevalier, did you say?"

"That's what he said," Summer replied.

"You come with me into the lobby and we'll plug this thing in." He turned to John. "Get checked in while I have at it on this computer. I'm starving!"

"There's a lot more to tell you," John said. "Somebody has been nosing around in your things."

"And sending you threatening emails and stealing your home computer" Rosalind added.

"My Power Mac! Well, I've got a lot to tell you too, but it can wait for later. The hotel dining room has already closed, and the staff recommended an excellent Italian restaurant if we can get there in time. Stuart, can you give them a hand?"

Chapter 24

Nobility

"Etienne de Chevalier," Summer sighed. The waitress filled her glass with Provençal wine. "He's real nobility," she said just before sipping it.

"Petty nobility," Rosalind said.

"Nobility is nobility!" Summer replied.

"You're right," Barry agreed. "A cousin twice removed from the great grandson of a count is real nobility, distant or not."

Summer had grown to like Barry. He had a real talent for making people like him.

"I'm worried about you," she said to him. "They broke into your cave over here and stole your computer in Ohio. Are they after this statue you just brought back?"

"They could be, but I don't know how they would have known about it. They may be after a statue that some people erroneously believe I smuggled out of Egypt last year."

"The email Paul read me made reference to that other statue but implied that you had just returned with something new," John said.

"Come on Barry, tell us about it," Rosalind urged.

"If you keep it to yourselves. Hans Bueller summoned me because of the statue he had found. It's a very ancient statue of a woman of unknown identity, but we think she has an important identity, perhaps extremely important."

"Nobility?" Summer asked.

"More than nobility. We think the statue is a representation of a hitherto unknown goddess. Hans sent me back here with her hoping I would be able to discover who she is."

"That would be the find of a lifetime." Rosalind said. "Your name would be recorded forever among great archeologists, perhaps alongside Howard Carter. But why here and not there?"

"We don't think she's Egyptian. She looks European, a black European."

"Tell them about the verse," Stuart said.

"Yes, here, I've got it in my pocket." He pulled out a piece of paper and read,

> "She looks upon herself who is not there.
> But sees instead before her all the world.
> Whatever was, whatever will be is in her care.
> For she is the maker of the world.
> Within her face all faces, all time, the cosmic burst of creation.
> She holds the mirror of the world."

"It reads almost like a riddle," Rosalind said. "'She looks upon herself who is not there.' What could that mean? Looks at herself but is not there," she puzzled. "Hmm, she sees herself even though she is invisible?"

"Good, keep going," Barry said.

"Well, I see why you think she may be a goddess. She can see all, even those things others can't see. In fact, she herself is what others can't see, but she is there nonetheless."

"What else is unseeable?" Summer asked.

"Many things," John said. "Cells, atoms, distant stars and planets. Then there are the things that aren't there that we do see, colors, for example."

"What's the second line again?" Rosalind asked.

"But sees instead before her all the world."

"Interesting. She can see herself even though others cannot, but the self that she sees is all the world. So the meaning goes beyond things of science. When she looks at herself she sees not the small particles of science but the whole thing, all the world."

"That could be a lot more than one big globe," Summer added. "It could be expansive, like all time, like everything that ever happened."

"That's right," Barry said. "The next line reads, 'Whatever was, whatever will be is in her care. For she is the maker of the world.'"

"She is the maker and everything is in her care," Rosalind repeated.

"Whatever was, whatever will be—she could be watching us right

120

now!" Summer said.

"'Within her face all faces, all time, the cosmic burst of creation,'" Barry read aloud.

"She is all and observes all, forever," Rosalind said.

"She is either the cosmic burst of creation or she can see it. If we could see her face, we would see it too," Summer said.

"Like looking though the Hubble," John said. "Looking back at the beginning of time, the big bang."

"'She holds the mirror of the world,'" Barry read.

"It's almost as if she is the Hubble telescope and more," Rosalind said. "She mirrors all—Telescopes have mirrors don't they? She is also the 'all' that is mirrored. Oh Barry, this is fantastic! Can I see her?"

"I have her put away, and it's a good thing too after everything you've reported."

Stuart who had been quiet up to now, spoke up, "Do you know who would have sent that email and taken your computer?"

"I have an idea, but I can't be sure. The fact that the email originated in Rome lends weight to my thinking. He would have contacts in the U.S. that could have swiped my computer. I don't want to say anymore for now. This is all speculation."

Chapter 25

The Royal Ball

"You're not going to get me into one of those things," Barry said to Summer when he saw her fingering the fabric of a black tuxedo.

"Why not?"

"Because I refuse, that's why!"

"Come on Summer. A tuxedo is over the top," John said.

She gave up, which she didn't like to do. But it was unanimous so she didn't argue. She was happy enough that everyone agreed to go.

"What's wrong?" Rosalind asked.

"Oh, nothing really. We're going. That's what counts. I just hope we make a decent appearance, that's all."

"Okay, okay. What about these pants," John said pulling a pair of well tailored brown dress pants off the rack, "with a dress shirt."

"I like this shirt," Stuart said, pointing to a charcoal gray shirt with thin, silvery threads woven into the fabric.

Summer studied the pants, felt the fabric, walked over to a table piled high with shirts, and looked back at the pants. "Can't they at least be black with a suit jacket?"

"All right," Barry replied before John had a chance to answer. "Black pants it is." The salesclerk began measuring the arms, waists, and the inside leg of his customers now that a decision had been made.

Satisfied, Summer and Rosalind headed toward the door. "We'll see you back at the hotel," Rosalind said. She looked back at the salesclerk. "They might need dress shoes and socks." The clerk looked down at Barry's boots and shook his head in agreement.

Buying women's clothing was another matter. Summer pored over some swank evening gowns that Rosalind cautioned against, arguing that they should not be more formally dressed than the men. Summer relented and settled on a classic black sheath after the salesclerk assured her that such a dress is always chic at any occasion. Rosalind found some lovely black crepe bell-bottoms and a silk pearl tank top. The salesclerk dressed it up with a lovely red shawl in case it became chilly. She sold Summer a deep purple wrap, the color of royalty, she said.

Les Baux, once a thriving medieval city, now lay in ruins perched on a steep hillside that they had to ascend by foot, which was all for the good since their rented van hardly looked suitable for a royal affair. They climbed up the steps unsure where the festivities were to be held until they arrived at the top. Lights were strewn across the remnants of castles and other old structures creating a beautiful outdoor setting. In spite of the chill in the air, it was fabulous.

"I had no idea royalty still existed in France," Rosalind said as she surveyed the crowd.

"Yeah, I thought they all met the guillotine a long time ago," Stuart replied caustically.

John showed the invitation, and they were politely admitted to a very formal gathering.

"I told you tuxedos would be appropriate," Summer scolded. "Gowns would have been appropriate too."

"We can introduce Barry as the Duc de New Orleans of Louisiana," John joked. "He looks distinguished enough in his new shoes."

Barry looked down at his polished black wingtips and winced, the joke having made the shoes feel all the tighter.

Smiling broadly, Etienne walked towards them from out of the crowd wearing an extremely well tailored tuxedo. "You came," he said, looking admiringly at Summer before taking her hand. "And you brought others. Will you introduce me?"

"You've met my sister and my brother-in-law." He bowed his head, and they bowed theirs in return. "These are their friends whom we met in Aix, Dr. Barry Short and Stuart—I don't believe I know your last name."

"I don't believe you do," Stuart said, breaking the monotony of polite introductions.

An awkward silence ensued as everyone waited for him to offer it. Summer, mortified, explained that he is an investigator with the United States government and may feel the need to keep his identity to himself.

"An investigator!" Etienne said. "Perhaps you are a spy too?"

Stuart said nothing. Summer redirected Etienne's attention. "Barry is an archeologist doing work here in France."

"In France, you say, and for how long have you been here?"

"For several months now. I'm studying artifacts and caves in the Perigord region."

"Prehistoric. Tell me, what period. The Magdalenian?"

"No, I mean yes and no. You can hardly be in the region without exploring the Magdalenians, but I'm more interested for the purposes of my current research in the earlier Solutrean culture."

"What is your current work if you do not mind that I ask? It is unusual, you see, to have an American here doing archeology."

"There are those who believe the Solutreans may have influenced the development of North American indigenous culture. I'm here to see if I can find anything that would support that claim."

"That is quite original. I've never heard such a thing. What else might you be doing?"

"I hate to interrupt, but I really need a drink," Stuart said.

"How thoughtless of me," Etienne apologized. "Follow me if you will."

He took Summer's hand and led her into a beautiful ruin of a building that lay open to the stars. "You will find anything you might like to eat or drink just inside."

Rosalind, John, Stuart, and Barry entered the ruin, leaving Summer alone for a few minutes with her prince. There was champagne enough that Rosalind and John delighted in making up toasts while Stuart pulled Barry aside for a few minutes of conversation.

"I don't know about this guy," Stuart said. "He asks a lot of questions."

"He's only making conversation," Barry said.

"No, he's got a motive, and I'm not sure what it is."

"His motive is to impress Summer, that's all."

"He met her in a hotel."

"A hotel restaurant. It was perfectly respectable, and she's a lovely girl. That's why he invited her here. You are letting your imagination get the better of you. Let me offer a toast," Barry said turning back to

John and Rosalind. "To Summer's good fortune and to ours for being able to come along."

"It is a beautiful place," Rosalind said, taking in the illusion of grandeur the artificial lights cast upon the ruins. "It certainly stimulates the imagination, speaking of which...."

Christabel, poking her head out of the traveling bag slung over John's shoulder greeted Summer and Etienne with a round of barks. Etienne petted the playful dog. "You have nothing to eat. Let me take you over to the table and please serve yourself. I am sorry about the informality of the buffet but with so many guests..."

"Don't apologize," Barry said. "It looks wonderful."

Etienne gave the dog a few pieces of beef and watched while the others filled their plates. "Let me get you a table."

He led them into an adjoining area full of linen draped tables surrounding an empty bandstand and a makeshift dance floor. Chandeliers hung from posts. The setting reminded Rosalind of movie sets of 1930's New York dinner clubs. "Very elegant," she said.

"I'm glad you like it," he said with a slight bow. He seated them at the table he had reserved.

"Etienne told me he too has many archeological interests," Summer said, reintroducing the topic of the earlier conversation.

"Oh, you do," Barry said. "What are your interests?"

"Not so much in France, I'm afraid. I have spent many months in Greece looking at Minoan art. My grandmother who resides in Italy has introduced me to Rome's ancient past."

"Barry has done a lot of work in Egypt," Rosalind said.

"The institute I'm employed by has a campus in Luxor. But I spent most of my time on the Giza plateau, near the Pyramids."

"Yes, they are fascinating," Etienne said. "So old and yet so solid and mysterious. When were you last in Egypt?"

"Some time ago. Nearly a year." Barry began to wonder by this line of questioning if Stuart had a point.

"There are no Solutrean remains in Aix-en-Provence," Etienne said.

"I came for the thermal baths."

"Looks like there's a great view of the valley from up here," Stuart said. "Would you mind if we go take a look?"

"Not at all. But it is a far better view in daylight."

"This will do," Stuart said, standing up and signaling Barry to come with him. "Better at night than not at all."

"Well, I guess we should take a look too," John said.

"I would really like to dance," Rosalind countered, noting the musicians returning to the stage.

"Not now," John said.

"I would love to dance too," Summer said.

"We shall dance then." Etienne rose from his chair and helped her up from hers. "Do you have a favorite song?"

"La Vie en Rose."

"Beautiful!"

Rosalind watched as he put his arm around Summer's waist and walked her up to the bandleader. When she and the others stood looking down from the parapet wall into a darkened valley, she concentrated her imagination on the music that wafted out to where they stood and imagined her sweet sister with Etienne, dancing very close, as if no one else were there, as if they were wrapped in clouds.

"This is perfect for her," she said to John.

Stuart overheard and countered, "It's too perfect."

"I fear you may be right Stuart," Barry said. "Where did you say you met this fellow?"

"We spent a night in Montauban before we came here," John explained. "We met him, or I should say Summer met him at the breakfast buffet and introduced us."

"In Montauban?" Barry said. "Why were you there?"

"We were on our way to Toulouse," Rosalind said, "coming from your place. I was driving, and I believed we were being followed so I took a quick turn off the highway and we landed in Montauban."

"Followed!" Barry said. "You didn't tell me that."

"Well, I'm not sure of it, but it seemed that way at the time. We had just come from your ransacked cave of an apartment."

"How did she happen to meet him?" Stuart asked.

"I saw the whole thing," Rosalind said. "Summer was holding a plate full of food while trying to pour a glass of orange juice. He walked up and grabbed the plate to free up her hands. They started talking, she brought him to our table, introduced him, and he invited us here."

"So they only knew each other for a few minutes before he offered the invitation?"

"Yes, only a few minutes. You should have seen them together. Instant chemistry. Summer hasn't been able to think of anything else since it happened."

"Love at first sight?" Stuart asked.

"Yes, it seemed that way."

"What's your take Barry?"

"I don't know, but this fellow is asking an awful lot of questions. I think it odd that she met him just after leaving my place. I find it odd too that he issued an invitation after such a brief encounter in a hotel restaurant. Not that Summer isn't an attractive girl. She's quite attractive but..."

"But what was he doing in that hotel restaurant in the first place?" Stuart asked. "He could have followed you all the way to Montauban."

"I think I would have noticed a car on my tail in Montauban," Rosalind objected.

"That's not how it works," Stuart said. "You are not supposed to notice. It's more subtle than that."

"I just can't believe this!" she said.

"Which?" Stuart asked. "The story being postulated that Etienne could be up to no good or the fairy tale going on in that room. Which is more realistic?"

"Neither," she said, sad that she no longer believed in fairy tales and sadder still that if Barry and Stuart's suspicions proved correct, Summer would not for long.

Barry put a sympathetic arm around Rosalind. "Look, we don't know what the truth is, but we probably should be cautious given the situation. The prudent thing is to leave and not to give much indication where we will be going. It's probably best if you don't say anything to upset your sister. Just tell her that I need to remain incognito, and therefore she should refrain from offering up too much information."

They walked back into the ballroom after the music went silent. Summer and Etienne were seated together at the table, playfully sharing a glass of champagne.

"I hope you don't mind," Barry said, "but I'm very tired and think we ought to drive back to our hotel. It will take at least an hour to get there."

"So soon?"

"You just arrived," Etienne objected. "I could arrange for you to stay here for the night."

"Thank you very much for the offer, but I really must get back."

"He's not well," Rosalind explained.

"I am so sorry to hear that," Etienne said. "Would you like me to get a doctor?"

"No, I just need some rest, that's all."

Summer felt Barry's head. "You do feel a little warm."

"I should find the powder room if we're going to leave," Rosalind said looking about.

"You will find it behind the stage," Etienne said.

"Summer, will you come with me?"

Etienne turned to Barry. "I am sorry you are not feeling well. Will you be staying in Aix-en-Provence for a time?"

"Maybe for a day or two."

"Where do you go from there?"

"North. I thought I would take them up into Burgundy to some Solutrean sites up there and of course the vineyards."

"Yes, my favorite vineyards are in Burgundy. Maybe I could see you there or in Aix-en-Provence before you leave. Summer tells me you are staying at the Aquabella."

"Yes, I'm taking advantage of their thermal baths."

"I have not tried them myself." His attention turned to Summer who had just returned from the powder room and handed him a note.

"My telephone number if you would like to call me. I will be back in Amsterdam in a week or so."

"I should like to see you before then," he said. "I will call your hotel tomorrow and perhaps come to Aix. We could drive out to the lavender fields."

"That would be wonderful!"

Summer, reluctant to leave the royal ball, walked slowly to the van waiting below. Before she climbed in, she took one last look up to the top of the hill where lights twinkled about the fallen ruins.

"We should be careful with our suspicions," Barry whispered to Rosalind, "to avoid damaged feelings."

Chapter 26

Escape to Narbonne

"**I** hated to do that to the young lady," Barry confided to Stuart in their room at the Aquabella.

"It's that jerk who's doing it—using her to get to you!"

"We don't know that for certain," Barry replied. "Maybe you're right," he sighed. "We'll see." He opened up his laptop and signed on to his email. "What! How could Mike Fuller have ever thought I would be so naive as to ask such a ridiculous question?"

"Maybe he thinks you're losing your marbles, ha, ha, ha, ha!" Stuart said.

"Very funny." Barry scrolled down and read the originating email. "Oh, it must have been Paul. Why can't that kid confine himself to his family's computer?" He would have to explain to Mike Fuller, but not now, he thought as he continued to open, save, and delete mail. "Here's a strange one. It's from Rome. It came only yesterday, and late. My god! It's him!"

Your little subterfuge to conceal your whereabouts did not work as you had so obviously planned. How you insult my intelligence. And to think you would use a small boy. Naughty old man. I will be contacting you shortly with a place and time. Be there with the object or risk all.

"Do you know who this guy is?" Stuart asked.

"I think I do. I've corresponded with him on a few occasions so I recognize his smug style. Not a very nice fellow. He's a thug, a rich one, but a thug nonetheless."

"Italian?"

"I'm afraid so. Comes from a good family with many connections, which he uses to take what he wants or take out anyone who gets in his way. Oh, he is an assassin all right."

"Mafia?"

"No, but he might as well be."

"You think he would take you out?"

"Well, he says here, 'risk all.' So I take that to mean if he can't get what he wants, he surely will try, one way or another. Hmm, he may only be referring to my standing, to my career, not my life."

"I wouldn't count on that, not with these smuggler types. I've seen it all. They'd as soon shoot their mother as each other."

"Are you implying something?" Barry asked.

"I'm not implying anything. Just saying."

"Either way, I'm not going to let him get his hands on this prize. We took huge risks getting her out of Egypt. We put others at risk too. I'm determined to find out who she is. Then maybe I will turn her over to a museum or some such place where she will be safe from the likes of him."

"Well, if you're serious about that, we've gotta go," Stuart said. "Rome is only a day's drive from here, and this email was time stamped at 9:47 tonight. It's one o'clock now. He could be here in the morning if he's so inclined."

"He sent it while we were at that party," Barry noted.

"Yeah, while we were at the party spilling the beans on ourselves. We're getting out of here now." Stuart picked up the phone. "John! Pack up! They've located Barry. Meet us in the lobby in fifteen minutes; we're going. Okay, I'll phone her room right away." He turned to Barry. "Do you want me to call her or do you want to do it?"

"She's probably dreaming about lavender fields and that fellow right now. I'll phone her."

Summer was very much awake, playing and replaying every detail of her magical evening when she answered the phone as if she thought it was him. "Hello?" she said in anticipation.

"Summer dear, I'm sorry. It's only me," Barry said. "Look, we've got to leave here tonight. Apparently these rogues have some idea where I am. Well, I can't say they know for sure I'm at this hotel. They weren't that specific, but we've got to leave just in case. No, not in the morning, right now. Can you meet us in the lobby, say in fifteen minutes? I would tell you to stay on here, but I fear that could put you in danger. Okay, see you in a few minutes. I'm sure your prince will understand. I'm sorry dear."

"Are you okay?" Rosalind asked when she went to Summer's room.

"We were going to walk through the lavender fields," she sobbed. "I've always wanted to do that. And with him!"

"You can another time. We've got to get Barry out of here right now."

"I know," she said. "He's in danger, and that's got to be our first priority."

Rosalind looked closely at her little sister, remembering her as a child who thought only of herself, at least from the point of view of an older sister.

"Summer, let me tell you something. I'm very proud of you. You've grown up to be a really good person. Can I help carry any of this stuff out to the van?"

"Sure, here," she said, flattered by the compliment. She handed Rosalind a smallish bag that seemed to weigh nearly two tons.

"What's in here, books?"

"No, my hand weights," she laughed.

"I hope none of you will be disappointed, but I've changed my mind, about Burgundy," Barry said once they were all loaded up. "We're going to a town called Narbonne, west of here. Hans suggested that I talk to the curator of a museum there who he thought could give me some direction. I need it now, and I need it fast."

"Narbonne," Rosalind said as she looked at the map. "That's right back where we came from. Just head out the same way we drove in."

"Is it near Montauban?" John asked.

"No, it's on the Via Domitia Highway," Barry said. "The first road the Romans ever built in Gaul."

"Narbonne must be old," John said.

"Antique. They called it Colonia Narbo Martius when the Romans built it 118 BC."

"Ancient," John replied. "We're on our way."

Night passed quickly. One of those particularly beautiful sunrises with spikes of white light shooting up from soft roses and golden yellows lay in the east when Rosalind walked Christabel in the grassy area in front of a roadside gas station cafe. The others were inside ordering their breakfasts of croissants; bread and jam; coffee or hot chocolate; and vitamins, meaning fresh squeezed orange juice. Christabel relieved herself and pranced inside to a plate of sausage overjoyed that in France she was as welcomed inside as out.

"I can't say where we will go after Narbonne," Barry said. "It depends on the direction I get. We should spend this night in as obscure a place as possible no matter where we are headed."

"Who did you say is in Narbonne?" John asked.

"The curator at their archeological museum, a monk. He's reputed to be an expert in the Black Madonna."

"The Black Madonna!" Rosalind said. "That's a coincidence. We had two encounters with her on our way to your cave. I mean your room. I had never heard of her before, and now you bring her up again."

Barry's face came to full attention. "How did that happen? These encounters, I mean."

"Purely by accident," John said. "At least it seemed that way, at least the first time. On our way south we stopped in a town called Mende. It was late when we got there, but the cathedral was still open. There is a spectacular Vierge Noire there."

"We probably wouldn't have even noticed her if we hadn't met an Anglican Priest who showed her to us," Rosalind interrupted. "I lit a candle to her and asked if she might tell me her story since it's shrouded in so much mystery."

"You what?" Stuart laughed.

"It was just an impulse," she said. "Not that I really believed she would or could. The Anglican had just explained that some believe her spirit lives inside the statue. Maybe I was testing his belief. I don't know."

"You say there was a second encounter?" Barry asked.

"In Rocamadour," John said. "The Anglican highly recommended the place when he helped us map a route to Les-Eyzies-de-Tayac. Said there was another Black Madonna there. It was getting too late to try to find your place so we stopped in Rocamadour for the night."

"We found ourselves among a large group of Polish pilgrims who began praying, chanting, and singing when they saw her," Rosalind said.

"We didn't expect that. I never would have imagined it if I hadn't seen it for myself."

"You say this Anglican Priest helped you plan your route to Les-Eyzies-de-Tayac?" Barry said.

"He worried we might get lost," John said.

"He warned us of the Beast of Gévaudan," Summer added.

"That's a very old legend in those parts," Barry replied.

"The Anglican said he meant it only metaphorically," Rosalind said. "Be careful not to take the wrong path! He frightened me. That night I had a grizzly nightmare of a beast carrying off the Black Virgin."

"Do you know this priest's name?" Barry asked.

"James Stroud," John said. "He seemed very knowledgeable and was very kind to us."

"So this statue you have," Rosalind said. "Is she a Black Madonna too?"

"She seems much older than that, certainly pre-Christian. But Hans must have thought there is some kind of connection to have sent me to see this monk."

"Can we see her now?" Rosalind asked.

"I don't see why not. Let's go out to the van."

Barry pulled a box out of his backpack. Inside was another box. He opened it and lifted an object wrapped in a velvet cloth. Unwrapping it, he held the object in the sunlight for all to see.

"She is more beautiful than either of the Black Virgins we saw," Rosalind said.

"I can see myself in her eyes. They're huge!" Summer said. "And she has a disc on her head!"

John turned her over in his hand studying all of her aspects. "Are these supposed to be wings?"

"Feathers or fish scales. I'm not sure which," Barry said.

"What do these runes mean?"

"Why do you call them runes?" Barry asked.

"I don't know what else to call them. They look like the geometric markings we saw in the cave near Les-Eyzies-de-Tayac where we met Yvette."

"I thought so myself," Barry said. "But I wanted to know why you thought that before I said anything. The cave paintings and geometric figures you saw were from the Magdalenian period, which was about 16,000 years ago. Runes came much later, but these markings in the caves also look like some kind of symbolic system, perhaps precursors to runic alphabets."

"She doesn't look that old," John said.

"She would have to be remarkably well preserved to be that old," Barry agreed. "And we don't have anything from that period that looks like her."

"The carving looks more sophisticated," Summer said. "But her lines certainly exhibit the same kind of gracefulness as those paintings in the caves."

"But they're all animals and she's a woman. It was just a thought," Barry said as he wrapped her back in velvet and put her away. "I'll have to wait to see where this exploration takes me."

Chapter 27

Brother Thomas

Brother Thomas had been curator of the Musée Archéologique for a very long time and looked it. He suffered from a natural stoop, the consequence of a habitual downward gaze. He had a tendency to mumble and to look the other way when he spoke or was spoken to, which could be quite disconcerting when trying to engage him in conversation. On such occasions one found oneself speaking to his bald head with only a rare glimpse into his eyes. Yet in spite of these oddities, his age, and other infirmities, those eyes had not suffered. They were youthful in their expressiveness, and his vision was sharp. He inspected the little statue Barry brought to him in every detail.

"I have not seen these markings before," he said. "They look like a language of sorts. That is most assuredly what they are; but I'm sorry, I cannot translate them."

"Are they runes?" Rosalind asked.

He did not look up. "They don't look like any runic language I'm aware of, but that is not to say they are not a language. They most assuredly are. They may be from a runic alphabet unknown to me. These other markings on her back appear to be fish scales or wings. Quite unusual and would indicate she is pre-Christian, quite so."

"Would that negate any connection with the Black Madonna?" Barry asked, curious what the monk would say, although he already knew the statue to be very old, much older than the Christian faith.

"I would say not."

"Not connected?" Barry asked to clarify the monk's meaning.

"To the contrary. They are all connected."

Barry was still not clear what the monk meant. "What do you think of her?" he asked, hoping a simple, direct question would draw him out.

"She is very remarkable," the monk said, raising his head and exhibiting a broad, impish smile. "Could you come to dinner tonight? I invite you all. If you could bring her with you, I have a friend coming to dine who may be of some help."

Barry was happy to accept the invitation although a little frustrated that he had learned so little from the purported expert. He did get a lodging recommendation though, a more than adequate hotel just across the avenue from Brother Thomas' apartment.

"This meeting could be fortuitous," the monk said as he ushered them out of the museum.

Not used to being ushered out, Barry was slightly perturbed. "I'm surprised Hans Bueller recommended this man. His perceptions were unremarkable. Anyone could have pointed out what he did."

"Maybe he will have more to say at dinner," John offered.

"I should hope so. Well, what do we do for the next many hours?"

"How about a beer?" Stuart suggested.

"There's the cathedral," Rosalind said. "We could wander through."

Barry, not being in the mood for beer or churches, nixed those ideas.

"Isn't there supposed to be an excavation of the actual Via Domitia around here someplace?" John asked.

"Yes, somewhere nearby," Barry said. "Over there," he pointed and led the way.

"I'm sure glad the Via Domitia we drove on was paved," Stuart remarked, reacting to the sight of the rough, uneven cobblestones.

"We weren't on the original road, just the route," Barry scoffed.

"I know," Stuart said, recognizing Barry's foul mood, which improved very little over the course of the afternoon while they waited.

At last six o'clock arrived. They crossed the road from their hotel to the building whose address the old monk had given them, climbed a flight of stairs and entered an oddly appointed apartment. No couch or lounge chairs were there to make them comfortable. No TV, radio, or record player was there to entertain. The living area was filled with books and furnished with only a long table and several wooden chairs. That evening the library table was nicely set for seven.

Something had caught Rosalind's eye when they entered. An umbrella with a finely carved twisted tree handle stood next to the entry door.

"I have made you a cassoulet," the monk said. "It is ready to be served. I've only been waiting for you to arrive. But first let me introduce you to my other guest. You will certainly enjoy his company. He has made a very fine study of the Black Virgin."

"James Stroud!" Rosalind said.

The old monk raised his bent head and looked intently into her eyes. "You know him?"

"We've only recently met." She pointed to Summer and John. "In Mende. We went into the cathedral there and he showed us the Virgin."

"Then you've seen her pregnant," Brother Thomas said.

Stroud's expression quickly changed from surprise to acceptance. "We meet again," he said. "Did you find your way to Les-Eyzies-de-Tayac without incident?"

"Your directions were very helpful," John said.

"I hate to imagine what could have happened to us if we had taken a less populated route," Rosalind added.

"People are surprised that there are still great stretches of France that remain nearly uninhabited," he said and turned his attention to Barry and Stuart. "You are the residents of the cave?"

"Not me," Stuart said.

"I am," Barry replied, "but it's really a room. I'm living there temporarily while I undertake some research."

"Into the Black Madonna?" Stroud asked.

"Well, no. That's not why I came to France. But for now that's where my attention has been directed."

"I can't believe this!" Summer exclaimed, no longer able to contain herself. "How can we be meeting up with you again?"

Rosalind looked at Summer hard and long attempting to communicate that she had crossed the boundaries of politeness.

"I don't mean to be impolite," Summer said looking first at Rosalind and then at Stroud. "I'm not averse to seeing you again Reverend Stroud, but this is just too unreal. I had never heard of the Black Madonna before I met you; and now, unexpectedly, here I am meeting you again. And this time we've come in search of information about her. On top of that, we did take your advice and went to Rocamadour and saw her surrounded by singing pilgrims!"

"Well, don't let it upset you," Stroud said. "Events happen that way sometimes. I'm happy to hear you were able to see the Lady of Rocamadour. She is very important."

"And quite venerated," Rosalind added.

"Yes, because she is so important. I am disturbed Summer that you are troubled to meet me again. I realize I said some things that frightened you. That was not my intention."

"I know," she replied. "It isn't that. It's just so odd to see you here. I'm sorry. I'm just a little freaked out right now about other things too."

"I find it a happy coincidence or maybe not," the Anglican said, addressing himself to all of them. "Later that night after we first met in Mende, my instincts told me that our meeting might not have been by chance. I thought maybe I was to guide you, which is why I went to your hotel early in the morning to give you proper directions. But perhaps there is something more. I was told that you have with you a remarkable statue of a lady that I should be delighted to see."

Barry warmed up to the Anglican immediately. He liked his way of thinking. "I have it right here," he said, impatient to share the statue with someone who might begin to help him untangle her identity.

"That will have to wait," Brother Thomas said as he placed an earthenware casserole dish on the table. "My best cassoulet, and it cannot wait so you must." He went back to the kitchen and returned with a large bottle of unlabeled wine and two loaves of bread.

"Good wine," Stuart said after sipping the glass he had just poured himself.

"That's a rare compliment coming from Stuart," Barry pointed out to his humble host. "I don't believe I've ever heard him wax enthusiastic over anything he eats or drinks."

"This is good stuff," Stuart mumbled, embarrassed to be so singled out.

The monk smiled as he served helpings of the sausage, lamb, and duck baked with white beans. "Get your own bread," he ordered.

Stroud placed one of the great loaves on a cutting board and sliced it into large chunks.

"Very good," John said, relishing the dish. "You say it's called cassoulet?"

"My specialty. When I lived with my brothers I was known for this dish."

"I believe it is a regional specialty too," Barry said, directing himself to John. Turning to the old monk he asked, "Why are you living alone?"

"There are not so many of us as there were."

"The monastery where Hans Bueller lives is still very active and large," Barry pointed out.

"The situation in Europe is quite different."

"There didn't appear to be a religious decline in Rocamadour," Rosalind said.

"It is ironic," Stroud said, "that the Black Madonna has inspired so much passion at a time when religious passion is on the wane."

"Why do you suppose?" Barry asked.

"She is authentic. People are looking for that. And she threatens no great divisions or bloodshed. You must remember Europe's history. Why, right here, near where we are sitting right now, the Church once turned on her own, the Cathars. Massacred them. Men and women, young and old."

"Why?" Rosalind asked.

"They held different views. Were seen as a threat. That's always the reason. The massacre of the Cathars occurred in the thirteenth century. Following the Reformation in the sixteenth century came the wars of religion that threw Europe into conflict for over one hundred years. Thousands and thousands were killed."

"I see what you mean," Rosalind said. "The Inquisition and the witch burnings. That even happened in America."

"Only for a short duration. In Europe these events went on for hundreds of years, ending finally with the Nazi slaughter of Jews not that long ago. Knowing their history, many Europeans have had enough of religion and the intolerance it can breed."

"So what's the deal with the Black Madonna then?" John asked.

"She is a manifestation of Mary," the Anglican answered. "She is merciful. People still seek mercy in religion because they find so little of it elsewhere."

"All the Mary's offer mercy," the monk said.

"All the Marys?" Rosalind said.

"Yes, of course," the old monk said. "Mary mother of Christ; Christ's disciple, Mary Magdalene; her handmaiden, Sarah; and the Vierge Noire."

"How does the Black Madonna figure in?" Barry asked.

"She is a link to the past," the monk answered.

"They are all out of the past," Barry argued.

"Further back," the Anglican answered. "Further back. Know that the notion of a divine mother is very old."

"You mean Isis?" Barry said.

"I do mean Isis but older still," the Anglican said.

"Can I show you my statue now?" Barry asked, addressing himself to the little monk sitting at the head of his table.

"Why yes," he said, as he passed a carving board filled with assorted cheeses and sliced pears around the table.

Barry opened the box, taking from it the smaller box. He pulled out the velvet wrapped statue and delicately unveiled her.

The Anglican's eyes brighten. "Can I see her?" he asked. He took the figurine into his hands and spoke these words:

> "Spirit of beauty, that dost consecrate
>
> With thine own hues all thou dost shine upon
>
> Of human thought or form, where art thou gone?
>
> Why dost thou pass away and leave our state,
>
> This dim vast vale of tears, vacant and desolate?"

"Shelley?" Rosalind said.

"Yes," he acknowledged as he stared into the statue's reflecting eyes.

"But the poem is about beauty's absence," she said.

"You see, the poem is more about hope for her return."

"And love?" Rosalind added.

"And love," he agreed, "the steadfast kind, the immutable."

"Is that what you see when you look at her?" Barry asked.

"Yes, it is in her eyes. We are looking at her."

"We are looking at who?" Barry asked.

"Intellectual beauty," the deeply moved Anglican answered.

"Look at her closely," Barry urged. "She is so old. The markings. The feathers and fish scales."

141

Stroud studied her every mark.

"She is very old," the monk interrupted. "I studied those markings this afternoon. I would say she is from the late Magdalenian period, some 12,000 years ago."

"I see what you mean," Stroud said. "She is very, very old, but I doubt that old. I'm no archeologist, but I would say the style of the carving is far too sophisticated."

"There has been some curious news of late that could change your view," Barry said. "They've recently found petroglyphs in Egypt, very like the Magdalenian cave paintings here in France. They're pre-dynastic, believed to be 15,000 years old. They're calling the find Lascaux on the Nile, although no one has gone so far as to suggest that the peoples of prehistoric Egypt had contact with the Magdalenians. I only bring it up because we brought her here from Egypt."

"Why not? Why don't they suggest a more direct connection if it is so obvious?" Stroud asked.

"Archeologists like to think of themselves as scientists so they require hard and fast evidence, particularly regarding matters that would change previous thinking," Barry said. "Of course, there rarely is that kind of evidence in matters so old. But let me tell you more. Hans found manuscripts associated with her that contain cartouches that he believes once held her name. In every case the name has been scratched out, obliterated."

"Ah, she was assassinated," Stroud said.

"What do you mean by that?" Summer asked, convinced the Anglican is obsessed with ghoulishness.

"What is the goal of an assassin if not to change history? Those marked for assassination have always been persons who were setting a course, a course someone or some others objected to. The assassination of your Martin Luther King has changed your history. So did the assassination of your President Kennedy. In this respect the assassination of your Abraham Lincoln failed. It came too late. The course was already set. But perhaps Lincoln's assassin had not fully realized that."

"So you think she was as important as King, Kennedy, and Lincoln?" Summer asked.

"Victims of assassination are always important. But don't take my remark too literally. It may be only our memory of her was assassinated, which is almost the same thing."

"I have something else," Barry said as he pulled a piece of paper out of his jacket pocket. "Hans found a poem he associated with her. I have a copy of it here." He read:

> "She looks upon herself who is not there.
> But sees instead before her all the world.
> Whatever was, whatever will be is in her care.
> For she is the maker of the world.
> Within her face all faces, all time, the cosmic burst of creation.
> She holds the mirror of the world."

The monk and the Anglican stared at each other as if they were communicating what others could not hear.

"What language was the poem written in?" Stroud asked.

"Hieroglyphics," Barry said.

"If you've come to me for answers, I'm afraid I have none," the monk admitted. "But if you've come to me for direction, that I can give. I think you must work backwards to find the connection. They are all connected, you know."

"Yes, quite right," the Anglican agreed. "This is your quest," he said to Barry. "Maybe the quest belongs to all of you. It is no coincidence you are together. It is no coincidence that I had previously met three of you. And it is no coincidence that we are all here tonight."

Stuart looked decidedly uncomfortable with such an inclusive assertion.

"Come to the museum tomorrow morning," the old monk said, as he lifted himself out of his chair. "I will help you begin your journey there in the privacy and complete solitude of its chamber."

"Not here, not now?" Barry asked, thinking there was plenty of solitude and privacy in this library room apartment.

"Not here and not now," the monk replied. "Tomorrow, when I'm refreshed. You must all go now."

James Stroud immediately rose from his chair, unfazed that he had just been asked to leave. The old monk escorted them to the door in a hush.

"We'll see you tomorrow," Barry said, nodding to the monk as they exited his apartment.

Chapter 28

The Acoustic Chamber

"I had a really weird experience last night," Summer said the following morning as they were driving to the museum. "An image came into my head, just sort of popped out in front of me."

"What was this important dream?" Barry asked with a wry smile.

"I wasn't dreaming. And no, it wasn't him," she snapped. "I was awake when it happened, laying in bed trying to get back to sleep. It came in two flashes."

"An epiphany?" Rosalind asked.

"Yes, it was more like an epiphany. First I saw the little boats hanging from the chapel ceiling in Rocamadour."

"Oh, I remember those," Rosalind said. "They reminded me of Mary Magdalene."

"Why so?" Barry asked.

"Because she was supposed to have traveled to France by boat. I put the two together."

"Then I saw something that I don't remember having seen," Summer continued. "Maybe you do but I don't. I saw an image of the Black Virgin in Mende, but this time she had a golden shell mounted above her, a really large shell too. It looked like a golden clam shell."

"Like out of Botticelli's Venus?" Rosalind said

"Yes, but this one was above her in a starry sky. Do you remember seeing it?"

"No, but it was dark. John, do you remember?"

"I don't recall it either. Are you sure that's what it was?"

"Yes, I could see it as clearly as I can see you."

"Yet you have no memory of seeing it when you were in Mende?" Barry asked.

"Like Rosalind said, it was very dark. When I saw the Black Virgin there, I was totally focused on the fact that she looked pregnant. But I remember the shell now, at least I remember what I saw last night."

"Hmm, boats and seashells and the Black Madonna," Barry uttered softly. In a more forceful voice he said, "Maybe Stroud will be here this morning."

The Anglican was not at the museum, but the monk was there reading an old text. After a few minutes he lifted his bald head and greeted them with a nod. Barry broke the silence and spoke up. "The young lady here had a dream last night that I had hoped the Reverend Stroud could have verified for me." The monk only stared, obviously waiting for him to continue. "She imagined that the Black Virgin in Mende has a large clam shell mounted above her."

"Quite so," the monk said. "There is a large golden scallop shell above her head. The setting they've placed her in is quite beautiful. Here, I have a picture."

He thumbed through a packet of photos of various religious artifacts he had collected, and there in brilliant color was the image that Summer had described.

Barry studied it for a few minutes. "You must have seen this. It didn't register consciously but it did unconsciously."

"That must be what happened," she said. "It was probably those fish scales on your statue that made me think of it."

"I see," Barry said. "The water is the link. Brother Thomas, what is the meaning of the shell?"

"In this context, it represents a pilgrimage site, which of course the Black Madonnas have become. The shell is used also for baptisms and sometimes for holy water. All three, the pilgrimage, the baptism, the holy water have their place on the road to purification, which is our holy mission here on Earth."

"In Botticelli's Venus?" Rosalind said.

"Well, that's another matter," the monk said. "I am no art historian, but I would imagine the image of Venus rising from the sea has more to do with life and beauty than rituals of purification. I believe the painting is fully titled 'The Birth of Venus.'"

"Water is life," Barry said. "Life arose out of the water."

"And love and beauty," Rosalind said.

146

"Out of the golden clam shell in the ocean of sky," Summer said. "It all sort of hatched."

"Good observation," Barry said. "I'm very glad you told me about the vision you had last night." He turned back to the monk. "We're here for our instructions."

"Only one of you," the monk said. "Follow me." He motioned them out of the museum. "We are going to the cathedral treasury."

They followed him into a lovely courtyard outside the entrance to Cathédrale Saint-Just-et-Saint-Pasteur. He pointed out a Madonna who guarded the entrance. "I believe she was whitened," he said pointing to the large black marks that appeared through whitewash. He shook his head. "How little they understand."

The monk took them to a stairway that led to the upper chamber, the cathedral's treasury, which housed ancient relics and a very unusual room that was neither square, rectangular, nor round. Instead, its corners were set at one hundred and fifteen degree angles or thereabouts, below a large, round domed ceiling. The walls were not gilded or frescoed but fashioned from bricks.

"I must apologize," the monk said, "but this is only for one of you." He escorted Barry across the room to one of the wide angled corners. Placing his hands on Barry's shoulders, he turned him inward and towards it. He then positioned himself in the corner opposite looking towards the wall.

The room was entirely silent as the others watched from a distance for possibly ten minutes, waiting for what they thought was some kind of prayer ritual to end and the conversation between these two men to begin. At last Brother Thomas broke the spell and moved away from the wall, but Barry remained where Brother Thomas had put him. The monk nodded his head to the others as a gesture of goodbye and exited the treasury room leaving the four onlookers bewildered. Barry began to rub his head as if he were massaging away a headache.

"Are you all right?" John asked and walked towards him. Barry put a heavy arm around John's shoulders and the two walked over to the others.

"What's this all about?" Stuart asked.

"Very strange, wasn't it," Barry said. "I suppose it was nearly as

147

strange for you as for me. You've heard the old phrase, 'If walls could talk?' Well, these walls can."

Stuart scanned the walls and ceilings of the room looking for wiring of some sort. There was none.

"That's about all I can tell you for now except that we are headed for Rome."

"Rome!" Stuart said. "I want to know more about these talking walls."

"It's an acoustic chamber. Brother Thomas and I could hear every word the other whispered, but absolutely no one else could hear a thing. It's foolproof. No one can listen in through the walls or in any other way."

"I thought you were praying," Summer said.

"Or undergoing some kind of initiation ritual," Rosalind said.

"Nothing like that," Barry replied. "No prayers, no initiation."

"Too weird for me," Stuart said. "Rome. Isn't that where that dude lives who wants to do you bodily harm?"

"Well, we're not going there to see him," Barry said.

"I think he will want to see you whether you wish it or not," Stuart cautioned.

"We're starting from the recent and moving backward," Barry said. "That's how it is. If you don't want to come, you don't have to. I'm not telling you any more than this. The fewer who know what we are doing and where we're headed, the safer we all will be and the more likely I will be able to complete this mission."

"So now it's a mission," Stuart said. "My mission is to get you home safely and not let you walk into the sea without a raft."

"My colleague probably isn't in Rome any longer anyway," Barry said. "He could be near here if he's figured out we really didn't go up to Burgundy."

"Why would he think we went to Burgundy?" Summer asked, detecting some kind of charge being made against Etienne since he was the only other person to whom Barry had mentioned Burgundy.

"Oh, no dear, I didn't mean to imply that," Barry said guessing her thoughts. "This man knew I was in Aix-en-Provence, and he may have asked after us there. He could have discovered our friendship with

Etienne, who could have told him where he believed we were headed, not knowing, of course, the intent of the inquiring stranger. This man I speak of is very artful. He shows his real self to very few. You haven't talked to Etienne since we left have you?"

"No, I haven't!" Summer answered emphatically. "But if I had, I wouldn't have told him anything since it's supposed to be a secret."

"I'm sure you would not have," Barry said apologetically.

"So if this guy thought we were headed towards Burgundy then he should be northeast of here. So why did you say he could be nearby?" Stuart asked.

"For one thing, he may never have been directed to Burgundy in the first place. But if he was, he may have ignored it because he's smart, because he knows I wouldn't be that interested in the vineyards right now, and because he might have figured out it was a dodge."

"So we're driving back towards where we've just come from and on to Rome. Heck, we might pass him on the road. You two could wave to each other."

"That's enough Stu," Barry said. "You don't have to come if you don't want to."

"I don't want to, but I'm not going to let you get yourself killed."

"Thank you," Barry said calmly. "We're not going back the way we came. We are heading into the Pyrenees so we can cross into Spain inconspicuously. From there we can make our way to Barcelona where we can enter Rome though the backdoor by ferry."

"I've always wanted to do that," John said. "I've heard the stars are fantastic when you're out there on the Mediterranean."

"Are the rest of you game?" Barry asked, less sure after Stuart's outburst.

"I'm game," Rosalind said. "I love Rome. How about you Summer? Do you want to come or would you rather fly back to Amsterdam?"

"Are you kidding? I'm coming!"

"Let's get out of here then," Barry said. "We can stop along the road for lunch."

Barry took over Rosalind's duties as navigator since he knew exactly where they were headed. Instead of continuing south along the path of the old Roman Via Domitia towards Barcelona, they headed west towards Toulouse. Barry had two purposes for this detour, which he explained when they stopped along the highway for lunch. Besides his desire to avoid one of the few formal border crossings left in Europe, where an interested party might look out for a license plate number or a car model type, he wanted to visit a Magdalenian cave in the area to compare its runes or geometric figures—he wasn't sure what to call them—with those on his statue. It had been a long time since he had been to the Grotte de Niaux in the French Pyrenees, he said, and he wasn't sure if he remembered the marks correctly. After a quick lunch, they bypassed Toulouse and headed south on the A 20 toward Tarascon.

Chapter 29

Niaux

"Up there!" Barry said, pointing up to a large cave opening in the upper reaches of remote foothills of the Pyrenees. John put the van in low gear and steered it up the winding lane made narrow by jutting rock. He parked in a nearly deserted gravel lot situated just outside the cave's entrance. Barry made a beeline for the small ticket office building, which roused the sleeping dog who began to bark as soon as Barry stepped outside of the van, her volume only increasing when she spotted him returning. Parked car barking had become a bad habit she had developed, but it seemed intensified here.

"You will need jackets or sweaters," Barry shouted over the din of the dog's pitched howl.

"Christabel! Quiet down now," Rosalind urged.

"That's all right girl," Barry said, petting the little dog. "You can come too. She's shivering. Do you have something to keep her warm?"

Rosalind quieted Christabel while she pulled the dog's red sweatshirt over her head, plucking her long white ears out from beneath the neckband they were caught under.

Summer's satellite phone buzzed for the first time in days. "It must be Jos," she said as they piled out of the van and began rummaging through their suitcases looking for warm clothes. "Etienne," she spoke into the phone. At the sound of his name everyone went silent. "How did you get this number? Oh, Jos gave it to you," she said out loud so everyone could hear. "Uh, no, we're not in Burgundy right now. I'm not sure where we are," she said, her face beginning to flush. "Just a minute. I will ask John." Summer dropped the phone down to her waist. "He wants to know where we are," she whispered. "What should I tell him?"

Barry puzzled over her question for nearly half a minute. "Tell him we're on our way to Bourges. That's due west of Burgundy. Tell him

John wants to see the astronomical clock there." Turning to John. "That sounds like something you might want to do."

"We're going to see an astronomical clock at Bourges," she said. "Oh, the Duc de Berry is your ancestor. Well, if he lived in the fourteenth century we're not likely to meet him," she laughed. "A man was looking for us? Oh, looking for Barry. An Italian Count. I will tell him. Yes, I'm sorry we had to leave too. I will phone you when I've returned to Amsterdam. I'm not sure when that will be, but I will phone you then." The call ended. "An Italian Count!" she shouted.

Barry looked embarrassed. "He isn't really an Italian Count. They no longer tolerate that sort of thing in Italy. France is far more liberal in that regard. He's rich though and well connected." He paused for half a minute. "So he did go looking for me in Aix."

"You knew as much," Stuart said. "Where did you send him off to?"

"Bourges is well north of here. I assume Etienne told him we went off to Burgundy; perhaps he told him we left suddenly and unexpectedly." He paused for a few seconds. "Hmm, I doubt Felix will buy that story."

"Felix!" Stuart said. "That name doesn't sound Italian."

"No, it doesn't. The upper classes intermarry a lot. Class before country."

"How did you come to know this upper class count anyway?" he asked.

"I don't know him well, but it's impossible for people in my line to not know him at all. We cannot just walk into Egypt and start digging, you know. We must be approved, and Felix has become a kind of gatekeeper between the Egyptian government and those of us who seek their approval. They trust him. I don't know why but they do. Of course, I never believed the rumors I would hear about him before I came to know him better."

"What happened?"

"You were there. That incident last year. Felix was convinced that I walked out of Egypt with a valuable artifact. He tried to blackmail me even as I pleaded innocent. Well, apparently he never really believed me, but he eventually left me alone after warning me that he had his eyes and ears on me. If I was lying and tried to sell it, he threatened it would be all over for me. Nothing happened, of course, because I hadn't

152

walked out with an artifact so there was nothing to sell."

"So he's been keeping an eye on you since?" Stuart said.

"Hmm, it looks that way."

"Did he want you to return said artifact to the Egyptian government?"

"Hardly, at least that's what I hear from Bueller who knows more about these things. He told me that Felix would have sold it to one of his own clients or kept it for himself."

"What a thug! I hate those kind."

"Yes," Barry agreed. "We had better get a move on now. Summer! Don't you have something better to wear than those sandals? It could be pretty darn slippery in there."

"I would have brought my hiking boots if I had known we were going spelunking," she quipped. "I've got my running shoes with me. Will they do?"

"They'll do better than those sandals. We've got to get going," he said impatiently as the others pulled on sweatshirts and jackets. "It was lucky they would let us in at all. Fortunately, they seem to remember me although I must confess I don't remember them."

"You're a memorable guy," John said.

"Well, yes, I've made quite a few contacts in France. But it's been years since I did any work here at Niaux, and it was only for a short time. Heck, those two young ladies don't look old enough to have been around back then."

"How could they have remembered you then?" Stuart asked.

Barry considered the question for a minute. "They must have been here, mustn't they? It's a good thing too because they never would allow anyone other than a trained archeologist inside after hours and without a staff person."

"They're not taking us in?" Rosalind asked. She was not fond of cold, dark, wet places and was keenly aware that her rubber-soled moccasins were not particularly appropriate shoes for hiking, but they were the best she had.

"No, they're closing down for the evening."

"Well, you sure are lucky they know you then," Stuart said hesitantly.

The two young women came out of the small building with arms full of lanterns.

"I'll just ask them about it," Barry said before strolling over to collect the lanterns and the key. He returned quickly, panting under his awkward load.

"They asked that we not stay long," he said as he passed out the lamps. "It's our breathing they're worried about—The effects of carbon dioxide. And they asked me to remind all of you not to touch the artwork. Oil from your skin can damage the cave paintings."

"Did you ask them how they knew you?" Stuart asked.

"I didn't put it quite like that. They claim to have heard that I might be coming. That only yesterday they were contacted by someone who was looking for me."

"We know who that someone is," Stuart said.

"Yes, Felix must be calling around to any location he can think of where I might be working. There aren't that many, and he knows them all. I told you he's smart. Smarter than me it seems. If I had thought about it, we wouldn't have come here. We didn't have to, you know. We could have gone directly to Rome and avoided this prehistoric site altogether, and he wouldn't think to find me in Rome of all places."

"What did you tell them to say if he contacted them again?" Stuart asked.

"I didn't think to tell them anything. That wasn't very smart of me either. It just didn't occur to me that he might call back; but now that you mention it, why of course he will."

"Let's get the hell out of here now," Stuart said. "It's close to sundown already."

"Oh, come on Stuart. We're here now. We might as well go in," Barry said.

"Right!" Summer said. "I loved Font-de-Gaume. I want to visit here too."

"We all do," John said.

"Okay, but we'd better look at whatever you've come to see real fast," Stuart said. "And Barry, rely on me a little more. Two heads are better than one when strategizing these sorts of situations."

They moved through cavernous rooms whose floors appeared to slope down into undetectable reaches, along paths that defined more limited spaces, and into narrow openings where a command to duck was often the only thing that saved John from a severe blow to the head. Barry's warnings of "duck," "slippery," and "water" echoed back in greater frequency as the trek grew more precarious.

Rosalind began to tire. "How much further?" she called ahead.

"It's a ways yet," Barry answered. "But not too far."

"How far is not too far?"

"The Salon Noir is a good 800 meters from the entrance. How far do you think we've come already?"

"How far is 800 meters in feet or yards?" she said.

"800 meters is half a mile," Stuart shouted back.

Christabel's bag slid off of Rosalind's shoulder and down her arm, undermining her balance. She slipped on the wet limestone, but John caught her before she landed smack on the ground.

"Let me take Christabel," he said and steadied Rosalind back up on her feet. Summer walked back to make sure she was all right and then marched ahead to catch up with Barry and Stuart.

"I'm sorry," Rosalind said to John. "I wasn't prepared for this. I thought it would be like going inside Font-de-Gaume."

"If you had better shoes."

"But I don't."

"Are you all right back there?" Barry shouted.

"Could you slow down?" John shouted back.

The three lanterns in front of them turned in their direction lighting the way so they could ease forward more quickly and catch up.

"We're going to have to cross some water up here," Barry said. "We have one more low passage to get through and we'll be there."

Puddles of water were scattered helter-skelter making the damp path all the more treacherous for someone improperly shod. Rosalind carefully stepped around the puddles and remained stable even on the slipperiest of stones. At last they reached a low passage way. From there they entered the Salon Noir.

It was huge, a kind of domed cathedral with sacred painted walls. It reminded them of the great cathedrals of Europe, built over generations and adorned by artisans who gladly gave of their skills in devotion to their faith. The Salon Noir seemed like such a place: an immense natural structure where Paleolithic artists had come some fifteen thousand years before to bestow reverential paintings of gentle, beautiful animals. The bison, horses, deer, and ibex appeared nearly as transcendental as the saints, angels, and glorious biblical scenes inside those grand churches. The effect was achieved through the elegance of their curves and the peacefulness where they stood silently together. Here was evidence of an expression of a much older faith, a faith in the transcendent beauty of nature.

Barry pulled a small flashlight from his pocket and shone a narrow beam of light along the cave walls as he sought out what he had come for. "Over here," he said.

"What is it?" Summer asked.

"It looks like a red line to me," Stuart said.

"Yes, but see that slight bulge on the side. It's called a claviform. Here, take a look at the markings inside that Bison over there." Barry moved nearer and focused his light.

"They look a lot like what we saw at Font-de-Gaume," Rosalind said.

"Oh, yeah, that straight horizontal line with an arrow pointed up in the center," John agreed. "Look, one side of the arrow is shorter too, but they aren't resting on a horizontal line like they did at Font-de-Gaume. They sure are similar though." John looked Barry squarely in the face searching for answers.

"I don't know what they mean," Barry said. "I wish I did." He sat down on the damp floor and pulled the box out of his backpack, disrobed the statue and began carefully studying her carved symbols with his flashlight. "There!"

"You're right," John said. "That's the same arrow shape, but it's carved, not painted. And it rests on a horizontal line like at Font-de-Gaume. It looks, well, it looks..."

"More refined," Barry said.

"Yes, more refined. As if the technique of the artist who carved it was more sophisticated."

"More developed. And here we have the claviform."

"That one looks pregnant," Stuart laughed.

Barry looked taken aback. "That's an interesting observation," he said.

"It was only a joke. It's just where that curve pops out on that straight line, well...."

"No, I mean it," Barry continued. "People have imagined all kinds of things. That the claviform symbolizes time, the sun, the moon. The moon maybe, because well, if that line is a stick figure representing the female human form, then the curve may be a pouch, a pregnancy."

"What would that mean?" John asked.

"Who knows? What I do know is this statue is old. The Magdalenian period ended some 11,000 years ago."

"What ended it?"

"No one knows for sure," Barry said. Sensing John's dissatisfaction, he offered what he could. "There's very little record left. It could have been disease, conquest, climate. I tend towards the climate explanation myself. There were huge extinctions in North America. The North American Clovis people disappeared. Some major event must have taken place."

"It could have been disease," John countered. "If it found a way to spread, it could have affected humans on both sides of the Atlantic."

"There were massive extinctions of animal life too. Did you know there were once indigenous camels in North America?"

"Camels!" John laughed, "Maybe they hung out near those pyramids in Teotihuacan."

Barry ignored the flip humor. "I wonder," he said and paused.

"Wonder what?" Rosalind asked.

"I wonder if the language, symbols, runes, whatever these markings are, were understood for a while after what we term the Magdalenian period had ended? The culture may not have been destroyed all at once. Fragments may have been carried forward into cultures that followed."

"Unless, it was entirely decimated," Rosalind said.

"Yes, that's true. But her carvings are so curious they indicate it wasn't. The manuscripts Hans showed me with her damaged cartouche appeared by their hieroglyphics to be from the Third Dynasty. So she must have been known in Egypt throughout the Early Dynastic period before her identity was destroyed sometime later. But the lack of any sort of hieroglyphics carved into the statue indicates her origins are much older than Hans' papyrus manuscripts and likely rest outside of Egypt.

Yes, she must be Predynastic. That would place her sometime after the Magdalenian culture but before the Egyptian Empire began. If she came from the time between, after this cave art was created but before the meaning of these symbols was entirely lost, she could be 6000 or 7000 years old or even older!"

"The time in between," Summer said breathlessly, as if the words were romantically charged.

"Given her crown is fabricated from copper, the earliest I could place her would be the late Neolithic period, sometime during the Copper Age," Barry said. "But these symbols, symbols that in all likelihood will never be fully explicated, indicate that she carries with her meaning that is much older."

"When we were talking to Stroud, didn't you say something about Lascaux on the Nile?" John asked.

"Yes, I did. She may be evidence of a connection. She may represent an exchange of ideas and beliefs between North Africa and Southern Europe that began in the Paleolithic period and continued well into the Neolithic period, until her identity was snuffed out."

A long somber silence ensued until Stuart asked impatiently, "Have you seen what you came for?"

"Oh, uh, well, yes," Barry said.

"Okay. Let's get out of here before we have visitors."

"I guess you're right," Barry reluctantly acknowledged. He turned to look at his companions as if he were witnessing a scene from the distant past: a group huddled together in the dim light of the Salon Noir with his beautiful statue and these exquisite cave paintings. "Let's get out of here."

Chapter 30

Crossing the Pyrenees

"Where do we go from here, navigator?" John asked after Barry had just hauled the last of their lanterns to the side of the ticket office.

"We all could use a restaurant and a warm bed. How about spending the night here in Tarascon," Barry said.

"No, you don't!" Stuart said. He reached over the seat and grabbed the map out of Barry's hands. Barry whipped around ready to grab it back.

"Come on you guys," John said.

"I'll navigate!" Stuart said. "It's not safe to lodge anywhere near here. This Felix guy already knows where we've been."

"I'm not so sure of that," Barry said.

"I am!" Stuart replied "I'll bet you anything he asked those sweet young women to give him a call if you should show up."

"Okay, so where should I go?" John asked. "I can tell you one thing, I need gas."

"How low are we?" Stuart asked.

"It took all we had to get here."

"Then drive into Tarascon to fill up. From there we can head south towards Barcelona."

"Barcelona!" Barry said. "It's a wilderness between here and there, and it's late and I'm tired. We all are."

"We can't risk being followed," Stuart said.

John drove up and down the streets of Tarascon with no gas station in sight. "Man, if we can't find one, we're in trouble."

"Why didn't you stop and fill up sooner if we were running so low?" Rosalind asked, irritated that this was the second time they had found themselves in this situation.

"Because Barry was in a hurry."

"Yes, it was all my fault," Barry said. "I admit it, but those girls left not more than ten minutes after we arrived. If we had stopped, they would have been gone."

John slowed the van next to a group of teenagers to get some help.

"Andorra," one of them said.

"I'm empty," he replied.

Understanding at least that much, one of the youths said, "Expensive," and another pointed him back to a bridge he had just passed.

He did a U-turn as directed and crossed a bridge into a different part of town. A young girl attendant pumped the high priced fuel at the combination gas station car wash.

"This is nearly twice what I paid on my last fill-up."

"No wonder those kids suggested Andorra," Barry said. "I've heard they've got no taxes there or something like that."

"You really pay a premium here," John said when he handed the attendant his credit card.

"Why don't we go to Andorra for the night?" Summer said.

"Let's get on the road and see how it goes, what I feel comfortable with," Stuart said.

Traffic on the N20 going south was heavier than Stuart had expected. A steady stream of lights followed them, which disturbed his peace of mind. He turned around and stared at the lights through the rear window as if by doing so he could discern the intent of the drivers. "Slow down. Let them pass," he said.

"They're probably all going to Andorra," John said, as car after car sped past them, sometimes creating a hazard for oncoming traffic.

Recognizing the danger Barry said, "Maybe you should drive a little faster. Keep pace with them."

"No, keep it slow," Stuart repeated.

"This is as fast as I want to go in these mountains in the dark," John said, which quickly settled that dispute.

"You're probably right. They're all headed for Andorra," Barry said. "Never been there, but I've heard they've got cheap everything and it's all duty free."

"Sounds more like a discount shopping mall than a country,"

Rosalind said.

"They've got tourism as well, mountain biking in the summer and winter sports later in the year," Barry added.

"Sounds great. Let's go!" Summer said.

"No way!" Stuart replied.

"Why not?" she said, her voice raised.

"Because if that's where everyone goes then we shouldn't go there. Look at this map. There's nothin' else around. If they're looking for us down here, that's where they'd expect to find us."

"Since when were you named captain of this trip?" she shot back.

"All right, all right, that's enough," Barry intervened. "I know we're all tired but keep a grip. Stuart's probably right this time. John, do you need help driving?"

"No, I'm fine."

"Okay, then we'll stop when we reach someplace no one goes. Is that okay with you Stuart?" Stuart didn't reply.

An inconspicuous border sign with no gate or guards separated France from Spain a short distance past the turnoff to Andorra. It read "Catalonia." The next sign indicated they were on the E9, and the next one directed them to Barcelona.

"Lots of new construction, but no one around," John pointed out.

"It's like they had a lot of money and didn't know what to do with it," Rosalind said.

"Maybe they're trying to encourage people to move out here," Stuart suggested. "Take the strain off of some of the bigger cities. Let's stop at that roadside restaurant coming up."

John slowed down, looped the van around a newly built exit ramp, and pulled into an ultra modern roadside rest stop situated in this desolate wasteland of new construction. The restaurant was big enough to hold hundreds, but no one beside themselves was inside the diner.

"Hello! Hello!" John called out.

There was a case full of sliced meats and cheeses. And apparently people had eaten there earlier because tables were piled up with dirty paper dishes, crumpled napkins, and empty cups.

"Hello! Hello!" John called out again.

A young man darted from out of a back room surprised to see them.

"Can you make us some sandwiches?" Barry asked.

The boy nodded and took a rag and wiped off the countertop, embarrassed, it appeared, that he hadn't wiped it earlier. And embarrassed, perhaps, that whatever he was doing in the back room had kept him from clearing and wiping down the tables.

"Let's keep it simple. Ham, cheese, on a baguette, for five," Barry said.

"I'll just have cheese," Summer said. "And could you put some of those mushrooms on mine and lettuce and tomato? Maybe some hot peppers if you've got them. Oh, I see anchovies. Could you throw some of those on too?"

"What will you all have to drink?" Barry asked.

"I'll have a glass of wine," John said. "Whatever the regional favorite is."

"Same for me," Rosalind added.

"Beer for me," Stuart answered.

"Something white. Do you have a good white wine or champagne maybe?" Summer said as Christabel nudged her head through the zipper opening of the bag she was carrying.

The boy nodded and then directed Summer to a sign, "No es permeten mascotes a l'interior," it said with a picture of a dog crossed out.

"Here, I'll take her," John said. "I'll just put her back in the van. Sorry Christabel. No acceptée in España."

The sandwiches arrived and were eaten quickly so as not to keep the dog waiting long. They piled back into the van and fed Christabel tidbits of ham and cheese, gave her some water, and steered the vehicle back out on the highway.

There was just enough traffic to make Stuart nervous. He was fixated on a car that had pulled out of the gas station next to the restaurant just as they were leaving and continued behind them no matter how slow or fast John drove.

"They probably know the make and color of van by now," he said. "

"You're getting paranoid," Barry said.

"No, I'm telling you how it is. We've got to dump this van. Get another one after we leave this car behind us."

"Wait a minute," John said. "I rented this van. It's in my name."

"Who did you rent it from?" Stuart asked.

"Hertz."

"Good. You can park it somewhere, phone Hertz, and tell them you're having car trouble. They will send someone to pick it up. They may charge you a little extra, but they do this all the time. Nothin' to it."

"Park it where? And how will we get to Barcelona?"

"I think this is entirely unnecessary," Barry said. "But if you think that's what we ought to do, I have a suggestion. We can go to Montserrat. They have a very famous Black Madonna there, and it's not too far from Barcelona. Trains run back and forth all day long. We could leave the van and take the train into the city. Barcelona has an excellent metro system, so we won't need a vehicle again until we arrive in Italy."

"You're thinkin'!" Stuart said.

"Another Black Madonna!" Summer said.

"This one is quite famous. Montserrat is a major Vatican pilgrimage site. Unlike what you've seen up to now, the Black Madonna of Montserrat is fully authorized. She has been signed, sealed, and approved."

"I don't know if I like the sound of that," Rosalind said.

Summer nodded off with Christabel snuggled in her lap. Stuart was silent, his eyes focused on the lights that in his mind stalked them like a panther. Rosalind kept her eyes simultaneously on Stuart, the lights, and John. He should not be driving under these strenuous conditions without sleep, she thought. Barry again offered to take the wheel. John, stubborn as always, refused to give it up. So Barry kept him engaged in quiet conversation about the history of astronomy, which he knew John had a keen interest in. Eventually the subject led back to Bourges and the astronomical clock.

"It's as beautiful as it is ingenious," Barry said. "It still works, you know. I believe Jean d'Orleans painted the clock face with signs of the zodiac, but Canon Fusoris created the mechanism nearly 600 years ago."

"I would love to see it," John said, wishing he were driving north back into France where his real interests lie.

"We will go there, I promise, when this whole thing is over. You

163

probably would have had a lot in common with Fusoris. He was a kind of computer programmer in his own day. I read somewhere that he built some kind of astronomical computer to determine planetary longitudes. You would have liked him, but if I remember right he ended up being accused of conspiracy with the English or something like that and was exiled."

"He was a spy?" John asked, thinking of the guy sitting in the back seat whose real occupation had always seemed a bit elusive.

"Probably not," Barry said. "He probably talked to other astronomers, some of whom happened to be English. They were pretty suspicious back in the fifteenth century."

"We have a print called 'The Hours of the Duc de Berry.' It's got an astrological representation at the top and below is a beautiful country scene. It looks medieval," Rosalind said.

"That's Etienne's cousin," Summer mumbled half asleep.

"We got it in Paris a number of years ago," John said. "It is from the Très Riches Heures du Duc de Berry, 'The Book of Hours.' That's an illuminated manuscript, a prayer book, not very scientific."

"You couldn't always separate science from religion back then," Barry said. "The astronomical clock resides in the Cathedral of Bourges, the same place the Duke of Berry was entombed."

"I would love to see it," John repeated.

"The print we have is incredibly beautiful," Rosalind said. "Rich blues, greens, reds, and golds, with a lovely medieval couple standing in an idyllic landscape exchanging rings and a castle in the background."

Summer sighed.

"The sun's rising," John said, his eyes resting on a thin pinkish line on the horizon. "What's that ahead of us?" he asked, noting the silhouette of a towering shape, curved like a multitude of squat, muscular fingers reaching upwards.

"That's Montserrat. That's where we're going," Barry said. "We should be there in another hour. We can park the van in their lot. Then we're going to have to figure out how to remove our bags unnoticed."

"Is there a hotel?" Rosalind asked. "We could look like we're checking in. Then it won't matter so much if we're noticed or not."

"Excellent idea," Barry said. "It might even be worth it to pay a porter to remove our bags for us. That would fool them."

"If there's really anyone to fool," John said, glancing at Stuart through the rearview mirror.

"Lights are still behind us. They've been trackin' us for miles."

Chapter 31

Unwelcome Guests

Christabel pranced and posed, happy to be under the camera eye as photographers snapped photos of a bride and groom from every conceivable vantage point in the courtyard outside the abbey at Montserrat. Priests crossed through the crowd of celebrants, making their way from one building to another, looking intent on matters of business.

The weary travelers watched for a few moments and then turned towards the magnificent views of the valley below and the high peaks above whose cliff sides jutted up and about the monastery complex like protective walls. Mountains that from a distance looked like stubby fingers took on the appearance of huge, irregular knobby knees attached to great columnar thighs that encircled the angular architecture of the abbey and monastic residences. Montserrat was designed to stand apart from nature, the architecture making no effort to harmonize with the mountain's natural shapes.

A line had formed to pass before the shrine of La Moreneta, the Black Madonna that resides within the abbey. Her placement in the cathedral was remote and could only be reached by a narrow staircase that limited her audience at any given moment to only a few. Pilgrims pushed impatiently as they climbed the stairs, waiting their turn to pose for pictures in front of the Madonna they had come to see. At last they too climbed the final steps and stood momentarily in front of La Moreneta. The baby Jesus sat on her lap holding a small globe in his hand. She held a much larger one. She looked Romanesque, made in the late twelfth century, although local legend would dispute that late date. She stared out through her glass case, her eyes looking past the crowds, past the abbey, past the whole monastic complex.

Rosalind sensed that something was wrong here. Was it the impatient crowd? Was it the glass case that interfered? Her eyes staring off distantly? Her placement being so remote? No throng of Polish pilgrims could gather round in prayerful song here. She was isolated.

They left the abbey and went in search of a restaurant. Their plan was to eat lunch, pick up their luggage at the hotel, and take the train to Barcelona. The restaurant would not seat them, however. They were too early the waiter said.

"Well, then who are all of these people seated in your dining room?" Barry asked.

"They are here for breakfast," the waiter answered. "It's too early for lunch. Not for another hour."

"Then we will have breakfast."

"I'm sorry, but you are too late for breakfast. We stopped serving ten minutes ago."

"Oh, I see. Well, then, we will go where we are wanted. Thank you very much. Let's get out of here," he said to the others and led them out of the restaurant and towards the hotel.

"I feel really uncomfortable here," Rosalind said.

"It's an official place, designed for tourists," Barry said.

"I felt more at home in that Paleolithic cave at Niaux," Rosalind said. "But there's more to it. I don't feel wanted. Yet no one here knows us so how could we be unwanted?"

"I feel the same thing," Barry said. He signaled the desk clerk. "I'll ask the clerk to have our luggage transported to the cable cars, and we can get out of here."

"Hold on just wait a minute," Stuart ordered. "Let's step outside and talk a bit. You don't mind do you Barry?"

"Why no," he said and awkwardly signaled the hotel clerk "not now."

Stuart led them out to a long stone bench at the edge of the plaza. "Rosalind asked a good question," he said looking directly at Barry. "How could you be unknown and unwanted at the same time?"

"It was just a feeling," Rosalind said.

"Barry feels it too. And we haven't exactly been given a red carpet reception."

"Tourists get treated badly all the time," Barry said, thinking Stuart must be referring to what had happened at the restaurant. "Especially in tourist traps like this place."

"Is that all there is to your feeling?" Stuart asked Rosalind. "You didn't feel it before we tried to eat?"

"I felt it when I stood in line at the abbey," she admitted.

"And you Barry?"

"I felt quite uncomfortable ever since we got here."

"It may only be my imagination, but it feels to me like we are being watched," Stuart said.

"You feel it too?" Summer asked.

He nodded. "I have been suspecting it for some time, but I've been unable to verify my suspicions. I prefer facts, but since a number of us are feeling uncomfortable, that's about as good."

"Facts," John said skeptically, "like believing a car behind us on a major highway full of cars is following us."

"That car was behind us for more than one hundred miles," Stuart argued. "That is a fact. While I have not seen anyone following us while we've been here, windows sometimes have eyes. And I feel..."

"So do I," Barry interrupted. "And my feelings are usually right. Let's get out of here."

"We need to find a way to leave unnoticed," Stuart said. "I suggest we check in as if we are planning to stay for a few days. When it's dark, we leave inconspicuously, even if we have to leave our luggage behind."

"What!" Summer shouted. "I bought all of these clothes new for this trip."

"You can buy more new ones later," Barry said. "Stuart is right. We need to slip out of here unnoticed. If we check-in, let's say for three nights, they may let down their guard."

"Who are 'they'?" John asked.

"I don't know," Barry admitted.

"I think Barry and Stuart are right," Rosalind said looking at John. "I can feel it too."

"Feel what?"

"I'm not sure but something is wrong."

***

John lay stretched out on the bed, using his pillow to block what remained of the ebbing sun.

"It's time to go," Rosalind said.

Christabel raised her weary head in disbelief. She nestled close to John and began to lick his beard in a gesture of sympathy.

"Come on, get up," Rosalind said, giving him a little nudge. "We can sleep once we get to Barcelona, but we can't miss the train or we're stuck here."

John ripped the pillow off his head and sat up. "What time is it?"

"It's seven. We're supposed to be ready to leave at eight."

"Are you ready?" he asked.

"Just about. I thought we could keep Christabel on her leash so I can stuff our toiletries and underwear in her carry-bag."

"What about our clothes?"

"Summer suggested we layer what we can and leave behind what we can't."

"I hope Stuart's right about this," John complained. He climbed out of the bed, grabbed a few things, and headed for the bathroom.

Rosalind looked at her clothes. She layered two long sleeve knit shirts under her long white cotton shirt, slipped on her jeans, moccasins, and jacket. She looked longingly at the lovely outfit she had bought in Aix-en-Provence that lay spread out on a chair. She tried pulling the black crepe bell-bottom pants over her jeans and stood up on the bed to look at herself in the mirror. All that bulk felt heavy, but there was enough crepe in the dress pants to make it unnoticeable. She took off her three layered shirts, pulled on the silk pearl tank top, followed by the two long sleeve knits and the white cotton blouse. She turned around in front of the mirror. There was a knock. She quickly stuffed her dress shoes in Christabel's bag before answering it.

"Oh Summer, it's you. It's only 7:30."

"I was just wondering if John has a coat or a large jacket I could wear. Mine is too tight."

Rosalind grabbed a neatly folded black trench coat from John's suitcase and held it up. "He hasn't worn this since we've been over here. I was going to leave it behind."

"It will work great," Summer said, and grabbed it out of Rosalind's hands.

"Just a minute." Rosalind tapped on the bathroom door. "Is it okay if Summer wears your trench coat?"

John came out of the bathroom, dressed and fresh from bathing, wearing his burgundy sweater over a long sleeve white cotton shirt layered over a dark blue knit shirt and his most comfortable black pants. "It's okay with me. I was going to leave it and wear my jacket. But I wouldn't mind keeping the thing. It wasn't cheap."

"Yes, it's nice," Summer said. "I'll be back in a jiffy."

"You look like you've put on a little weight," John said. They both laughed but not as hard as they laughed when Summer returned, her bulging frame cinched tight with the trench coat belt. She plunged her overstuffed handbag down on a chair.

"What do you have on?" Rosalind said.

"Just about everything. I can't afford to replace all my new clothes. I hope no one notices," she said, mildly amused and wondering if they were going to get away with this deception.

The three of them left the room, Christabel prancing in front of them on her best leash. Summer transferred her heavy bag from hand to shoulder and back to hand, unable to carry it comfortably. Rosalind's jacket pockets bulged with items she usually carried in her handbag while her handbag was stuffed with Christabel's food, brush, foldup water dish, toothbrush, and toys. She wore her beautiful red Provincial shawl around her shoulders.

"Why didn't you put Christabel's belongings in her bag?" Summer asked.

"Because I've got our toiletries and underwear in there."

"Why didn't you...?"

"I know! I know! Because I'm new at this. How did you manage to wear that dress you got in Aix in all those layers?"

"I'm resourceful."

"Do any of you have some spare cash?" Barry asked. "I want to leave enough here to cover our rooms for one night."

"How much do you need?" John asked and opened his billfold.

"About 200 euros will do it."

"I sure hope the maid doesn't mistake all of that cash for a tip," Rosalind cautioned.

"Here," Barry said grabbing a piece of hotel stationary from a drawer. "I will write a little note and explain in case she doesn't figure it out."

"That would be one huge tip!" Summer laughed. "You could make her day."

"Yes, well, you have to trust that there is a little honesty left in the world." He looked over at her and did a double take. "What are you wearing?"

"She's got everything on that she owns," Rosalind said and began to laugh.

"You don't look so slim yourself," he said.

"Do you think they'll notice?"

"I don't think so," Stuart said. "Stepping out without our luggage will blind them. They don't even realize we're on to them."

"I'm sure not on to them," John said. "I haven't noticed a one of them yet."

"People see what they expect to see unless they're given significant reasons not to, or unless they don't know what to look for," Stuart said, looking directly at John.

"Okay, I acknowledge that you could be right. Even if it turns out you aren't, it's better to play it safe. But I can't see how we are going to get away with this if they're really watching us?"

"Because of what I just told you," Stuart said. "Look, we've checked into the hotel for three nights with luggage. When they see us leave without luggage, dressed for dinner with the dog on her leash, they will have no reason to imagine anything more than what appears to be the case, that we are stepping out for dinner, a walk, maybe an evening prayer. That's what visitors here do. They will be caught off guard, won't suspect a thing until tomorrow. That's when the shit will hit the fan, but we'll be long gone by then."

"Let's get out of here," Barry said. "If we're lucky, tomorrow we'll be on a ferry to Italy.

Chapter 32

Revelation

An hour and half later they were in the center of the sprawling city of Barcelona, better named Gaudi City from Rosalind's point of view as she surveyed his unique designs along their pathway through the town. If the architects of the monastery at Montserrat chose to ignore the shapes in the surrounding landscape, Gaudi had not. He brought the rounded, undulating forms into the city, creating urban magic in the buildings he designed; but it was his famous cathedral La Sagrada Familia that held her attention.

La Sagrada Familia looks at once new and old, avant-garde and traditional, individual and collective, playful and holy. The whole process and duration of its construction is reminiscent of Europe's great cathedrals, the building of which lasted decades and reflected the skills and generosity of multiple generations of benefactors and artisans. Begun in 1882 and still not completed, La Sagrada Familia was not yet finished in Gaudi's lifetime.

Rosalind, transfixed by its enchantment, gazed at the great edifice under the magic of twinkling evening lights. Gaudi did not care that he had not seen its completion, she imagined. She understood instinctively, it was the doing, not the having. Real art is in the process of its making. At the instant of that recognition, La Moreneta flashed into her mind, pushing her way through the edifice's tall spires as if she were coming out of a forest into the light. She looked into Rosalind's eyes in the way she had not when they had arrived at the top of the stairway and stood before her in Montserrat. Rosalind intuited her meaning, why the captive Black Madonna had looked beyond the abbey and past the throngs of worshipers who came to see her, as if she longed to be elsewhere more befitting the power of her spirit. As if she longed to be here, Rosalind thought.

"Are you all right?" Barry asked her.

"Oh, I'm sorry," she said.

"You seem lost in thought. We were beginning to wonder if you would come back to us."

"Oh, I was just thinking about La Moreneta, about Gaudi, about this cathedral, about the nature of art, about magic."

Barry smiled. "Worthy thoughts but not now. I want to get all of you secure in your rooms while I arrange for our departure to Italy. You can attend to your meditation later."

Barry had made the hotel reservation at Avenida Palace while they were still at the train station. He said it was a good hotel, centrally located, and the only hotel he had ever stayed at in Barcelona, which was a good enough recommendation for the others. They were so extraordinarily tired they could have slept anywhere that night, on a park bench under one of Gaudi's street lamps if they had to. They ate tapas at a little bar around the corner from the hotel before they surprised the doorman, having brought with them no luggage.

"He was probably looking for a tip," Barry whispered. "Wait here while I check us in. That will expedite the process."

They were surprised to overhear his mastery of the soft tones of Catalonian Spanish.

"No wonder he thought it better that he do all the talking. I would have assumed they spoke English," Summer commented as she looked around the swank lobby.

"It is a nice place," Rosalind agreed, "in an old fashion way."

The officious young woman behind the desk eyed them coldly. The porter stood intent, ear bent to hear every word of her conversation with Barry. Barry seemed to be explaining something. They guessed that it had something to do with their lack of luggage, lack of a car as well. He handed the clerk a credit card, which she carefully swiped and waited patiently until the payment was approved. She smiled and handed him several sets of keys, looked in the direction of the others, and stiffly smiled.

"They required full payment in advance," he said, looking a bit flustered.

"Because we don't have luggage?" Summer said.

"Because they run a respectable place."

"You mean they thought..." she said, her mouth left wide opened in mid-sentence.

"I'll buy us some luggage tomorrow before we leave. Here are your keys. The porter will show you to your rooms. Be sure to tip him. I'm going to head down to the port and arrange our travel before I turn in."

"For god's sake Barry, you were up all night," John said. "Can't it wait until the morning?"

"I'm itching to get out of here and don't want to run the risk that by the time we get there tomorrow the ferry will be booked up."

"Why?" Rosalind asked, looking around at the gold and marble lobby. "This seems like a very nice place to spend several days if we have to."

"My goal is to get us to Rome and get there quickly. What happens after that, I don't know. But I want a chance to follow the lead Brother Thomas gave me before I run smack dab into trouble. I have some business there anyway. And I don't intend on being chased all over Europe."

"What do you intend to do about it?" Stuart asked.

"I'm not sure. Right now I'm going to cross the street to that ATM over there, get some cash, hail a taxi, and go to the port. I will let the hotel doorman hail the taxi so I can tip him. That'll make him happy."

"I'll go with you," John offered.

"Me too," Stuart said, inspired less by John's altruistic motives and more by his own suspicions that Barry was contemplating another reckless act.

"No, get some sleep. I'll do this myself. There will be fewer complications that way."

"What do you mean by that?" Stuart asked.

"I don't mean anything! Look, John has these women and a dog to look out for. I know the language here. I just want to keep this transaction simple. I'll get the money, have the taxi driver take me to the port, and wait while I buy our tickets. I'll be right back."

"I don't have any women to look after," Stuart said, although in the back of his mind he was thinking about the woman who charged him with looking out for Barry. "Besides, we've come this far together. It wouldn't hurt you to have a little backup."

Barry had to acknowledge while they rode together in the taxi, that Stuart's help had been invaluable, that he may never have escaped Egypt without it. In fact, without Stuart's assistance he might be sitting in some dank Egyptian cell or worse. Yet on this night the transaction Barry had contemplated went without a hitch. An hour and half later when John and the women were fast asleep, Barry and Stuart crawled into their twin beds having successfully secured tickets on the next evening's departure to Italy.

"We should find a secluded place to visit in the morning," Stuart said before he dozed off. "If they haven't already found out we eluded them, they will tomorrow. Barcelona is the logical place to look for us."

"I just want to get to Rome," Barry said. "They may track me down there too, but at least I will have made it to my destination." He turned off the light. "The first thing I'm going to do tomorrow morning is buy us some luggage."

"You can't go shopping in broad daylight."

"I'll go early before anyone is up and about," Barry muttered and drifted off into a surprisingly peaceful sleep.

It is sometimes the small things that define a man's character. Barry's fortitude and single-minded determination were just a few of those things.

Chapter 33

Barcelona

A smattering of light filtered through thick clouds when Barry rounded the corner near the market. Tightly packed stands and the scent of fresh flowers, fish, and produce were a welcome relief from the cool and clammy December morning outside. Most of the goods were on full display in the large, brightly lit space that housed myriad stalls packed with merchandise; but a few vendors were still busily arranging their goods. A pleasant looking woman brought up handfuls of potatoes from below her stand that she carefully placed next to piled high displays of peaches, plums, berries, avocados, asparagus, and green beans. She looked like a garden fairy wearing a crown of pineapples. He drew near, attracted to bunches of bananas, bags of oranges, and ripe pineapples hanging down from above on a horizontal aluminum pole that ran the length of her counter. She popped back up from below, hands loaded with potatoes. She winked and smiled. He smiled and nodded at the pretty lady before turning towards a booth that smelled of freshly brewed coffee.

Boys in white aprons stood behind a long glass shelf loaded with plates of breakfast pastry in anticipation of customers who had not yet arrived. They poured cups of coffee for merchants who carried them back to their stalls. Barry saw a pile of fresh oranges and asked for orange juice and coffee, pointed to one of the flakey pastries and sat down at the long counter. A boy plunked the large pastry before him along with a knife and fork, brought him a cup of coffee, and began to feed four perfect oranges into an electric squeezer. He brought Barry a glass of juice along with a little slip of a paper and went back to what he was doing. This juice tastes like sunshine, Barry thought.

In less than an hour crowds would fill the aisles and make getting a seat at the counter where he now relaxed and enjoyed his coffee nearly impossible without a wait. His eyes were drawn to a display of cheeses across the way. He had rarely seen so many cheeses together in one place and regretted he had no apartment in Barcelona to take them to. He placed a few euros on his check and began his search for luggage.

Meats dangled from poles. Baskets upon baskets of mushrooms whose type and origin were a mystery to him were on display. More stalls piled high with fruit and produce and more restaurant counters preparing for their morning clientele filled the aisles he wandered down. When he reached the fish he began to make sense of the organization of the place and realized he had made a wrong turn. A vendor sent him to the other side of the building where he passed racks of shirts, displays of scarves and shoes, but nothing resembling luggage until dangling leather handbags suggested he might be close. Next to the handbags were straw and cloth totes designed to carry home purchases from the market. He made an inquiry.

The friendly vendor pointed to the totes. Barry wondered if he had used the wrong word. He elaborated. The vendor reached down and brought out a canvas duffle bag from below the counter. Duffle bags were as good as he was going to find, the vendor said. If he wanted real luggage, he would have to wait for the shops to open on the elegant streets he had walked down the evening before.

"Summer will hate this!" he exclaimed. The vendor who knew little English fortunately did not understand. He could wait for the shops to open, he thought, but Stuart would never approve. It's a good duffle bag, he noted, sturdy, with leather trim and handle. It was navy blue too, a color he liked. He ordered four more. The vendor bent down to retrieve what he had from under the counter. He heaved a second, then a third, then a fourth navy blue bag up on top of the counter. The fifth was red, all that he had left, he apologized. Barry smiled and paid him, thinking maybe he had solved the Summer problem and slunk out of the market and back into the hotel with a large package containing five duffle bags stuffed under his arm.

"You are back, sir," the desk clerk said when Barry asked for the key to his room.

"Yes, of course. I just went out to browse around the market."

"The market is very nice early in the morning. Pardon me if I'm being too inquisitive," the clerk said in perfect English unlike the woman from the night before, "but someone was just here looking for you."

Barry turned pale. "Who? What did you tell him if it was a him?"

"He was a him, sir and very elegant. He left no name and offered no card."

"Spanish?"

"I think Italian, but since he spoke in English I couldn't say for certain. He was dressed very smartly, yes, very elegant."

An image of Felix flashed through Barry's mind: thin, emaciated, hardly what Barry would describe as elegant. Then another image overtook Felix's visage, one that more aptly fit the description the desk clerk offered.

"Could he have been French?"

"That is possible, sir."

"Did he ask after a girl?"

"He asked for you by name, sir."

Barry paused to reconsider the motive of Etienne's inordinate interest in his work and future whereabouts.

As if to recapture Barry's attention from some foreign place, the desk clerk blurted out, "I told him you left early, for you had, hadn't you?"

"Yes, of course," he said, now quite pleased with himself for having gotten up and out of the hotel so soon. "If he should come back, please phone the room. But please, don't give him the room number."

"Yes, of course," the desk clerk said. "Will your party be staying on? I see you are only registered for one night."

"Did you tell him that?"

"No, he did not ask, and I would not have disclosed that information had he. It is not our policy to report the comings and goings of our clients."

Barry was about to tell the clerk their immediate plan. Then he thought better of it. It might not be the hotel policy, but if the desk clerk were offered money, the policy could be adjusted. Besides, it had not been his policy when the first inquiry was made. Better that he did not know.

"We arrived late last night. We had just come from France and are not yet sure if we shall stay a few days or go on to Madrid. I will let you know later if you don't mind."

"Very well, sir."

"By the way, do you have the time?"

"Certainly. It is half past nine. Breakfast is being served in the lounge if you would care to have some."

"Maybe later."

He pushed open the door to his room, dropped the large package of bags on the floor, and shook Stuart. "You're right! We're being followed, and they've come here." It took Stuart a few moments to process what Barry had said, but when he did he sat up and gave Barry his full attention. "I went out early this morning to pick us up some luggage. When I returned and asked for the key at the hotel desk, the clerk said a man had been here asking for me. The clerk told him I had gone out."

"What time is it?" Stuart asked.

"It's 9:15."

"Did he tell you any more?"

"Only that he sounded Italian but could be French and was well dressed. The clerk asked after our plans, but I thought it best not to reveal too much in case the fellow comes back. I told him not to give out our room number but to call if the inquirer returns."

"Good thinking. Can you let the others know we're leaving while I take a shower?"

"I certainly will. I suggested to the desk clerk that we are headed to Madrid. We should stick to that story. Oh, and here's a bag," he said as he handed Stuart one of the blue canvas duffle bags. "I'll see to it that the others get theirs as well. Where shall we go to wait it out?"

"Hell, you know this place better than I do. Find a place where we won't be noticed; off the streets is best."

Barry looked through the window at the thick, gray clouds. "On a day like this the park might do."

By mid-afternoon the clouds let out a torrent of rain. The small group of travelers sat huddled under a Gaudi designed outdoor pavilion with modified Doric columns holding up its roof. Gloomy Barcelona looked almost foreign to Barry who had never been there when the sky was not brilliant. The only sun shining on them now was a colorful mosaic wheel set in a ceiling composed of what looked like large serving bowls

179

arranged on an upside down buffet table. His elbows resting on the railing, his face resting in his hands, Barry's mind was elsewhere until his reverie was broken by the sound of Summer's satellite phone.

"I thought I told you to keep that thing turned off," Stuart scolded.

"Sorry," Summer said. "I recharged it overnight and forgot. Can I answer it? It's probably Jos wondering where I am."

The voice on the other end was not Jos' voice, it was Etienne's. "I thought surely you would be returned to Amsterdam by now," he said. "I have become very worried about you."

She paused as she tried to think of what to say.

"Summer, are you there?"

"Yes, I'm here," she replied as she searched Barry's face for some hint of what she should say. "I'm fine. We're just traveling about."

"Where are you?"

She paused again and looked at Barry, mouthing the words, "Where are we?"

"Rome, tell him we are going to Rome," Barry whispered.

Relieved that she no longer had to lie to this man she felt deeply about and trusted to the bone, she repeated Barry's words.

Stuart looked at Barry as if he thought he had gone mad. In fact, it was Stuart who was mad, mad as a hornet.

"I am not far," Etienne said. "I will leave for Rome today and meet you there. Where will you be staying?"

"I don't know where we will be staying," she said.

Barry reached over and took her phone before she could say another word. "Etienne, it's nice to speak to you again. You wondered where we would be staying. Yes, well I usually stay at the Albergo Del Senato when I'm in Rome. I can see no reason to stay anywhere else. No, I don't have reservations, but at this time of year it's hardly necessary. It's at the Piazza della Rotonda, across from the Pantheon. Good. I look forward to seeing you again."

Barry handed the phone back to Summer. Her face grew animated. Stuart, on the other hand, looked livid.

"We need to have a little talk," he said as he escorted Barry away from the others. "What are you doing? Are you crazy?" he shouted.

"I'm quite rationale. Look, I can't keep hiding. I know we don't

180

know much about this Etienne fellow, but that doesn't matter. I will never solve the riddle I carry if all of my plans and energy are devoted to hiding. I can't do this any longer. No, once we get to Rome I will be very public, if I ever truly was undercover. It seems to me that they, whoever they might be, have had that advantage more than I. They are the ones who have remained undetected, not me. My plan is to force my opponents out. Then it becomes an open challenge as to who will prevail. I'm determined to prevail Stuart, and I hope you will continue to assist me. But this game of hide and seek has got to end. By the way, how long have you had your phone turned off?"

"Since we left Narbonne. I thought we'd be safer if we were entirely undetectable."

"Well, turn it back on. It's time we become detectable to our friends."

"Whoever they are," Stuart said with a hint of sarcasm.

"That is precisely what we must learn."

The sky had not cleared entirely, but the rain had stopped. The group gathered themselves and their duffle bags and climbed the pathway that would lead them to the park entrance and a taxi. The air smelled sweet though no flowers bloomed. Tropical leaves glistened under the last rays of a sinking sun. Perched high up on the pathway overlooking Guell Park, they said goodbye to the ornate rooftops of Gaudi's magical castles.

Chapter 34

At Sea

Barry lit a cigar, puffed it a few times, and slowly exhaled.

"I didn't know you smoked," John said, as he took a sip of brandy.

"I don't," Barry answered. "At least I haven't for years." He inhaled again and let out another long puff. "I deserve it," he sighed. "I haven't truly relaxed in quite a long time." He sipped his brandy.

"You seem like a relaxed kind of guy to me," Rosalind said.

He looked at her and smiled. "So I wear a pretty good mask, eh? You learn that in academe. You need to always look confident, always act calm. If you don't, you will be eaten up."

"Hmm, I had always imagined academics to be a polite sort of people," Summer said. "Now, in my business, the music industry, talk about eating people up, talk about stress. My college professors by comparison seemed so, well, 'refined' is the right word to describe them."

"It's all part of the disguise," Barry laughed. "I have to admit that we don't act like music moguls. No, we're more subtle, every bit as competitive but more subtle."

Barry shouted to Stuart who stood apart looking out at the murky blackness that lay ahead. "Hey, come on over here and take a look at those lights back there before they're gone. Barcelona looks beautiful lit up like that." He turned back to the others who were relaxing and sharing brandy before looking up again to see if Stuart had relented and was about to rejoin the group. He had not.

"What's wrong with him?" John asked.

"He thinks I don't respect his judgment. I do most of the time, but he has to learn to respect mine at least some of the time."

"He's upset because you told Etienne where we're staying," Summer said.

"Yes, and the general principle of the thing. I told him to turn his phone back on too."

"It makes me angry that he would suspect Etienne of anything," she fumed.

"Well, we don't know much about the fellow," Barry admitted.

"I do!" she said.

"What do you know?" Rosalind asked. "You hardly know him."

"I know he's wonderful, and I know he wouldn't be involved in any plot against Barry. He likes him. He likes all of us."

"I only said we don't know much about him," Barry said. "I didn't say I thought he was involved in a plot against me." Although secretly that's what he wondered.

"The hotel clerk did say it was a Frenchman looking for you," Stuart said as he walked towards them. "And he did coincidently call Summer later in the day to find out where we are."

"To find out where I am!" she corrected.

"Let's not fight about it, not now," Barry said. "Sit down and have some brandy. Do you want a cigar?"

"Don't mind if I do."

Stuart lit up, took a couple of quick puffs, and watched as Barry poured some spirits into a brandy snifter. Barry looked around at the rest of them. "Does anyone want anymore?"

"I do," Rosalind said holding out her glass. "I didn't know it was a Frenchman at the hotel."

"That doesn't mean anything," Barry chuckled. "There are millions of Frenchmen. It could have been any one of them. Besides, the hotel clerk thought he could have been Italian. He spoke English with an accent, that's all."

"You're arguing semantics," Stuart said.

"Maybe," Barry said. "But you never know."

In the few minutes they debated, a transformation had taken place. The lights of Barcelona had entirely faded, and in their place the stars brightened as if nature had turned up her dimmer switch.

"Look at those stars!" John said. He laid back in his deck chair to get a better view.

"Look at the water!" Summer shouted.

The rest of them looked up at the sky and then out towards the sea, which like the sky was ablaze with starlight.

John raised himself up from his chair to view the whole picture at once. "You can hardly tell where the sky ends and the sea begins."

"It looks like Nuit is holding us close to her heart," Rosalind sighed.

"You're right," Barry said. "It feels like that." He poured more brandy in each of their glasses, laid back in his deck chair, and puffed his cigar.

"Do you think it's a sign?" Rosalind asked, "A cosmic message that we're on the right path?"

"And that we are pursuing her identity as we should, openly," Barry said.

"Recklessly," Stuart charged.

Ignoring Stuart, Barry continued. "If I do not pursue her identity openly, I run the risk of keeping her buried as she has been for hundreds perhaps thousands of years. I must bring her into the light. That is my task."

"You might be right about that, but I smell danger. And my task is to make sure nothing happens to you."

"You forget what I do for a living, Stuart. There is always danger in discovery. Sometimes it's to my reputation. At other times it's more."

"I never thought about my professors that way," Summer said, who had only recently graduated college. "I thought of them as refined, slightly dull types with liberal social views, but not as adventurers, not as fierce competitors, not as wearing masks, and not as putting themselves at risk."

They sat silent for about an hour taking in the night, their imaginations now joined in common commitment. One by one, as the evening wore on, they each drifted into their tight cabins, their snug beds. Then morning broke, and the hours of daylight had begun to race towards noon then afternoon. They had arrived. They were in Italy.

Chapter 35

Arrival

U mbrella pines signaled they were nearing Roma Termini Railway Station. What a welcoming sight, Barry thought. These slender trees with their canopy tops symbolize the city and mark a more ancient time when according to legend, the city's founders, Romulus and Remus were suckled by La Lupa, the she-wolf.

Rome is the eternal city, and that is no misnomer or legend. All you have to do is look about you. Empire replaced empire, religion conquered religion; and yet all of its ghosts reside in temporal coexistence, the veil between its fabled epochs being so very thin.

Barry was reminded of which Rome they were in when their taxi lurched to a stop to avoid hitting a group of pedestrians who leaped into the street in a bid to cross it. Motor scooters buzzed past the jam up, weaving in and out of cars and pedestrians alike. These present day occupants may live in historic buildings, walk on ancient streets, celebrate in antique piazzas, but they will never own them. The past owns Rome.

The statue of Vittorio Emanuele astride his horse announced their proximity to the old city where narrow mostly pedestrian lanes feed into wide piazzas that in warmer months are full of tables where locals and tourists alike eat and drink as they gaze upon fabulously beautiful Bernini fountains. The taxi driver let them out at their hotel, housed in a nineteenth century building that sits across the piazza from the far older Pantheon, a temple to the gods built in the year 126 of the current calendar.

Etienne waited inside for Summer. Under his direction the hotel was holding her their best room, the only room with a balcony that looked out onto the grand Piazza della Rotonda. He wanted to please her. He had thought of nothing else since he held her in his arms in the ballroom at Les Baux. Even after these many days her scent would come back to him, haunt him with its foreignness, mix as it did that evening with the familiar fragrance of lavender. He remembered her as a flower from another land with the face and hair of a Botticelli. An angel, he thought, a beautiful angel.

His grandmother would not approve. He knew that. Summer had not a trace of the aristocrat and yet there was something in her of a queen. She had a career, which excited him, and yet there was nothing overbearing or belittling in her behavior. Great queens were surely like that and were able to gain the respect and dedication of their subjects. Surely his grandmother would see this in her. "She is a queen," he said softly, his dark eyes flashing when she entered the front door of the hotel with her entourage and the little white caniche prancing in front of her.

Her eyes brightened when she saw him. "When did you get here?" she asked.

"I arrived this morning," he said, pleased to see how she looked at him. He greeted the others. "I hope you do not mind that I reserved a room for your sister. I wanted to make sure she has the best view."

"Oh, I don't mind at all," Rosalind said, while dividing her attention between his face and the face of her sister.

Barry held out his hand, which Etienne heartily shook as if they were best friends meeting up after a long separation. "I'm glad we meet again," Barry said.

"I am so very glad too," Etienne said before addressing them all. "Do you have plans? I know a lovely place we can go to dinner."

Barry took a quick read of the situation. "Maybe tomorrow night. There is somewhere I want to go after I check-in, and I think some of the others will wish to accompany me. Why don't you take Summer to dinner? We can all go out together tomorrow."

She looked at Barry, her eyes saying thank you.

"He really does like her," Rosalind said to John when the elevator door closed.

"Do you think we should leave her alone with this guy?" he replied.

"I think she will be fine."

***

"Why are you in such a hurry?" John asked.

"I don't want to be late," Barry said. "Come on you guys. Get with it." He led them out of the hotel door and into the piazza where he waved down a taxi. "We're not far, but we're cutting it pretty close."

"Piazza del Gesù," he told the driver.

"Chiesa del Gesù?" the driver asked.

"Sì."

"Oh, so this place we're going to is a church," John said. "I was beginning to think we were late to a performance, a play perhaps."

"I will tell you now. Brother Thomas said I should go to the Church of the Jesuits in Rome and study a statue of a woman holding a mirror. He was vague about it; spoke in riddles. I remember that he distinctly used the word 'study' rather than 'look at.'"

"That's all he told you? Why were you so secretive?" John asked.

"He said I should keep it to myself as long as I could, implying that the longer I kept it to myself, the sooner I would solve the riddle. He merely tempted me to keep quiet, that's all. He knew I would tell you eventually."

"You kept quiet a good long time considering that we've been in each other's company since we left Narbonne," John said.

Maybe that's a good omen," Rosalind suggested.

"Well, it's been a long time in people time, but I'm not so sure it's been nearly so long in monk time," Barry said.

"Brother Thomas is a curious sort of person," John said.

"Hmm. You're right about that. I've had to stew on it alone, and the more I stewed, the more curious his remarks seem. He implied that the answer will be right in front of me but hard to find."

"Hidden in plain sight," Rosalind said.

"Yes, something like that. You're probably aware that the Church of the Gesù is the home of the Jesuit order. It's enormously famous, world renowned."

"No, I wasn't," John said as he climbed out of the taxi and looked up at its baroque facade. Once inside, *Il Gesù's* gold, marble, statuary, and elaborate frescos overwhelmed his senses. Every conceivable place he rested his eyes had something to contemplate or admire. In spite of this wealth of holy art, he could not help but notice high above in the dome that crowns the nave a statue of a woman holding a mirror with one hand while her other arm is entwined with a snake.

187

"There she is," he pointed. "Who is she?"

They all looked up. "That's the question. Who is she?" Barry said.

John, spotting a very old priest sitting in a booth went over to speak with him. Rosalind was about to follow when Barry held her back. "Let him go alone," he whispered. "Their conversation will be more intimate that way. Let's just stand here and admire her."

"She must be very important to have such a notable position in this church," Rosalind said. "I can't imagine who she must be."

"Maybe she isn't all that important," Stuart said.

"Look where she is!" Rosalind said. "If she is unimportant, why is she looking down on the whole church? She's practically the first thing you see."

"Only if you're looking up," Stuart said.

"Up is a very important place in a church," she argued.

John returned and told them that the old priest did not know who she is and directed him instead to the ceiling fresco, Gaulli's "Triumph of the Name of Jesus," imploring him to focus his attention there. When John persisted in his inquiry, the priest relented and said a book is available in the gift shop that describes all the artwork in the church. He should look there for answers.

They followed John into the gift shop. Barry and he began to scour the book the priest had recommended while Rosalind perused the postcards looking for the statue's likeness but not finding it.

"Nothing here," Barry said. "Everything else in this church is pictured and described in detail, but she isn't even mentioned in passing."

"See, I was right," Stuart said. Rosalind shot him a glance.

A man entered the shop, took his place behind the counter, and looked at them suspiciously as if he feared they might walk off with something. Barry took the opportunity to ask after her identity. "Io non lo so," the man answered.

"This truly is a mystery," Barry whispered.

Stuart repeated his assessment. "It's no mystery; she isn't that important."

"She is too!" Rosalind argued. "If she wasn't important, Brother Thomas wouldn't have sent Barry all the way to Rome to see her."

188

"Well, she's not in the book," Stuart quipped.

"Don't you see, that is what's so curious," Barry interjected. "If she is so unimportant as to not be in the book, why give her such an important place from which to look down? Everything in this church has meaning Stuart. The question is, what is hers."

"Maybe she's Eve. She's got herself a snake," Stuart replied.

"She's not Eve," Rosalind said. "She's fully dressed and holding a mirror."

"Saremo chiusi per la notte. Dovete andarvene ora," the man behind the counter said.

"Grazie," Barry said. "They're closing. Let's take another look on our way out," he whispered.

They circled the entire nave of the church and saw from those vantage points three other statues positioned in the dome, one opposite the other.

"Justice, Temperance, and Fortitude, the four cardinal virtues," Barry said. "She must be Prudence."

"Doesn't Prudence represent truth?" Rosalind asked.

"She does," Barry said, "but I think we will find there's more to it than that. Let's grab a bite and go back to the hotel and rest. I've got somewhere to go early tomorrow."

They walked over to the Campo dei Fiori, to a restaurant John and Rosalind remembered from another trip to Rome. That visit had been in the summertime when tables lined the piazza. There were no tables outside this cool evening, but there were a few available inside. The owner sat them at a window overlooking the Campo.

"What you have?" the owner said.

"Do you have menus?" Barry asked.

"Si, but I make anything you like."

"I want spaghetti. It's been a long time since I've had any," Rosalind said.

"We will both have spaghetti pomodoro and some antipasto," John said.

"Meatball?"

"Yes," John said.

"Sure, sure."

"Do you have lasagna al forno?" Barry asked.

"Si, I can make."

"With salad. Or maybe I will start with today's soup."

"Zuppa, good." The owner looked at Stuart.

"I will have the same as him," he answered. "That'll keep it simple. And a beer."

"A bottle of house wine with three glasses for the rest of us," Barry added. "And a liter of water with gas."

"Grazie," the proprietor said before walking off to the kitchen.

The Campo was empty, lit only with low lights that illuminated a nearby statue of a hooded man in a Dominican cowl.

"That's Giordano Bruno," Barry said, looking grim for a man who is usually in high spirits. "Funny we should be dining with him tonight."

"Why? Who was he?" Stuart asked.

"He was a friar, scholar, writer, and heretic. He was burned at the stake right where you see his statue."

Rosalind put the piece of bread she was about to eat back down on her plate.

"He was a free thinker," Barry said. "It was dangerous to be a free thinker back then."

"When was then?" Stuart asked.

"They burned him around 1600. He was just a little younger than me. A Pantheist, they called him. He thought everything was imbued with God. He adhered to Copernicus's view that the Earth revolved around the sun. He even thought there were other planets out there that probably supported life."

"That's heretical?" Stuart said. "I thought you were going to tell me that he didn't believe in God or that he was a witch."

"It didn't take much to be labeled a heretic in a time of religious turmoil," John said. "I think it was really about power, a challenge to authority. Any view that contradicted orthodoxy was suspect. And anyone who held such a view was brave to hold it publicly."

"Maybe that explains why Brother Thomas was so careful about his communication with Barry," Rosalind said.

John turned to her. "They don't burn people at the stake anymore."

"No, they don't," Barry agreed. "But she has a point. You have to be careful in such organizations. You could be excommunicated or marginalized."

"Or labeled a subversive in the political arena," Stuart added. "There really isn't as much freedom of speech as most people think."

"Only at a price," Barry agreed.

After dinner, they stood before Giordano Bruno for a few minutes to get a better look and pay him homage. His visage tore at their hearts as they were reminded of the pain he must have endured.

"He couldn't recant what he believed to be true," Barry said. "What isolation he must have felt."

"And look what he got for it," Stuart added.

"At least he stood on the right side of truth if the wrong side of orthodoxy," John said. "He must have gotten some satisfaction knowing that."

"Enough to die for?" Rosalind said.

Chapter 36

Nanodiamonds

Barry took an early morning bus to Janiculum Hill to keep an appointment with Dr. Rosa Palazio, a colleague who teaches archeology at the American Academy in Rome. He had met her a number of years ago when she was in graduate school in Chicago where she had come to study North American indigenous culture, now her specialty. His recent interests had led to an exchange of research materials from time to time and as he had recently learned, led to the erroneous exchange between Rosa and his near nephew Paul.

Her dark eyes afire, she laughed as much at herself as anyone else. "I wondered after the questions he asked that you would not have known the answers yourself. But then I thought, well, maybe I have more expertise than I give myself credit for."

"Paul is a bright boy. I will give him that, but this was entirely a mistake. I had asked him to watch over my house while I've been away in France, and apparently he has been watching over my computer as well."

"He still writes me now and then," she said, sweeping her dark hair away from her face. "I heard from him only a few days ago."

"From my account?"

"Yes, I think so. Let me see." She searched through her email. "Yes, here it is. Your signature is at the bottom."

Barry looked at his automated signature. "This is odd. He reported my computer stolen, and he was told to keep away from my house."

Rosa looked at him curiously.

"You're not the only person he had a correspondence with from the academy," Barry said. "I believe Felix sent several rather threatening emails. Next thing my computer was stolen. Then Felix contacted me over here, apparently after having learned that I'm still in Europe. He has been dogging me ever since."

"He isn't a pleasant man," she said. "I dated him for a few months several years ago. That's when I learned the kind of person he is. We remain collegial; that is all."

Barry bristled at the thought of what Felix might have put her through but restrained his anger. "You rather have to remain collegial I suppose."

She stared off for a few seconds. "He seemed charming until I got to know him."

"I'm sure that once he revealed himself, you sent him packing."

"Yes, I did!" she said, smiling approvingly at Barry's characterization. As if a cloud suddenly overtook the sun, her joyful expression changed to concern. "Why is he threatening you?"

"It's simple. I've got something he wants, and he is as determined to get it from me as I'm determined to keep it from him. I was wondering if you spoke to him recently about the email inquiries Paul had made, and if that could be the reason he thought I had returned to the United States."

"I may have spoken, not to him directly but to a group of us at lunch. Your email, at least what I thought was your email, was so funny!"

Barry blushed. "Do you remember him saying anything?"

"Let me see. Yes! He said he thought you were in Egypt. I said I thought you had left Egypt nearly a year ago. That's all."

"I wonder?" he said. "I was just in Egypt but only for a short time. I wonder if he could have found out, if that's what he was referring to?"

"I have no idea. I never meant to cause you any trouble if I have," she said. "I was only making conversation, a little joke."

"Oh, I know. You didn't cause me trouble, not much at least. But whoever informed him I was in Egypt did because he seems to know that I've brought something back with me."

She stared at Barry a few awkward moments, fully aware that archeologists are not permitted to bring artifacts back except in the rarest of circumstances.

"This is a very unusual case," he explained. "A friend living in a monastery made a rare find and asked me to identify it. That's what I'm trying to do now."

Her eyes widened.

193

"Here, I will show it to you. Maybe you can help." Barry unslung his backpack from his shoulder and pulled out the box containing the statue.

"May I touch her?" Rosa picked the statue up and carefully turned her around. "She's exquisite. How old is she?"

"I don't know, but I would guess very old, older than what you might think. She was found with some papyrus verses that suggest she is a goddess of unknown identity. Every reference to her name on scrolls that accompanied her has been scratched out."

"What about the stone?"

"I haven't had her looked at yet."

"There is a fine geologist here. I will see if he is in." She picked up the phone and made a call. "Success! Follow me."

Barry walked with Rosa out into the hallway and down several flights of steps to the basement where they entered the laboratory of Dr. Espezi.

"Buon giorno, Rosa."

"Buon giorno, Henri. May I introduce my American friend, Dr. Barry Short? He has something he would like you to look at to see if you can tell him anything about the stone it is made from. He's trying to date it."

"Certainly, buon giorno."

"Grazie," Barry said, and handed over his statue.

Dr. Espezi gave it a quick perusal. "Basalt and copper," he said before he brought out his microscope and placed her under it.

"Ah, nanodiamonds," he said.

"What?" Rosa said.

"Nanodiamonds! Come see." She peered through the microscope. "Can you see?" he asked.

"Yes, but they are very small. They look like specks. Barry, come here."

He bent down and looked for a few minutes before turning the statue very carefully, studying it in its entirety. It sparkled from end to end under intense magnification like sand under a brilliant sun. He looked up. "Pretty nifty instrument."

"Very expensive," Dr. Espezi replied before he carefully placed it back in its case.

"Nanodiamonds. I've never heard of them," Barry said.

"It has only been recently that we've been able to see them," Dr. Espezi said.

"What can they tell us about her?" Rosa asked.

"That the stone she is made from is very old. That she must be very old."

"I knew that, but can you tell me anything specific?" Barry asked.

"They only exist in sediments that were on the surface 12,900 years ago when they were formed by the hot explosion of a comet strike. This period began what is know as Younger Dryas."

"That's when the Clovis culture disappeared," Rosa interjected.

"Yes, and many animal species," Henri added. "Temperatures cooled exceedingly, which may have depleted available food."

"Or the explosions themselves may have killed them," Rosa said. "At any rate. You have a partial answer. The stone your statue is carved from is very, very old."

"But the detail of the carving," Barry said. "Its intricate style doesn't look that old."

"It doesn't as far as we understand," Rosa agreed. "But there is so much we don't know. The stone would not have been used until there was some kind of cultural stabilization following the catastrophe, maybe 11,000 or 12,000 years ago."

"What about the copper?" Barry asked.

"Yes," Dr. Espezi said, looking at the statue and considering the obvious problem. "I would suggest the crown was added later, much later perhaps. The stone is much older."

Barry carefully wrapped the statue, returned it to its box, and tucked it back in his bag. "You will not say anything to Felix if he should ask?"

"I will say nothing," she said.

He thanked her and made his way out of the academy towards a lookout on Janiculum Hill. Towers, domes, and antique buildings of the Roman panorama lay below, but his imagination was elsewhere. She is older than this city, he thought as he pondered the little statue tucked in his backpack; older than the ghosts that haunt it; older than the pyramids. He thought about her finely polished eyes, her feathery hair, her copper crown, and her runes. How could this be, he wondered, and who were the people who carved her? The memorial to Vittorio

Emanuele towering in the distance caught his attention and near it the dome of the Pantheon. His friends were in the hotel behind the dome, he thought. He turned and made his way back to join them.

When he had arrived back at the Senato he seated himself in the lobby and opened his laptop. He determined that the most efficient way to reach young Paul was to send an email to his own account since he had just learned that Paul was still actively using it.

Hello Paul,

This is Barry. You might be happy or unhappy to know that I visited your friend, Dr. Palazio in her office today. I say unhappy because she informed me that she is still receiving correspondence from you on my account. I thought my computer was stolen, and I thought you were given orders to stay away from my house after the theft took place and after the threatening email was sent? Young man, I expect you to explain yourself.

Your Friend,
Barry

At the very moment he pressed the send button, Summer came bouncing down the stairway into the lobby.

"You needn't have waited for me but thanks anyway," she said.

He was not sure what she meant until he learned she had come to join the others for breakfast. He quickly put his laptop back into his backpack and followed her into the dining room.

"Where've you been?" Stuart asked.

"I had an appointment this morning and didn't want to disturb you," he said, dropping his jacket and bag on a chair before going over to the buffet table.

"With whom?" Stuart asked.

"A colleague of mine at the American Academy. I learned some interesting things I will tell you all about after I get a plate." He went off to the buffet table, leisurely poured himself a glass of orange juice and loaded up his plate with pastry, fruit, and cheese. He asked the waiter for espresso and pointed to where he would be sitting.

"The American Academy," Stuart said when Barry returned to the table. "Isn't that where the threatening email came from?"

"That's the place," Barry said.

"You went over there this morning without letting any of us know where you were going?"

"I told you I had an appointment with Dr. Rosa Palazio, not Felix. He wasn't there. She hasn't seen him for some time. She does believe however that he may have overheard one of her conversations about the email she was receiving from Paul that she thought was from me."

Stuart said nothing. He only looked at Barry, wondering what he might do to rein him in.

"Speaking of Paul," Barry continued. "Rosa told me that he has continued to write her using my account. She heard from him only a few days ago. I just sent him an email asking him to explain himself when Summer invited me to breakfast."

"I thought your computer was stolen?" Rosalind said.

"I thought so too. That's why I asked Paul to explain himself. By the way Stuart, have you heard much from Natalie?"

"Not at all," he said, trying to disguise his discomfort with the question. "I'll phone her after breakfast and see what she knows." He did not phone her, and he was not certain why.

"I have a surprise for all of you," Summer said. "Last night Etienne took me to a fabulous restaurant. It was so fabulous that I asked him to take us all there tonight. He made a reservation for us at eight."

"What's it called?" John asked.

"Ciampini's."

"I believe I've heard of it," Barry commented. "But I've never been there. Tell Etienne we look forward to it."

"You can tell him yourself when he comes down."

"You said you learned something interesting," John said, changing the subject.

"I did, I did," Barry coyly suggested as he took another bite of his roll.

"Well?" Rosalind said after several moment's of silence.

"Have any of you heard of nanodiamonds?" There was silence. "Neither had I. Rosa thought I should have a colleague of hers, Dr. Espezi, take a look at my little statue. She thought that as he is a geologist he might be able to tell me something, and she was right. The lady is full of nanodiamonds."

"Rosa?" Summer asked.

"No, the statue."

"Hidden inside?" Stuart asked.

"No, no, they're nanodiamonds. Nano, small, infinitesimally small. You can only see them under a high-powered microscope. What's really interesting is what they tell us about her age. The geologist guessed the stone could be over 12,000 years old."

"All stones are old," Stuart said.

"Dr. Espezi explained that nanodiamonds exist in sediment layers dating back over 12,000 years. That's the only time they are known to have existed. Since then they have been covered over in layers and layers of new sediment. The point is that at the time the stone was gathered and carved, it had to be accessible to the carver, which would make it very old, maybe not 12,000 years old, but very old indeed."

"I still don't get it," John said. "Why do these diamonds only exist in sediment 12,000 years old? And why would the stone only be accessible back then? People mine diamonds all the time that were formed thousands of years ago."

"These aren't regular diamonds; they're more like particles of dust than the diamonds we know. Dr. Espezi says they were caused by a giant comet strike the heat of which was so intense it caused the formation of these minute particles that spread all over the earth."

"Stardust!" Summer said. "What a beautiful image: shimmering, billowing, glimmering particles of dust settling on the earth."

"It's not so beautiful when you think of what else happened," Barry said. "They believe this same comet explosion led to mass extinctions and marked the end of the Clovis culture in America."

"Oh!" she said.

"So, if the explosion was that massive and destructive, how can you square that with the production of art?" Rosalind asked. "Wouldn't the remaining people be more focused on survival than art?"

"I've wondered the same thing," Barry said. "I doubt that such carving would take place until after a period of cultural stabilization."

"Unless," a new voice was heard, "the piece of art was more than a piece of art; unless it was intricately connected with their survival, or so they thought."

The voice was Etienne's. He had been standing and listening for several minutes, not wanting to interrupt the very interesting conversation with an announcement of his presence.

Barry grew stiff and stood up. "Ah, Etienne, you're here. Please, get a chair and join us."

He happily obliged, pulling a chair up and taking a seat.

"You could be right," Barry said, surprised that such an insight came from a man who claimed archeology only as a hobby and not as a profession. "We're too simplistic sometimes when we think of the necessities of survival. Their mythology could have been as important to these people as food and shelter."

"Yes, and what we call their mythology was for them their religion," Etienne added. "It goes back to that age old question. What would you choose to save if your house was on fire?"

"You're right about that. It wouldn't be canned goods and clothing," Barry said. He could tell the man had tremendous insight. He longed to tell him more but cautiously played his cards close to the vest. "Then there's the issue of the remarkable style of the found object. It's far more sophisticated than objects that have been uncovered several thousand years later."

"Very curious," Etienne admitted. "Have they tried to compare it to anything from the same period?"

"There isn't too much available to compare it with. Of course, the assumption is that art objects of an earlier date would necessarily be more primitive."

"Well, then," he said, "if they can prove the antiquity of the date, that would indicate earlier people were far more sophisticated than what has been imagined, that artistic skills had progressed and later were forgotten and declined."

"That makes sense," Rosalind said. "She may have been carved by the people who survived the comet strike and who retained their skill and believed it very important to perpetuate their beliefs. Maybe most of their other religious objects had been destroyed in the firestorm."

"In which case she would have been doubly important," Barry added.

"She, who is she?" Etienne asked. "You have such an object?"

"We'll talk more about it later," Barry said. "The question for us now is what are we going to do today?"

"If you have no plans, I can take you around and show you some things," Etienne offered. "Rome is so very historical."

"That would be wonderful," Summer said, looking imploringly at the rest of them.

"Yes, that would be very nice," Barry agreed. "I hear you have a wonderful restaurant lined up for us tonight."

"I thought we would go to Ciampini's. Summer enjoyed it very much."

Chapter 37

Galileo

A large Egyptian obelisk atop a great fountain stands at the heart of Piazza della Rotonda. Gushing mouths of sculpted dolphins and grotesque masks that surround it keep the water flowing and send a clear message: Keep off! Except for a pigeon or two, that request is honored. Stuart stared into one of these horrific masks as if he could see into the secret eyes behind it. He studied the roguish men who lounged about the steps below the fountain with their attention trained on what Stuart imagined to be hapless tourists preparing to go inside the very famous Pantheon. Some of these miscreants looked down on their luck while others appeared just plain suspicious, he thought, as he trailed behind the others before going inside the great building into which they had just entered.

"No matter how many times I visit this place, I can't help but be impressed," Barry said standing inside the large domed structure with the sun streaming through its oculus.

"Fantastic!" Summer agreed. "How old is it?"

"Nearly 2000 years," Etienne replied. "It is an ancient temple that later was made a church. The painter Raphael is entombed here. So is Vittorio Emanuele."

"Vittorio Emanuele again!" Rosalind said. "I'd never heard of him before I came to Rome. Now he's everywhere."

"He is like your Abraham Lincoln to Italians: The king who united Italy. Let me take you to a historic site connected with someone you will have all heard of."

Behind the Pantheon in Piazza della Minerva stands a large sculpture of a baby elephant holding an obelisk on its back.

"Bernini created the elephant, but the obelisk like that on the fountain is Egyptian," Etienne said.

"What does it mean?" Summer asked.

"I do not know what Bernini intended. Probably no one does. So Summer, you must give your own meaning to it."

"The obelisk reaches up into the sky," she said, gesturing upward with her arms, "but the poor little elephant that carries it looks burdened, as if celestial striving is a burden fallen upon the innocent."

"An interesting interpretation," he said, looking admiringly at the girl. "The story about how they found this particular obelisk is quite amusing. It was originally brought here by the Romans from Egypt but was lost, probably when Rome was sacked. It was later rediscovered by a group of Dominican nuns who were connected with that church over there." He pointed to the church across the piazza. "They found it buried in the ground while they were gardening right here in what used to be the convent garden. No one knows how it got here, if it fell by accident or if it was buried to protect it from marauders. Picture in your mind their surprise when they were tilling the soil and uncovered this thing."

"A miracle!" Summer exclaimed full voice. "They might have thought it was a sign of some kind, a celestial message."

"Yes, yes, they may have," Etienne said with a chuckle.

"That reminds me of the legendary origins of many of the Black Madonnas we saw in France and Spain," John said. "Some legends have it that they were found in some natural place like in a tree, in the forest, or in a cave. They are believed by some to have great magic."

"But those are legends, and this is a true story," Etienne laughed. "This obelisk was found right here in the convent garden! Let me take you inside the church. It is very famous." He opened the door for them. "Welcome to the Basilica of Santa Maria Sopra Minerva." They were quiet for a few minutes, the grandeur of its starry vault having silenced them.

"Beautiful!" Barry said breaking the silence.

"Minerva, wasn't she a Roman goddess?" Summer whispered.

"Most certainly," Etienne said.

"Odd that they should name a Catholic Church after a Roman goddess."

"Not so odd really. The church simply absorbed a very old tradition."

"She was the Roman equivalent of Athena, wasn't she?" John said.

"Yes, very much like her. Actually, most historians believe it was an

Isis temple and not Minerva's that once stood here. That obelisk out there now on Bernini's elephant was supposed to have marked the entrance to the Isis temple."

"Why didn't they call it the Basilica of Santa Maria Isis then?" Summer asked.

"They are too similar."

"What do you mean?"

"Before the Virgin Mary was designated such, Isis was said to be the queen of heaven."

"Oh, I see. They didn't want any confusion," she said, not entirely satisfied with her own answer.

"You said this location is associated with someone we all know," Barry said.

Etienne began to recite:

"I, Galileo Galilei, son of the late Vincenzo Galilei of Florence, aged 70 years, tried personally by this court, and kneeling before You, most Eminent and Reverend Lord Cardinals, Inquisitors-General throughout the Christian Republic against heretical depravity, having before my eyes the Most Holy Gospels, and laying on them my own hands; I swear that I have always believed, I believe now, and with God's help I will in future believe all that is held, preached and taught by the Holy Catholic and Apostolic Church."

"It happened here?" Barry said.

"In this very place. I had to memorize the abjuration as a schoolboy. I remember my schoolmaster taught that it was a good lesson in error. It was in error, he said, for Galileo to deny what he knew to be true. It was in error, he said, for the church to attempt to conceal the truth because the truth cannot be concealed."

"But Galileo might have been killed otherwise," Rosalind pleaded.

"Yes, he would have likely suffered the same fate as that other martyr to science whose statue we saw last night," Barry argued.

"I agree with you," Etienne said. "But my schoolmaster would not have. He believed in the nobility of martyrdom. I remember he had a great respect for Socrates."

"Poppycock!" Barry said. "There is such a thing as the good lie when it saves lives and limbs. And there is such a thing as a foolish lie when it serves the purpose to falsely elevate oneself. Because the falsity of such a lie will always be discovered, and the liar will eventually be laid low as the truth emerges. Galileo told the good lie; the church told the foolish one. There is a distinction to be made."

"Maybe I should not have brought you here," Etienne said.

"Oh, no," Barry said. "I'm glad you did. It was enlightening. I have walked past this church on several occasions and had no idea of its history."

"Its history is so tragic, and it spoils such a beautiful day."

"Beautiful days have to be more than illusion. This day is beautiful for the truth it reveals," Barry asserted full of conviction.

Etienne said nothing more. But what had transpired during their visit to Basilica of Santa Maria Sopra Minerva came to define both men's impression of one another. Etienne had come to feel a great deal of admiration for Barry Short, thinking him far wiser than his schoolmaster. Barry, for his part, had come to believe Etienne was a man of high character, a man he could trust.

"Enough of history," Etienne said as he took hold of Summer's hand. "Let's go have gelato."

Piazza Navona was only a short walk away down narrow cobbled lanes full of pedestrian traffic, tourists snapping photos, and vendors selling all manner of colorful wares. Their moods livened, except for Barry's and perhaps Stuart's whose mood rarely livened. Barry began to feel eyes upon him much like he had in Montserrat. He glanced to his rear and up into the windows of the buildings along the lanes but saw nothing of note; and yet he continued to feel uncomfortable. His discomfort increased as he thought about his activities that morning. He had not only trusted Rosa with the revelation of his statue but Dr. Espezi. People talk, he thought. They both had learned that he keeps her with him in his backpack. The weight of the statue upon his shoulder began to feel exceedingly uncomfortable. Anyone could steal her, even thieves expecting only money or a camera. He considered how casually he had put his backpack down on the chair in the hotel restaurant before going to get his breakfast. A waiter could have snatched it, and no one would have noticed. How reckless, he thought. But what else could he do but carry her? He did not trust the hotel safe, and he certainly could not leave her in his room. He tried to reassure himself by considering that he had brought her safely this far and under far worse circumstances, but he had not felt the eyes upon him when confined in the ship's hold of either barge or boat. The feeling grew more intense once they arrived at the gelato shop in the open and crowded piazza.

Traditional Romans serve these delicacies in three scoops, each one a different flavor. The trick is to choose three flavors that enhance each other, which can make the choosing a subtle art for someone not well acquainted with ice cream. Summer was not such a person. She stood in front of the case filled with gelatos and sorbettos choosing among an array of colorful ices.

"I will have a scoop of cioccolato, a scoop of fragola, and a scoop of — I'm not sure how to say it?

"Banana," the scooper said.

"Yes, I will try your banana. Please, in a cup."

Barry stood behind Summer as the group of six was gathered around the case choosing their flavors. While she was concentrated on making and ordering her selection, he discretely slipped the box containing the very ancient prized statue from his backpack into the large bag she wore slung over her shoulder. They wandered back out into the piazza and gathered around one of the exquisite Bernini fountains except for Barry who unexpectedly announced that he had another appointment to keep and would be leaving them.

"I'll go with you," Stuart said.

"I must do this by myself if you don't mind."

"I do mind."

"I'll see you all back at the hotel; or if I'm late, I'll meet you at the restaurant," Barry said before Stuart could even raise himself up from where he was sitting.

"I'm not going to let him get away again. I'll catch up with you all later," Stuart said, before charging off in the direction Barry had disappeared into.

John placed his half eaten cup of vaniglia gelato on the cobbled ground next to Christabel.

"What is this all about?" Etienne asked.

"Christabel loves ice cream," John said.

"No, that is not what I mean. Do Barry and Stuart always behave so strangely?"

"Not usually," John said. "They're having a conflict right now. Early this morning before any of us was up, Barry left the hotel to visit a friend at the American Academy, which annoyed Stuart who is determined not to let him run off like that again."

"Is Stuart his shadow?" Etienne asked

"My sister and my mother have asked Stuart to look after Barry."

"Do they think him incompetent?"

"No, not in most circumstances."

"They both are being a little rude," Summer said, embarrassed. "What's this doing in here?" she said when she reached into her bag to grab her change purse so that she might tip a nearby musician.

"Here, give it to me," Rosalind said, grabbing the box out of view and tucking it into her purse.

"What's going on here?" Etienne said.

Rosalind's eyes met John's. "We might as well tell him," she said.

"This is getting a little awkward," John admitted. "Okay, so Barry brought an ancient statue back from Egypt more than a week ago and has been pursued ever since. He's trying to learn what he can about the identity and age of the statue, but he's had to dodge thieves at the same time he's trying to do research."

"That's why he put it in my bag!" Summer said. "He must think they're following him right now." She paused for a moment while she considered what she had just said. "What if they saw him do it?"

"Not likely that he would have been so careless," Etienne reassured her. "He must have been trying to lead them away from it."

"In that case, I'm glad Stuart followed him," John said. "That's why I qualified my answer to your question about my sister's and mother's motives. They think him quite competent in most circumstances but not all."

"Can I see this statue of his?" Etienne asked.

"Not here," Rosalind said. "I think we should go back to the hotel."

Chapter 38

Paranoia

Barry caught a glimpse of a man who had been behind him since he left Piazza Navona. He quickened his pace until he finally reached the busy Corso del Rinascimento where the volume of people and traffic offered more safety than the narrow, empty lane that had brought him there. He looked back. The suspicious man was nowhere in sight. Satisfied, he slowed his pace and reflected on the skill with which he had sneaked the sought after statue into Summer's bag. He thought himself quite an artful dodger in reverse. Where would he go next? The Coliseum, he thought. It's surrounded by plenty of tourists and guards even in December. He turned onto the Corso Vittorio Emanuele in the direction of his intended destination when a hand grabbed his shoulder from behind. Startled, he turned around and stood face to face with Stuart.

"I told you I wanted to be on my own right now!" he shouted.

"Not if I can help it," Stuart defiantly shot back.

Barry realized the futility of trying to escape a friend too dear to let him run off halfcocked, as Stuart saw it. "They're on to me." he said. "They were following me back there."

"I didn't see anyone."

"Well, I'm not entirely sure I did either, but I believe I did. I'm nearly certain of it." He paused for a moment. "You were right that what I did this morning was reckless."

"I know I was right. But what brought you to that realization?"

"I not only disclosed what I have but that I was carrying her around Rome in my backpack. What a dope I am!"

Stuart looked at Barry's backpack still slung over his shoulder. "Have you done something with her?"

"I didn't have time to plan while we were out there on our grand tour so I switched her out of my backpack and into Summer's bag in the gelateria. She doesn't know, of course."

"Oh, good god!" Stuart groaned. "You put that little girl at risk?"

"No one saw me do it. Not even she. I made the switch so I could lead them off the trail of what they really want, which is the statue, not me."

"So you set yourself up as a decoy. Why don't you consult with me before doing these crazy things?" he grumbled. "You've put me in a very difficult position. Do I stay here and protect you, or do I go back and look out for Summer?"

"You know what you must do. She has no idea, but she will learn soon enough, the next time she looks inside her bag. You must see to her and the statue."

"If I go, who's gonna to look after you?"

"I'll be all right. I'm going over to the Coliseum. With all the tourists and guards they've got over there no one would dare try to touch me. After I've tired them out with waiting, I'll duck out and return in a taxi to the hotel. So, if you will my dear friend, please find a secure place to hide her while I'm playing decoy."

"Quit this scheme and go back with me," Stuart said. "We can hide her together."

"You know that won't work. They'd be right behind us."

"You could be right," Stuart acknowledged. "Are you sure you can handle it?"

"Of course I can. I know these people. They're thieves, not murderers." In reality he was not so sure.

"Hurry back," Stuart said before he turned to go back to the piazza.

"Don't be too obvious with the location," Barry urged. "No hotel safes or anything like that."

"Take care of yourself, and don't stray from the crowds. I'll see you later."

Barry continued down the Corso another block or two until he felt the eyes burning a hole in his back. Glancing over his shoulder he spotted a young man in his twenties dressed in khakis like hundreds of other tourists. He picked up his pace and momentarily looked back. The young man had kept pace. He saw the Chiesa del Gesù in front of him when an idea popped into his head. He walked past the venerable edifice with the man still following, stopped dead in his tracks, did an abrupt 180 degree turn, and walked back, passing the stalker along the way and entered the church. The man did not follow.

He stood in the rear of the church happy to have found another opportunity to look at the crowning sculpture standing in the church's dome. His gaze drew the attention of a priest. "E cosi bella," he said.

"She is," Barry agreed. "Who is she?"

"You English! She not Our Lady," the priest replied.

"Yes, I know. I think she may be Prudence, but that does not tell me enough."

"You intrigued?"

"I am. What is that phrase? Hidden in plain sight. I think that may apply to her."

"Some things hidden for a purpose," the priest said. "Not for us to know."

"In matters of faith perhaps. In matters of knowledge it's rarely the case."

The priest stepped back slightly, distancing himself from a man with whom he shared a fundamental disagreement. Barry studied the sculpture for a few minutes more. He looked closely at how she gazed into the mirror that she held, how the snake curled itself harmlessly around her arm. He wondered what it could mean, why she was there, and why no one at the church could tell him about her. With all of his questions unanswered, he left.

He sat on the steps at the monument to Vittorio Emanuele at the end of the Corso he had just walked down and began to wonder if he could start a dialogue with Felix, reach an agreement of some sort, shift his monetary interest in the statue to an intellectual one. Perhaps if the facts were presented dramatically and with enough detail, he could entice Felix to join with him in his pursuit to solve the mystery of her identity. In his heart of hearts he doubted such an agreement was possible, but this chase had become intolerable and it had to stop. He pulled his laptop out of his backpack in the off chance he could pick up a Wi-Fi signal.

A couple sitting nearby who had watched his futile effort to get online suggested he try a cafe with Wi-Fi just off the Corso from where he had just come. He would only need to buy a cup of coffee, they said, and he could surf the web to his heart's content. He thanked them, crossed the piazza, walked back down the Corso, and turned right onto Via del Gesù.

It was a nice cafe, more of a bar really with light Italian lunch fare. He ordered a cup of coffee and signed on to his computer filled with anticipation that perhaps Felix had written and was about to make a more reasonable offer when instead he found a reply to his email to Paul.

Hi Uncle Barry,
I have not gone inside your house since you told me not to. I just come over to collect your mail and other junk that gets dropped there and take it to my house. Somebody left your computer in a big box on the front porch. I took it to my house since you told me not to go inside your house anymore. I didn't think you would mind me using it. You haven't gotten any more bad emails so I think everything is safe now.
    Paul

Barry felt a little guilty and shot back:

That's fine Paul. You've been a great help to me, and I shouldn't have accused you of not minding me. You are a good boy. Please enjoy my computer until I get back. I must say that I'm surprised the thief returned it. It sounds like he wasn't such a bad thief after all. Give my regards to everyone there. Tell them we are all in Rome now, and I look forward to seeing them when I get back.
    Best Regards,
    Barry

He sat drinking his coffee and wondering what to make of Paul's message. It's positive, he thought. No more threats, and they even returned his computer. Maybe Felix is softening with age. Maybe there is nothing really to worry about as long as he can guard her location. He even began to wonder if he had only imagined he was being followed. Perhaps he had become a little paranoid. Stuart's company can do that to you, he considered. Regardless, he thought it wise to spend his day as he said he would at the Coliseum with all the tourists.

A walloping shove propelled him into the back seat of a car just after he exited the cafe. Before he could look to see where it came from his head exploded in pain and he lost consciousness. The car that carried his limp body pulled slowly away from the cafe, continued down the Via del Gesù until it reached the Piazza del Campidoglio and from there Via del Teatro Marcello further south towards the Aventino, one of the more obscure Roman districts. When he awoke he found himself alone in the back seat of a large car that was slowly being driven up the hill of Via di Santa Sabina.

Chapter 39

Concealment

Summer opened her balcony doors wide while Etienne studied the statue Barry had slipped into her bag. "What do you think?" she turned to him and asked.

"She is marvelous. I have seen nothing like her. Are these feathers on her back?"

"Barry isn't sure if they're feathers or fish scales," Rosalind said.

"Yes, they are quite worn," he noted. "Her hair almost looks like a mass of feathers gathered around her face. These markings look like some sort of glyphs."

"Barry calls them runes," Summer said.

"Maybe. How old is she?"

"That's one of the questions he's trying to answer," John said. "How old is she, and who is she?"

"He thinks she's very, very old," Summer said. "He thinks she was a goddess whose identity was intentionally destroyed."

"That is quite possible. There is plenty of evidence of that sort of thing all over Egypt. We only know of those attempts that were not successful, of course. But how many attempts were so successful that the identities remain unknown is a matter of conjecture. She could be such a case."

"Barry acquired her in Egypt, but he thinks her origins are here in Europe," John said.

"Astonishing! I presume she is filled with the nanodiamonds he spoke of earlier, but I see no traces."

"You need a high powered microscope for that," John said. "He thinks she could be older than the Egyptians. The presence of the nanodiamonds would seem to confirm that."

"We saw markings very much like these in Magdalenian cave paintings in a Paleolithic cave Barry took us to," Rosalind said.

"Impossible! She looks nothing like what I have seen from that period, which is not much I confess. There is so very little left."

"Barry theorizes that the meanings of those runes inside the caves somehow survived the extinction of the Magdalenian civilization and were passed down to whoever carved her years later," John explained.

"She may have come from the time in between," Summer said. "After their culture declined but before the old language and beliefs were entirely forgotten."

"How could she have ended up in Egypt?"

"He doesn't know," Rosalind said. "Maybe she came from whoever the people were that lived in the land that later would become ancient Egypt. There had to be people there."

"You are suggesting that a people with highly developed artistic skills existed there before the known Egyptian Empire. That would be most incredible if it were true. It is possible but very unlikely. It is probably nothing more than wishful thinking on Barry's part."

"There's a poem he brought back with her," John said, reaching into the box the statue was in but finding it empty. "He must have it with him. I don't remember most of it, but I do remember that it said she holds the mirror of the world."

"The copper crown. Yes, I see. And her eyes! They are so highly polished. I know someone who may be able to help us identify her. I will tell Barry about her tonight."

"What should we do with her now?" John asked. "Barry must have thought he and she were in danger or he wouldn't have put her in Summer's bag."

"Which means we are all in danger," Etienne said. "I have a friend here in Rome, a trusted friend. I will take her there now," he said raising himself up from his chair. "We will all be a lot safer for it."

John was not entirely sure he could trust Etienne, but he agreed that keeping her in the hotel or on their persons would be too risky. Reluctantly he agreed.

"Right. Then I will go now. I promise we will find the truth. This is fascinating."

"I will go with you," Summer said.

"No, not this time."

There came a tap at the door and then it opened slightly. "I'm glad you're all here," Stuart said as he stepped in. "I was looking all over the piazza for you."

"Did you find Barry?" John asked.

"Yes, he's fine. Summer, can I see your bag?"

She pointed to Etienne. "He has her."

"Good," Stuart said, as he reached out to take the box. "Barry asked me to hide her for him. He's pretty sure he's being followed."

"Where will you take her?" Etienne asked, not yet relinquishing the box.

"I'm not sure. Maybe a bank vault."

"Etienne was just about to take her to a trusted friend," Summer said.

"I'm a banker, and I can tell you she will be safer there than in an Italian bank vault."

"Who is this friend?" Stuart asked.

"My grandmother," Etienne admitted. "She has an apartment near the Villa Borghese Gardens where she has her own vault. There is no worry about inquisitive employees there. She is the only one who knows the combination." Sensing Stuart's discomfort, he added, "Why don't you and John come with me?"

Summer blanched but held her tongue. He was oblivious to the slight. His mind must be on other matters, she thought. She watched from her balcony as Etienne signaled a taxi and the men rode off.

"I'm sorry," Rosalind said when she turned away from the window. "He's probably concerned about your safety."

"Barry put the statue in my bag. He obviously felt I was competent to deal with it. Then Etienne, almost a stranger, just walks off with it."

"He wasn't alone. Anyway, it could have been something else."

"Like his grandmother. He obviously didn't want to introduce me to her."

"Let's get out of here and do something," Rosalind said. "Have you ever seen the Garden of the Vestal Virgins? I once had something remarkable happen to me there."

Chapter 40

Abduction

"Quit shoving me! I'm quite capable of getting out myself."

Barry might as well have been talking to a wall. Two men continued to shove him out of the car and inside a very old basilica. An organist, apparently undisturbed by the commotion, rehearsed Bach's "Toccata and Fugue in D minor" in an otherwise empty church. Barry thought the melodramatic notes a tad overdone. His expression turned from anger to amusement at the sight of skulls and crossbones on the granite floor he was being dragged across.

"X marks the spot," he said to the consternation of his captors who pushed him down a flight of steps that led into a crypt. He marveled at Felix's sense of drama, but then he considered it was not so new as he recalled the dramatic nature of the email Felix had sent. His captors led him into a large room filled with empty chairs that must have been a meeting room of sorts, but for now it was empty except for him and the men who had brought him there. As if to answer his impertinence, one man pushed him down into a chair while the other yanked his backpack from his shoulder and left the room.

"I had hoped this would be a friendly meeting," a third man said upon entering the room carrying Barry's backpack. He was slight of build, tall, pale, with regular features, and steel blue eyes. He looked to be in his fifties, slightly bohemian, clean, but his shirt and trousers were a bit rumpled. He wore a long scarf wrapped around his neck and shoulders, shawl like.

"Abduction is hardly friendly," Barry replied, wondering who this stranger was.

"I needed to see you alone, which was quite impossible with all of your friends gathered around you."

"You could have made an appointment."

The man smiled and returned the backpack. "Well, here we are together now. I see the artifact is not with you."

"No, I don't carry her about with me everywhere."

"A verse is here. Quite interesting, 'For she is the maker of the world.'"

"Yes, it's both interesting and beautiful."

"I've been told that you were asking many questions at Il Gesù."

"If you don't mind, we haven't been formally introduced. Who are you?"

"That is not important now. Let me just say, I am a person very interested in keeping things, well keeping the world safe for..."

"What? For democracy?" Barry laughed.

"This is not so funny as you might think," the man said.

"I'm sorry," Barry apologized. "It's just well, you begin to sound like a stock phrase."

The man stared into Barry's face and then quietly spoke. "There is much chaos in the world today, don't you think? Dangerously so," he continued. "Some of us are vested with the responsibility to minimize it when we can. If we can get your assistance, it would do you well."

"Oh, come on now. Where's Felix? This is getting ridiculous."

"I am not with Felix. I can assure you of that."

"Well then, who are you with?"

"That is not your business."

"If that's not my business, why is my business yours? I am no radical. I'm not sent here to topple governments."

"I think that is not your intention, which is why I speak to you now. But if you go too far with your research, that may be the outcome. That is why I hope you will reconsider."

"You had better explain yourself."

"I know what you've brought back from Egypt, and I know where you got it. I can tell you that what your friend Hans Bueller found and gave to you was meant to be hidden. It should have remained hidden if not destroyed."

"Go on," Barry said his voice steady.

"You are an educated man. You more than most understand the fragility of culture. The world to most people seems permanent, immutable. You and I know that is not the case, don't we?"

216

"Well, yes, you're quite right about that, but I don't see the connection."

"What you and I understand, most people do not; and they do not want to. They require stability to maintain their existence. Without it existence for them becomes chaotic. Without it they will believe all sorts of demagoguery and can be mobilized to commit heinous acts that serve no one but those who manipulate their fear and confusion. That is the source of much of the suffering in the world today. Would you agree?"

"I think what you are talking about is worldview. Yes, people in my field recognize how important it is to people to believe that how they see the world is how the world really is."

"Exactly. Shared worldview is the source of stability in those places that remain stable, and to maintain it requires an unconscious if not conscious acceptance of order. The kind of order the church provides or your United States government. For the well-being of the people, that order must remain immutable."

"I understand what you say up to a point, but there has to be some kind of flexibility in that orderliness to avoid, well, authoritarian rule. You must acknowledge that the United States of America was formed out of rebellion against too much authoritarianism."

"Yes, yes, I know precisely what you mean. We Europeans must remain flexible enough to allow a certain, how should I say, controlled change. We cannot afford to degenerate into what we were in the past."

"I can understand that," Barry said. "I'm still not sure what any of this has to do with the statue I've brought back."

"Governments are one thing; religion is something else," the man continued. "The bloodiest wars have been fought by men of strong religious conviction. One's deeply held religious beliefs go to the soul of a man. He will kill and die for them as nothing else."

"European history unfortunately speaks to that," Barry acknowledged.

"How would it be if what is fundamental to religious belief, not just Christianity, but religious belief as it is widely held around the world, were to be undermined?"

"Are you saying? 'She looks upon herself who is not there. But sees instead before her all the world. Whatever was, whatever will be is in her care. For she is the maker of the world,'" he recited. "Are you

217

telling me that?"

"I am telling you that our present beliefs were forged through great suffering and sacrifice. I cannot permit a repetition of the past. Will you cooperate with me in this?"

Barry considered what this man had argued. Unfortunately, he had to acknowledge that no force in nature or elsewhere has ever been more potent than religion in bringing out the best or the worst in people, the worst more often arising when a religion believes itself under siege. That was never his intention, but he had to consider whether knowledge of his statue would result in such a catastrophe. He could not know while so many questions about her remained unanswered. But this man thinks so, he considered.

"What would you want me to do?" he asked.

"You would cease your exploration, turn over the statue to me, and pretend that none of this has happened. Don't write on the subject. Don't even acknowledge that you were recently in Egypt. Simply go back to what you were doing."

"And if I don't cooperate?"

"We will take her from you. If you dare write about her, make charges, anything of the kind, your reputation will be ruined. Without evidence no one will believe you, and you will be made a fool of. So, you have a choice to go on with your honorable career or see it destroyed."

"You say we will take her from me. Who is we? Who do you represent?"

"I would rather not say. Rest assured we are a powerful force and our motivations good. You will be rewarded for your cooperation in subtle ways: grants that will be made available to you, publishing contracts for your more worthy endeavors. I can assure you that we will do our best to elevate your name among your peers. But if you choose not to cooperate, the opposite will happen."

Barry, unfortunately, had little reason not to believe this man whose manner was far too forthright to be ignored. "You leave me little choice," he said. "As you see, I don't have her with me. I think I should need some time to think further about what you've said, although I must admit you've made a very good case. And I must retrieve her. I have her hidden away in a place only I have access to."

218

The man smiled gravely, convinced that his argument had been effective. "I can give you only a few days," he said. "I will have my men take you back to where they found you, and I will contact you soon. You still check your email account I see?"

With that remark, Barry became convinced that this man had something to do with Felix. "You know Felix then?"

"You might be happy to know that as a result of our intervention Felix no longer represents a threat to you."

"Well, thank you for that. Can I go now?"

"Yes, you may. I will ask the men to escort you to the car and drive you back."

"If you don't mind, I would rather walk. I have a lot to think about, what I will tell my friends and all."

"It's a beautiful day. Enjoy your walk. And don't forget, I will be contacting you very soon. I trust you will have her for me at that time."

Chapter 41

Roman Goddesses

Barry was overcome when he stepped outside the decrepit basilica. The place had infected him. Free and open air acted more like an emetic than a tonic. He felt faint. His head throbbed. He leaned against a tree and vomited. His feet were heavy weights although more than anything he desired to flee the place. He would have to find somewhere to rest and recover. A little restaurant lay ahead, Apuleius. He would get something to eat and drink, he thought.

"Apuleius," he said to the waiter who seated him. "Didn't he write a novel about a man who turned himself into an ass?"

"Ah si, *The Golden Ass*," the waiter said to his only customer, it being late afternoon. "Lucius dabbled too much in magic. He was too curious, and he accidentally turns himself into an ass."

"How does it turn out for him?"

"Okay. After a long journey, Isis grants his wish, and she turns him back into a man."

"That's good. Isis did that, eh?"

"Si. What would you like?"

"Something light with some wine."

"An antipasto?"

"What do you recommend?"

"Our chef just prepared seafood cakes for this evening, very good, very fresh, with his special pumpkin cream."

"Pumpkin cream! That sounds seasonable."

"Si, very fresh."

"I will have seafood cakes with pumpkin cream and a glass of Frascati."

"No Frascati. Pinot Grigio?"

"That will do."

The waiter walked off to the kitchen leaving Barry alone in a dining room that was decorated with columns and marble walls. He returned with his wine and placed it on the table. "The cook is just taking the seafood cakes from the oven."

"Your decor looks like a temple," Barry said. "It's very agreeable."

"It was a temple," the waiter said. "This was the site of the Temple of Diana."

Barry looked around him. "This was a temple? I've seen temples transformed into churches but not into ristorantes."

"We sit above it," the waiter said. "Come, I show you." He took Barry to look through the floor into a glassed-in area underneath. "That wall there is two thousand years old. We keep it preserved."

"Wasn't there another Temple to Diana a few miles outside of Rome near a lake?"

"Lake Nemi. It's only 16 kilometers. Women would walk there in great processions seeking Diana's blessings. È bellissimo!"

"The ruin?"

"Ah, the lake. Diana's mirror. It reflects the moon."

"She was a moon goddess?"

"Certo! The procession was in August under a full moon."

"That would have been a sight to see. What would Diana do for these women?"

"She makes their lives easier. She was close to nature and so too the women with their babies."

Satisfied that Barry was content with his story, the waiter disappeared back into the kitchen to see if the seafood cakes were ready.

Barry thought about Diana and the Roman women who once had a goddess to look after them. That must have been comforting, he thought, particularly given the pain of childbearing. He too felt pain. Would that there was a goddess to come to his rescue. Was he, like Lucius, becoming an ass? Each time he imagined himself turning his glorious statue over to the likes of the man who he had just threatened his career, he saw himself becoming one. Just another ass among asses, he thought.

The fish cakes were served with their pumpkin accompaniment. They were delightful and refreshing. He thanked the waiter and was on his way.

Inspired by tales of Isis and Diana, Barry determined he would walk through the ancient Roman ruins to give himself time to think before returning to the hotel. On his way he walked past the portico of the church of Santa Maria in Cosmedin where the Bocca della Verita sits. He had visited the Bocca della Verita many times, always delighting in taking new visitors there and daring them to place their hand inside the mouth of the round, stone river god. Legend has it that if you are a liar, he will bite it off. He paused, turned around and returned to the portico, and placed his hand confidently in the mouth of truth as he had done many times before. Would he be able to do that in the future?

***

Etienne embraced his grandmother. "It has been too long since I've seen you," she said. She spied two gentlemen over his shoulder.

"Grand-mère, I would like you to meet two American friends, John and Stuart."

She smiled at the two strangers who returned her smile.

"I have come to ask a favor of you."

"Sit down," she said taking them into her living room.

The room was soothing to the senses: soft blue walls; delicately made French provincial chairs covered in blues, aquas, and greens; a parquet wood floor topped with a large, hand woven beige and ivory rug with dusty pink and green accents. It was flanked to the north by a row of long windows that let in diffused light through the white organdy drapes that dressed them. If one were to squint one's eyes, the palette resembled one of Monet's water lily scenes, all nature green and blue water.

"What favor can I do for you?" she asked.

Etienne opened the box, unwrapped the delicate statue, and handed it to his grandmother.

"Where did you get such a thing?" she said as she turned it about in her hands.

"A friend just brought it back from Egypt. The statue is very old."

"I can see that. Who is she?"

"That is what my friend is trying to find out. He believes she is a representation of someone or something quite significant."

"She must be. The workmanship is exquisite. What favor do you ask Etienne?"

"My friend and these others believe they are being followed by those who would steal her. We need to hide her for just a little while, and I believe your safe to be as good a place here in Rome as I could find."

Madame Conti smiled. "Some people laughed, I remember, when I invested in my own safe. You even said it was better than what they have at most banks."

"I know Grand-mère. I did say that, and I was right. You have the top of the line."

"If I remember right, you thought it a bit...didn't you use the word, 'overkill?'"

"I probably did say that," he admitted. "But that is why I brought her here. I could not think of a safer place in all of Rome."

She smiled again, a beautiful smile for a woman her age, which had to be well into her eighties, although she did not look it.

"I will put her there right now," she said, taking the box and wrappings from Etienne and leaving the room for a few minutes.

Noting her absence, John felt free to speak. "This apartment is spectacular. The girls would love it. Too bad they're not here with us."

"I thought to bring Summer along," Etienne said, "but I felt it might be distracting."

"Yes, these are some digs," Stuart agreed. "Kind of like a big aquarium."

"I had never thought about it that way," Etienne said and began to laugh.

"The maid will bring us some tea," the grandmother said when she returned to the room. "She is put safely away now. When do you think you may come back for her?"

"I am not sure, but I think soon. When we leave Rome." Etienne turned to the others. "My grandmother has lived here in Rome for some time, since she married."

"Yes, since I married your grandfather. It has been very long ago but seems so recent," she said looking off as if she were staring back into time.

"She knows Rome as well as anyone might. She has made it her project."

"When you are in a place long enough, you must find ways to keep yourself entertained."

The maid poured hot tea in delicate china cups and served the room full of men. Stuart fidgeted awkwardly with the cup but ate a cookie in spite of his discomfort with the china, the chair he sat in, and the general ambiance.

Etienne's grandmother couldn't help but notice and only smiled more.

"She knows the art, history, mythology, everything," Etienne continued.

"Well, it is a fascinating place," she modestly replied.

"Would you know who the woman is, the statue of the woman in the dome at the Jesuit church?" John asked.

"Why of course. That is Prudence. Why do you ask?"

"Barry is fascinated with her, and no one in the church seemed to know who she was when we visited there."

"Barry is the archeologist I told you about Grand-mère. The one who brought the statue back from Egypt."

"I am not surprised they did not know. The church has so little interest in women these days, except for the Virgin, of course. At their peril, I believe."

"It seems odd that the statue would be in such an elevated position and yet they know nothing about her," John continued.

"Someone knows about her. Why else would she be there?" the grandmother said. "The symbols that accompany her, the snake and the mirror are very meaningful and represent enormous power, which is why she is not ignored entirely. What we usually associate with Prudence makes her a safe vehicle for their presentation."

Madame Conti had managed to pique even Stuart's interest in the subject, which was a great talent of hers.

"What do you mean safe vehicle?" he asked.

"Well," she said, preparing herself for what Etienne knew would be a long explanation. "The snake has many meanings. We all know that in the biblical garden it represents temptation and human weakness, but in medicine it stands for healing. We have all seen it wrapped around the Rod of Asclepius in medical situations. As a symbol, it is full of contradictions. The Medusa's beautiful hair was turned into evil snakes when she was cursed. But for the Roman goddess Minerva and her Greek counterpart Athena, the snake represents heroic virtues, symbolizing both women's wisdom and their willingness to protect the cities they guard."

Desiring to bring his grandmother to the point at hand, Etienne interrupted, "But what is the meaning of Prudence's snake?"

"Of course, meaning is always subjective. It depends on how you interpret it. The standard interpretation is that Prudence's snake comes from the Book of Matthew, 'Be ye wise as serpents,' and the mirror represents self-knowledge. That is why I say Prudence is a safe vehicle for the representation of these symbols. Their meaning is reduced to 'be prudent.'"

"In the states we have an insurance company by that name," John offered.

"Yes, then you know what I mean. The symbolic meanings of the woman, the snake, and the mirror are reduced to insurance," she laughed.

"So, that is all she means?" Etienne said.

"No, of course not dear. Some, not many, see the mirror as a representation of vanity and the snake as phallic. That is a rather Freudian interpretation if you ask me and too modern. I think it better and more classical to understand the mirror as an instrument of reflection and the snake as the symbol of wisdom. But what wisdom is it reflecting? The truth is Prudence is more in line with Sophia, and that could explain her prominent position in the church."

"Sophia! You mean the Sophia?" Etienne asked.

"Yes, that is who I mean, and I'm not the first to say so."

"Who is Sophia?" John asked.

"It is not so much who she is as what she is," Madame Conti explained. "Sophia, whether you understand her through the Greeks, the Christians, or the Gnostics embodies wisdom because she stands close to God, at least from an earthly point of view. She is His last emanation, and the only one in heaven who reaches down to us here on Earth. Some say she brings with her the light of God out of which the material world was formed. You have heard of the Oracle of Delphi have you not?"

"Of course."

"Well, the Greeks associated Sophia with the Oracle of Delphi because she too was believed to be an intermediary of sorts. So, understood as Sophia, Prudence is likewise an intermediary, and her mirror a reflection of the divine wisdom."

"Some might consider what you suggest blasphemous," Etienne said to his grandmother.

"How can the seeking of truth ever be so?" she answered back sharply.

"You've got to talk to Barry about this," John said. "What you say makes sense given that she stands at the highest point in the church. But why wouldn't anyone there have known that?"

"Why did you not know it or your learned friend Barry? Women have lost their cosmic identity. Of course, so too have men. We are all so commercially invented now—so physical. All we have of the spiritual is what our churches have chosen to give us, and they have so simplified it for us that we have forgotten. Oh, it is sad, I tell you, very sad. I would have loved to have lived in the days of the goddesses with great processions and much celebration. It is not that I'm really a pagan," she blushed, "but there would have been so many more possibilities for me."

"Grand-mère, you've had a wonderful life," Etienne scolded.

"I know I have," she answered. "Look where I live, and look what I have! When I see those poor gypsies out there on the streets, I am so grateful. I tell myself, there but for fortune go I. Yet I live in this museum of a city that is a reminder of so many other times, richer times, and I don't just mean materially. I mean richer in the magic of the spirit, which we all have, rich and poor alike. We do not realize it any longer, most of us that is."

Madame Conti fell silent after this last remark. None of the men knew quite what to say. Etienne understood his grandmother to be a brilliant woman, but he found her explanation of why so little is known about Prudence too generous. If his experience in business had taught him anything, it is that little goes on among men by accident. Our lack of knowledge of these things is by design, he thought to himself. Stuart felt an awkward embarrassment that he was happy not to acknowledge, so he said nothing. He recalled how he had argued at the church that the statue probably was not important in spite of the fact of its prominent position. Was he just being obstinate, he wondered, or was the lack of information available about her an adequate explanation for his attitude? It may have seemed so then but not now, which caused him privately to question his investigative judgment. John's reaction was mixed. He thought back to the statue of Giordano Bruno they had seen in Campo dei Fiori as a reminder of a past when one could be burned at the stake for entertaining scientific knowledge. He thought of the stories he had been told as a young boy in Sunday school about early Christians being thrown to the lions in the Roman Coliseum. He considered the Inquisition and the European religious wars. He was not so sure he shared Madame Conti's perspective on the glorious past. Surely he did not. But he had to acknowledge that in many ways she was correct. Look at the art and architecture early religion had produced. And yes, she may be right that women had an opportunity for more exalted roles when goddesses were still believed in. For all the thoughts these three men entertained, they said nothing. The visit had come to an end.

"Thank you for your help Grand-mère," Etienne said as he kissed her on the cheek.

"Don't be gone long. I enjoy our visits."

"I will be back very soon."

***

Flowers were still blooming in the Garden of the Vestal Virgins even though it was well into December. The two young women sat together with their little dog on the remains of a stone wall and looked at the statues, now mostly headless, of the women who once inhabited the place.

"Can you feel the power here?" Rosalind asked Summer who quickly assented.

"I can feel their spirits. It's like they're still here."

"That's what I think," Rosalind said. "Once, when John and I visited Rome, we had walked all over for days, and it was blazing hot when we arrived at this very spot. I remember there was purple wisteria blooming

227

here then. My feet were a mess of blisters. I didn't know how I was going to continue. But I wasn't thinking about that when we sat here and talked. I was thinking about Rome. It was only my second time here, and I had just begun to realize how magnificent the city had once been. We had explored the aqueducts and drove to the city on roads the Romans had built. John told me that they even made some of the tunnels we had driven through to get here. Before I had only thought about the great human tragedies that had occurred here. But at that moment I was astonished by Roman genius and talked about it in this very garden. The next morning when I awoke, my feet were healed."

"Wow! What do you think that meant?"

"I think I had been blessed by something very powerful in appreciation of the perspective I had gained. Of course, I cannot prove anything of the kind. But I've never before or since experienced my feet healing themselves so quickly."

"If what you say is true, then these women had real power and still do."

"I think so," she replied. "We think of it only as ritual power, the power that came from the respect bestowed upon them by the city. But maybe it was something more."

"The Vestal Virgins kept a fire lit, didn't they?" Summer said. "And the fire was supposed to protect the city, wasn't it?"

"Yes, that's what I've read, but there was more to it than the fire. They protected a statue of Athena that was brought here from Troy in very ancient times. The Romans renamed her Minerva, and it was believed she would protect Rome."

"Her name lives on," Summer pointed out. "We were just at Basilica of Santa Maria Sopra Minerva earlier today, but Etienne said the church was actually sitting on top of an Isis temple."

"I didn't want to argue with him about that, but it could have been both," Rosalind said.

"Both?"

"Well, yes in a way. Isis is so widely known. She has always been so. Some scholars argue that Isis was the basis of Athena. And we know Athena was renamed Minerva in Rome. So in a sense all three are the same. It's like they broke off a piece of Isis and out of her created

Athena, and the Romans carried Athena off and changed her name to Minerva."

"That's interesting to think about," Summer said, "Isis was originally Egyptian and later made Greek and then Roman."

"Very adaptable those ancients," Rosalind laughed. "But that makes her and all of them a construct, a fiction, something to be shaped to conform to culture and politics and passed from empire to empire as one rises and the other falls. Yet, my blisters were miraculously gone the next morning."

"If only I had their power," Summer said.

Rosalind looked closely at her sister, her beautiful sister. She had always thought Summer's power intrinsic, a given. "What's wrong?"

"What do you think of Etienne?" Summer asked.

"He's very handsome but a rather an old fashioned sort of man. The knight of your dreams perhaps?"

"Perhaps, but he didn't take me to his grandmother's today. I'm not sure how to interpret that."

Christabel began to bark. The women looked up and saw a man with a slow gait making his way through the fallen columns. He looked as old as the ruins he walked through. It was Barry, years older than when they had seen him only a few hours earlier at the Piazza Navona.

"Barry!" Summer shouted to get his attention.

Rosalind let go of the little dog's leash, knowing what she would do and instinctively realizing this might help him. Christabel ran straight to Barry, leaping up and down at his knee, tail wagging, asking to be picked up so she could greet him properly. He obliged, and the little dog licked his face. He smiled.

"What happen to you?" Summer asked. "You looked as old as Methuselah walking up here."

Barry smiled, unable to disguise his admiration for her impertinence although his words said otherwise. "Is that anyway to speak to your elders?"

She broke out in laughter and he joined in. "I didn't mean to insult you," she said. "But you look pretty bad."

"You do, Barry," Rosalind agreed. "Are you walking back to the hotel from the Coliseum? Maybe we can get a taxi to take us the rest of the way."

"I never made it to the Coliseum."

"What happened?" Rosalind asked.

The smile on his face did not fit the words coming out of his mouth. "I was abducted, threatened, and then finally let go on the promise that I would give her up."

"Your statue?" Rosalind asked.

"Yes."

"Did Felix do this?"

"No. I don't know who he is. He wouldn't tell me. Whoever he is I think he's part of some kind of powerful organization. He said if I don't give her up my career will be destroyed, and I believe him. I believe he and whatever he is part of can do that to me."

"What are you going to do?" Summer asked.

"I don't know yet. Did you find her in your bag?"

"Yes, but Etienne has her."

"I sent Stuart back to take charge," Barry groaned.

"Don't worry," Rosalind said. "Etienne, Stuart, and John are together. Etienne is taking her to his grandmother's apartment."

"His grandmother's!"

"She has her own vault," Summer explained. "According to Etienne, it is safer than any vault in Rome."

Barry's tension lessened. "Good," he said.

"Why do they want her?" Rosalind asked.

"I can only explain this once," he sighed, as if recounting the ordeal would tax him. "Let's go to the hotel, and I will tell all of you together."

Chapter 42

The Unwinding

Two taxis arrived at Piazza della Minerva within minutes of each other. One carried three men; the other carried two women, a little dog, and a ragged and drawn Barry Short. Stuart was immensely relieved to see that Barry had returned as promised, a little tired but safe. And he was tremendously interested to learn what had transpired since he left him earlier on the Corso Vittorio Emanuele. But Barry was having none of it.

"Do you mind if I take a little nap before dinner. We can talk then." He walked towards the hotel in the Piazza della Rotonda leaving the others standing near Bernini's elephant.

Stuart looked surprised and slightly peeved. "Since when is Barry ever too tired to talk?"

"He was abducted today," Rosalind whispered.

"He was what?" Stuart shouted.

"Shush! I don't want him to hear us talking about him. He told us a little bit about it when he came upon us in the Roman Forum."

"We were in the Garden of the Vestal Virgins," Summer added.

"If you think he looks tired now, you should have seen him lumbering through the ruins," Rosalind said. "They threatened to destroy his career if he doesn't turn her over to them."

"Felix?" Stuart asked.

"It's not Felix. He believes a very powerful group is behind them."

"Them, who?"

"He doesn't know."

"Is he going to do it?" Stuart asked, realizing now that Barry had looked more than tired, he had looked beaten.

"I don't know," she said. "He's exhausted and wanted to wait and recount the whole story when we're all together. I guess we will learn then, but it seems to me that he must be thinking about it or why would those men have let him go."

"After what my grandmother told me today, I can begin to imagine what the stakes might be," Etienne said.

"What did she say?" Rosalind asked.

"She knew about the statue in the church. She knew it is Prudence," John said.

"Even more," Etienne elaborated. "She knows Prudence's suppressed meaning. I know a bit about the tactics of suppression, and I can tell you that while the loss of certain profoundly important bits of information is made to look like an accident of history, it rarely is. It is an act of will perpetrated by forces that would rather we forget. Something like that may be at work here." He looked at his watch. "Our reservation is at eight, and it is now half past six. We should go to our rooms and rest and meet in the lobby in an hour."

***

Sunny skies gave way to a clear but chilly Roman evening, making it nearly impossible to enjoy the view from the outdoor terrace of Ciampini's. Still, the window next to their indoor table offered a commanding view of the dome of Saint Peter's Basilica from the outer rim of the Borghese Gardens.

John grabbed his black trench coat from the back of his chair and put it around Rosalind's shivering shoulders. Etienne sat next to Stuart across the table from Summer. She eyed him coolly as if thinking something she would rather not say. She was upset. Barry, who sat at the head of the table, looked tired but improved.

"It has been an eventful day," Rosalind said, squeezing her sister's hand under the table as if to comfort her.

"I need a steak," Barry said, and put down his menu. "And a glass of wine. That's all I need."

"For the first course everyone must try Tonnarelli Cacio e Pepe," Etienne said. "It is marvelous. Let us begin with an antipasto. I will order wine for everyone."

No one argued.

"Cacio e Pepe and Bistecca Alla Griglia," he said. "Il miglior vino

232

della regione."

"Perfetto!" the waiter replied.

"It's been a very eventful day," Rosalind repeated.

"I suppose they told you that I've been threatened," Barry said looking around the table.

"I hear they've threatened to destroy your career," John said.

"Not only that, they say I could destabilize the world's religions and cause massive wars."

Stuart began to laugh. "How are you gonna do that?"

"I don't know. The guy talked like my statue would replace God or some such nonsense. He seemed to make a good argument at the time. But upon reflection, I think he's full of it."

"What exactly did he say?" John asked.

"He talked about the fragility of culture. He argued that when people lose their cultural moorings they become vulnerable to demagoguery. And the fiercest button demagogues can push is religion. He seems to think that this little lady I brought back is very important, important enough that if she becomes known, well, the doorbell to hell on earth would never stop ringing."

"He's nuts!" Stuart said.

"Or very worried," Etienne suggested. "My grandmother discussed Prudence with us when we visited her this afternoon, the statue that you are interested in that stands in Il Gesù."

Barry's eyes fixed themselves on Etienne. "She knows about it?"

"She claims the symbols associated with the virtue are far more meaningful, and I might add, more magical than what we are told. I could not help but think as she spoke that our limited understanding of Prudence is by design."

"What did she say about the symbols?" Barry asked.

"She sees Prudence as a Sophia, and she says she is not alone in that."

"A Sophia?" Barry said. "I'm sorry, classical anthropology is not my specialty."

Etienne looked surprised. "I thought nearly everyone...?" He paused for a moment and remembered that Barry Short is an American. "According to the Gnostics, Sophia is God's final emanation and the only one to reach the earth. That makes her the divine link and many say the source of the material world. If the connection is there as my grandmother says it is, then the snake wound around Prudence's arm represents divine wisdom and her mirror is the device by which it is reflected and revealed."

Barry looked startled. "Whatever was, whatever will be is in her care. For she is the maker of the world," he recited from memory. He smacked his fist down on the table. "I thought that fellow was crazy! I should have known it was something like this. I must talk to your grandmother."

"We are not far. I will phone her."

"Here, use mine," Stuart said, handing Etienne his government issued satellite phone.

"If you don't mind, I will go to the lobby," he said swallowing the last of the wine remaining in his glass then refilling it with the remainder of the bottle.

The waiter uncorked more wine and brought out the antipasto. The mood at the table was much brighter when Etienne returned.

"My grandmother is most agreeable. In fact, she is quite excited to meet you," he said to Barry. "She says she has done a little research since we were there and has found out something spectacular about your statue that she wants to share."

Cacio e Pepe was served. The tonnarelli pasta was rich with eggs and clearly homemade; the cheese was of the highest quality.

"Thank you for recommending this dish," Barry said, relishing every bite and obviously back to his old self.

Grilled steaks were served garnished with fresh vegetables.

"Grilled to perfection," an exuberant Barry proclaimed.

At the close of the meal, the waiter brought out Tartufo and brandy.

"I've never had such a wonderful rich, chocolaty delight," Rosalind swooned, when the waiter brought out the bill.

"We are famous for our Tartufo," he said quite pleased with her enthusiasm. His expression changed at the site of Summer's half eaten sweet still remaining on her plate. "Signorina, are you not hungry?"

"It's all very good, but no I am not," she said.

They walked briskly from Ciampini's to the Piazza del Popolo and around the corner to the apartment of Etienne's grandmother located three flights up in an antique building. Summer stood back while Etienne unlocked the door and held it open to let the others in. "We will be a few minutes," he said. He let the door close, leaving them alone together on the empty street.

"Are you angry with me?" he asked while insinuating his hand into her hand.

"I just felt a bit left out today, that's all."

"I never meant to make you feel that way, quite the opposite."

"I thought you didn't want to introduce me to your grandmother."

"It was business earlier. I only took Stuart and John because I knew they didn't trust me, but I thought you did."

"I'm sorry," she said, feeling quite penitent. "We had better go inside. Your grandmother must wonder what has happened to us."

"Let me kiss you first," he said and pressed her against the wall of his grandmother's apartment building.

Madame Conti hugged Etienne as if she had not seen him in weeks. "Where have you been? Your friends say they left you at the doorstep just outside."

"I was showing Summer the sights in the piazza, the obelisk and the park above."

Madame Conti doubted his explanation, her sharp eyes noting Summer's disheveled hair and a hint of lipstick on her grandson's face.

"Have you met everyone?" Etienne said. "This is John's wife, Rosalind and her sister, Summer. Of course, you've already met Stuart. And here is the archeologist I told you about, Barry Short."

"I'm a folklorist and a writing professor," Rosalind said shaking Madame Conti's hand. "Summer manages an American record label here in Europe, in Amsterdam to be precise."

"I'm delighted to meet such accomplished young women," Madame Conti said. Turning to Barry. "You must be the archeologist who brought this magnificent find back to Europe."

"You said 'back' Madame, as if you know that Europe is her place of origin," Barry replied and shook her hand.

"Yes, I did say that. I will show you what I found, and then you will understand. First, come and sit down. Would you like some coffee or tea?"

"Tea would be nice," Summer said.

"Good, I will send for some."

"I love this room," she said. "The colors are beautiful."

"What can you see from the windows?" Rosalind asked.

"Come here, and I will show you."

Summer and Rosalind joined Madame Conti at a long row of windows. She went to the center of the row and drew back the filmy organdy that covered them. "This one opens out into a small balcony. When it is warm, I keep it open."

"I can see the obelisk in the piazza," Summer said. "There are so many in Rome."

"This one is very important. Augustus brought it to Rome from Heliopolis several thousand years ago. I believe Ramesses the Second had it made."

"Here we stand looking at it right now," Rosalind said. "It's amazing."

"They remind you of the deep historical connection between Rome and Egypt," Madame Conti said.

"Isn't that the Villa Borghese gardens behind it?" Rosalind asked.

"That is the Pincian Hill. If you climb the steps to the top, you will find the gardens to the rear."

The maid brought in a tray filled with china, spoons, napkins, sugar, lemon, cream, cookies, and a large pot of tea.

"We will serve ourselves," Madame Conti smiled. The maid left the room, relieved of the duty of serving. "Let me show you what I've found," she said as she picked up a book lying on the table next to her reading lamp. "Please, take a cup of tea," she offered as an afterthought. "Have you heard of the work of Marija Gimbutas?" she asked Barry.

"I've heard her name, but I'm afraid I'm not acquainted with her work," Barry replied.

"I was looking at your statue earlier this evening, and I could not help but notice the markings. I thought I recognized them, and sure enough I found them depicted and described in one of her books. Here, let me show you."

Barry walked over to where she sat holding her book. She turned to a page she had marked. "Do you recognize these?"

236

"I've spent a great deal of time poring over those markings myself. They look a lot like what we saw at Niaux, particularly that one."

"That was the one that caught my eye as well. It is so definite and so often repeated on your statue." She paused, and then looked up and thanked Rosalind for the cup of tea she had just brought her.

"Oh, my god," Rosalind said looking down at the book. "That looks exactly like what we saw at Font-de-Gaume. The markings at Niaux are similar, but this looks exactly like Font-de-Gaume!"

John looked on. "You're right. It does."

"So what does it mean?" Summer asked.

"That's exactly what I've been trying to figure out," Barry said. "But no one knows the meaning of these symbols."

"I can see you have not read Marija Gimbutas books or you would know," Madame Conti chided before getting up and going into the next room to retrieve the statue from her safe. Returning she began, "The V, whether standing or inverted, represents the goddess; in one of her earliest representations, the bird goddess. Not only does your statue have these same markings, but look at how they are arranged. They give the appearance of conveying some sort of written message."

"Yes, they look that way to me too. I only wish I could decipher it," Barry said.

"Look at these dim markings on her back. They look like wings, and her hair looks like feathers."

"I'm aware of what she looks like," Barry said. "But I've never heard this interpretation of the markings. A bird goddess, you say. Well, that makes all the sense in the world except for one thing. The markings, if they are Magdalenian in origin, could be up to 18,000 years old; and yet the style and workmanship of this statue makes dating her that far back impossible."

"I can see that," she agreed.

"A geologist at the American Academy looked at her this morning and noted a peculiarity about the stone she was carved from. It contains nanodiamonds, a kind of cosmic fallout from a major comet strike some 12,000 or more years ago. He speculates that the stone would have been in the upper sediment and available for carving some 11,000 years ago and that her copper crown was added later. But when you look at the delicacy of the carving, that seems improbably old."

"Yet everything else points deep into antiquity," Madame Conti said.

"Into prehistory," Barry corrected. "If I didn't know better, I would say she appears to be a very ancient goddess carved very long ago by a skilled craftsperson whose ability was well beyond what we could even speculate. And that craftsperson also retained knowledge of the meaning of these symbols from the Magdalenian period. I would have to suppose their meaning was known by others as well since they clearly were meant to communicate."

"Until the knowledge was extinguished," Madame Conti said.

"Yes, until it was extinguished," Barry agreed.

"Barry, why do you say if you didn't know better?" John asked. "What's to prevent your hypothesis from being correct?"

"Two obvious points. We don't have evidence of carving that is this sophisticated until much, much later. If my hypothesis were true, I would have to assume that the skills that we see here were lost and reemerged later. The second assumption we would have to make is that the language of the Magdalenians outlived their culture."

"It could have been carved as their culture was dying out," Madame Conti said. "Maybe as an effort to resuscitate it."

"But the sophistication of the style?" Barry reiterated.

"What killed off the Magdalenians?" John asked.

"We don't know. Maybe it was that comet strike that rained down nanodiamonds."

"Maybe their art was more sophisticated than what we know?" John surmised. "Their cave paintings are incredible, but maybe there was more that didn't survive."

"Maybe," Summer said softly. Her voice strengthening, "Maybe this statue was created by a handful that survived the devastation after the culture was wiped out, in the time between their decline and the rise of later cultures. Earlier today Etienne asked what would you save if your house were on fire? The answer is obvious. You would save what is most important to you, and this goddess is it. That would explain how she survived for so long when almost nothing else did. Barry, I think your hypothesis is correct."

"She has survived this long because she was hidden away in a remote part of Egypt," Barry said, having gained some enthusiasm for his own idea. "The fellow who had me forcibly taken to him told me it was known where she was and that she was to have stayed there. Ironically, she survived because of the measures taken by those who wanted to suppress her. He suggested that they should have destroyed her. I can only wonder why they hadn't since that would have eliminated the threat she represents to them."

"They could not destroy her," Madame Conti declared. "They fear her too much. She has too much power. They could only bury her."

"What power?" Rosalind asked.

"She is the Bird Goddess after all, not a replication, but likely the real thing," the grandmother passionately argued. "We know the owl was one of Athena's symbols, along with the snake and the helmet. Athens depended on Athena for its life."

"Like the Palladium," Rosalind said and turned to Summer. "What we were talking about at the Garden of the Vestal Virgins today. The statue of Athena was brought to Rome from Troy and renamed Minerva. The Vestal Virgins guarded this statue because Rome's safety depended on it. When she was stolen from Troy, Troy fell. Legend has it that she was eventually taken from Rome by Constantine and buried in Constantinople, and we all know what happened to Rome."

"Are you ascribing real power to it?" John said.

"The ancients did," Rosalind said.

"This one has the mirror in her crown and in her eyes," Madame Conti said. "What the geologist told you explains the necessity for both. Her highly polished eyes were the only representation of a mirror possible 11,000 or more years ago, until later when copper metallurgy was discovered and a reflective crown could be fashioned. If she is who I think she is, she is the wisest of beings. What is more important is our entire existence depends upon her since she brings existence into being. One who knew that or feared it, would not dare try to destroy her."

"But she's only a statue, a representation," John argued.

"I would not bet my life on that," she rejoined.

"What should I do?" Barry said. "They say I must turn her over. They say the world order depends on it. They say they will destroy my career if I don't act willingly. They say they will take her by force if necessary."

"They are wrong," Madame Conti declared, "on all counts. The world depends on her preservation, as do you," she scolded. "We must take her where she will be safe." She looked up at her grandson. "I think we should take her to Cinzia."

He shook his head in agreement and explained to the others, "Cinzia is my sister. She lives in France. She is an expert in these things and knows how to be discrete."

"How do we get her there?" Barry asked. "They will be watching my every move until they have her."

Etienne looked over at his grandmother. "Can you take her there?" She shook her head yes. "Can you leave tonight?" She again shook her head.

"I will just pack a few things and call my driver," she said and turned to Summer and Rosalind. "The two of you should come with me."

"That would be a good idea," Etienne said, "in case things get rough."

"I don't feel right leaving you here. We're a team," Rosalind said to John.

"No, you go. You need to get Christabel out of here anyway."

"John, you can go with them," Stuart said. "You can look out for them and leave Barry to me."

"No way! I'm staying with Barry."

"That settles that," Etienne said, looking over at Summer.

"I've got to go get my clothes," she said.

"Don't worry about your clothing," Madame Conti said. "It would draw attention to our plan if we were to pull up at your hotel. We will get you clothing in France."

"Apparently the fates have declared that you will lose your clothing no matter how hard you try to hold onto it," Rosalind laughed.

Summer looked at her defiantly. "John can pack up my things and bring them with him when he leaves Rome. You will be rejoining us in France, won't you?"

"If he can dear," Madame Conti said.

"How is this going to work?" Rosalind asked. "When and where will you join us?"

"I will have the driver bring the car around to the rear," Madame Conti said, avoiding addressing her concerns. She looked at Etienne. "It would be wise for the three of you to stay here a little longer, until we have gone. I will have the maid bring you an evening snack."

"Do you have any beer?" Stuart asked.

"I think the maid might have some. I will ask her."

Madame Conti made a phone call and went to her room for a few minutes returning with only a small travel case. John kissed Rosalind and petted Christabel who licked his mustache. Etienne assured Summer that she was in the best of hands. At that, the two women followed Madame Conti out of her apartment and down the hall to a rear staircase where her driver took her case and led them to a large Mercedes-Benz limousine. The car slowly pulled out into the near empty street and away from the piazza in the dim midnight light.

"We need to trick them into complacency. Make your captor think he has already won," Etienne said to Barry as the four men sat together in Madame Conti's blue aquarium waiting for a sufficient amount of time to pass before they would leave.

"He said he would contact me by email," Barry revealed. "If he has, I could reply that I agree with whatever he proposes."

"La mia nonna ha il servizio di internet qui?" Etienne said to the maid who was by then serving pilsner glasses filled with Italian beer. She shook her head no and returned to the kitchen.

"You will have to wait until you are back at the hotel to check," he said. "But that is a very good idea. Then we will need to engineer a plan to prevent any harm from coming to you when they realize they have been duped."

"What would that be?" Stuart asked sipping the white foam head off the top of his glass.

"I don't know yet," Etienne said.

"I will just have to trust it to the fates," Barry said. Thinking again of Lucius' rescue he said, "I think I will trust it to Isis instead."

Chapter 43

Escape

The white Mercedes purred through dark Roman streets and tunnels until it roared out onto the highway headed north.

"I love your car," Summer said as she reclined in one of two soft leather seats the driver had pulled down across from the rear seat where Madame Conti sat.

"It's quite old now," she said. "The driver takes very good care of it. My husband purchased it nearly forty years ago."

"It's beautiful," Rosalind said, noting the suppleness of the leather. "You would hardly know it's this old." She finally ventured to ask a question she had wanted to ask ever since she met Madame Conti. "About your husband?"

"He has been gone for many years now," she answered. "I do have contact with him from time to time. I always leave a place for him." She rubbed the leather on the seat next to her.

"He lives elsewhere?"

"Yes, one might say that, but his spirit returns to me."

Rosalind dropped the subject immediately as an image formed in her imagination of an elegant gentleman sitting beside the lady that sat across from her. She now understood why she and Summer were seated across from Madame Conti. Although there was plenty of room for three on that rear bench seat, there was not enough room for four.

"Would you like to stop anywhere en route?" the driver asked.

"Not until we are well out of Italy. How long will it take us to reach Cannes?"

"No traffic this late. Six hours tops."

"Call the Carlton and book our rooms if you will."

"Your granddaughter lives in Cannes?" Summer said.

"Oh no, no. She has a house in Sainte-Maries-de-la-Mer, very remote, nothing there. I thought we would rest up in Cannes and do a little shopping before we go out into that wilderness." She looked into Summer's sleepy face. It is a pretty face, she thought and quite lacking in pretense. "You might as well rest. I think I may doze off."

The last thing Summer remembered before drifting into sleep was the muffled voice of the driver making their hotel reservation and the sensation of liftoff as he pressed his foot to the accelerator.

***

Barry fired up his laptop once they arrived back at their hotel. "My Dear Dr. Short," the email began. "Please respond immediately with your guarantee to honor the solemn commitment you made to me this afternoon. Please also answer whether you will deliver the object tomorrow as you have promised."

"I never made such a promise or commitment!" an indignant Barry shouted forcefully throughout the hotel lobby. John, Stuart, and Etienne bent over Barry's shoulder to read his email.

"Quite presumptuous of the guy," John agreed.

"There is a strategy here," Etienne said, looking as if he had gotten a whiff of a foul odor. "But I believe he has misjudged his opponent."

"He certainly has," Barry barked. "What nerve!"

"What's the strategy?" Stuart asked.

"Clearly Barry's captor is used to people bending to his authority, whatever that may be. He imagines Barry will agree to his framing of the events that took place today, that's all."

"Why would he?" Stuart asked.

"Barry wouldn't. But many others would. Those who lack confidence and place too much confidence in others, particularly in fellows like this one who have more confidence in themselves than they rightly deserve."

"You're quite the psychologist," Stuart said. "Go on."

"There's nothing new here. It's the art of taking and holding power. Men have been dominating other men by these means for thousands of years. For it to work, the power taker must have some real power to wield. The question becomes, what power does this man believe he has over Barry?"

"My reputation. He said if I did not hand her over, he would take her from me and destroy my career. If he can do that, that's real power."

"We've taken care of the first problem but not the second," Etienne admitted.

Turning to Barry, Stuart asked, "Is it that easy to do?"

"I've never seen what I knew to be a plot to undermine an academic," Barry said. "I've certainly seen a number of careers sink. Usually it's the result of a naive scholar overstepping his or her boundaries, asserting too much outside the parameters of what has already been established without due regard for the politics of the situation."

"How is this done, this academic assassination?" Etienne asked.

"Well, it's kind of a gang up, a consensus arrived at and communicated in published criticisms of the scholar's work."

"There's always debate among scientists and academics," John said. "It's a necessary part of the process, isn't it?"

"You're right about that," Barry agreed. "A debate will not destroy a career. In many cases it will advance it. What will destroy a career is a ready consensus that the assertions made, how should I say it, are so off base that they aren't worthy of debate. A scholar who finds himself or herself in such circumstances has two options, either recant or not."

"What would be the outcome of 'or not'?" Etienne asked.

"The scholar runs the risk of being expelled," Barry explained. "If you are not already tenured, you are not likely to be. You could expect that your research won't be published in respectable academic journals. And you will never get any book contracts unless you wind up in the popular press; and if you do that, that will seal your fate. I have seen this happen to not a few budding scholars. It meant the end of a career often before it was fully launched, and then the beginning of another, usually as a librarian or the more ambitious may try the law. One sad fellow I knew sunk into depression and alcohol. I haven't heard from him for years so I don't know how he ended up."

"They can't do that to you," John asserted. "You are tenured!"

"That I am," Barry agreed. "But I could lose my research funds, which is what allows me to do my work. What would be worse is losing my reputation, being reduced to a joke. That's what finally drives people out. But I don't see how any of these dreary scenarios applies."

244

Etienne said nothing, but the expression on his face spoke volumes to anyone who happened to take notice. Fortunately, Barry had not. After a few moments he said, "We will have to think about what we can do for your career, but for now, you must answer the email."

They gathered around Barry's computer as he hit the reply button and a fresh screen popped up.

"I won't type dear anything since I don't know what the man's name is," Barry barked.

"Why not 'My Dear Abductor,'" John laughed.

"Now, now, we can't appear snide," Barry said sarcastically.

"Just begin with the message and keep it simple," Etienne said. "That will seem honest."

"How about this," Barry said and began to type, "I will meet you tomorrow at 4 p.m. at...." He paused for a moment and looked over at Etienne as if he expected him to name the place. Etienne remained quiet so Barry continued unprompted, "at the Basilica of Santa Maria Sopra Minerva," he typed. He looked over at Etienne again. "I thought that an appropriate place."

Etienne smiled and nodded. "Good. Now we've got to figure out what to do with you."

"Maybe we should follow the girls' lead and have him leave Rome tonight, look like he's going out for espresso and leave," John suggested.

"We did that already when we ducked out of Montserrat," Stuart said. "This time they will be watching this hotel and Barry like a hawk."

"Hidden in plain sight," Barry said. "Why don't we put a twist on one of their strategies?"

"What do you suggest?" Stuart asked.

"Well, you said they would be watching me and this hotel like a hawk. Why don't we give them something to watch, build up their confidence a little too much?"

"I see what you mean," Etienne said. He looked over at John. "You and Barry are about the same height and build."

"You think I could disguise myself as Barry?" John asked incredulously.

"With the right clothes, a little gray added to your hair, maybe some sunglasses, you might pass."

John looked dumbstruck, but once he thought about it he realized that such a scheme might just work. "You will have to give me your backpack," he said to Barry. "That's your trademark. But I don't want to walk into that basilica tomorrow afternoon and come face to face with this guy. No disguise could be that good."

"You will not have to," Etienne said. "We will put you in Barry's clothing tomorrow morning. We will send you out somewhere, maybe on the bus to the American University. That would seem convincing enough. They will think you have gone off to retrieve the statue from its hiding place. Yes, the American University will do. While they are following you, Barry and Stuart can leave unnoticed. Barry, you will have to wear John's clothing just in case they leave someone watching the hotel. Maybe you can wear a hat. I will put a little shoe polish in your hair and beard to tone down the gray. You and Stuart can get on a train and leave Rome."

"Leave for where?" Barry asked.

"Take the train to Nice. If you and Stuart can get that far on your own, John and I will meet up with you later."

Stuart laughed at the absurdity of even suggesting that the two of them might not be able to pull off such a simple stunt. This was a solid plan. He could have kicked himself for not having thought of it first.

"One thing though," Stuart said, "while your plan will get Barry out of here, I can't see how it's going to save his reputation if these guys have the power they claim they have to wreck it."

"I'm afraid we are going to have to deal with that problem later. For now, I am most concerned with saving his hide," Etienne said.

"What do I do after I've gone to the American University?" John asked, resigned to his fate but concerned for his safety. "I want to help Barry, but I don't want to swap my hide for his."

"You won't. You simply return to the hotel. I will be here, and together we will take you out of your disguise and leave well before the afternoon appointment."

"Sounds like a good plan if you are up for it," Barry said to John.

"I'm willing to give it a try. I have one more question. Once I get to the American University, what should I do and how long should I stay?"

"Go visit my colleague Rosa. Tell her I sent you to ask if she has heard anything from Felix; tell her I'm looking for him. That will give you two something to talk about for long enough."

"Are we set?" Etienne asked.

Barry pressed the send button and went up to bed. Etienne postponed sleep for an hour or two to make a quick trip back to his grandmother's apartment to get a few items to assist in the disguises.

Chapter 44

Disguise

"Just a little dab here and there is all it takes," Etienne said as he smeared white powdery muck through John's hair creating subtle gray streaks.

"You've done this before?" Stuart said.

"I used to be in involved in a little play acting, amateur sorts of things. I had to learn to do my own makeup. Do you have a hat he can wear?"

"No, but here are my sunglasses," Barry said handing them over to John who gazed at his own figure in the mirror dressed in Barry's jeans and navy blue sweatshirt.

"I hardly recognize myself."

Barry stood with his chin in his hand evaluating John's appearance for a minute or two and then handed him his jacket. "Put this on," he said. John put on the worn, rumpled jacket. "Here, sling this over your shoulder," he said, handing him his backpack.

"I believe you have captured the look," Stuart said.

"I don't know if I should take that as a compliment or not," Barry noted, seeing himself now as others see him.

"There is a certain seediness in his appearance," Etienne agreed. "But you have been traveling for quite some time in difficult situations without a change of clothes."

"I had to leave them back in the hotel in Montserrat when we made our discrete getaway."

Truth be told he had not left much, only the clothing and tight shoes he had bought in Aix-en-Provence the day of Etienne's party. He handed John bus directions to the American University and directions to Rosa's office. "I want you to know how much I appreciate this," he said and patted him on the shoulder.

"I will be here waiting for you when you get back," Etienne said.

Barry, Stuart, and Etienne looked through the window onto the

248

piazza and watched as John walked in the direction where he was to catch a bus. They knew their plan had worked when they saw two men follow him from behind.

"You're already transformed," Stuart said to Barry who was dressed in John's neat black pants, blue shirt, and burgundy sweater.

"Ha! Ha!" Barry said.

Etienne worked some waxy brown shoe polish into Barry's disheveled hair. Combed it and lifted it in the front in a style reminiscent of John's more polished look.

"I'm not so sure you look like John, but you certainly don't look like yourself," Stuart said.

"The train for Nice will be leaving at nine so the two of you had better be off," Etienne said. "If you miss it there will be another at ten, but the sooner you leave Rome the better. I want both of you to stay out of view once you arrive. Go to the Hotel Excelsior. It is near the train station. Pick up food and wine on your way there and stay put until we arrive. I'm afraid we will not catch up with you until tomorrow morning because the night train is all that will be available by the time John gets back. Don't forget, the Hotel Excelsior."

Etienne returned to the same window where he and the others had earlier observed John's departure. He watched Barry and Stuart hail a cab, which he calculated would get them to the train station in fifteen minutes. They would just make the nine o'clock train, he thought. No one had followed them. He collapsed on his bed to wait for John's return.

***

Christabel barked incessantly. "Who is it?" Summer asked, her voice full of sleep.

"Room service."

She grabbed one of the terry robes from the bathroom and opened the door while holding Christabel in her arms. The waiter set up a table laid out with a spread of croissants and rolls, whipped butter, fruit, and cheese. He placed a small dog dish filled with what looked like beef filet on a mat he spread on the floor.

"Madame Conti was not sure whether you would prefer tea or coffee but decided on tea. She said to tell you it is better for you. She asked me to inform you that she has made appointments for all three of you in the salon before you go shopping. You are to meet her there in an hour and a half. Is there anything else I can do for you?"

"No, that will be fine," Summer said and let him out of the room.

"Wake up!" Summer cried as she shook Rosalind mercilessly. "Breakfast has just been delivered, and we have to get ready to go to the hair salon."

"Hair salon! What time is it?" Rosalind asked.

"It's noon. Summer flung open the drapes. "Look at this view! Too bad the weather isn't better."

"What's it doing?" Rosalind asked.

"Take a look."

She sat up in bed and looked out at heavy clouds and rain. "This is the kind of day for curling up and reading a good book."

"Taste one of these!"

The buttery croissant melted in Rosalind's mouth. She poured herself a cup of tea. "I wish I had hot chocolate."

"The waiter said that Madame Conti believes tea is good for us."

"How sweet of her to be concerned."

"I think she likes me."

"I'm sure she does," Rosalind said. In an effort to tamp down what she feared might be misplaced expectations, she shifted the topic back to the main subject. "It's surprising he hasn't married yet. He's old enough, and he's certainly attractive and quite eligible. There must have been many women who pursued him. You will be careful, won't you?"

Summer made no reply and instead prepared to go down to the hotel salon.

"Madame Conti is having her massage," the receptionist said when they arrived. "Can I take your dog?"

"What would you do with her?" Rosalind asked.

"We have a groomer on staff. I can have her bathed, trimmed, and brushed."

"She does look a little scruffy," Rosalind said and handed over her leash.

250

"I will take you back for your appointments before I deliver your dog. Would you like something to drink?"

"What do you have?" Summer asked.

"I can get you coffee, juice, or if you like, champagne."

"Champagne!" Summer exclaimed. "I could get used to this."

Madame Conti appeared with her head full of curlers. "I thought I would check with the two of you before they put me under the dryer. It is a dismal day. We could do a little shopping for some more appropriate clothing, have dinner here at the hotel, and wait until tomorrow to leave when the weather is scheduled to improve."

"That's fine with me," Summer said.

"Me too," Rosalind agreed.

"I want to thank you for getting us such a lovely room," Summer said. "The view is wonderful."

"If only the sun would shine. We should all be finished here in another hour. I will see you in the reception area, and we will be on our way," Madame Conti said before returning to her stylist.

"Did you hear that Rosalind? We're going to shop for appropriate clothes. Maybe Etienne's sister lives in one of those French country estates with sprawling lawns and gardens and huge patios. She may have horses. We might need riding clothes, and garden dresses, and formal dinner outfits."

"I think you're letting your imagination run away with you," Rosalind cautioned.

"Or maybe she lives in one of those ancient castles with a moat."

Chapter 45

Second Escape

John poked his head through Rosa's open office door. He pulled back into the hallway when he saw she was not alone. Rosa, curious, went to her door and peered into the hall.

"La posso aiutare?" she said to the unkempt, nervous stranger.

She's beautiful, John thought. Barry had not mentioned that. "Dr. Palazio?" he asked.

"Si."

"You have someone in your office. I should come back later."

"No, no, he's just a colleague," she answered in English. "Can I ask who you are?"

"I'm a friend of Barry Short," he said, relieved that he no longer had to maintain the pretense that he was Barry, at least not in Rosa's presence.

"Come in," she said and opened the door wide. "We were just speaking of him." A slight figure of a man sat in a chair by her desk looking attentive. "Dr. Assi, a friend of Barry's."

Dr. Assi extended a limp hand. "How do you do," he said.

"I just saw Barry only yesterday morning," Rosa said.

"I left him this morning," John replied. "We're traveling together. He asked me to drop by and see you about something—ah, someone—if I had a few extra minutes." John paused to consider how much he should say with a stranger present, but then he thought he had very little to say anyway. "He asked if you might know how he could reach Felix. He would like to talk with him about something or other."

"He could have phoned me and not put you to all this trouble," she smiled. "Since you are here, I would like to present Dr. Felix Assi."

"I suppose he wants to reach me about that statue of his," Felix said indignantly.

"That's probably it," John said. He looked into Felix's face and saw none of the attributes his imagination had ever associated with a count, save one, arrogance.

"Felix has been telling me it is a fake," Rosa said, "although I saw it only yesterday and thought it looked quite authentic."

"It is a very good fake, then," Felix proclaimed. "I have it on the highest authority that it is a total fabrication. That my old friend Barry is in the business of attempting to perpetrate a fraud on our profession does not surprise me, but the very idea that he thinks I could be defrauded by such fakery is an insult."

"Barry Short would never do such a thing!" John said and rose from his chair.

"The man's a thief! He has been banned from Egypt ever since he smuggled a valuable artifact out of the country last year."

"That is not the Barry Short I know!"

"Then you don't know him! After committing a crime that threatens the integrity of our profession, he and his partner, that disreputable Hans Bueller, saw fit to try to pass a statue off as something other than what it is. I have it on highest authority that their real intent is to threaten the church. To think he is seeking me out to be an unwitting participant."

"You, unwitting! My nephew told me about the threatening emails you sent to Barry demanding that he turn over that fake, as you now call it."

"How dare you!" Felix said as he stood up in an outrage. "I specified nothing in those emails. I only offered to help him find a buyer, but that was before I knew it to be a fraud."

Rosa's eyes grew large and grave. "Please, both of you sit down. You offered to help Barry sell an illegal artifact? Why you both could be thrown out of our profession not to mention jailed for such a crime."

"I was only trying to help him," Felix said, looking earnestly into Rosa's dark eyes as he seated himself beside her. "The deed had already been done. Barry has not been quite right since the episode last year. I only wanted to save him."

"No, he has not been the same. He gave up Egyptology entirely and with no explanation," she said looking earnestly at John. "All of us have known that he would not have done so for no reason and could only assume he had gotten himself into very big trouble in Egypt."

"It's not what you think," John said.

"I hope you are right. I have always admired Barry."

"That was before you knew him to be a fraud trying to perpetrate a fraud on to our profession and on to me!" Felix blurted out. He turned to John. "Tell your friend I will no longer do business with him. Any offers I have made have been rescinded. Warn him...no, tell him that in the name of our past friendship, I will say nothing more about this fraud unless he makes further attempts at trickery and foolery. If he does, if he does not desist, I will be the first to denounce him."

John was speechless. He had heard far more than he could tolerate from someone he had not expected to meet. Silent, he rose from his chair to leave. Rosa escorted him into the hall, her bright eyes softened and full of pity.

"You will send Barry my love and tell him to be careful," she said before returning into her office.

He stood nearly frozen in the corridor. He knew it would not take long for the men who had followed him to learn that they had been duped. He wondered what they might do. Try to capture him? Go back to the hotel in search of Barry? He must talk to Etienne immediately.

The hallway where he stood was lined with closed doors. He took the stairway down to the next floor. There were only classrooms. He went down to the first floor and saw an open door to a large administrative office at the end of the corridor. He told the clerk inside that he was lost and wondered if he might use their phone to call his friend at their hotel to get directions.

"I can place a call for you if it's local," she said.

"It's the Senato hotel at the Piazza della Rotonda. I don't know the phone number but the room number is 419."

The clerk rang up the operator. "Albergo del Senato. Grazie. Buongiorno. La camera quattro cento diciannove. Grazie." She smiled, handed the phone to John and went about her business.

"Grazie," John said. "Hello Etienne," he whispered. "There's a situation here. Felix was in Rosa's office when I arrived. He was angry and accused Barry and his statue of being frauds and threatened to publicly expose him if he does not desist. He said he had it from the highest authority. Yes, that's what I thought. He's in contact with those fellows. I'm afraid to step outside the building. He might have phoned them right after I left. Okay, I will try to sneak out the back. You think I should wash it out before I leave? Yes, I'm sure I can find the memorial to Vittorio Emanuele. How could I miss it? A bridge across the Tiber, the Ponte Sisto. I will ask someone here before I leave. I will see you soon—I hope."

"Grazie," John said to the clerk and handed her the phone. Do you know how I can get to the Ponte Sisto?"

"Si. I will draw you a map."

The clerk methodically mapped directions from the American University to the bridge and handed them to John. "It is a pedestrian bridge, very beautiful," she said. "Can I make more maps for after you cross?"

"No thank you. I can find my way from there."

"You have not been to Trastevere before?"

"No, I haven't. Is there a bathroom in this building I can use before I leave?"

She came out from behind the counter and directed him down one of the corridors to the rear of the building near the exit to the gardens.

The odor of the institutional soap was strong, but it did the job. The grayish white powder flowed down the drain as John slicked back his wet hair, washed his face, and dried himself as best he could. He took off the sunglasses and rumpled jacket to make himself more presentable before he exited the door into a garden where students gathered around tables. They were so engaged in conversation they hardly noticed when he walked past and left the grounds through the gardener's side gate.

The air was cool against his damp hair when he began his descent down the Janiculum Hill. He passed academies, embassies, fountains, and memorials never stopping to look, so fast he walked along the winding Via Garibaldi. Parks and greenery gave way to hotels, restaurants, and shops when he had reached the heart of the Trastevere district and the Ponto Sisto. By then his hair was dry.

Halfway across the Tiber he allowed himself a few minutes to take in the beautiful view the bridge afforded. On the side of the river he had just left, the dome of Saint Peter's Cathedral rose majestically, half in shadow and half in light. He turned away from the mighty church and soon was in a place he was better acquainted with, Campo dei Fiori. He passed the statue of Giordano Bruno near where they had eaten dinner their first night in Rome. The sight of it sent a shiver through him as he imagined Bruno come alive, his spirit resisting as his flesh succumbed to the flames of a cruel orthodoxy. He soon intersected with the Corso Vittorio Emanuele and began his march toward the memorial. He knew he was near when he saw the Church of the Jesuits; and although Prudence beckoned him with her mysteries hidden in plain sight, he did not enter. Less than an hour after he left the American University he had arrived at the Piazza Venezia.

Etienne stood on the steps of the monument to the great unifier. He waved John to stay where he was and made his way across the intersection with the assistance of a traffic cop who took pity on him. The two climbed into a taxi and went directly to Roma Termini. The large clock on the wall of the train station read half past two. They both wondered what would occur at the four o'clock appointment at the Basilica of Santa Maria Sopra Minerva when Barry's abductor would soon discover the basilica empty and silent, void of further apologies and recantations.

"Follow me," Etienne said. "We must board immediately."

"This train says Genova," John said.

"We cannot risk waiting for the evening train to Nice. We go there tomorrow."

The two men boarded a first class car for their five-hour trip to the northern industrial city. The hotel near the Genova train station was anything but first class; however, it offered them clean beds, a good night's sleep, and escape, which was all they required.

.

Chapter 46

New Clothes

S tuart bellowed, "Man, I'm hungry. If they don't get here soon, I'm going to risk it and go out to get something to eat." He rose up off the edge of his bed and paced in their very cramped room.

"Oh, sit down. It's probably no risk for you. It's me they're after," Barry said and continued to recline in his twin bed and watch babbling television commentators. "I hope they made it out okay," he added. "They should have been here by now."

"Crap happens," Stuart said, shrugging off Barry's concerns. "They'll show up soon enough, or I'm out of here. Man, I could use another beer." He walked over and flipped off the TV. "I can't handle any more of this French stuff."

"You could have asked me first," Barry said.

There was a tap at the door that Barry believed must be the maid come to make the beds. "She shouldn't bother," he said to Stuart as he rolled off the bed to answer it. At first he narrowly opened the door, but seeing John and Etienne standing in the hallway, one disheveled the other quite dapper and both a little damp from the rain, he opened the door wide and offered a full-throated greeting, "Welcome!"

"Sorry, we're late," John said. "I'm just glad we made it here."

"Did you think you wouldn't?" Stuart asked.

"I truly wondered when I was confronted by Felix in Rosa Palazio's office yesterday."

"For god sakes! Felix was there?" Barry said.

"He called you on the carpet right in front of me. What a ridiculous position I was in having to say I came to ask about Felix, and there he was bigger than life."

"I'm sorry John. I hadn't imagined that."

"On top of that, Rosa made me look a fool. She asked the obvious. Why hadn't you just phoned her if you had a question? I had to fumble through that one. Then I had to elude two men who had followed me all the way from the hotel if I didn't want to risk being kidnapped myself."

Hoping to diffuse John's passions, which had exploded like a time bomb, Etienne added, "John handled the situation remarkably well. His quick thinking got us out of Rome unscathed."

"Unscathed!" Stuart shouted. "I knew this was a boneheaded plan sending John to the American University. He could've just as well gone to a restaurant or a museum for a couple of hours while I got Barry out of town."

"If you thought the plan was so boneheaded, why didn't you say so?" Barry argued. "Anyway, I don't agree with you. It wouldn't have looked half as convincing. And by the way, I could have gotten myself out of town without your assistance."

"That's enough!" Etienne shouted. "What is all of this quarreling about? We are all here and unharmed. The statue is safely out of Italy. The plan worked. It was a complete success."

"I just wanted Barry to know what a dangerous situation I was in," John said.

"Believe me, I know," Barry replied, this time in a softer voice. "I never would have imagined in my wildest dreams you would walk into Rosa's office and find Felix. I wonder what the hell he was doing there? She doesn't like him much, you know."

"They were talking about you. That's what she said when I arrived. Then Felix turned on me. He called you a fraud, your statue a fraud. He claimed you intended to perpetrate a fraud on him and your entire profession."

"What?" Barry shouted.

"That's what he said. He said he had it from the highest authorities. He ordered me to tell you that if you continue, he will denounce you."

"Oh, now I'm beginning to see the outlines of their plan," Barry said. "That fellow who had me kidnapped told me he had gotten Felix off my back. What he didn't tell me was how he did it. He told him the statue is worthless. That cad acted like he had done me a big favor when in fact he had a two-pronged strategy. He wanted to get Felix out of his way, and he wanted to set in motion rumors that would ruin me."

"It's worse than that," John said, his anger turning to pity. "Felix called you a thief and said you were thrown out of Egypt last year for artifact smuggling."

"Well, you know I didn't do that. I put it back!" In a softer voice he asked, "How did Rosa react to all of these accusations?"

"She told me to send you her love and tell you to be careful. But unfortunately, I think she kind of believed him. She said that everyone was surprised when you gave up your Egyptian work last year and could only assume that you had gotten into some serious trouble."

"Well, of course I did get into some serious trouble, but not that kind. But I can't tell her or anyone else what went on without setting off a gold rush on the Giza plateau with everyone and their uncle trying to find that statue I put back."

"You put a valuable artifact back from where you uncovered it?" Etienne asked in astonishment.

"Yes, but that's another story."

"You are a noble soul," he said, and then brought the topic back to the matter at hand. "Our plan was a partial success anyhow. And at least we don't have to guess any longer about the means by which they plan to destroy your career. We are clear on that now." He took a few steps back and addressed the two men. "We are safe and the statue is safe, so we have accomplished quite a lot."

Noble soul, Barry thought, liking those words just ascribed to him. "Yes, we are safe and the statue was safely gotten out of Rome. That's quite an accomplishment," he agreed.

"Yeah, but we can't stay in this hotel room any longer," Stuart complained. "I'm hungry."

"It is very small," Etienne acknowledged. "I think we should rent a car and be on our way. Maybe stop someplace along the highway, get cleaned up, get some food, and tomorrow morning head for my sister's house."

"Man, I can't wait. I need something to eat now," Stuart howled.

"I will pick you up a roll or something when I go after a car, but we need to go somewhere less public and soon," Etienne said.

"I need some fresh clothes," Barry said.

"You can have your clothes back," John said.

"I don't believe I want them," Barry replied as a new self-image was taking shape in his mind. "Etienne was right. They look seedy."

"Thanks Barry! Not only did I have to go through a horrendous experience on your account, I had to wear your seedy clothes. They smell bad too. Did you know that?"

"I'm sorry John."

"Oh, I can hardly blame you. I can't wait to take them off. I tell you what. Since we're the same size, how about I go shopping and get you some new clothing while Etienne gets the car."

"After what happened yesterday, you're far too recognizable," Stuart argued.

"Who is going to recognize me? I was made up to look like Barry."

"You're probably right," Stuart admitted.

"You might be surprised," Etienne added. "Information travels fast on the internet."

Stuart stared at Etienne for a moment wondering if he really is only a banker. "Tell you what John. Get out of Barry's smelly clothes and take a shower. I'll buy him some new ones. I might even buy some duds for myself," he said, after taking a whiff of his own underarm.

"Good plan," Etienne agreed, feigning a cool, calm demeanor, although all the squabbling was wearing on his nerves. "I'm happy everyone has settled down. Stuart, you come with me."

Taking Stuart in tow on the streets of Nice turned out not to be such a good idea. If Etienne had been alone, he might not have been noticed. If Stuart had been alone, he probably would have gone unnoticed too. But the two of them together made them both highly recognizable since photos taken in Montserrat had been circulated on the internet for a number of days now among certain secretive parties. And just two days ago a new batch of photos had been released, taken in Rome near the Piazza Navona, which included pictures of Etienne and Stuart.

Thanks to this unfortunate lapse in judgment, Stuart was identified as he made his purchase of pants, shirts, sport jackets, socks, and underwear, all charged to his federal government expense account. Etienne was observed renting a large van, big enough to hold the entire group once they were together again. Their hotel quickly became known, as well as the fact that they checked out later that day. The route they took when they drove out of the city did not escape notice either.

But for some unknown reason the car that had followed them out of Nice picked up speed and passed them on the highway before they had reached the environs of Cannes where they would stay the night.

***

Instead of garden dresses and gowns, Madame Conti bought all three women identical slacks, shirts, sweaters, jackets, sensible shoes, and flannel nightgowns. The weather had grown quite chilly, she explained, and Cinzia lived away from the fineries of city life. Summer was not sure exactly what she meant. Did she mean fineries of only city life or did she mean fineries of life in general? She hoped only the former as she surveyed the empty landscape they drove through from the window of the limousine.

The driver had just circled Arles and was now headed south along a much narrower highway. "We should be there shortly," Madame Conti said. Dappled sunshine broke through fast moving clouds and spread across the great swath of flat, marshy land on either side of them. "This area is known as the Camargue," she said, assuming rightly that neither of her traveling companions had ventured into this remote place.

"Madame," the driver said. "A car has been behind us since we turned south from Arles."

"So? We are not the only people going to Saintes-Maries-de-la-Mer. There is no surprise in that."

"Madame, I would not have mentioned it but the same car has been behind us on the highway all the way from Cannes. I thought little of it until it turned south behind us."

She looked out of the rear window of the limousine. "I do not see anything."

"It has stayed well behind us. When the road curves it disappears only to reappear."

"There is probably nothing to it," she said uneasily.

"Look! White horses!" Summer said, pointing to a herd galloping in the distance.

"There are hundreds of horses such as these in the Camargue," Madame Conti said. "I believe they are indigenous to the area. They

261

run wild, or sometimes the gardians mount them to help tend their bulls."

"Bulls!" Rosalind said, having noted that they had passed a bullring in Arles. "Who are gardians?"

"Your American word might be 'cowboys.' They breed bulls here for the ring in Arles and Saintes-Maries-de-la-Mer. It's a very popular sport down here." Noting her companions' distressed faces she said, "They don't kill the bulls here as they do in Spain."

"Oh, good. Are those Flamingos?" Rosalind asked.

"Driver, slow down," Madame Conti ordered. The car slowed while they observed an entire flock of the pink and white birds standing on twiggy legs near a marshy pond. "You are lucky to see them. People come here from all over to see the Flamingos."

"Oh, they're beautiful!" Summer said.

"Madame, that car again."

Madame Conti bent around to look out of the rear window, this time seeing the car her driver had warned her of. It slowed behind them nearly to a stop as if its passengers were likewise interested in observing the birds.

"Very suspicious," she said. "But there is nothing we can do now. We are almost there."

The driver sped up. The car to the rear of them began to move too, cautiously at first, until it achieved the same distance behind the limousine that it had earlier.

The long flat plains of the Camargue stretched out for many miles with no sign of a country estate or any other structure until they arrived in the modest seaside village. Summer's hopes were dashed when they pulled in front of a white washed stucco two-story row house with a clay tile roof that looked much the same as all the other houses that lined the street, except that it had a lavender door.

"I would not know it any other way," Madame Conti said of the lavender. "They all look so much alike."

Standing inside the front door when it opened was a very pretty girl, with brown eyes and long dark hair who looked to be in her late twenties.

"Cinzia darling!" her grandmother said.

"Mamie," the girl replied and threw her arms around Madame Conti in a most exuberant manner. Then she looked up at the other guests.

"These are your brother's friends I told you about."

Cinzia smiled, threw the door open wide and stood back. "Welcome to my house. I have rooms made up for you upstairs." Christabel eagerly jumped up and down at her knee, instinctively recognizing a friend. "Ah, a petite caniche!" she said, picking the little dog up and letting it lick her face.

Christabel looked like a petite caniche even more so now since her grooming session at the Carleton. She had a poof on her head, a poof on her tail, and a little poof above each paw.

"There will be little luggage," Madame Conti said while holding on to her night case. The driver carried their shopping bags up to their rooms.

The cottage, while simple, was elegant in its simplicity. Two off-white couches flanked the stone fireplace that was burning a low steady fire to keep the chill off. A walnut coffee table topped with two neat piles of books, magazines, and journals stood between the two couches. The rug was creamy white with brightly colored red, French blue, and yellow patterns. French blue and off-white checkered curtains with yellow ribbon trim hung from the windows and were pulled far back on their iron rods admitting all the light possible on a cloudy day. A large vase of dried lavender stood on a stand near the door emitting its sensuous relaxing scent. The kitchen was simple, with walnut cabinetry and an old fashion sink. Yet it was equipped with top of the line kitchen appliances, no doubt a gift from grand-mère, who nonetheless continued to complain about the charming home her granddaughter chose to live in.

"Come, sit down. I have made some soup for you," Cinzia said, ushering them into the dining room. There was a large, heavy rectangular table made out of the same fine walnut as the coffee table. The place settings were Provencal, with red, yellow, and turquoise mats and napkins. But what really caught one's attention was a black iron chandelier twisted to look at once like an anchor and a heart. Pieces of cut crystal and colored glass hung from its rungs, capturing the passing sunlight that entered the room through the large rear window when the clouds opened up. Outside were the remains of a well-tended garden in another season, with a few hearty herb plants still producing.

"I love this house! It's perfect," Summer said.

"Cinzia has a talent for doing quite a lot with very little," Madame Conti admitted. "She has had this talent for as long as I can remember. She used to enjoy making her dolls when she was a child. I could never understand why. She has made all of her own curtains here."

"They look very nice," Rosalind said.

Cinzia placed a large white soup tureen on the table with scenes from the sea painted in blues and greens, trimmed in Provencal yellow, with a large yellow fish for a handle. She lifted the lid and served steamy bowls of bouillabaisse made with shellfish caught that morning. The broth was clear and enhanced with tomatoes, leeks, potatoes, and garlic. A plate of freshly cut bread was piled high, and each of them was given a small bowl of a spread called rouille, made from olive oil, garlic, and saffron with red pepper. A sumptuous fruit tart sat on the sideboard across from the head of the table. Before she sat down to join them, she placed a plate of sausage and a bowl of water on the floor next to the table for a delighted Christabel.

"I thought a simple meal would do," she said. "We can dine out at one of the restaurants tomorrow. They do so need the business in the off-season."

"Do not be modest," her grandmother said. "This is a feast." Cinzia blushed. "I am hoping you will take us for a walk to the church after dinner and tell the girls about the local legends you have studied." At that, the quiet girl quickly regained her composure. There was nothing she liked better to do.

"So that's what you do here," Rosalind said, curious as to why she lived in this out of the way place. "You study the local legends."

"That's what I have done since I was twenty-two. I came her to do a university project and fell in love," she gushed.

"What happened to him?" Rosalind asked, seeing no trace of a man anywhere in her home.

"It was not a man she fell in love with. It was this place, the people," Madame Conti explained. "She has quite a reputation here as a scholar and guide."

"Yes," Cinzia said, her complexion now crimson. "It is the place that I love. It is hard to explain, but it was as if I found my soul mate in its culture, not in its men. They are too rough."

264

"Rough?" Summer asked.

"They are fishermen and gardians. They are not scholars."

"Many are gypsies," Madame Conti added.

"Gitans," Cinzia corrected.

"Gitans are French gypsies," Madame Conti replied. "They don't appreciate the idea of a woman being such a scholar as my Cinzia has become. But there was one, not too many years ago, a musician I believe."

Cinzia blushed again, but this time without the exuberance that characterized her smile. "Yes, him. He played beautiful Flamenco guitar. He was self-educated, a poet."

"What happened?" Rosalind asked.

"Oh, he said something like his life was a journey while mine was to stay here."

"Many musicians come here for the festival in May," Madame Conti said. "Mostly gypsies, so they do not stay."

"He was not Gitan," Cinzia said. "But he wanted to live the life. He comes to see me sometimes when he is passing through. We are still friends."

"I'm sorry," Rosalind said, seeing in Cinzia's face the pain the memory of this man aroused. Turning to Madame Conti she asked after the festival she had alluded to.

"Let Cinzia explain."

"It revolves around the three Marys and Sarah. Have you heard the legend that Mary Magdalene came to France after the crucifixion?"

"How can you be in France for any time and not hear of it?" Rosalind said.

"You are right about that," she laughed. "But she was not the only one. According to legend Mary Magdalene, Marie Salome, and Marie Jacobe along with Lazarus, Joseph of Arimathea, and others were forced to escape persecution in the Holy Land and sailed from Alexandria across the Mediterranean, landing here in Saintes-Maries-de-la-Mer. That is of course how the town got its name. Mary Magdalene and the others were to have traveled further into France. Exactly where is in dispute. But Marie Salome and Marie Jacobe remained here. Their relics are in our local church, Notre-Dame-de-la-Mer."

"What do you mean by relics?" Summer asked.

"Their bones," Rosalind said.

"Oh...so who is Marie Salome and Marie Jacobe?" Summer asked.

"They were Jesus' disciples. As to their exact identities, that remains in dispute. Some say Marie Salome was his aunt and that Marie Jacobe was the sister of Mary mother of Christ, which of course would make her his aunt too. So others say Marie Salome and Marie Jacobe are really the same person. Regardless, here in Saintes-Maries-de-la-Mer they are venerated saints who are believed to have great power. Every May their statues and relics are paraded through the streets in celebration while pilgrims try to touch them to receive their blessings."

"Tell them about Sarah," Madame Conti said.

"Sara-la-Kali, Saint Sarah. I did not know about her before I came here, but she is why I have stayed."

"Who is she?" Summer asked.

"She is the patron saint of the gypsies," Cinzia replied. "I guess I did not tell you. The religious celebration here is known as pèlerinage des Gitans, the gypsy pilgrimage."

Summer's eyes grew wide. "Oh!" she said. "What's it like? Is there music?"

"Oh yes," Cinzia answered. "There is lots and lots of music, and it is fascinating to see. They take Sarah down to the sea as if to purify her. Do you want to see her? If we leave now, we can walk to the church before it closes."

Chapter 47

Weaving the Tapestry

Winter's nip did not bother the women, nor did the two gypsies wrapped in shawls who stood in the lighted plaza outside the Romanesque church asking for money in a dialect none but Cinzia understood. She told them to be gone and pulled her new friends inside the fortress-like building whose architecture contradicted the delicacy of its name: "Our Lady by the Sea." She led them through the dark, stone crypt to where Saint Sarah stands crowned and robed outside the sanctuary. Hundreds of devotional candles radiated light onto her crown, her robe, and her face, promising to bless all who seek her aid. Her expression tells a sad story, her prettiness amplified in hints of sorrow.

"She's another Black Madonna!" Summer said.

"She's dressed the same," Rosalind said, admiring her crown and glittering gown.

"You know the Black Madonna?" Cinzia asked.

"Do we ever," Summer said. "We first saw her in Mende. That was creepy."

"We saw her again in Rocamadour and again in Montserrat," Rosalind said.

"You have been on tour," Cinzia said. "You must be on a pilgrimage, yes?"

"Of sorts," Rosalind answered. "An unintentional one."

"She does look like them," Cinzia said. "But Sarah is said to be a Saint, by the gypsies anyway. The church doesn't recognize her as such."

"But she's here in the church," Rosalind said.

"Outside the official sanctuary. They tolerate her because, well, if they did otherwise, they would lose their flock of gypsies."

"What does the church say about her?" Rosalind asked.

"Very little. The official legend claims that Sarah was an Egyptian servant who accompanied the three Marys from Alexandria."

"Official legend! That's an oxymoron," Rosalind said. "A legend by its very nature is unofficial."

"Religious legends are a little different," Cinzia explained. "While their stories are not biblical, their characters are. There is no biblical account of the three Marys leaving the Holy Land for France, for example; but there are references to the three Marys in the Bible. When these two elements, biblical and non-biblical, combine into a single legend that serves to validate the history the legend purports, the church tolerates these hybrids, which is what I mean by official legend. But they don't tolerate legends that spring wholly from outside the Bible. There is no biblical account of Sarah, and yet she is adored by the gypsies and put up with by the church, who have reduced her to a maidservant on the ship that brought the Marys."

"It seems almost racist," Rosalind said.

"The motive may only have been to provide her a small part. I came here to study what I now call the official legend because that was all I knew. But when I discovered the unofficial account, the one with no biblical basis, the one that the Gitan tell, it led me to so many places I never had intended that my mind became free, almost like a gypsy," she laughed.

Summer could barely contain herself. "What does it say, the unofficial one?"

"That Sara-la-Kali, as they call her, was a Gitane like themselves, a sort of priestess or queen with visionary insight. On the night when the ship carrying the disciples approached the coast, there was a great storm that caused their ship to capsize. The priestess Sarah, using her visionary gifts, was able to see the entire event in her mind's eye and brought help to the disciples who would have otherwise drowned. This great event wedded Sarah and the disciples, and thus Sarah to Christianity. It is why the Gitan worship here, why they are Christian at all."

"You called her Sara-la-Kali. Isn't Kali an Indian goddess?" Rosalind asked.

"Yes, she is. The Gitan originally came from India hundreds of years ago. It means blackness."

"And the Black Madonna," Rosalind said. "Sarah looks like one, and the stories the Gitan tell about her remind me of the Black Madonna of Rocamadour who is supposed to protect seafarers."

"You see, that's what I have learned," Cinzia said. "These stories, legends, and beliefs are all so alike and yet they are different in subtle ways. But these subtle differences have little to do with the kernel of the legends and more to do with the cultures where they exist and the passage of time. If I could only see the whole, I think I would see into the great mystery obscured by time and culture, maybe war and conquest too, and who knows what else."

"Mesdames, nous sommes de clôture," said a priest who seemed to appear out of nowhere. "Puis-je vous aider?"

Cinzia turned to the others. "They are closing now. We have to leave. We can go back to my house and talk."

Maybe it was the rush of the wind or maybe it was the plaintive chords of a violin coming from across the street. Whatever the cause, the night had come to feel melancholy. No violinist was in evidence. Even the two gypsy women had disappeared into the warmth of their homes. Perhaps the sounds came from someone practicing or someone playing for the joy of it behind closed doors, although there seemed little joy in the music being made. Yet there was a deep beauty. Before they left the desolate plaza they surveyed the exterior of the church.

"It looks like a fortress," Rosalind said.

"It was at one time both church and fortress."

Rosalind spied a cross affixed on one of its walls and recognized it from the extraordinary chandelier in Cinzia's dining room.

"Your chandelier!" she said.

"No, the Cross of Camargue. I had my chandelier made from its design."

"It's most unusual."

"It represents the spirit of the place. The cross at the top is at once a cross and trident, a tool used by the gardians when they herd the bulls. The anchor at the bottom is for the fishermen. The heart in the middle, I take to be the heart of Sarah and the two Marys whose crypt we just visited. It is a good heart that will protect us all."

"No wonder you stay here."

"Yes, but it is cold now. Let us go home."

They gathered around the fire that Cinzia had stoked into hot flames and had tea and hot chocolate and ate fruit tart. Summer was wrapped up in a blanket on the couch she shared with Rosalind and Christabel. Cinzia and her grandmother sat together on the couch opposite. Dishes were still spread across the dining room table and dirty pans filled the sink, but there was hardly time to clean up, so engaged the women were in conversation.

"I wish I could say the berries came from my garden, but as you can see we are passed the growing season," Cinzia said.

"You said something that really interested me back at the church," Rosalind said. "You said that since you've been here you've learned to see the whole picture."

"Maybe not the whole picture but a much bigger one," Cinzia said. "I first became interested in the sea motif because it is so common. It is not just our Marys here in Saintes-Maries-de-la-Mer. As you mentioned, the Black Madonna of Rocamadour is thought to protect fishermen and other seafarers. One could say that it all has to do with occupation, as fishing can be very dangerous and the sea in general is unpredictable. But I began to think there was something more to it. There are so many sea goddesses...the legendary mermaids. And there are others, many others, Yemaja, for example."

"Who?" Rosalind asked.

"Yemaja. She is Yoruban, their divine goddess of the sea. She is similar to the great earth mothers, but in her case a sea mother. Her children are like the fish, meaning there are great multitudes of them."

"Oh, a fertility goddess," Rosalind said.

"More than that. In Yoruban tradition, Yemaja brought forth life, all of it, including the other gods. So I reason she cannot be understood simply as a fertility goddess. No, there is a finer point here. Yemaja is thought to be the source of life, not just its perpetuator. In Brazil and some other parts of the Americas, African slaves associated her with the Virgin Mary once they came into contact with Christianity. For them the two are one."

"Why did they link them?" Rosalind asked.

"Probably because their Portuguese masters often referred to Mary as

Nossa Senhora dos Navegantes, Our Lady of the Seafaring. Their description of Mary was so like Yemaja that for these Africans the two became synonymous. Sometimes Yemaja is portrayed as a mermaid. So I asked myself, how can this be? Mary, mermaids, Yemaja, all with different names yet combined into one. How many times have myths commingled in this way? Or more importantly, how many times has one goddess been fragmented into many?"

"So, you're saying the Black Madonna at Rocamadour, the Virgin, the Marys here, Sarah, Yemaja are fragments?" Rosalind asked.

"Yes, that is what I'm saying."

"Remember the dream I had about the Black Madonna in Mende?" Summer said. "I dreamed there was a golden clam shell above her, and we found out there is. It was just so dark when we saw her that I hadn't noticed, at least not consciously."

"There you have it," Cinzia said. "Venus rising from the sea. She is everywhere!"

"Well, Cinzia, this will fascinate you further," Madame Conti said as she opened her night case. The firelight glimmered on the statue's copper crown. Her eyes blazed.

"Oh Mon Dieu! Where did you ever find such a thing?"

"I did not." Madame Conti looked over at Rosalind and Summer. "I should say we did not. It came to me quite by accident. A friend of your brother's, and I might add their friend too, brought it back from Egypt. An old monk found it in the cellar of a Christian monastery near the Red Sea. He asked our friend, a noted archeologist, to bring it to Europe and try to identify who she is. Someone else, who wants it badly it seems, threatened this man in Rome. Your brother asked me to take it out of Italy and bring it to you."

"Grand-mère, now you are a smuggler."

"I am no such thing! Barry Short is the smuggler but with good intentions. So, what do you think?"

"I think she is amazing!"

"Look at the runic marks on her. I found them in one of Marija Gimbutas' books."

"Marija," Rosalind said. "Isn't that another form of Mary?"

"Yes, the Lithuanian form of the name," Cinzia replied.

"I'm beginning to feel like I'm swimming in Marys."

Cinzia, who by now had become used to swimming in Marys did not comment. Instead, she continued her discussion with her grandmother. "Then she is very old."

"The runes are Magdalenian, but we think she might have come later, shortly after their decline but while the language was still known."

"Are these feathers or scales?" Cinzia asked, looking at the markings on her back.

"It is difficult to tell, but I think she could be one of Gimbutas' bird goddesses, perhaps the original. Look at her hair."

"Yes," Cinzia agreed. "Maybe she is both, goddess of the sea and sky. Her eyes!"

"They are very reflective," Madame Conti replied. "And the crown. It is a mirror."

"How do you know that is how it was meant?" Cinzia asked.

"Well, it is made from copper, is it not? That is the material they used to make mirrors. The poem is quite telling. One line is definitive. It says that she holds the mirror of the world. Cinzia, I believe her to be a Sophia, maybe the Sophia."

"Grand-mère, do you know what you are saying?"

"I know very well."

"I thought Prudence was a Sophia?" Summer said.

"She is my dear," Madame Conti replied. "They all may be. They are just not given credit."

"Oh, yes, Prudence with her mirror," Cinzia said.

"Your brother's friend had become quite interested in the Prudence figure who stands in the Jesuit Church in Rome. I explained to him the deeper meaning of her symbology."

"Barry was directed to that statue by a monk who lives in Narbonne," Rosalind explained. "Hans Bueller, the man who found this statue in the cellar of a monastery in Egypt, asked Barry to contact this monk because he might know something. Well, Barry did, and the monk told him to go to Rome and study the statue. He didn't even identify her for him; he only told Barry the location. It was all very secretive. The rest of us were left in the dark until after we had arrived there."

"It was bizarre," Summer said. "Barry stood in one corner of this large room and the monk, his name is Brother Thomas, stood in another. It looked like they were just standing there silently diagonally opposite each other, but Barry told us later that Brother Thomas was talking to him, and his voice somehow traveled through the walls and ceiling of the room from one corner to another, but we couldn't hear anything."

"They were speaking in an acoustic chamber," Cinzia said.

"It just looked like a brick room," Rosalind said.

"It is very ritualistic to do such a thing," Cinzia said. "This Brother Thomas must have thought that what he wished to tell Barry was very esoteric."

"Look at where it led him," Madame Conti said. "Telling him to go there raised his curiosity. He was determined to find out who Prudence is, to really find out who she is."

"Why couldn't anyone at the Jesuit Church identify her?" Rosalind asked.

"As I have said before, none are given credit," Madame Conti replied. "They have not been for so long that their true meaning is all but lost. I doubt that those people in charge at church were trying to deceive you. They did not know themselves. Benign neglect, I call it, or perhaps intentional neglect. Only a few know the truth about anything, and many of them keep it from us. All they have accomplished in their keeping of secrets is to make most of us ignorant and to make these goddesses seem so inconsequential that we pay little attention to them and, as a consequence, to ourselves."

"Or it could be the passage of time and the prejudice of culture has erased our memories?" Cinzia said.

"It all works together," her grandmother said. "Time, prejudice, and intent."

"It is interesting that you should bring up Prudence's mirror," Cinzia said. "Yemaja holds a mirror too. Yet its meaning has been reduced in ritual ceremonies to represent vanity. Believers throw cosmetics as offerings into the ocean of this queen of the sea."

"They have forgotten," her grandmother said. "They understand the mirror only in a functional sense. It is a wonder that they bother to have any ritual at all. Look at Sarah. If you think she was only a servant, hardly deserving to be on the same boat with those she served, she is of little consequence. Yet we have the devotional candles of the Gitan as evidence that they think otherwise. They must have a long memory to have maintained their beliefs."

"Grand-mère, the Gitan were not forced into slavery on the other side of the ocean."

"Yes, yes, I know dear. But who pays any attention to them. They too are marginalized and so too are their beliefs. Yet what they say feels true because it is so like the other legends, the old ones. These women bring forth the light. Their mirrors are their instruments."

"What do the mirrors symbolize?" Cinzia asked her grandmother.

"Their souls of course, their minds. They can see backwards and forwards with insight and foresight that they mercifully bring to bear on us poor mortals through their compassionate soul."

"And they bring forth life, all the fishes in the sea and the birds in air," Cinzia added. "And not just as fertility goddesses or holy wombs."

"You are right!" her grandmother proclaimed. "Not through fertility but through creation. The light is creation, and that is who the Sophia is. She is the last emanation, and through her light becomes material. If she has that kind of power, those who fear her would believe she also has the power to withdraw herself. We could all be obliterated in an instant."

"So is she the Sophia?" Summer asked looking at the statue's wide eyes and delicate turns.

"She may be it. Let Cinzia read the poem when the others come."

"She does look a like a bird," Summer remarked, looking intently at the statue as if she had just met up with a long lost friend and was studying the ways time had changed her. "And birds fly high, sometimes into the sun."

"Into the light," Madame Conti declared, "into the heavens."

Chapter 48

Invasion

Plates, mugs, and the remains of the tart still lay on the coffee table when the women went up to bed after an exhilarating peek behind a door too long closed. Bowls, plates, silverware, and the fish knobbed soup tureen were spread across the dining room table, unmoved from where they had been left after their late day meal. The kitchen sink and counter was a jumble of pots and pans and cutting boards and knives. Madame Conti had urged Cinzia to go to sleep and leave the cleanup for the next morning when she would help, and that is exactly what she had done.

All was quiet but for the occasional crackle of embers in the fireplace. Christabel, who had been upstairs asleep, rose to get a drink of water from her bowl in the kitchen. She stopped at the top of the stairs and surveyed what lay below in this cozy but unfamiliar house before prancing downstairs to her bowl. She lapped the water, stopped and froze in an attentive position. She relaxed, took a few more laps of water, froze again. Her eyes stared off in a fixed direction as if she thought she had heard something but wasn't sure. A muffled thud against the front door set her wild with barking. The next thud was louder. She barked and barked, focusing her attention on the door, whose center pushed inward as if a great boulder were about to shake it from its frame. She ran upstairs to safety and barked to alert the women. Her bark faded into a guttural growl when Summer came out into the hallway.

"What's wrong Christabel?" She reached down to pet the dog, hoping to calm her.

"What's going on?" Rosalind said when she joined them in the hall.

A loud thud and then a huge crash came from the downstairs. Rosalind screamed. Cinzia and Madame Conti came out into the hall but were hard pressed to be heard over Christabel's barking.

"You're being broken into!" Rosalind shouted.

"What?" Cinzia replied, unable to comprehend such a crime in her sleepy little town.

"Do you have a weapon?" Madame Conti asked her.

"Only these," Cinzia said. She opened the hall closet door and took out a broom and a dust mop.

"I will take that," Madame Conti said and grabbed the broom, held it stick forward, and slowly climbed down the stairs.

"You cannot go alone," Cinzia said and took the dust mop and followed her.

Rosalind picked up Christabel and shut her in the bedroom, and she and Summer followed behind.

"Qui est ce?" Madame Conti shouted as she neared the bottom of the stairway.

Three men stood in the living room looking up at the women as they slowly came down the steps. One of them, a tall, thin man with angular features and thinning hair stood apart from the other two who were stoutly built. Instead of a jacket, he wore a dark gray sweater and a long crimson muffler that wrapped around his neck and hung to his waist. He looked at the women with an air of confident composure, as if he had every right to be where he stood.

"Sorry to disturb you," he said in a tone dripping with sarcasm. "We have come for something that belongs to us."

Cinzia, holding her dust mop, moved in front of her grandmother. "This is my house. Nothing here belongs to you."

The man ignored her and looked towards her grandmother. "That stolen statue that the thief Barry Short absconded with belongs to me. Hand it over now!"

Cinzia spoke up, "If it is stolen as you say, why did you not send the police?"

"I hoped to avoid having Barry put behind bars. I hoped to appeal to you good women to do what is best for him and turn it over."

"If this is such a friendly request, why did you not knock? Why did you break into my house like thieves in the night?"

His eyes went steely gray for a few seconds and then softened as he regained his composure. "There was no time. You would not have heard me at the door," he said, apparently unaware that the incessant

276

barking of the dog now shut in the bedroom upstairs rendered his words false.

"Do not lie to me!" Cinzia shouted. "I am not stupid. You are the thief, not this man you speak of, this Barry Short."

His expression turned to stone but soon morphed into a sneer. He signaled one of his compatriots with the wave of a hand. The burley thug snatched Cinzia in a flash, knocking the dust mop out of her hand when he yanked her arm behind her back wrenching it so badly she grimaced in pain. "Now, Madame Conti, I had hoped this might be a friendly exchange, but it will not be so friendly if you do not turn the statue over to me immediately."

"It is not here," she said coolly. "If you really believed that it was, you would have your man here quit these theatrics and search for it."

"Madame, rest assured that I know you brought it with you from Rome. If it is not here, as you say, you had better get it fast if you want to minimize the damage done to your beloved granddaughter."

His thug wrenched Cinzia's arm again, this time hard enough to make her cry out in pain.

"I am sure I do not know where it is or why you would say such things. But you had better let her go right now or I will see you behind bars," she said, her temper flaring.

"Perhaps I need to make myself more clear on how far I'm prepared to go. He signaled his second man, a brute in his muscularity.

The man leered at Summer, delighted it seemed to be ordered to do his obviously preplanned part. He ripped the sleeve from her flannel nightgown as if a prelude to tearing it off, forced her to the floor with his full weigh upon her and silenced her screams with a rough kisses as she fought in vain to push him off.

Madame Conti, unable to contain herself any longer and willing to risk it all to prevent the outrage unfolding before her, beat him mercilessly with her broom until at last he let Summer go. Streams of blood ran down his face. Hands that had torn at Summer now protected his head from further blows. He was done with this fight. Her eyes fierce as if she had been driven to near madness, Madame Conti next beat the arms and hands of the man who held her granddaughter until he freed her and cowered under heavy wallops that did not cease even after he let her go. She beat him and beat him, stopping only when the broom handle split. Furious, he picked up the fallen piece and struck Madame Conti with it across the face.

Cinzia grabbed the weapon nearest her, the heavy clay platter with leftover tart and smashed it across her assailant's face. Following her lead, Rosalind took the two heaviest books from a pile next to the wall and hurled them at the man who had accosted her sister. Summer spied their leader backing away towards the front door and snatched the nearby vase, lavender and all, and flung it against his head. He began to bleed and became fierce.

Like angry bulls, the men repositioned themselves into one solid block, backing the women into the dining room, pushing them towards the table still covered with dirty dishes. Each of the women picked up a plate and lobbed it at the approaching menace as they were being herded into the rear of the room.

"It is ours!" the thin man shouted. "It has been ours for centuries. You have no right to it!"

"We have every right to her!" Madame Conti shouted back.

"We know who she is now!" Cinzia screamed, tears streaming from her eyes. "You cannot steal that away. It is too late!"

"No one will believe you," he said in an indignant tone.

"Why?" Summer argued, "I do. I know who she is, and knowing that has taught me who I am. Deep down I think I always knew, but it took her to awaken my memory."

Her statement articulated a truth that had grown in the women during their night of conversation, had filled their being with the budding joy of a new found purpose not fully realized or understood. It must be added that it filled these men with dread and fury. They rushed at the women, who grabbed bowls that had earlier held soup and threw them at their heads.

"Leave!" Cinzia shouted, moving forward, her eyes a cold blaze of determination. "Leave now!"

The two men looked at their leader as if seeking another signal. Recognizing fear in the eyes of his compatriots, the tall man grimaced, backed into the kitchen, and grabbed the large knife Cinzia had earlier used to cut and clean shellfish. He came at her with it, overwhelmed with anger at the humiliation these women had wrought upon his companions. She threw her lovely soup tureen in his face. Stunned by the blow, he pulled back, which gave her time to slip behind the table with the other women. His face contorted into a malicious grin; he signaled his two companions to join him. All three men violently shoved the heavy walnut table forward with the intent to pin the women against the dining room wall. Recognizing what was about to happen, Cinzia shouted, "Push!" The women pushed back as hard as they could, causing the rest of the plates and cutlery to crash to the floor and rattling the low hanging chandelier with the force of their bodies. The men shoved back in a fierce counteroffensive, their weight crashing harder against the chandelier that had begun to spin and swirl so forcefully that its chain dislodged, dropping its iron mass into the chest of the man who stood under it. The hook of the anchor of the Cross of Camargue had plunged into the heart of the leader. He did not suffer. His death was immediate. The two remaining men looked in horror at his bleeding body slumped over the table, pierced by the chandelier that still lay under him.

"Witches!" one of them shouted as they backed away and fled through the front door they had earlier pushed in.

Chapter 49

Aftermath

Cinzia reached down to pick up fragments of the platter she had served her fruit tart from the night before.

"You mustn't do that dear, not until the police have come," her grandmother warned. "They said it would be only a few minutes."

The sun was rising, but a chilly melancholy had spread across the house. Summer and Rosalind sat together on one of the white couches wrapped in blankets with Christabel between them. Cinzia stared at her broken crockery lying shattered on the floor. She looked past the corpse as if it were not there, as if he had never been there. Sirens blared.

"They are here now," Madame Conti said, putting her arm around her granddaughter while walking her over to the other couch. "You sit down. I will get the door."

Madame Conti opened the broken door carefully so as not to pull it further from its hinges. Three police officers entered, the younger stopped to inspect the lavender portal.

"Là bas," Madame Conti said, pointing to the dead man on the table.

"Je n'ai jamais vu rien de pareil!" the sober faced officer in charge said as he studied the body that lay pierced through the heart with the black iron Cross of Camargue.

"We have some Americans here," Madame Conti replied. "If you could speak English, it would make it easier."

"Oui Madame. How did this happen?" he asked gravely.

"They had us pinned behind the table," Cinzia said, her words quivering as if she were very cold, very frightened or both. "They were shoving us against the wall when we pushed back. They pushed forward harder and the chandelier broke from the ceiling and struck him."

"They?" the officer asked as he looked about.

"There were two other men with this one," a more composed Madame Conti said. "They fled right after the accident."

"Why were they pushing you against the wall?"

"They wanted to kill us!" Summer said and began to sob.

The young officer who had been photographing the body pointed to the large kitchen knife still grasped tightly in the corpse's hand.

"He threatened you with that knife?" the lead officer asked.

"Yes," Cinzia answered. "He took it from my kitchen."

"After they had already grabbed her and wrenched her arm behind her back," Madame Conti said.

"Another one tried to tear my nightgown off," Summer said raising her bare arm.

"I believe the threat to you was greater than that, my dear," Madame Conti said coolly.

The grave officer looked about at the broken dishes, the snapped broom stick, the dust mop, the spatters of blood on the rug, the hurled books, the cut across Madame Conti's cheek and said with a momentary wry smile, "It looks like you put up a very good fight." His tone stiffened. "Do you know these men?"

"I have never seen them before," Rosalind said, rubbing Christabel's white furry tummy, as she lay sprawled out on her lap. "My little dog here woke us up barking as they were breaking into the house."

"Christabel saved the day," Summer concurred. "Otherwise they would have found us in our beds." The thought sent chills down her spine as she recalled the weight upon her, the foul taste of the man's mouth.

The officer looked over at Cinzia.

"No, I did not recognize them," she said. "They claimed I had an artifact that belonged to them. I told them I have nothing that belongs to them."

"You are a researcher in the historic?" the officer asked, having already recognized her, as she was rather well known in town.

"Yes, I am, but I am not a collector of artifacts."

The officer looked around her house. There were plenty of books but no artifacts on her walls, shelves, and tables, which seemed to satisfy him.

"He is not from here," the officer asserted, never having seen the deceased before in the Camargue. "We will search him for identification at the police station. My officer will take photos and ask each of you a few questions for our written report; then you may clean up. I will send someone to fix your door and perhaps reinforce it in case the others should come back, but I do not think they will. You did a remarkable job of frightening them off."

"Thank you officer," Madame Conti said.

Barry, Stuart, John, and Etienne had pulled up in time to see two officers place a stretcher in the van they had parked behind. They spied the lead officer sitting inside his vehicle on his phone as they cautiously looked on. They didn't pinpoint the exact location of the trouble until Etienne observed the broken lavender door ajar and knew it was inside his sister's house.

The officer lowered his window when Etienne began pounding it. "That is my sister's house!" he said in a panic.

"She is fine," the office said. "She has been broken into."

Relieved, he waved at the others who got out of their van and joined him inside.

"You are here! I am so happy," Madame Conti cried as she wrapped her arms around her grandson.

Summer turned while still sitting on the couch answering police questions. She lifted her arm to show him her ripped nightgown.

"What has happened here?" he asked his grandmother.

"They broke into the house looking for your statue. I denied everything. They employed every means of torture to extract her whereabouts from me. They twisted your poor sister's arm to the point I thought they might break it off. But worst of all a brute of a man nearly raped your friend Summer. Right here on the floor too! Right in front of us! He would have too if I had not beaten him nearly to death with my broom."

Summer's tears turned to sobs at the sound of the word and the image painted of the near deed. Strange she had not thought of it herself until Madame Conti said the word. Not so strange really. It was too intolerable to imagine. Even now she tried to block the thought, tried to convince herself that was not her assailant's intent. He was only trying to frighten her and make them talk. But the word once uttered had power to bring the horror back and defeat her attempt at denial. She relived the violent rip of her gown, the chill air against her naked arm, his

282

massive weight pressing hard against her, and the foul taste of his kisses. Unable to continue with the interview, she rose from the couch and stumbled towards the stairs. Etienne caught her as she nearly fell.

"I think I'm going to be sick," she said.

"I will help you," he said and led her up the stairway. He waited outside the bathroom listening to her retch. "Are you all right?" he called from the hallway.

"I think so," she said and came out into the hall.

He gently kissed her head. "I should never have let you go on such a dangerous mission, none of you." Then he too began to sob. "I nearly lost you, my grandmother, my sister as well."

"Etienne!" his grandmother called up the stairs. "Your friends are wondering where you are."

"Go clean yourself up while I attend to things," he said and kissed her cheek.

"I will talk to the police," he told his grandmother when he returned downstairs.

"You need not bother dear. We have told them the whole story except we did not tell them about the statue."

"Do you have it?"

"Why of course. It is upstairs in my travel case."

Barry sighed. "It's a wonder they didn't find it."

"They did not look! They were too busy torturing the girls and trying to intimidate me. They let their desire to vent their spleens overtake their judgment."

"Take me upstairs and let me have it," Barry whispered. "I will tell the police it was with me all the time."

Madame Conti looked at her grandson. He concurred. Barry followed her up the stairs. Both returned downstairs in only a few minutes. "The officer in charge is outside in their van," she told him. "He seems a very nice man."

Barry tapped at the officer's window. "I have information relevant to this case."

"Can you identity the deceased?" the officer asked.

"I'm not sure. I would have to see him."

The officer took him around to the rear of the van and asked him to

283

look.

Barry grew pale. "I've never seen such a sight," he said surveying the body not yet free of the object that impaled it. "This is the man who had me abducted while I was in Rome. He threatened me if I did not give him an artifact a friend had asked me to identify."

"What is his name?"

"I don't know. He didn't offer it."

"You say he is from Rome?"

"Yes, well my abduction occurred in Rome so I assume he lives there—lived there."

"If he abducted and threatened you, as you say, why are you here now?"

"I tricked him. I acted as if I would cooperate but instead I left Italy. And here I am now. He must have found out where I was going but got here before I arrived."

"So you were coming here with the artifact?"

"Yes, officer."

"Why did you not report it to the authorities in Rome?"

"For several reasons. I doubted that they would believe me because I had very little evidence or information to give them. I thought that both the artifact and I would be safer here than in Italy so I didn't want to initiate an action that may have kept me there. Also, Etienne, that's Cinzia's brother, thought she might be able to help me identify her. You see that's what I have been doing. I've been trying to date and identify this statue."

"It must very valuable. Can I see it please?"

Barry pulled his backpack off the shoulder of his new tweed sport jacket, opened it, and took out the box, which he unwrapped, revealing the bird goddess. "I really don't know her value yet because I haven't fully identified her. But evidently he thought her valuable enough to kidnap, kill, and die for. That gives me hope. My intention has never been to turn a profit on her. I'm an archeologist by profession, not a thief or an artifact smuggler."

The officer looked intently at the object and then at Barry. "I believe you. If you had been either, as you say, a thief or a smuggler, this man laying here dead would not have let you go. And you would not be talking to me now. Tell me, what did he threaten you with?"

"He said if I didn't turn her over willingly, he would forcibly take her and destroy my academic reputation."

"Which is important to you?"

"Yes, very important!"

"You must be a scholar," the discerning officer said wearily. "Do you mind if I ask for your academic credentials for my report?"

"No, I don't mind if you do," Barry said, pulling his identification card out of his wallet. "Actually, I'm doing work here in France, near Les-Eyzies-de-Tayac."

"Oh, the caves," the officer said as he wrote down pertinent information from the ID.

"Yes, in the caves."

"I have no reason to hold you or it," the officer said handing him his statue and identification card. "I will have this man's photo sent to Rome to be identified. If I need you for further questioning, will you be in France?"

"Yes, of course. I will leave my address with one of your men."

"Thank you for coming forward with this information. You could have not done so. If you were a thief and a smuggler, you would not have. Your story will exonerate the girl. Not that I thought there was any question about her innocence, but the prosecutor may not have seen the situation as I have."

The two other officers were leaving the house as Barry reentered it. He handed one of them a card that he retrieved from his backpack with his address in Les-Eyzies-de-Tayac. The others inside were at work picking up shards of china.

"I will get something to clean this rug with," Madame Conti said. "Who will clean the dining room table?"

"I will," Etienne said.

"I could never eat from it again," Cinzia groaned. "We should throw it out."

"I will clean it off and leave it outside for anyone who wants it," Etienne said as he began wiping it down with the bucket of hot, sudsy water his grandmother handed him.

"Oh, good, the blood is coming right up," Madame Conti said as she scrubbed the rug.

"What about your face?" Cinzia asked.

"I have not looked yet," she replied.

"Go upstairs and clean yourself up. I will finish the rug," Cinzia said.

Etienne looked at his watch. "Here, give me that china before you cut yourself," he said to his sister. "You and Rosalind should go dress. We haven't eaten all day and it's getting late. If we hurry, we can still get a late lunch."

***

Father Paul loaded Hans Bueller with all of his belongings into the monastery van having received a message from a higher up to remove him immediately, that very day if possible. He decided to drive him to El Quseir himself where he would personally hand him over to Doctor Omar Shabaka. He had never before been ordered to remove someone from the residence he managed, and certainly not someone as old and frail as Bueller nor someone he liked so well. "Bueller is a thief," the telegram had read, "who stole from the charitable institution that had been kind enough to take him in despite his unsavory reputation and his history."

"I don't understand," a disconsolate Bueller cried.

Father Paul, not known to raise his voice, shouted, "You don't understand? We believed you were reformed from your old ways. We offered you a home and friendship, and you betrayed us."

"I am changed!" Bueller argued. "I did not take her for myself. I gave her to Barry Short to be identified. You showed no interest in her. I did it not to betray you but for our betterment, for z'e advancement of our understanding of z'e past."

"Why did you not ask my permission then?" Bueller was silent. "Because you thought I would not give it, that's why."

"Because I feared you would not be allowed to give it. You knew noz'ing of her, not even z'at she was in your care. But I feared z'at z'ere might be oz'ers who did know and reasons z'ey wiz'held it from you. Z'ey could stop you and me, but me alone z'ey could not stop."

Father Paul sat silent for a few minutes. It was true that he had not been aware that the monastery housed an object of such immense value. If he had known, he never would have left it to molder in the cellar of the library. He would have placed it in a respectful place, high up in the church nave where it could have been guarded under the prayerful eyes of his monks.

"So you stole it from us," Father Paul said. "The rest are excuses."

Hans was silent but only for a few minutes. They were arriving at the hotel parking lot in El Quseir where they were to meet Doctor Shabaka.

"You are right. I stole it. But please as you remember me, z'ink of my motives. Z'ey were not selfish. Yes, in z'e past z'at was true but no longer." His eyes welled up in tears. "She spoke to me to free her from z'e darkness, to discover who she is and bring her back into z'e world. I set about to do z'is z'e only way I knew how. It was not to deceive you but to free her. You have been wonderful to me, and I have loved z'is retreat you offered me and will z'ink of you always in z'e kindest of ways. I hope you can z'ink of me likewise."

"I will pray for you," Father Paul said.

Doctor Shabaka looked closely at his charge once he and Father Paul had removed his things from the monastery van and packed them into his. He looked tired, older, and in a mild state of shock.

"When we arrive at my father's house I will make you tea, bathe you in oil and honey, and give you a good massage. You will be as good as new tomorrow."

"Where will I go, and what will I do?" the frail man asked.

"I don't know," Omar said as he patted him on his arm. "We will find a place."

***

The men carried the table outside to the road with a note advising any passersby that it was theirs for the taking. They gathered up the bags of broken china and other debris and put them in the garden trash cans. Stuart mopped the floors while John washed and put away the pots and pans and other cooking utensils left in the sink from the night before. When they were done, the house was spotless if a little empty. The carpenter arrived and set about repairing the front door.

The women came downstairs looking much better than when they had gone up, dressed in their new slacks, shirts, and sweaters. Madame Conti's cut was found to be only superficial once it was cleaned.

"Are you ready for lunch ladies?" Barry asked, he having been ready for several hours.

Etienne asked the repairman to leave a bill in the mailbox if he should be done before they arrive back, and they were off.

"Let us go to Restaurant L'Amirauté," Cinzia said. "It's so cheerful there."

Large restaurant windows opened out to the seaside letting in plenty of light even though the menu had already changed over for dinner. Brightly painted seaside scenes adorned the interior walls, and a mannequin captain stood near a real dining room captain who greeted customers as they entered. It was for tourists, of which there are many who visit this town. For all the cheerfulness of the decor, Cinzia was not consoled.

"I think you must leave this place, get back into the mainstream of life," Etienne said to his sister.

"I know, but I will miss it."

"You can visit," her grandmother said.

"Yes, that is what most people do," she said looking at the customers in the dining room.

"Or is it him you will miss?" her grandmother asked.

Cinzia looked down at her plate and said nothing.

"He is not worth it," her brother said gently.

"I agree with that," Madame Conti concurred. And then as if the thought of one bad man led to thoughts of others, she said, "We thought we were so smart. We thought we had fooled them."

"I wonder how they figured out we had the statue?" Rosalind asked, although she doubted that anyone could answer this perplexing question.

"I do not think they knew it immediately," Etienne said as he reflected back on events. "If they had, they would not have followed John the next day, believing he was Barry. I would say they began figuring something was amiss when John ditched them. Or perhaps they learned from Felix that the man they had thought was Barry was not."

"They would have known something was up for sure when I didn't

288

show up at our appointment," Barry added.

"Still, how did they figure out that we had it, and how did they know where we were?" Rosalind asked.

"Apparently, they followed you," Stuart said. "They must have followed us to Madame Conti's apartment from the restaurant that night. They knew Barry was still inside when they saw her car leave with all of you women. Just to play it safe, they had someone follow you."

"All the way to Saintes-Maries-de-la-Mere?" Summer asked.

"Apparently."

"The driver thought someone may have been following us as we crossed the Camargue," Madame Conti said. "What a fool I was. I dismissed it. Yet I'm not quite sure how they knew we had the statue?"

"Why else would you have left like that in the middle of the night with Barry still inside your apartment?" Etienne said. "That must be what they surmised the next day after they caught on to our tricks."

"Do you think they will leave us alone now?" Cinzia asked.

"I think they will," Etienne said, his brow furrowed.

"I sure hope so!" Barry said.

"The death of that man, whoever he is, is more publicity than they would have wanted," Etienne asserted. "Men like these work in the shadows. Their actions are made to look like accidents while they remain anonymous. I am very surprised he attacked you with a knife," he said to his sister. "That is not their usual method."

"I do not think it was his original intention," Cinzia said. "Remember, it was my knife he attacked me with. He did not bring one of his own."

"He lost it," Rosalind said.

"His knife?" Madame Conti asked. "How do you know?"

"No, I'm sorry, 'lost it' is an American slang expression meaning he lost control of his emotions."

"Oh, yes, that he did," Madame Conti concurred. "He was just plain angry, so angry that he 'lost it.' And we put up too good a fight. They knew we were not going to give her up easily. They would have to take her by force."

"It felt personal," Cinzia said. "When he came towards me with that knife, I felt his personal animus."

"It's a good thing that soup tureen was handy," Rosalind said. "Or it may have been you instead of him."

"Yes," she said softly.

"Maybe you reminded him of someone or something," Barry replied.

"Who?" she asked.

"I don't know. Maybe an ex-lover. Or maybe the statue that they so desired."

"Why would they even have thought we would give her over?" Summer asked.

"I asked myself that same question," Barry said. "Why did that fellow think I would just turn her over to him? Then I had to admit that I did think about it for a few minutes. He made a pretty good argument if you didn't stop and think it through. Then there is my career, which does concern me, the loss of funding and all. How would I do what I do? And what would I do if I couldn't do it? But then, I said to myself, what is the good of my work if I let fellows like him steal if from me, worse, steal it from all of us?"

"They read all of you wrong," Etienne said. "They are used to dealing with people who buy their arguments and take their threats more seriously. As we have seen, there is good reason to fear them. They thought you are like the rest."

"You sound like you've had experience with these kinds of men," Stuart said, eyeing Etienne suspiciously.

"I have, but that was another life. I will tell you about it sometime Stuart. Later."

They enjoyed their fresh catch of the day as much as possible under the circumstances and returned to the house. The lavender door was back in place, but its color looked cooler and grayer in the faded light. The dining room table was gone, taken away by someone who would never guess what had lain upon it only a few hours earlier.

"I cannot stay here tonight," Cinzia said. "Not after what happened."

"I don't either," Summer agreed.

"You will be safe with all of us here," Etienne assured them both.

"That is not what I mean," Cinzia said. "I have to get away from here. The thought of what happened sickens me."

"Let us go back to Cannes," Madame Conti suggested.

"That would be all right with me," Summer said.

"Hold on," Barry interrupted. "We are not that far from Narbonne, are we? I should go back there and see Brother Thomas if that's all right with everyone. I do want to thank him for his help and tell him what I've learned. He deserves to know."

"I think I should go back to the Carlton," Madame Conti replied. "I am so very tired." She looked at Summer. "Would you like to come with me?"

Summer looked at Etienne and then at her. "I should continue on with Barry if you don't mind."

She eyed her grandson critically. "She should come with me," she said to him.

"She is coming with me Grand-mère."

"Whatever you want," she said. "And you Cinzia, would you not rather go with me to the beach?"

"It's too cold for the beach. And I have so much invested in this now that I think I too should go with Barry."

"That is all right. I will call for my car and the rest of you can go on together if you like. My driver will phone the Carlton and have my room readied."

"Grand-mère, you talk as if we are abandoning you," Etienne said. "You can come if you like. This adventure is not over."

"I have had enough," she said. "After experiencing a break-in, watching an attack on my granddaughter, preventing a rape, and witnessing an accidental death that seemed no accident at all in a cosmic sense, I think I have had enough for now. Later perhaps. You can phone me at the Carlton. I do not think I will be going back to Rome soon."

"I know what you must feel," Cinzia said. "I feel it too. I am very tired, and this has been overwhelming. And you Grand-mère were the mightiest fighter of all of us. But I must keep going."

"Of course you must," her grandmother said. "It is your future."

The old monk picked up his keys and gathered up books of poetry he planned to take home that evening to read. He walked through the halls of the museum as he always did at the close of the day, switching off lights as he passed from room to room. This had been his routine for twenty odd years now, and this day had been no different from the others. He relished the routine, the steady pace of an orderly life that had ticked by like a well-made clock, steady and accurate. But on this day he found two patrons still remaining in the museum past closing, which was unusual anytime but more so this time of year when few tourists were there to visit.

"Messieurs, le musée est fermé," he said with a patient smile and an intonation as polite as he could make it. They smiled back and acknowledged his remark by turning and walking towards the door. Just as he reached the top of the stairwell leading down into the basement, he felt a massive push against his back and shoulders that sent him tumbling into the dark.

Chapter 50

The Naming

Their journey to Narbonne brought the weary travelers to an inn just outside the city. There they ate, drank, and talked before retiring early, so early that Cinzia rose in time to greet the sun. She lay herself down on a grassy spot, her dark brown hair shimmering while she focused her attention on nature's beauty. Such meditations gave her strength, she said. On this clear morning the sunrise was particularly striking, a brilliant golden yellow rapidly overtaking the soft pinks and corals of its beginnings.

***

Madame Conti awoke in the rear seat of her limousine, her head throbbing. "Driver! Driver!" she called, but there was only silence. She pushed open the partially jammed door and climbed out to find herself in the desolate winter fields of the Camargue. Her walking shoes sunk in a marshland that threatened to swallow the car. Quick to gather her wits, she climbed into the front passenger seat and tested the silent driver's phone. It still worked. "There has been an accident," she told the operator who passed the information on to the police. She slogged her way back to the road and waited for help. As she did, she recalled what she could. The last thing she remembered was a great force crashing into the rear of the car, pushing it rocking and bouncing off of the road and into the marsh. She recalled that they had been traveling very fast. The driver had warned her that they were being followed just as he had the day before. She remembered having apologized to him for doubting his judgment earlier and instructing him to do what he must. The police said her driver might have survived if the limousine had been a newer model equipped with airbags.

"My husband bought this car for us many, many years ago. He loved it, and I hated to give it up," she sobbed.

***

Etienne joined Cinzia for the last few minutes of the sunrise before bringing her inside to join them for a simple French breakfast.

"Who is this Brother Thomas we are going to see?" she asked.

"He runs the museum in Narbonne. A very quiet sort of man," Barry said.

"Peculiar," Rosalind added.

"That too," Barry said. "Hans Bueller, the fellow who asked me to identify the statue, suggested that I visit Brother Thomas. He thought he might be of some help."

"Was he?"

"Oh, yes, yes, he was."

"In a peculiar sort of way," Rosalind added.

"Well, yes," Barry said. "He wasn't exactly straightforward. It was he who sent me to Rome. He told me to go to the Church of the Jesuits and look for a statue of a woman holding a mirror that stood above the nave of the church."

"What were you supposed to do when you found her?"

"I should study her, he said. That's all."

"Peculiar," Rosalind repeated.

"Yes, ahem," he cleared his throat. "Of course, the first thing I wanted to know is who she is, and finding that most difficult to ascertain, well, that aroused my curiosity. I did figure out that she is Prudence through no help from anyone at the church."

"They all claimed they didn't know who she was even though she stood above the nave looking down on everything else they did know about," Rosalind said. "It was your grandmother who explained her real significance, who Prudence really is."

"The deeper meaning of the symbols associated with her, the mirror, and the snake," Barry explained. "Madame Conti's help has been invaluable."

"Brother Thomas told you only to seek her out, nothing more?" Cinzia asked.

"That's all the direction he gave me."

"Well, what do you make of it? Why are you so grateful?"

"That's a very good question," Barry acknowledged. "This may sound a little odd, but my work is generally cumulative. One thing leads to another sort of thing. Yet the most important part is that one significant clue from which the mystery unravels and the item in question reassembles itself in a new light. I believe that is what Brother Thomas gave me. And I believe he understood that was what he was giving me."

"Everything followed from there, meeting my grand-mère and all?" she said

"And of course Etienne. It is doubtful that we would have met your grandmother without first encountering him. That happened before my meeting with Brother Thomas. I wasn't even there," Barry said eyeing Summer. "Maybe we would have found our way to the same destination following a different path, but I have my doubts."

"So many things that were meant to be," Cinzia said. She sat quietly for a few minutes.

"What are you thinking?" her brother asked.

"I was just thinking…I don't know," she said. "This Hans Bueller you mentioned. Where did he find her, the statue? How did you get her?"

"He is pretty peculiar too," Rosalind said. "But you can't help liking him in spite of himself."

"Yes, Rosalind, I would have to agree with you," Barry said. "He lives in a monastery in Egypt, which is where he found her."

"Oh, he is a monk too?"

"No, ahem. He had been an Egyptologist. He is very old now. The monastery has allowed him to take up residence there. An act of charity you might call it. They made him their librarian since everyone who lives there works at one thing or another. He called me down there when he uncovered the statue buried in boxes in the library cellar along with several manuscripts that were obviously associated with her. He wanted me to solve the mystery of her identity since, well, he is too old for much travel these days."

"Manuscripts?" she asked.

"Yes, papyrus scrolls that were obviously about her. At one time her name had been written in hieroglyphs inside cartouches located in the texts, but all the hieroglyphics have been removed, scratched out."

"She does not look Egyptian."

"No, she doesn't, which is why he told me to search her out in Europe. She must have been brought to Egypt some time ago."

"Tell her about the poem," Rosalind said.

"Yes, my grand-mère mentioned it."

Barry cleared his throat and began to recite:

"She looks upon herself who is not there.
But sees instead before her all the world.
Whatever was, whatever will be is in her care.
For she is the maker of the world.
Within her face all faces, all time, the cosmic burst of creation.
She holds the mirror of world."

"Oh, that is why Grand-mère thought her a Sophia!"

"Maybe the Sophia," Etienne offered. "She thinks of Prudence as a Sophia, with her mirror and snake. But she thought this one an original with her mirror like eyes, her reflective copper crown, her fins and feathers."

"Originals, copies, what do you mean? Who is she?" Summer asked while her thoughts were asking the more personal question, who am I?

"No, no, it is not that Prudence is a copy. No, no, that is not what he means," Cinzia explained. "The meaning of the Sophia became hidden. I am not sure why, but it happened as if it was forcibly suppressed and eventually forgotten. Yet one can see her trying to reemerge throughout history in myriad other goddesses, including the goddess of my church, Mary and all the Marys associated with her. It is as if she refuses to be forgotten or people refuse to give her up. But what we have left of her is only in fragments. Thus, some believe she is diminished."

"Some believe it diminishes all of you," Etienne said, looking at the women.

"Diminished," Summer quietly said.

"Like all the Black Madonnas we've seen," Rosalind said. "They each have their own legend, and they are said to provide blessings and protections from various dangers. So one chooses which one to pray to according to their need. Yet we saw people on pilgrimages who were visiting many of them. Making prayers to them all."

"People will travel many kilometers to seek out a miracle. It has always been so," Cinzia said, "long before the Virgin Mary and all the Marys that have followed."

"We saw that in Rome at the garden of the Vestal Virgins," Summer said. "I could still feel their presence."

"And the processions to Diana's temple," Barry added. "I ate a snack next to the wall of one of her temples soon after those men released me, and then there is Isis and Nuit."

"I visited the site of the Oracle of Delphi once when I was in college," John recalled. "She was a big deal in Ancient Greece. People would travel miles through treacherous rocky slopes to seek out a prophecy or an answer to a perplexing question. Then there is Athena!"

"The protectress of Troy and Yemaja, the protectress of seafarers," Cinzia said.

"Funny you should mention Yemaja," Barry remarked. "A very wise fellow I met in Egypt mentioned her too."

"Yes, all of them," Cinzia said. "They have all been there for people, offering hope, solace, and direction. My grand-mère's contention, which has become my own, is that all of them derive from the one whose role was far greater. Like your poem suggests, 'she is the maker of the world.'"

"God?" Rosalind asked.

"Oh, no, not God. The Gnostic gospels say she is the last emanation, that which stands closest to humankind, somewhere between God and Earth, that which reflects the light of heaven out of which creation is born."

"A high priestess?" Summer said.

"The highest priestess," Cinzia replied, thinking more deeply than ever before about her grandmother's words, words that in the past had seemed more fantasy than real. "A partner of God in this creation. The bringer of light, life, compassion, and knowledge. Both the Bird Goddess and the Goddess of the Sea," she said as she began to articulate an image that had formed in her mind. "She brings down the first light, a light so powerful that you or I could not bear to look upon in its pure form. She casts its heat on the cool waters of the sea where it shatters into a million lights, visible to us in their sparkling dance out of which the multitudes are created, thought is created, and the kindest emotion."

"What a beautiful image. Can I see her again?" Summer asked.

Barry took her out of his bag. Her eyes shone as they never had before. Her copper crown turned golden under a ray of morning light breaking through the restaurant window. Her feather-like hair looked as if it could lift her up in flight. The faint scales carved into her back seemed to mark the place where life began.

"Why would she have been suppressed?" Summer asked.

"Why is anything suppressed?" Etienne said. "So that you would not know her and act on that knowledge."

"Act powerful?" she said.

"In a manner of speaking," he said. "Know yourself a queen and not a slave. The sad truth is we become only what we can imagine. The easiest way to control the destiny of an individual or the destinies of whole peoples is to limit what they can imagine about themselves. To set their sights so low as to reduce them."

"That's evil!" Summer exclaimed.

"From your point of view but not theirs," he replied. "It is a most efficient method to control those you might otherwise fear. Make them believe that their greatest endowments should be shunned, and they will first forget them out of shame and later from disuse."

Stuart was intrigued by Etienne's insight, insight that he recognized as true as soon as he heard it. The women he had known, and there had been many, had set their sights so low they were content with lives superficial and vain. They had their appeal, he had to admit, since he was often the object to which they directed their carefully cultivated sexual allure. Natalie had been an exception in all but one way, her willingness to tolerate him. Why, he had wondered, would she settle for him when there were better men? His estimation of women had always been lowered by that fact, even his estimation of Natalie.

"What should we do now?" he said, feeling a bit jittery in spite of his effort not to be taken in by mumbo jumbo. "If what you say is true, I doubt that these men will end their pursuit."

"We shall see," Etienne said. "They may have other less overt methods. For now, let us go visit Brother Thomas. The more people who know and understand what we have uncovered, the better."

"We still don't know her name," Barry said. "After everything we've learned, her cartouche remains empty."

"I doubt that we will ever learn that, at least not her original name," Cinzia said. "We should name her, give her one for now at least."

"What would that be?" Barry asked.

"I do not know," Cinzia replied.

"We could call her Queen Goddess," Summer said.

"Somehow I think that kind of raw grandiosity would violate her spirit," Barry said.

"I think you're right," Summer said upon reflection. "Let's see. She has no home, at least that we know of, and she is part of the line of Marys. In fact, she heads it."

"Gitane Marie," Cinzia blurted out in a fit of inspiration.

"She is no gypsy," Etienne replied.

"I know she is not," she said. "But she has had to exist like one. She has been buried in the shadows away from her homeland, unnoticed and neglected, and yet she may be the Mary of Marys."

"Gitane Marie," Barry repeated. "I like it."

"So do I," Summer said.

Cinzia dipped her fingers into the glass table vase that held only a single flower. "I name you Gitane Marie," she said, sprinkling a few drops of water on the forehead of the delicate statue.

Chapter 51

Return to Narbonne

"Fermé," a sign posted on the museum door read. "I see a note. Pull over and let me run up there and read it," Barry said.

Etienne hugged the curb so other cars could pass. He watched as Barry climbed the steps to the museum door. He watched him read the note, peer inside the window glass, and pound on the door's wooden frame. He watched him wait for a few minutes, look inside once more, and return to the van.

"The note reads closed until further notice," Barry said. "There's no more explanation, and there's no one inside."

"What do you want to do?" Etienne asked.

He looked over at the cathedral. "Let's go into the church. Someone there should be able to tell us something. If not, I know where Brother Thomas lives."

An eerie chant that sounded more Buddhist than Gregorian filled the cathedral environs. "Pardon me," Barry said to a woman walking through the vestibule. "Would you happen to know when the museum will be opening?"

"Je suis désolée. Je n'en sais rien," she answered and quickly walked away.

Seeing no one else to ask, he left the others in the vestibule and walked into the nave of the cathedral looking for information as well as the source of the chant that continued unabated in a long, drawn out monotone. He studied the bent heads and shoulders of a small group of people seated near the altar silently bowed in prayer. He spotted an umbrella hanging from one of the pews with a handle made from a tree branch polished to a glorious shine.

As if he could feel his eyes, James Stroud turned around and came face to face with Barry who stood in the rear of the cathedral next to the holy water. The ecumenical Anglican crossed himself, got up, and walked towards him.

"This is a sad day indeed," Stroud said.

"What has happened?"

"Oh, I'm sorry. I thought you knew and came to join me. Brother Thomas has died."

"How?"

"Last night the cleaning staff found him at the bottom of the stairway leading down into the museum basement. They surmise that he must have tripped on those treacherous steps while making his closing rounds. Such a very sad loss indeed," the grim faced man replied.

"I'm very sorry to hear that," Barry said, notably disturbed. "Is that what all this chanting is about?"

"It is the custom of his order to insure an easy passage. It will continue until he has been buried, which is scheduled for later this week."

"Where are they?" Barry asked looking around.

"Up there," Stroud said, pointing to the carved wood panels high up in the church. "They stay concealed. Are you alone?"

"No, I've come back with the others. They're out in the vestibule. I thought Brother Thomas would like to know that we discovered the identity of the statue I brought to him, who she is if not her name. The direction he gave me proved invaluable. I thought he would want to know that. I'm so sorry I wasn't able to tell him before he passed."

"He would have been exceedingly interested to know," the Anglican said as they walked together up the aisle. "I certainly am." Seeing Summer standing with her sister in the vestibule, he couldn't resist the urge to tease her even at this most solemn time. "I see that you still have your head."

"Huh?" she said.

"The wolf, the Beast of Gévaudan hasn't run off with it yet," he chuckled

"Oh," she replied not appreciating the joke. She added, "The wolves almost got us the other night."

"We've had a difficult time, particularly these women," Barry said. "I was kidnapped in Rome by a shadowy group of rogues committed to wresting the statue from me. To protect her, I sent her off to France with the women, thinking they and she would be safer there. My captors followed them and attacked them. Their leader was killed in the process. These are the wolves Summer is referring to."

"Oh, my! You have had quite a time of it, " Stroud said, looking visibly disturbed. "I suggest we go outside. It's a little chilly but pleasant, and I would feel freer to speak."

"Good. I wouldn't mind getting away from this drone of a chant," Barry said before he delivered the bad news to the others.

"I knew something terrible must have happened," Summer said. "The locked museum and these sad sounds." She turned to Stroud. "I'm sorry for your loss."

"Yes," he said, his eyes momentarily looking distant before he brought them to a sunny spot in the pleasant little church courtyard. "Were these men who kidnapped and attacked you ordinary thieves?" he asked.

"They're thieves, all right, but I don't think they are the ordinary brand," Barry said. "The one I spoke with—I don't mean to speak ill of the dead—but he seemed driven more by ideology than anything else. He was very aware that our statue had been buried away in a monastery in Egypt and wanted her to remain there unseen and unknown. He seemed to think that if she were revealed it might destabilize the entire planet, or so he said."

"This man has died, you say?"

Cinzia's pink cheeks faded to a ghostly alabaster. "When they attacked us in my house, he and the other men tried to pin us against the wall using my dining room table. We pushed back. When they lunged at us a second time, my chandelier let go of its chain and ripped into his heart."

"The cross of Camargue," Summer added.

"I saw it myself," Barry said. "It has a peculiar looking design, a cross at the top, an anchor at the bottom, with a heart in the middle. The hook of the anchor got him."

Stroud grimaced, and the girls began to sob. "And the others?" he asked."

"They got away," Summer said. "They left this man sprawled out on the table. They didn't even try to help him."

"His death must have been quick and obvious," Stroud said.

"Yes, it must have been," Barry said and put his arms around the girls. "You have to understand they're still pretty shaken. This happened only two nights ago."

"Two nights! Is there a chance these rogues knew of your meeting with Brother Thomas?"

"Well, I don't know. The fellow didn't mention him when I spoke to him in Rome. What are you suggesting?"

"Revenge," Stroud said in a fit of agitation. "Brother Thomas had gone up and down those stairs hundreds of times. It has been impossible for me to fathom this so called accident. But revenge, that I understand. You say the women were attacked. How about the fellow who gave you the statue?"

"I would have to write him," Barry said. "The monastery is off the grid as they say."

"We could call Doctor Shabaka," Stuart suggested. "He could drive over and warn him."

"I have his phone number with me in my pack." Barry ripped off his backpack and pulled out his notebook. "Can you make the call?"

"Sure, I juiced her up last night at the roadside inn. What's his number?"

"It's his office number," Barry said, preparing Stuart for what he thought could be a long wait.

"Is Doctor Shabaka in?" Stuart asked. "Tell him it is very important, that Barry Short needs to speak to him immediately." He handed Barry the phone.

"Omar, is that you? This connection is breaking up. Here, I will try moving and see if that helps."

He crossed the street and sat down on the steps of the museum. Curious, the others followed.

"He wants to know if someone can get Hans on a plane?" Barry said to them. "He says he's weak and confused so he's reluctant to let him fly alone. He's been evicted from the monastery. I'd go myself if I could. Stuart, could you fly down to Luxor and bring him back?"

Stuart nodded.

"He can leave anytime," Barry said into the phone. "Okay, he will try to leave today or tomorrow, depending on when he can get a flight.

He will be there either tomorrow or at least by the day after. Thank you so much Omar. Get back to your patients."

"At least he's all right," Rosalind sighed.

"Have you ever heard of such a thing?" Barry said. "Being evicted from a monastery."

"That answers my question," James Stroud said. "It was revenge."

"At least Hans didn't have a little accident, Stuart said while looking out at the town. "Well, here we are in the middle of nowhere. Where can I get a flight?"

"Toulouse is only an hour and a half away," Stroud said. "Call the airport there and see what they can do for you."

"Surely this is not a coincidence," Barry said.

Stroud, looking resolute said, "Surely it is not. May I ask who she is?"

"The Mary of Marys," Barry said. "The Sophia."

"She exists! Are you sure?" Stroud asked.

"As sure as you can ever be about matters that date back into prehistory."

"I have been looking for evidence of her over the course of the last twenty years and had begun to think she exists only in legend," Stroud said.

"Apparently, these men wanted to keep it that way. Ironically, the way they threatened me gave it away. One would not make those kinds of threats over a legend."

"Or kill for one!" Stroud said.

"Let's get out of here," Stuart interrupted, having just made his arrangements. "I've got a flight leaving Toulouse at 3:30 this afternoon. I'm scheduled to arrive in Cairo early tomorrow morning, and from there I fly to Luxor arriving around noon," he read from his notes. "The flight back is better, more direct. We leave shortly after I arrive and get into Paris that evening."

"So the two of you will arrive in Paris late tomorrow," Etienne said as he calculated the driving time and distance. "We can be in Paris by then. No problem."

"Could you come with us?" Barry asked the Anglican whom he found enormously good company.

"I would enjoy continuing our conversation," Stroud said. "But I mustn't go on to Paris now with the funeral scheduled later in the week."

"Of course not." Etienne said. "We have a little time yet," he said, looking at his watch. "Let us go to one of the cafes for an early lunch."

"My favorite is just across the street," Stroud said. "You might try their cassoulet. It's very good."

Barry thought back to his dinner with Brother Thomas and how the old monk had bragged about his recipe. He was right to have done so because it was delicious. He worried that he had failed to thank him enough for his culinary effort, so focused he had been at learning any secrets he could about his statue. He turned down what he knew would be the cafe's inferior version of the dish on this regretful day.

"Are you all right?" Stroud said, detecting Barry's sadness.

"I'll be all right. I think I will just have a sandwich."

"I thought you were only about the Black Madonnas?" Summer said after placing her order for a bowl of bouillabaisse.

Stroud turned to Summer. "I believe there may be a connection. I had hoped that I could discover the Sophia through the Black Virgins; or that one of them, perhaps put away in a private church vault somewhere, might prove to be the prize I had sought. And here you had her, showed her to me, and I did not recognize her," he said turning to Barry. "Could you show her to me again?"

Barry unpacked the object. "Ah," Stroud swooned. "She is lovely. I suspect my friend recognized her or thought he did, and directed you to something he believed would guide you if in fact she turned out to be who he conjectured she was," he said, feeling a pang of bitterness that the monk had not done as much for him. "May I ask what direction he gave you?"

"He sent me to a statue of Prudence in Rome at the church of the Jesuits."

"Why, he sent me there too," Stroud said looking perplexed. "Many years ago that was. I cannot imagine how that helped you."

"It wasn't so much the statue itself as the questions it raised and the direction those questions took me. No one in the church could or would identify her. I eventually identified her myself, but it was no easy matter since I got absolutely no help, only stubborn resistance. This roused my curiosity and led me to a description of Prudence I had never before heard, which ultimately allowed us to make the link between what I carried in my bag and the Sophia."

"From my grand-mère," Cinzia interjected.

"Yes, Cinzia and Etienne's grandmother is an expert in these things. She knows the deeper significance of Prudence's symbols and helped me make the link. My kidnapper had already convinced me the statue was more valuable than I had imagined; and there were other pieces of evidence, especially the runes carved into her, which we were eventually able to identify as late Magdalenian. If I remember correctly, Brother Thomas had surmised as much about the runes. I just couldn't see it at the time. It had seemed impossible that she could be that old, but I had to accept it with the discovery of the nanodiamonds."

"Nanodiamonds?" Stroud said, looking quizzically at the statue he still held in his hands.

"I had a geologist look at her in Rome. Apparently the rock she's carved from is full of these things, but they can only be seen under a high-powered microscope. That identification helped him date the age of the stone she's carved from, which confirmed the rest."

"Hmm, it's hard to imagine what cannot be seen. And she is very black indeed."

"Black she is, but she doesn't look particularly Egyptian or African."

"That is not my point," Stroud said. " Although I'm not surprised you should think it given the popular legends about crusaders bringing these Black Madonnas back from the Holy Land as if their origin explains their blackness. No, it is evidence of more than ethnicity."

"Marija Gimbutas thinks black is the color of the earth and therefore associated with fertility," Cinzia said.

"I believe the meaning is far more metaphorical as a means to express a nearly unfathomable mystery, Stroud said. I'm reminded of a few lines from William Blake:"

> "When I from black and he from white cloud free,
> And round the tent of God like lambs we joy.
> I'll shade him from the heat till he can bear,
> To lean in joy upon our father's knee."

"Songs of Innocence," Rosalind said. "Black can better absorb light's white heat."

"Exactly! She can stand close to its source and shade us from the intensity of light we could not otherwise bear. That is what has excited me so about the Black Madonnas and now her."

"The final emanation, the one that touches the Earth," Barry said.

"Creates the Earth!" Stroud said slapping his hand on his knee. "The Sophia! She who makes life possible! But such talk is unorthodox."

"Why?" Barry asked. "The image is beautiful."

"It is beautiful," Stroud acknowledged. "And in a lessor way that beauty is retained. That's why people pray to these Madonnas, asking them for compassionate intervention."

"It is the exalted position of the Sophia that is at odds with orthodoxy," Etienne said, who up to then had remained quiet. "Her gender and perhaps even her color. I had never considered that aspect since I had not made the connection to the Black Madonnas before having the pleasure of meeting this learned man," he said, nodding approvingly at James Stroud.

"What the two of you are saying is that the Sophia does not conform to men's prejudices about race and gender. So what is left of her has been reduced to better fit the desired profile," Barry said.

"Certainly, it both reduces her and elevates ourselves," Etienne said, referring now to his own gender.

"Chauvinist pigs!" Summer uttered in disdain.

"Are you guys traitors to your own gender or what?" Rosalind asked.

In a very serious tone, one far more serious than is the norm for him, Barry replied, "Some of us have always been more interested in the pursuit of truth than erroneous prejudices, no matter how comforting such misconceptions might be."

"Now we have proof!" Stroud said.

"If what happened in my home is an accurate indication, followed by the death of this monk and the expulsion of your friend, I don't think it will be easy to go forward with this proof. Who will believe us when we come under attack?" Cinzia argued.

"Yes, that is the problem," Stroud admitted. "Who will believe us?"

"We will write an article together," Barry said to Cinzia. "Maybe a book. No, a book would take too long to write and publish. It will have to be an article."

"Why not both?" Cinzia said, excited by the prospect of collaboration, something that until then had been outside her scope.

"Yes, you must get the word out," Stroud agreed. "Perhaps a press conference to exhibit her to the public."

"I might be able to arrange that," Etienne said. "Yes! I could arrange that in a hurry in Paris."

Chapter 52

Flight to Paris

"Only this morning I called Brother Thomas peculiar, and here he was..."

"Rosalind! I've seen you do this to yourself before. You must stop," John said.

"But I feel so bad."

"We all do, but you are not responsible for what happened. And the fact is you weren't exaggerating. Brother Thomas was a little peculiar."

"I was thinking 'is,' not 'was.' It was insensitive of me."

"You didn't know what had happened. None of us suspected he was in danger or we would have warned him." He paused for a few minutes. "He might have been a little bit odd, but his heroism is what we will remember him for."

"He probably knew that it was no accident that knowledge of the lady has been kept under wraps for centuries," Barry said. "That's probably why he was so careful about what he told me and how he told me. He knew it was dangerous to reveal what he knew. And it cost him his life." He paused to wipe away tears and then began to orate, "Brother Thomas! If your spirit is with us now, as I suspect that it is, please accept Rosalind's apology." He turned to her. "Does that make you feel better?"

She shook her head as she too wiped away tears.

"If the old monk could speak to us now, he probably would agree that his behavior was at times odd," Barry said. "I think he cultivated the trait myself. It may have been part of his cover. I also think him a modest sort of man, too modest to easily accept John's fine assessment of him. So let me tell you Brother Thomas if you are still listening, you are a hero to us. If it had not been for you, I may have never found the truth."

Silence filled the van as it pulled around to the boarding area of the airport.

"Be careful," Stuart said before climbing out.

"You be careful too Stuart," Barry said. "They may be following Bueller."

"We'll be fine. We will fly out of there only a few hours after I arrive. Unless these guys are into blowing up planes, they won't be able to touch us. It's you that I'm worried about. My advice, don't dally. Go straight to Paris. Where are you camping out in Paris anyway?"

"I have an apartment there," Etienne said. "Unless anyone objects, I thought we would all stay there. It is large enough."

"I should have known," Stuart said as climbed out of the van. "Look, I will call you from the airport when Egypt Air drops us off at Charles de Gaulle. See you then."

"That's very nice of you to offer to put us up in your apartment," Barry said.

"No problem. I will enjoy it."

The interior of the van fell uncharacteristically quiet. The silence was finally broken once they were north of Toulouse.

"There's the exit to Montauban," Summer said, recalling the restaurant at the hotel where she had met her prince. It seemed like months ago and yet it was only weeks.

"If it were evening, I would suggest that we stop in for an anniversary dinner," Etienne said. The two laughed together.

"It was odd that we happened to meet there as we did," she said. "It didn't seem so strange at the time, but after everything that has happened—What were you doing there anyway?"

"I had a business meeting the evening before we met. Speaking of business, your business partner Jos has not called for a long while."

"I should give him a call."

Jos answered after only two rings. "Hi guy," she said into her phone. "Haven't heard from you for a while so thought I would check in. I'm getting closer. We are on our way to Paris right now. Yes, tonight. I know. It's been some time. How are things going? Oh great! You closed that deal. You've become a real pro. How is the shipping going? Good, on schedule. That's great that you were able to book a few winter shows. Have you made their travel arrangements? Good. Oh, they're doing two shows, Christmas and New Years. I'm sure the company is happy about that. Okay, I will let you get back to work. See you soon I hope." She put away her phone without comment.

An awkward silence fell over the travelers again but only for a few moments.

"It sounds like Jos has things under control," Rosalind commented.

"Yes, it does."

Rosalind pointed to the sign for Rocamadour. "It's such a beautiful village to look at, jutting out of the rock the way it does."

"It's quite a sight," John agreed. "I think we got some good photos."

"That puts us near the turnoff for Les-Eyzies-de-Tayac," Barry said. "If we've got the time, I wouldn't mind stopping by my place and picking up some more clothes. It's only a few miles west."

"Hardly!" Rosalind said. "I drove part of the way back to the highway. It took forever. Round and round and round I went."

"There are many roundabouts," Barry admitted.

"And forests," Rosalind added, remembering the woodlands that grew more menacing after they discovered Barry's apartment ransacked. "Barry, did anyone remember to tell you that you were to call Yvette?"

"I don't believe so or I would have done it. When did she tell you this?"

"Ages ago, just before we left."

"Barry, I'm really sorry," John said. "There was just so much else going on when we got to Aix that I forgot. She asked us to have you call there because Aveline was very worried about the mess in your cave."

"Mess in my room?"

"I think I did mention that. Yvette thought it could be kids, but Aveline was upset about it."

"I should phone her," Barry said. Summer handed him her phone.

"Thanks," he said as he rummaged through his backpack searching for the notebook where he kept his list of important phone numbers.

"Bonjour Yvette. Barry, Barry Short. I know it's been a while. I got the message to call only this minute. The police came by? Yes, there was a death. No, it wasn't a murder; it was an accident. I probably should have thought to let Aveline know they might try to contact me there. So that was the last straw, huh? What were the others if I might

311

ask? Yes, I heard that someone had broken in. Some men interviewed you? Well, then, maybe it was best that I hadn't phoned earlier. Better that you had nothing to tell them. They threatened you how? Oh, your funding. Yes, they've threatened me too, and I'm beginning to think they are making good on it. No, don't send them. I will pick them up when I figure out where I'm staying. Don't be sorry. It wasn't your fault. Okay, Ciao." He handed the phone back to Summer.

After a few moments of silence she said, "That didn't sound good."

"No, it wasn't. I've been evicted."

"Oh, I'm really sorry. I can't believe I forgot to pass the message along sooner," John apologized again.

"Don't worry about it," Barry said. "It wouldn't have made any difference. What finally did it was the police showed up to question me further about the events at Cinzia's home. Unfortunately, when they didn't find me they checked with my landlady. Yvette said that Aveline phoned her right afterwards and asked her to remove my belongings. She's got them at her place now."

"Your landlady can't just evict you like that for no reason," Summer said.

"Well, that might be true, but there is a little matter of the rent. I haven't gotten around to paying it for the last several months. I would have gotten caught up, of course, when I got back there. But apparently Aveline has a new tenant lined up—one more to her liking—a nice French farmhand. May they be happy together. Then there is the matter of threats being made against Yvette's funding. Needless to say, I'm not too popular over there right now."

"Do you want me to drive over so you can get your belongings?" Etienne asked.

"No, not now. Let's keep going."

Everyone but Etienne dozed off, lulled by the soft purr of the highway. They took no notice of the steady stream of cars that whizzed past or the sign for Limoges that signaled they had traveled a third of the way to Paris. Etienne considered whether they should stop for dinner but decided to press on. When the van approached Chateauroux, a sign appeared pointing to the first exit for Bourges, which opened up a new, unexpected and embarrassing topic that roused them out of sleep.

"The sign says Bourges is just ahead. That must remind you of your earlier visit," Etienne remarked. Summer bit her lower lip. "John wished to see the astronomical clock as I remember. How did you like it?"

There was a long pause and finally Barry spoke up. "I'm the guilty party. That was all a bit of a story I asked Summer to tell you because, well, at the time, I wasn't too sure of you. It is true at least that John had wanted to see the astronomical clock."

"I'm sorry," Summer said.

"That's all right, but never lie to me again," he said and patted her arm. "So you thought I might be a villain?" he shouted into the rear seat over the hum of the passing traffic.

"No, not exactly," Barry said. "I had just learned that Felix was on my tail. I thought it was possible that you might know him in a social sort of way and he could wheedle some information out of you. If he tried, I thought it better that the information should send him in the wrong direction."

"That is exactly what happened," Etienne said, "except that I did not know him. When he came to me, he claimed a relationship with a dear friend who had given him my private number. I was surprised by the inquiry since I had only just met you, but I was not at all suspicious."

"I was far too suspicious," Barry admitted. "Tell me, did you follow us to Barcelona?"

"Barcelona? You thought you saw me in Barcelona?"

"Not exactly. Oh, never mind," Barry said. "I was just wondering."

Not answering the question, Etienne said to Summer, "I was quite worried about you. Your departure was so abrupt, and I felt very much that something was wrong."

"I couldn't tell you anything. I had to protect Barry."

"I know. I would have done the same. Did I tell you that the Duc de Berry is my ancestor?"

"I think you said something about it."

"Yes, Bourges is one of my favorite places. There is a restaurant there I particularly like. Let me propose that we go there for dinner and allow John to see the astronomical clock."

Before anyone could agree or disagree, Etienne had turned off of the

A 20 in the direction of the town. He pulled in front of the Hotel de Bourbon, a lovely, old, and stately building surrounded by gardens and trees. The van seemed to sink into the curb, as if its entire steel body, plastic trim, leather seats, and six passengers and dog had together let out a collective sigh of relief. They had arrived safely in the North of France, having escaped the danger that lurked in the South.

"The building has so much character," Rosalind said.

"And history," Etienne said. "It was once an old abbey. Wait here for me. I will see about a reservation."

A few minutes later he was back. "We have a reservation at eight," he said through the window. "That should give us time to go to the Cathedral and examine the clock. I would suggest that we stay here the night. They do have rooms available, and that will allow me to enjoy my dinner and rest before we drive into Paris in the morning."

"That's fine with me," Barry said. "I'm in no hurry."

"I wonder if they sell nightgowns anywhere around here?" Summer asked.

"I need one too," Cinzia said.

The hotel staff directed them to a shop just around the corner where Cinzia, Summer, and Rosalind each bought a pair of cotton pajamas, the selection of sleepwear being rather limited.

"Hurry up," Etienne said, "before the cathedral closes."

They stashed their purchases in their rooms and walked briskly in the direction of the cathedral.

"Isn't that impressive?" Barry said when its flying buttresses and tower came into view.

"It is a World Heritage site, you know," Etienne said.

"No, I didn't know. I've heard about the place but never visited."

They entered through a garden at the rear whose rows of rose bushes, though not in bloom, were lovely in their orderliness on this mild winter evening. A plaque bearing the cathedral's full name appeared, Cathédrale Saint-Etienne de Bourges, it read.

Summer looked up at Etienne amazed. "You told me about your fourteenth century ancestor the Duc de Berry but not about Saint Etienne."

He laughed. "No, Saint Etienne is no ancestor."

"Wow!" John said once they stepped inside.

"They have survived intact for some eight hundred years," Etienne said as they looked upon religious scenes pieced together from brilliant red, blue, and golden stained glass.

"Some of them look pretty horrific," Barry said. "I don't remember reading any of this in the Bible." He was referring to carefully cut and soldered people bound up in ropes, burned alive, freshly beheaded, or forced by industrious devils into the mouth of a devouring beast.

"Their religious imaginations sometimes took them well outside the Bible," Etienne said. "Think of the drama of it!"

"They give me the willies," Rosalind said. "I prefer the serene paintings of animal life in the Paleolithic caves. Much more spiritual to me."

"Yes, and far more life-affirming," Summer agreed.

"Follow me," Etienne said. "I will take you to the clock."

"It's beautifully painted," Rosalind said, marveling at its reds, blues, and golds.

"The designs!" Summer said. "They're so astrological. I love the crescent moon."

"This will interest you John," Etienne said, taking him over to a glass case that housed the original internal mechanism. "The clock went into service in 1424 and continues today."

John studied the clock's huge wheels and gears, then stood back to take in its whole appearance. "It's incredible," he said, studying the mechanism from every angle and examining the tall clock case both front and rear.

"So now you have seen it! No need now to say you have when you have not," he said, and looked down at the precise timepiece on his wrist. "If we leave now, we should arrive at the restaurant right on time."

The brief tour put the big lie behind them. They relaxed, believing their long journey had come to an end.

Chapter 53

The Beasts of Gévaudan

"This place reminds me of the dining hall where Hans Bueller lived," Barry said after finishing a fine dinner in a splendid hotel dining room that had been fashioned out the ruins of a seventeenth century monastic chapel. "May I offer a toast to Hans? Hear! Hear!" he said.

They all drank. The waiter swept by and refilled their glasses.

"If I close my eyes I can see tables filled with jovial monks. They made an excellent vintage of their own down there in Egypt. Not as good as this though," he rattled on, swallowing more wine. "Let's drink to the monastery that for centuries was Gitane Marie's home and for nearly one year the home of my dear, dear friend."

They all toasted again, Barry drinking twice as much wine as the rest of the table. The waiter refilled his glass. "What happened is very, very sad," he lamented. "He was happy there. What's gonna become of old Hans now?"

Rosalind looked about the dining room trying to imagine the place as Barry was seeing it, which was impossible for her to do since she had never visited Hans Bueller's monastery and Barry's laments were not descriptive enough to transport her there. What she did notice was the extent to which their table had gained the attention of other diners. Even the staff had fixated on them, as had two men who sat quietly nearby who would turn towards their table each time Barry grew excessively boisterous.

"Maybe we're being a bit too loud," she whispered to John.

"You mean he's being loud! The cavernous size of this room is probably amplifying his voice and making it even louder," he said, as he too looked around at all the people looking at their table. Barry was about to lead them in song when Etienne mercifully suggested otherwise. John nudged Rosalind, "You suppose we could get him to sleep if off?"

She rolled her eyes and stood up. "I'm getting tired. It must be all the wine."

"Oh, don't poop out on us now. The night is young!" Barry chortled.

Etienne followed up on Rosalind's prompt. "I am tired myself. Barry, let me help you up to your room."

"No, no."

"Come now. We can celebrate again when we get to Paris."

"Why not now?"

"If you don't mind, I'm going to take a little walk before retiring," Cinzia said having just stood up herself.

As if in imitation, Barry tried to stand up too. "I'll go with you!" he said before falling back into his chair.

"I think you need to get your beauty sleep," she replied.

"Hold on to me," Etienne said as he lifted him up. "You are going to your room."

"I don't need any help," Barry said as he let himself be dragged along.

"I'll see you later in our room," Cinzia said to Summer as she took her departure.

"I can go with you."

"If you don't mind, I need a little time alone."

Outside the air was fresh and crisp but warm enough that Cinzia felt comfortable wrapped only in Rosalind's red shawl. She crossed the street to the park and entered the still open gate. The sky was both dark and bright; the moon cast its light on a tree here and a bush there making the park navigable. She was used to living alone in a town where she had little connection. That would all change now, and it was probably better that it did; but she required a period of adjustment after riding all day in a van full of people. She made her way over to a bench under a very large tree, whose leaves in summer would have shaded her from the midday sun. Tonight the shadow of its wide trunk and bare branches shaded her only from moonlight. She gathered her knees up and pressed them close to her chest for extra warmth. That night the stars told no stories; they spoke only of beauty.

Voices encroached on her solitude, but whose voices she did not know. She listened intently as they grew nearer. They were male voices speaking Italian, which thanks to her grandmother she had learned very well. She heard the name Barry Short spoken. She strained to hear more, but it was nearly impossible unless she moved closer. She dared not. She stayed quiet as a mouse as they drew nearer. They called him an ass and mocked his behavior in the restaurant. She detected vindictiveness in their tone. She heard one say that Barry's gross behavior will only further their plan. What plan, she wondered? Once they passed her she could hear no more. She quietly left the bench and headed for the open gate, slipped into the hotel lobby, and climbed the stairway up to her room.

"What happened?" Summer said when she saw her shivering and distraught.

"There were men out there speaking about Barry and some kind of plan they are making."

"Who were they?"

"I don't know. It was too dark to see them, but they must have been in the restaurant because they described seeing him there. We need to warn him."

"He's too drunk to understand or care. We had better tell your brother."

Etienne was startled out of his sleep by loud pounding on his door and was startled more when he opened it to find his sister there shivering and Summer with her.

"Let me put a blanket around you. Where have you been?"

"I went over to the park after dinner," she said. "I was sitting on a bench looking at the stars when I heard two men speaking in Italian. I could not make out most of what they said, but I heard them make jokes about Barry and say something about a plan they were devising and how if he acted as he did tonight that could only help them."

"What did they look like?"

"It was dark. I could only make out their silhouettes. They looked tall and of medium build."

"We should go out there and get a better look at them."

Cinzia looked very tired. "They must be following us. How long will this go on?"

"I don't know. Okay, you go to bed. I will take a look around myself."

"I will go with you," Summer said

Summer and Etienne made a futile search up and down the empty streets around the hotel.

"We should do as my sister did; station ourselves in the park and allow them to come to us rather than our trying to search them out."

"Maybe they're inside now, gone to bed," she whispered. "Oh, my god! They may have followed us here, been in our restaurant, and I didn't even see them." She clung closer to Etienne.

"They cannot be the same men who assaulted you," he said trying to calm her. "You would have recognized them, but you must be right about the other. We are being followed."

They crossed the street and entered the park, its gate still open, perhaps always open to lovers and other creatures of the night. Darkness was broken only by moonlight and the glare of nearby street lamps that cut through the naked deciduous trees on the park's edge. They found the very bench Cinzia had sat upon and seated themselves quietly waiting to see if they would hear Italian voices as she had; snatch part of a conversation as she had; but unlike what she had done, follow those voices and identify the men.

Silence was interrupted by occasional street sounds when a car or two ventured alone on the roadway between the park and the hotel. A robin warbled urgently as if it had a message to deliver that neither could understand. Eventually those sounds were gone as time moved more deeply into the hidden hours of the night. Mists rose, covering shrubs and bushes in a milky hue then enshrouding the lamps of far off streetlights while clouds rolled over the moon. She believed she heard a wolf howling.

"What's that?" she cried.

"It is only a dog," he said.

By then the blackness had nearly enveloped them. Summer, not used to such darkness, let it envelop her mind.

"If it had not been for us and our pursuit, Brother Thomas would still be alive, Hans Bueller would be welcome at his monastery and that man who was slain by the Cross of Camargue..." she sobbed. "And I almost..."

"But you were not!" Etienne said comforting her in his strong arms.

319

"There is always a price for seeking the truth. It has always been so. They who would keep the lie guard the truth well. You uncovered it in spite of them. It is they who are responsible for the good monk's death, not you and the others. The poisoned breath of revenge has taken his innocent life and displaced another."

The couple sat throughout the dark night giving solace to each other. Just as dawn lit the sky, they returned to their rooms, wiser in their evening's contemplation.

Chapter 54

Confessions

The van skirted past the Paris suburbs, crossed the Seine onto the Boulevard Saint-Germain and drove down that famed avenue until it arrived at Etienne's home in one of the well kept eighteenth century buildings on the Left Bank. His apartment was spacious, boasting plenty of windows, three large bedrooms, an expansive living room and separate dining room. Its high ceilings and beautifully carved fireplace suggested feminine elegance, which was tempered by the muscularity of a wall of cherry wood cabinets and bookshelves, two comfortable leather chairs, and a long leather sectional sofa that wrapped around the fireplace. It was most definitely a man's home; and by the look of the tidy, well equipped but under stocked kitchen, a man's home that had not been lived in for a while.

"I sure could use a cup of coffee," Barry said.

"You will have to excuse me," Etienne apologized. "I have nothing here to offer you, but we can go to a cafe for coffee and pick up some things while we are out."

He took them to his favorite cafe on the boulevard. The six of them gathered cozily around a table for four. Once the coffee, hot chocolate, and pastry were served, he sprung the bad news. "We are being followed," he announced.

"I'm not surprised," Barry said, looking around at the other tables. "How did you find out?"

"I will let Cinzia explain."

"I heard two men talking together after dinner last night. They mentioned you Barry."

"What did they say about me?"

Cinzia looked over at Etienne. "Tell him," he said.

"I couldn't hear too much and they were speaking in Italian, but I did overhear them say that your behavior last night would be good for their plan."

"Were they referring to our party at the restaurant?"

"I think so."

"I did drink a little too much. I'm not used to so much wine," he offered as an apology.

"Don't worry about that," Etienne said. "At least there is no plan to murder you, and they provided a few clues as to what they intend to do. That is what matters. It sounds like they plan to make good on their threat to undermine your credibility."

"And I helped them along."

"Have you looked at your email lately?" John asked.

"No. Why do you ask?" Barry said.

"Oh, I don't know. I was just thinking about that creep Felix."

"Good characterization. I doubt he will email me any more threats after what has happened, at least not the same kind. But you're right; I should check my email when we return to the apartment. I should also give that police officer down in Sainte-Maries-de-la-Mer a call to let him know where I am and find out what the house call in Les-Eyzies-de-Tayac was about. They may have gone by your home looking for you too," he said to Cinzia.

Summer handed Barry her phone.

"Does anyone have their number?" he asked.

"Ask the operator," Etienne said.

Barry was unable to connect with the officer in charge of the case. Instead, he left a message with his name and Summer's phone number, told him where he was, and invited the officer to phone him anytime.

They strolled down the Boulevard St. Germain and around the corners of abutting streets, peering into the shop windows of stylish boutiques. Summer nearly bought herself a silky gown to replace the plain cotton pajamas she had bought in Bourges that replaced the flannel nightgown her attacker had spoiled. Just as she was about to make the purchase, to Rosalind's astonishment, Summer had second thoughts and put the gown back in the case.

"What's wrong?" Rosalind asked. "Do you need money? I can lend you some."

"No, I've got the money. I just don't feel right about it, that's all. I can't explain it, but I just don't feel right."

"If you need my help, just ask me."

Standing outside the shop, Summer looked into the window but instead of seeing the fashionably dressed manikin she saw herself: not once, not twice, not three times. Images of herself filled the shop window all staring back at her as if they were trying to tell her something that she did not understand.

Etienne spotted a notice on a nearby lamppost announcing a winter solstice concert at Saint Sulpice the following day.

"We should go," he said. "You will love it. They always have fine musicians and the church is beautiful."

"Let's go then," Summer said, relieved their window-shopping was over.

"Isn't that the church built on the site of a temple to Isis?" John asked.

"No. You must be thinking of the Abbey Saint-Germain-des-Prés. Legend says that it was built over such a temple site. Let us walk over there and I will show you."

The gate of the churchyard was still open when they arrived, so they entered and sat down to rest for a few minutes outside.

"You said legend has it as if you aren't convinced," Rosalind said.

"I am not too sure," Etienne said. "Such places are far more commonplace in Italy. Here, some even claim that the name 'Paris' is a form of the word 'Isis.' While they do sound alike, one cannot help but wonder if the comparison and such stories arise more from longing than reality. Either way, I think Paris an appropriate location to display the Gitane Marie. Paris is truly admiring of women. If a temple to Isis was never here, it should have been."

"How should she be housed?" Barry asked. "And where? Should we give her to the Louvre?"

After a few minutes Cinzia offered what was to become the plan. "I should want her here on the Left Bank near the Cluny."

"Why near the Cluny?" her brother asked.

"It houses those lovely tapestries of the Lady and the Unicorn. I have always loved their beauty and their expression of the female imagination. The two would complement each other. Our museum should tell the story of women."

"The story of women's accomplishments?" Etienne asked.

"No, it should tell a more spiritual story."

"Like a museum of female saints and Madonnas?"

"Not that sectarian," she said. "It should tell their whole story, drawing on all religions and mythologies. What I would like most is for those who enter our museum to leave understanding the Gitane Marie as I do, understanding she is the whole and the beginning, the presence who turns light into creation, the Sophia, from whom all the manifold female saints and goddesses have descended. I want them to experience this for themselves through the exhibition. It should assist them in their own discovery. Let them weave it together as we have."

"That way they may internalize it," Barry offered.

"Yes, internalize it! That's what I want. When they have learned who we are as I have, they may be changed and uplifted by that knowledge. They will have a new model to aspire to that could release the potential that has been hidden away like she was, buried in a remote cellar with her identity defaced. Someday, once all of that potential is realized, the possibility will exist to transform this lonely planet into something better, not so full of strife as it is now."

"That's a tall order. You think this knowledge could have a calming effect?"

"Yes, I do," Cinzia asserted with a self-assurance Barry had never seen in her before. "It must!" she cried. "It has to! It only makes sense! Like lovers finally uniting after a long separation, neither having been sufficient without the other, like a body reuniting with its soul. I tell you it is not only women who have suffered from this loss, all of us have. It is as if we all have existed as half a man."

"The fellow who died on your chandelier had the opposite view. In Rome, when he tried to persuade me to hand her over, he argued that knowledge of her, no doubt the very knowledge you desire to communicate, would have the opposite effect. It would destabilize our worldview, which would lead to war and strife."

"Did you believe him?" she asked.

"For a few moments I considered it, and then I thought of all the strife and suffering that exists right now. The belittlement of women certainly

324

hasn't resulted in world peace. So no, I was not convinced. Nor am I convinced that the revelation of Gitane Marie can bring about all that you hope for, but it is a noble endeavor that I would be proud to be a part of."

"I cannot fault you for thinking as you do," she said. "It is hard to imagine such change in a world where hope has been squeezed out of us drop by drop after each sordid revelation of human degradation, after every hurt we experience at the hands of another. It has been hard for me too to find that wellspring of hope. My grand-mère tried to give it to me, to both of us," she said turning to her brother. "But her words alone were not enough to counter the experience of the loss of my parents."

"What happened to them?" Barry asked, his voice softened.

"I can hardly remember them," she sobbed. "They were doctors, committed to service, who went to Africa to tend to the wounded refugees in one of the civil wars. They never returned."

"It has been more than twenty years ago," Etienne said. "They went to Rwanda."

"I'm so sorry to hear that," Barry said looking at the sad girl. "They must have been very brave, very compassionate people."

"They were," she acknowledged, wiping away tears. "I fear they were rare. In a sense, your discovery, this Gitane Marie is a confirmation of what my grand-mère taught me, what I had always professed to believe but really never did until you brought her to us. She has helped me rediscover what I lost too many years ago. Without hope, I could protect myself the only way I knew how by hiding myself away. So I cannot fault you for not believing."

Barry looked studiously at her passionate brown eyes, her serious expression softened by her melodious voice and tender smile, and hoped beyond hope her vision would be fulfilled.

Confession over, they left the Abbey and continued their walk down the boulevard. Rosalind spied a grocer whose window was full of fresh poultry and insisted they buy two chickens to roast that evening with fresh herbs, potatoes, and onions. Summer bought a base to prepare a broth and virtually every kind of vegetable they had on hand: tomatoes, garlic, celery, broccoli, cauliflower, carrots, green beans, and a variety of greens. She was going to make a big soup, she declared. Etienne selected some fine cheeses and suggested that they visit a nearby bakery for fresh bread and some very good éclairs.

The setting at the apartment became quite domestic. Summer and Rosalind were in the kitchen chopping vegetables and stuffing buttered chickens. John was at Etienne's computer searching for everything he could find about the astronomical clock in Bourges and frustrated at the lack of depth and scarcity of what was available. Cinzia sat cross-legged on the blue Persian carpet meditating on Gitane Marie, who sat atop the mantelpiece above the crackling fire below. Barry laid back in one of the soft leather chairs, propped his feet on the footrest, and searched around on his laptop while Etienne relaxed in the other chair. They all were awaiting Stuart's phone call.

Summer was unusually quiet until she finally spoke her heart to Rosalind. "I'm feeling confused," she said. "I want to go back to Amsterdam, but I want to stay here too. Nothing feels quite right to me."

"I thought you loved your job? And you've got that amazing apartment there."

"I did love the job, particularly when I first got there and had to put the whole Amsterdam office back together. It was quite challenging," she said.

"I remember you telling us how filthy the apartment was when you first got there."

"Not only that, but the company had not paid taxes for years. And there hadn't been anyone aggressively collecting payments due, so they weren't coming. I had to fix all of that."

"Sounds like a lot of work."

"It was! It was a challenge. But now the whole operation is running so smoothly that my assistant has mastered my job in the few weeks I've been gone. But you're right about the apartment. I would miss it."

"What would you do here?" Rosalind asked.

"I'm not sure but Cinzia's ideas sound exciting."

"They do if she can pull it off. What about him?"

"I don't know. He seems more than perfect, a real prince of a man, and yet...?"

Rosalind felt the same hesitation. "Don't move too fast or presume too much," she counseled.

Their conversation was interrupted by a yowl coming from the living room. "How dare they even suggest!" Barry shouted. "Those!"

Christabel's head pushed out from between the two pillows she had sandwiched herself between, she having an aversion to leather and all things firm and slippery. Startled, she eyed Barry, released herself entirely from her pillows, stood up on the hard couch, and barked. Summer and Rosalind came out from the kitchen to see what was going on. Cinzia returned from wherever her meditation had taken her, and John pulled himself away from the computer screen.

"They've stopped my money!" Barry said reading from an email he had just received. *"You have been suspended until further notice upon the investigation of your alleged unethical and perhaps illegal conduct."*

"Why?" Summer asked.

"It says it all right here: *This committee has determined to take this action not only on the basis of the current allegations of artifact fraud but from previous rumors purporting smuggling and unsavory connections. We ignored the earlier rumors since no actual evidence was presented and your reputation until then had been spotless. But the current charges suggest a pattern of misconduct that cannot be ignored. We have no choice but to act now and to act decisively."*

"What does this mean?" Cinzia asked.

"It means I've been fired!"

"Without a hearing?" Rosalind said. "Don't cases of academic misconduct require a hearing before a penalty can be imposed?"

"That's the usual procedure. But they're arguing that previous unproven rumors are enough for them to fire me first and ask questions later. That just goes to show how fair and impartial such a hearing might be. Guilty until proven innocent!"

"Who are your unsavory connections," Rosalind asked. "Us?"

"I'm afraid they're referring to Hans Bueller."

"Who is this Hans Bueller, and what are these allegations of smuggling?" Etienne asked, well aware that Hans Bueller, whoever he is, would be making an appearance at his apartment that evening.

Barry rubbed his head not sure how to explain the matter of Bueller. "Well, they're right about Hans. I have to admit that he does have an unsavory reputation. In the past I made it my practice to remain cordial but distant. But last year that became impossible and a number of us," he said looking over at Rosalind, "unwittingly got tangled up in what could have been another one of his smuggling affairs. The irony is that our involvement helped prevent that from happening; and interestingly, Bueller had an epiphany, which is the only way I know how to describe it. He reformed. Now I find myself one of the few friends he has in the world. And since he has given up his illegal activity, he has no means of support. That's why it's so tragic that he was booted from the monastery."

"Surely you can explain all of that to your superiors," Etienne said.

"Well, that's hard to do without giving too much away. The only way I could convince them that Bueller did not steal said artifact is to produce it myself. I can't because I put it back and don't want anyone to know where it is. It was special, you see, and could have been put to dangerous use if it had fallen into the wrong hands, so it needed to go back to where it was buried."

"No one puts an artifact back," Etienne said. "They would never believe you."

"That's my problem. It has been my problem ever since the incident. Even some of my own colleagues suspect me. Even Rosa!"

"You have this one to show them," Etienne said.

"Yes, I do, and I must present it to them," he said with an eye on Cinzia. "They will determine who really owns her and where she goes."

"What are you saying?" Cinzia blurted out. "She must stay here as we planned."

"That would be the best choice if it were mine to make. But I won't be in a position to make it now that this action has been taken," Barry reluctantly concluded. "The monastery likely will claim her as their property. Egypt may claim her since that is where she was found, although it is abundantly clear that she is not Egyptian in origin. She appears to be European in origin, but since we cannot pinpoint an exact location, who knows how many claims might be made."

"Possession is nine-tenths of the law," Etienne said. "Let us be proactive. If we all agree she should stay here in France, I will attempt to set the wheels in motion. I have a friend, a curator at the Louvre. Let me see what I can arrange with him. If I can demonstrate that we have a real plan for a museum to house her in Paris, we can get the needed political support as long as we can put together the financial backing."

"That doesn't sound so easy to do," Barry said. "Such a plan will cost a fortune to implement even if we are modest in our endeavor. The real estate alone in a city like Paris is astronomically high."

"Yes, raising such a sizable amount of money will not be easy," Etienne said. "And we are working against time. I will get Grand-mère on the phone to see what she might be able to do to help. I am quite sure she will be supportive."

Etienne went into his bedroom to phone his grandmother in Cannes. Summer and Rosalind returned to the kitchen with Christabel at their heels, who by then had caught the scent of roasting chickens. John went back to his internet search, Cinzia unsuccessfully tried to resume her meditation, and Barry read more of his email.

He sorted through the junk email first, deleting as he went through the list while being careful not to delete replies to the emails Paul had sent. The boy had been quite busy, he noted, as he looked at the volume of replies he had elicited. His parents are going to have to get him his own email account and soon, he thought. He spotted an email from Rosa with a message line that read, "Paul, this is for your Uncle Barry." He immediately opened it.

Felix let me know what he intends to do in regard to pursuing an action against you. I tried to persuade him otherwise but to no avail. I have taken an action of my own in your support. I asked Dr. Espezi to write a report about his findings when he examined the statue you brought to me. I have forwarded his report along with my own assessment of the age of the statue to your institute. This will at least help dispel the charge that your statue is a fraud. As to charges related to how you came into possession of the object, that's another matter that I'm afraid I cannot help you with. If there is any more you can think of that I can do, please don't hesitate to ask. I enjoyed meeting your friend John. I'm afraid the circumstances were not good and wish you to apologize to him for me.

Best Regards, Rosa

Barry nearly wept. It was not just for the splendid argument that Rosa had made to the institute but for the knowledge that she was still his trusted friend. He thanked her for letting him know and asked her to thank Dr. Espezi. Just after he hit the send button Etienne walk out of his bedroom.

"Grand-mère was in an accident," he said in a near whisper.

"What! Is she all right?" Cinzia cried.

"You might say so, but the car was destroyed and her driver is gone."

Cinzia stared in shocked disbelief for a few moments before she asked her brother what had happened.

"It was very bad and the implications are worse," he said. "She says she remembers only that they were being followed after they left us in Saintes-Maries-de-la-Mer. Her driver sped up and apparently was run off the road into marshlands. She has little memory of that. She says that when she awoke, she saw her driver dead and called for emergency help."

"Were they the same two men who were at my house?" Cinzia asked.

"We do not know," Etienne said. "I suspect it was them. In which case their revenge knows no limits."

"Where is our grand-mère now?"

"The Carlton. She feels safe there and plans to stay on for some time. It is probably best since she has friends nearby. Certainly better than being alone in her apartment in Rome."

"Maybe I should have gone with her."

"Do not even think that Cinzia. You could have died too."

His sister turned pale.

"So, what do you think we ought to do?" Barry asked.

"Be vigilant," Etienne said.

Minutes later the phone rang. Etienne answered thinking it was his grandmother calling him back but instead it was Stuart. He and the notorious Hans Bueller had arrived at the airport and phoned while they waited to claim Bueller's luggage.

"You are just in time," the always polite host said. "The chickens are in the oven. Yes, it would be best if you take a taxi."

The dining room table was set for eight when the bell rang. The taxi driver carried two very large bags up the two flights of steps to Etienne's apartment followed by Stuart, who carried another very large bag. Hans hopped along behind them. Etienne gazed at the very elderly man and his luggage and knew right away to offer him his own bedroom. He directed the taxi driver and Stuart accordingly, tipped the driver and sent him on his way.

"That was good of you," Stuart said.

"I cannot put a man of his age on the couch."

"You can put me on the couch," Stuart offered.

"No, I will take the couch," Etienne laughed, the couch having become prime real estate in his crowded apartment. "You, John, and Barry are going to have to share a room together. Did your trip go as planned?"

"It was a cinch. The old guy is a little upset, that's all."

"You will have to introduce me."

Bueller was reclining in one of the leather chairs recounting his ordeal to Barry and the others when Stuart and Etienne reentered the living room. Cinzia had poured him a glass of wine, and he looked quite comfortable and not a day older than when Rosalind had last seen him nearly a year ago.

"He was quite angry with me. He had all of my z'ings packed and ready to go in less z'an two hours, but I was able to pack away z'e papyrus scrolls in another bag without his knowing. Z'ank heavens for Omar Shabaka and his faz'er and all of you," the grateful man said as he took another sip of wine.

"Did Father Paul tell you how he learned you had given me the statue?" Barry asked.

"He would tell me noz'ing. He had shown no interest in her when I found her. He knew noz'ing of her and was not interested in my questions. I did not z'ink he would have cared if he had known I sent her with you. She is very beautiful," he said as he gazed at the statue sitting on the mantelpiece.

"She is," Cinzia agree. "We named her you know. We are calling her Gitane Marie since she was taken far away from home."

"You were right Hans," Barry said. "Her origin is European. I learned that she is very, very old, older than you would have thought. Our strongest speculation is that she represents the Sophia, the original female goddess, a bird goddess of sorts."

"She is the Sophia!" Cinzia insisted and crossed her legs as she sat below her on the blue carpet.

"Z'e Sophia, ah!"

"Hans, I would like to introduce you to Etienne de Chevalier," Stuart interrupted. "He's letting us stay here."

Bueller tried to get up but sunk so deeply into the chair that he would require assistance.

"Do not raise yourself," Etienne said. He walked over to the chair and shook Bueller's hand.

"Z'ank you for your generosity. I have heard z'at your family is funding a museum for my treasure."

"My grandmother has many friends who might be interested in the project."

"Dinner!" Summer said, poking her head out from the kitchen. Can some of you come in here and help carry it out to the table?"

They feasted on homemade vegetable soup, roasted chicken and potatoes, followed by an assortment of cheeses and chocolate éclairs. Of course, there was plenty of wine. The conversation was lively, avoiding the darker aspects of their respective experiences. Dr. Bueller discussed his work in the monastery library and the books he had written that were under contract but as of yet unpublished. The others described the high points of their adventure as they sought to uncover the identity of the Gitane Marie. Etienne invited Hans and Stuart to join them for tomorrow's concert. When the evening was done, Etienne could hardly believe that the charming Hans Bueller was ever thought to be notorious by anyone.

"I told you," Barry said, now a bit tipsy. "He had an epiphany. You, like most people, don't think these ancient statues have intrinsic power. They do! I tell you, they do!" Before he retired into the bedroom, Barry fired up his computer and read Rosa's reply to his reply:

I was just thinking. If you still have the threatening emails Felix sent you, you should forward them to the institute as evidence. They may prove nothing about the statue itself, but they certainly should undermine his credibility, which could only serve to strengthen your case, since it is your credibility he is after.

Love, Rosa

"Brilliant!" Barry shouted and began searching through his old mail. They were all there, every email Felix had sent. "Phooey!" he grumbled after noting that none were signed. Then he remembered what John had said. Felix had all but admitted he had written them in the presence of Rosa. He knew she would have no compunctions about reporting what she had overheard. Rosa had saved his ass, he thought while drifting off into sleep, far more relaxed now than even the wine in Bourges had made him.

Chapter 55

Crescendo

Sunlight would fade soon as rain clouds rolled into Paris, but for now the light had disturbed Etienne's sleep. He arose from the couch, back aching and hospitality stretched. Today he would bring in cots if he could not find nearby lodging for his guests. He tiptoed past his sister who lay curled in a blanket near the mantle underneath the Gitane Marie. To his surprise it was already ten, and the concert at Saint Sulpice was scheduled to begin shortly after noon. He started the coffee and reached into his cabinet for tea and hot chocolate. Cinzia soon joined him. Together they brought cups and saucers, a pot of coffee, a pot of hot tea, hot milk, and chocolate out to the dining room table. There was plenty of bread left from the night before, and that with butter and cheese would have to suffice for a light breakfast. Etienne entered his own bedroom to awaken Hans Bueller who lay sound asleep in the big bed. Cinzia woke the women sharing a bed in one bedroom and woke the men in another.

"I just dreamed of that clamshell again," Summer said to Rosalind as they still lay in bed. "It's funny how the only place I've seen it is in my dreams."

"I don't remember it at all," Rosalind said. "You know what! I think we should go back to Mende, just you and me, go on our own little pilgrimage to see the Black Madonna and her clamshell while we are fully awake."

"That's a great idea!"

"Did I tell you that when I lit that candle to the Black Madonna of Mende, I asked her to tell me her story?" Rosalind said.

"Did she?"

"Thinking back to all that we've learned along the way, I think she did. I'm not much at saying prayers, but I think my prayer was answered. I should thank her."

"We will go then," Summer said.

The rain began, and not just a little drizzle, it poured. Although Saint Sulpice was only blocks away, Etienne called for two taxis to ferry his charges to their destination. Before they left, the building manager phoned to say he had located a vacant two bedroom apartment several doors down that the owner was willing to let on a temporary basis and might consider under a longer term lease. He had also located cots that will arrive within days. That settled, everything seemed to be coming together in a comfortable and sensible fashion, which for Etienne was a good omen in spite of the dark clouds that blanketed Paris in a drenching rain.

The concert had not yet started when they reached Saint Sulpice, which gave them a few minutes before they took their seats in a back row of chairs. The church was a beautiful Baroque edifice named after its patron, Saint Sulpicious, the seventh century bishop of Bourges, which gave John an opening to say that he found very little on the internet about the astronomical clock in the city with the same name and thought it a good subject for primary research.

"Here, I will show you another astronomical instrument," Etienne said. He led the group nearer to the altar. "If the sun were shining, light would come through that opening up there," he said as he pointed to a small hole in the stain glass window at the south transept of the church. "It would travel along this brass meridian line inlayed into the floor, and today light the obelisk over on that wall to mark the winter solstice."

"A sundial!" John said. "What did they use it for?"

"As a calendar to measure the days and assist eighteenth century Parisian astronomers in making their calculations of the Earth's orbit."

Barry's eyes followed that brass line as it crossed under the grand piano that had been placed in front of the altar rail, then slid underneath the rail before reaching its final destination, the obelisk. His eyes quickly drew back to the golden altar now graced with a large arrangement of Madonna lilies, which resurrected the dream that had marked the beginning of this journey. It was no simple recollection either, more like his mind had returned to those sleeping moments when he had followed the bird child through the eye of the Madonna before landing in a field of

335

white lilies whose full meaning he had not comprehended. Have I arrived, he wondered? Is this quest finally over?

"Barry!" Etienne said, startling him out of his reverie. "We should be seated."

"Oh, yes, sorry. I was lost in thought."

Soft lights from golden chandeliers cast a diffuse glow. The musician stood in front of the piano, his dark brown curls encircling a serious but handsome face. His expression shy, almost self-effacing, he took a bow before a polite audience, sat down, and began playing Liszt's "Hungarian Rhapsody." He played with amazing dexterity and verve, his fingers pulling sounds from the piano that were hitherto unknown by most of the applauding audience. Then he began to play a composition of his own that had the quality of Debussy.

Cinzia, who was seated next to Rosalind, was enraptured but not enough to loosen her grip on the bag she clutched tightly under her arm. Barry had concluded that it was risky to leave Gitane Marie alone in the apartment and agreed to allow Cinzia to carry her since it had become clear that the two of them could not be parted.

Rosalind's mind drifted with the music. She looked past the musician, past the altar to a statue of Madonna and child peering through an opening in the draperies that lined the back of the makeshift stage. The Madonna bore the look of rapture as well, she thought, comparing her expression to that of the starry eyed woman who sat next to her.

The mood shifted as the pianist began to play a piece by de Falla, "The Fire Dance." It was as deep and passionate as the other piece was lithe and spiritual. As Rosalind listened to his fingers capture all the dimension and chaos of a flame, no, a fire burning out of control, she recalled the horror of the night Cinzia's house was broken into and her own nightmare image of wolves carrying away the Black Madonna. She looked again at the Madonna partially concealed behind the drapes, and using her mind's eye placed beside her the image of the Black Madonna of Mende, pregnant with female potentiality. Surely all of these events were no simple coincidence, she thought.

The pianist built to the finale, evoking all the fire the composer had intended. The audience, unable to restrain itself, rose from their seats in wild applause and shouted bravos. Cinzia rose with them, let loose of her bag, and then screamed, "He took her!" she shouted over the din of the applause and bravos.

Rosalind turned and saw two men racing towards the church doors. Barry, who sat on Cinzia's other side, followed their motions with his eyes.

"They took her!" Cinzia cried, her face in agony.

The three of them rose, knocking chairs out of the way as they burst toward the men who had just discovered the doors to the main entrance of the church had been locked to keep passersby from interrupting the performance. The men scrambled towards the side entrance door that had been left slightly ajar, and the three pursuers followed.

"Thief! Thief!" Cinzia shouted as the two men darted toward the plaza just outside the church.

One of the men pulled out a pistol and fired wildly as his partner ran ahead of him clutching the stolen bag. Cautious, Cinzia and Rosalind slowed their pace while Barry braved the bullets and lurched ahead of them. Running at an impossible speed he made a mighty leap, wrapping his arms around the legs of the man with the bag, pulling him to the ground. The few onlookers who stood outside in the rain looked stunned but then applauded when Cinzia bounded forward and pounced on the thief Barry had tackled, grabbing the stolen bag like a tiger retrieving her cub. The armed man lunged towards Cinzia, but Summer, who looked to have appeared out of nowhere, bravely yanked his arm forcing him to drop the gun. He flung her to the ground, picked up his weapon, and turned it on her when Etienne grabbed him from the rear and wrestled him down onto a park bench. Summer immediately piled on top of him effectively pinning him down. They were face to face when she recognized the man who had torn her nightgown. In a fury she tugged his jacket arm hard, ripping it from the shoulder.

Sirens that only minutes earlier had sounded otherworldly now surrounded her. The crowd began to differentiate. She saw Hans Bueller standing next to Rosalind who held an umbrella over him. He bent down and smiling said, "You are a brave girl," as a photographer snapped her picture.

"Brave no, determined yes," she replied, amazed at her own recklessness.

"I knew you had it in you," Rosalind said.

Etienne bent down and spoke tenderly, "Stuart will take it from here. Let me get something over you." He put an umbrella over her head.

Milling about were members of the concert audience, who, finding a second entertainment stood and watched, among them the arts reviewer from the newspaper and his photographer. He had ordered his cameraman to take photos, lots and lots of photos of this very dramatic breaking story. He then approached Cinzia who stood next to her brother, hands and arms pressing the bag tightly to her chest, and inquired after the details of the incident. She let Etienne do the talking and only reluctantly allowed the Gitane Marie to be photographed.

"Theft At Saint Sulpice!" the newspaper headline would read. This lucky reporter had gotten first dibs on the account. He not only covered the details of the attempted theft but got pictures and the story of the sought after artifact, which were published in the next day's paper along with a few of his own embellishments and misunderstandings. "The statue was retrieved from a hidden dungeon in Egypt," he wrote, "and returned to her original home in France where she was carved from nanodiamonds twelve thousand years ago by our Magdalenian ancestors. The de Chevalier family intends to present her as a gift to the nation and to raise the money to house her in a museum in her honor and to honor all women."

The rain abated after the police arrived who secured the criminals and ordered participants and witnesses back into the church to be interviewed.

"He would not drop his gun so I came to her defense," Etienne said. "He was wildly firing shots."

"It was he who brought the first man down," another witnesses said pointing to Barry.

"They had stolen our statue while we were here listening to the concert," Cinzia explained.

"Let me begin at the beginning," Barry said, stepping forward to the officer in charge. "I brought this statue back from Egypt where it was given to me with the understanding that I should learn its identity. You see, I'm an archeologist." He showed the officer his identification.

"It was buried away in a cellar cave at z'e monastery where I lived.

338

No one z'ere cared anyz'ing about her," Hans Bueller interjected. The officer rolled his eyes.

Barry continued, nodding at Bueller. "Hans gave her to me. These men have been following me at least since I was in Rome, maybe before. In fact, some of their compatriots had me kidnapped there. I sent the statue on to France to protect it, and while it was at this woman's home," he said pointing to Cinzia, "three men broke-in and tried to take it. I presume these are two of the three men; the other died at the scene." He paused for a moment and then went on. "The police in Saintes-Maries-de-la-Mer have a full accounting of incident. I suggest that you contact them."

The officer raised his eyebrows. "Téléphone immédiatement," he ordered his underling and then turned back to Barry. "This is a very serious matter!"

"Yes, it is. I'm very aware of that."

"These are the two men who broke into my house," Cinzia said in support of Barry's claim. "The other tried to kill me!" she cried.

"Officer, this is my sister," Etienne said. "She is very upset. You can understand."

"And who are you?" the officer asked.

"I am Etienne de Chevalier. My family was about to make a gift of this valuable statue to France when these two men tried to steal it."

The officer, recognizing the name, suggested that Cinzia take a seat and rest herself.

"Cinzia, go sit by the piano," Etienne urged.

"How are you able to make a gift of the statue if it belongs to him," the officer pointed to Barry, "or to him" he pointed to Bueller?

"With our permission," Barry said. "We have been looking for a good home for her."

Hans looked at Barry quizzically, unaware of the decision to relinquish ownership but said nothing under the circumstances.

"Do you know who these thieves are?" the officer asked. "They refuse to offer any identification."

"No, I do not," Etienne replied, "and neither does Doctor Short."

"La police de Saintes-Maries-de-la-Mer est au téléphone," the junior officer interrupted.

"Excuse me," the senior officer said as he walked to the rear of the church to take his call in private.

***

Cinzia sat at the bench, pulled the Gitane Marie out of Barry's bag and placed her on the piano while the others sorted through the day's events. She leaned upon the piano, her chin resting upon the back of her hands and studied the intricacy of the statue's feather-like locks as much to distance herself from the commotion that surrounded her as anything.

A young man with a shy smile bowed slightly before her, as if it took all of his courage to approach her. "Qu'est ce qui se passe" he asked.

She recognized him immediately. It was the pianist who had finished his concert less than an hour before.

She smiled. "Your concert was very beautiful. I particularly enjoyed the piece that is your own composition."

He smiled awkwardly, nodding his head as if to say thank you.

"It reminded me of her," she said, looking at the statue that shimmered under the light of the church chandeliers.

"She is very beautiful too," he replied in English. "Very delicate. Who is she?"

"The Mary of Marys, the Sophia, Gitane Marie," Cinzia said and began to recount the whole story to the sensitive musician.

***

"I have spoken with the officer in charge at Saintes-Maries-de-la-Mer who concurs with your account. You may go, but I will need your contact information. Will you all be staying in Paris?"

"Yes, everyone is staying with me. You may phone me at any time," Etienne said.

"Say, have they learned the name of the deceased?" Barry asked.

"No, they have not," the officer replied. "Nor has anyone claimed the body. They hope I might be able help them if I can persuade these two to cooperate."

Good luck, Barry thought but did not dare to speak.

The witnesses were dismissed followed by the police officers, leaving behind a church subdued and quiet and full of the subtle smell of lilies that might have been overpowering if not for its size. Only they remained and the pianist who shared his bench with Cinzia as their whispered conversation shifted back and forth between the statue and his music. Rosalind drew nearer as he played a few notes and tried to explain, as best he could, as best anyone can, the relationship between the notes he was playing and the harmony of the music of the spheres. At Cinzia's request he played his own composition once again.

All conversation ceased. Cinzia raised herself from the bench and moved away from the piano as he played. No one was near him now except the Gitane Marie who was perched under soft church lights just above where his fingers danced upon the keys. John tapped Rosalind's shoulder and pointed to the tiny hole in the stain glass window in the south transept. Light poured in and followed the bronze meridian line across the church, under the piano, and on to the obelisk to mark the winter solstice, the end of earth's long, dark day. Gitane Marie's copper crown caught its intensity and was emblazoned in sun as she, the pianist and his song for a few moments combined into something remarkable.

Chapter 56

Wax and Wane

Evening wore into the wee hours. The eight had gathered around Etienne's fireplace talking over the day's events while they drank champagne and nibbled on jambon-beurre, last night's cheese, and chocolate éclairs.

"I myself can hardly believe our good fortune," Etienne repeated for the second time. "A photographer! A reporter! Could we have asked for better publicity and with absolutely no effort on my part?"

"If you ask me those guys were just asking for it trying to pull off a heist in a public place in the middle of the day," Stuart said. "They risked it all and they failed."

"You can say that now after the fact, but we almost lost her," Cinzia grieved. "The publicity was hardly worth the fear I endured."

"But we didn't lose her," Barry said. "You girls went right after them. You showed amazing courage."

"It would have been a tragedy had z'eir plan worked," Bueller admitted. "After all z'e efforts we have made."

"It was a fantastic stroke of luck that they did what they did where they did it," Etienne said. "I am looking forward to tomorrow's papers."

"I'm not so sure it was our good luck or their poor planning," Rosalind said. "It almost worked out too well for that."

"What do you mean?" John asked. "It definitely was our good fortune and their bad luck."

"That's true," Rosalind said. "Heck, I'm not sure what I'm talking about."

"I am!" Summer said. "I think something more was at work here. It was more than our good luck." She looked up at Gitane Marie who sat on the mantle. "Maybe it was her good luck more than ours."

"Are you suggesting something supernatural?" Barry said.

"Maybe, I don't know. Rosalind and I have this idea that we should go back to Mende to visit the Black Madonna again. I think we should."

"I can drive you there," Etienne said eagerly.

"Let Summer speak for herself," Rosalind said. "But my idea is that Summer and I should go on our own little pilgrimage alone this time."

"That's my understanding too," Summer said. "It's for Rosalind and me to do."

Rosalind looked over at John. "I hope you don't mind."

"Not at all. I might go back to Bourges while you're gone. I'd like to spend the little time I have left in France looking over that astronomical clock. I can get better photos of its working parts."

"Perhaps I can drive John to Bourges," Etienne said. "Unless he minds my company too?"

"I don't mind your company," Summer said. "But this is a project for two sisters."

This last bit of conversation cooled the night off. They all went to bed shortly thereafter.

Who knows when the phone started ringing. It may have been hours earlier for all Etienne knew because his first inkling came in an incoherent late morning dream that incorporated the incessant sound with all kinds of disconnected images: the police whistle of a traffic cop in Rome, the tea kettle that threatened to burn up on his cooktop, a siren announcing some undisclosed danger, until eventually the ringing stopped. That is when he awoke and realized he had been asleep on his own couch and everything was fine. The telephone rang again, and this time he answered it.

The story had hit the morning papers, thrusting him and the others onto a stage they were unused to. "Where is the location of origin of your statue?" one reporter asked. "What are nanodiamonds?" asked another. "What exactly is the esoteric significance of this Gitane Marie?" the editor of a spiritualist journal queried. "Who is that woman photographed sitting on top of the thief?" asked a gossip columnist. The last question was easy enough to answer. As to all the rest, well, Etienne knew he was going to need help.

They gathered for breakfast at a nearby cafe with several newspapers spread across the table. Once the pastry, coffee, tea, and hot chocolate were served, Etienne tried to formulate a plan to organize a response.

He asked Barry and Cinzia to tackle the live television and radio shows that he was sure would request interviews. Cinzia's answer was no, absolutely not. She agreed that she would be happy to work with Barry on the book they had talked about but that she would never be comfortable in front of an audience answering questions on live TV or radio. They discussed the problem for some time and concluded that Barry could handle the more scientific questions; others of them could describe their experiences; but unless Cinzia was willing to do it, no one among them was prepared to try to address the deeper, more philosophical questions.

"Grand-mère!" Cinzia blurted out.

"Yes! She would be perfect," Etienne said. "I will phone her. I suspect she will be delighted to help in this capacity."

The conversation moved on to the more practical matter of the work involved in putting together the museum they envisioned. Cinzia was front and center here. She wished to be curator, she said. Etienne offered that he and his grandmother would be very well equipped to raise the needed funds particularly now that the dramatic story of the rescue of Gitane Marie had splashed across headlines all over France. But if he put in his effort there, who would go about the business of securing the exhibits necessary to tell the whole story that Cinzia wants to tell? He looked at Summer.

"Well, maybe," she said. "I would have to give my employer fair notice, and they might need me to stay on for a time."

"That assistant of yours—What's his name, Jos?—sounded like he had things under control the last time you spoke with him," Etienne said. "I can set you up in an apartment near me that you can share with Cinzia."

"I would like that," Cinzia said. "We were roommates in Bourges. We could be roommates here."

"Well, the project does sound inspiring," Summer said.

"Maybe I can help Summer deal with any transition she would have to make," Rosalind said.

"I've got to get back soon," John said. "I've got a project I'm due to begin."

"My situation is a little more complicated," Barry said. "I'm going to have to return to Chicago and try to straighten out those matters that threaten to sink my career. If all goes well, I don't think it will take too long. When I get back Cinzia and I can start on the book we've been talking about. If Summer takes up the task of trying to secure more exhibits, I can provide her invaluable expertise. Sometimes it takes a little nudge, a little personal touch to bring them around," he said with a wink. "That's my forté."

Unlike the rest, Stuart could not wait to go home. He had been thinking about Natalie for days now. She had not phoned him, and he was afraid to phone her and ask why. She seemed uninterested in what he was doing once she learned that Barry was out of danger. He feared it was only Barry she is worried about. He would have to see her in person to find out. As unmoved as he had hoped he would remain by all the "mumbo jumbo," as he had called it, he acknowledged that this experience had caused him to see Natalie and himself in a new light. She was the most perfect woman he had ever known, and he wanted to tell her so.

Hans Bueller did not talk about what he would do because he knew he was entirely dependent on the others. The question for him was what would they do with him, which was a question no one could immediately answer.

Chapter 57

Through the Eye of the Black Madonna

D iana's moon was full on the day the women boarded the train that would take them from Paris to Mende. If one had the imagination to see it, one could detect Diana's slender silhouette with her bow etched into the moon's bright surface.

Rosalind and Summer were oblivious to this sight however since neither had ever taken notice of Diana, who had been the goddess for other women in a different time. Yet Diana had been powerful enough that centuries later her story and the stories of the women who had gathered under her protective mantle would still be told in the casual setting of the Apuleius Restaurant that sits above the ruins of Diana's temple in the Aventino district of Rome.

Uppermost in their minds was the Gitane Marie, the goddess they had witnessed come into the light. It was her protection they sought along with whatever else the Black Madonna had to offer, that very same Vierge Noire they believed had made their quest possible. They ruminated over their experiences on their seven-hour train trip.

"I told you that when we were there before I lit a candle and made a prayer that she would tell me her story," Rosalind said. "I think she did, but I didn't find out what I would have expected to learn. In fact, I really didn't expect to learn anything because I didn't expect my prayer to work. I just thought I would give it a try. But I had thought that if I were going to learn something, it would be about how she was brought back from Palestine by a crusading knight or about how she was found under a tree in the forest."

"Why did I dream about the clamshell that I couldn't even recall seeing?" Summer said. "Why instead didn't I dream about the fact that she's pregnant or something else?"

Rosalind had no answer. She recalled that she had dreamed of the Black Madonna being carried off by the Beast of Gévaudan. Hardly symbolic, she thought. Just a horrific combination of images formed after their conversation with Anglican priest, James Stroud. Then she thought again. It must have been a warning. The clamshell seemed another matter since she could not recall having seen it either.

"What did Brother Thomas tell us about it when you asked? It seems like that conversation happened months ago."

"I still remember," Summer said. "He said they use them at pilgrimage sites. He said sometimes they are used for holy water and rituals of purification, but he said something more when we got to talking. I know! You brought up Botticelli's "The Birth of Venus" because it too has a large scallop shell that Venus floats upon. Do you remember that?"

"Not really, but it sounds like something I would bring up."

"And Barry made the connection between water and life. Brother Thomas thought the painting had more to do with life and beauty than rituals of purification. Now I remember what I thought: Out of the ocean and the sky, it all sort of hatched."

"Hatched! Don't you see? You knew of the Bird Goddess before we knew anything about the Bird Goddess," Rosalind said.

"Not really. It was more an intuition than knowledge, but yes, I intuited right. Out of the ocean and the sky could be taken to explain why Gitane Marie's markings look both like feathers and scales. They are both!"

"That's what your dream was trying to tell you. As I think back, the Black Madonna of Mende was not the only Black Madonna to speak. My most profound insight came to me at the shrine of La Moreneta at Montserrat and was brought into fruition in Barcelona. And that was not a dream!"

"You seemed completely out of it after we got there, like you had drifted off somewhere else," Summer noted.

"I was lost in thought. It was like Gaudi's art had carried La Moreneta's spirit into the city just as the shapes that he used in his architecture brought the landscape surrounding Montserrat there. Two became one. Her spirit joined with his art to become free of the confining religiosity that had kept her isolated on a small stage in the back of the church. I felt it so strongly both in Montserrat and

Barcelona."

"Hmm. Art, beauty, life, freedom," Summer said.

"And vision!" Rosalind added.

"Vision!" Summer repeated. "That reminds me of the story the gypsies tell about Saint Sarah and her crystal ball. She could see Mary Magdalene and her entourage about to drown at sea and sent rescuers to save them."

"Compassion too," Rosalind said.

"Compassion too," Summer agreed. "You told me when we visited the Garden of Vestal Virgins that on one of your previous visits they healed your feet."

"Well, it seemed like that. I've never before or since had blisters disappear overnight."

"I wonder how ancient Roman women perceived those virgins?" Summer asked.

"As powerful," Rosalind said. "Back then it was the spiritual seat of power with Minerva in its center. She and the living virgins protected Rome."

"Not only compassion but power," Summer said. "What about Prudence and the Sophia?"

"Everything! The beginning of the world!"

"That would be Gitane Marie's poem." Summer began to recite:

> "She looks upon herself who is not there.
> But sees instead before her all the world.
> Whatever was, whatever will be is in her care.
> For she is the maker of the world.
> Within her face all faces, all time, the cosmic burst of creation.
> She holds the mirror of the world."

Rosalind recalled what she had finally understood about Gaudi. Art is in the making not the having, which is why he was happy enough that the construction of the Basilica Sagrada Família could go on for centuries. "Maybe all this fragmentation, all these goddesses haven't been such a bad thing?" she said.

"They certainly have made it possible for women throughout time to

348

cast a new light on themselves," Summer agreed.

"Hmm," Rosalind said. "I think if I should tell Gitane Marie's story, first I would imagine that it's archetypal, a sort of cosmic script repeated again and again but adapted for the times of each enactment. Repeated, adapted, searching for a new context, a new ending that could break the cycle that binds us and buries our possibilities like so much dust in a box in a cellar with our names scratched out."

When their train finally arrived, they skipped the late lunch they had planned, so impatient they had become for their reunion that was about to take place at the Cathédrale Notre-Dame-et-Saint-Privat. As they approached the lady whom they had come to see, they were struck by the radiance of the golden scalloped shell above her.

"How could I have ever missed that?" Summer asked.

"You didn't, or it wouldn't have come into your dreams," Rosalind said.

A basket of white lilies sat next to the altar. Rosalind lit a candle and prayed to the Black Madonna of Mende that Gitane Marie's story should become a potent force in the world. They meditated a few minutes longer and suddenly in what seemed a brilliant flash, the door of the church swung open letting in sunlight along with a bird who flew around the church a few times before it perched just above the Black Madonna's golden clamshell and began to warble. As best they could, the two women joined it in song.

If the moon had been high in the sky that evening when they went back to the station to catch their return train, Summer and Rosalind no doubt would have seen Diana's slender silhouette etched on its surface, waiting there as she always has for centuries.

Epilogue

B arry was relieved to learn that thanks to Dr. Rosa Palazio the committee had dismissed all charges against him and apologized for ever having thought the worst. Most of his colleagues congratulated him on the smashing success he had become in Paris. There was one glitch however. The funding for his work had been permanently suspended. Not because of anything he did or was supposed to have done, they said, but because money was scarce and his research had not resulted in much. He had to acknowledge they were right and avoided mentioning that the reasons for his middling success had as much to do with his being distracted by another inquiry as anything else. In fact, they had funded his quest to learn the identity of the Gitane Marie without their permission or knowledge. He realized they had probably figured this out, but because her discovery proved to be such a success decided not to mention it. Embarrassed, he gracefully went about the business of winding up his affairs.

He had determined to sell his house. As romantic as it was to own an acre of former Indian land between the Scioto and Olentangy rivers in Ohio, it was totally impractical. For one thing, he was almost never there. For another, he did not know when or if he would again be traveling back and forth from Chicago to Meadowcroft Rockshelter. He determined that if the time came again, he would be better off renting an apartment, a living arrangement that had satisfied him for most of his life.

On the matter of Paul, well, that required a talk with his parents. Understanding that parents sometimes don't realize how remarkable their own children are, he met them for dinner at the local Mexican haunt to explain what their son had been doing as a way to tell them just how precocious a boy he is. He told them about Paul's use of his internet account. They apologized and said he would be disciplined.

"No, no! An apology is unnecessary. Discipline is hardly in order. He's a brilliant child and needs a computer with his own account." They didn't see it that way and wanted to ground him for a month.

Barry may not have understood the pressures parents face in raising children, but he did know something about general human psychology. "Until you get him one, Paul is free to continue to use my computer and my account," he then declared. His generous offer sent them immediately computer shopping. Paul had a computer with his own account within the week.

Barry did not stay in Ohio long, but while there he wrote a very long letter to Omar Shabaka and his father thanking them for all of their help and recounting in detail what he had learned. He invited them to Paris to see the museum once it opens. He had several dinners with Madeleine and both agreed that they should remain good friends, but Madeleine was adamant that he could expect nothing more from her. She told him he needed to come to terms with the fact that he was unsuited to marriage or to anything else but his work. He knew she was probably right but wondered what he should do in those moments when he is overcome with loneliness. "Just go to work," she said. "That will take care of it."

He hired a realtor and flew to Washington D.C. before returning to Europe. It was there that he met Stuart for dinner under the gaslights at the Old Ebbitt Grill. Stuart had arrived before Barry and was, as they say, crying in his beer. His intuition about Natalie had been correct although he presented the situation as if he had been completely surprised when he learned she had a new boyfriend. Not a casual boyfriend who informally met her for dinner on Friday nights but a real boyfriend. Natalie had not been at all secretive about it. She had arranged for Stuart to meet him at this very same restaurant where he and Barry were now eating clams and crab cakes.

"This had been our place," Stuart said fidgeting around in the velvet booth. "She had no difficulty turning it into their place."

"Natalie is not an insensitive woman," Barry said. "If she thought she would upset you, I'm sure she would have arranged the meeting elsewhere. Tell me about him. What's he like?"

Stuart took another slow drink of his beer. "He's everything I'm not. He is around forty, divorced, and makes a hell of a lot of money by the look of his suit and BMW. I can't even say that the fact that he is divorced is a mark against him. A friend of mine knows his former wife

351

and says she is one of those fickle types. It looks like she traded in a steady guy for a swinger who works in the same law firm."

"So he's a lawyer?"

"Yep, and with a darn good law firm. It's got one of those long names, and his is one of them."

"That makes him a partner," Barry said, realizing now that Stuart's assessment of his income was probably accurate.

"Natalie met him at work. He was representing the other side in a contract dispute his client was having with the government. She said her rapport with lawyers she is up against is usually pretty bad, but not so this time. They hit it off."

"Did the government lose the case?"

"I believe they did."

"That probably helped. So, what are you going to do about it?"

"What do I do about it?" Stuart paused, taking a hard look at his empty beer glass. "I don't know. I couldn't wait to get home and see her."

"Did you tell her?"

"No, how could I? The funny thing, I had been thinking that Natalie is perfect in every way but one, and that was the fact that she would put up with me. So now she's perfect in every way."

"Well, you know what they say about a shopper who can't make up his mind."

"Yeah, yeah, yeah. She was perfectly justified. I don't think she even thought I would care."

"You'd better tell her," Barry said.

"Why?" Stuart asked, convinced that it would make very little difference and only create humiliation for him and awkwardness for her.

"Because that's your only hope."

Dinner over, Barry had a plane to catch to Paris. He wished Stuart good luck and invited him to visit anytime.

***

Money poured in after a very charming and dignified Madame Conti made several television appearances along with the charming if less dignified Barry Short. A large building had been located at a suitable site about halfway between the Musée de Cluny and L'Université de la Sorbonne. And since the Gitane Marie had been made a gift to France, France decided to make a gift of the museum building where she would be housed. It was fortunate that they had because the cost of the building along with the cost to retrofit it with high tech climate and security systems was well beyond what anyone had imagined and far exceeded what even Etienne and his grandmother could raise. That money would be used instead to begin to establish the collection. Summer learned that establishing the collection was going to be far more expensive and take far longer than anyone had imagined. Not many churches were interested in giving up their very rare and sacred Black Madonnas. It became clear that if the museum were to open anytime soon, it would have to rely on lent items.

Difficulty is often the impetus to new ideas. As letters came back from museums and churches, some offering to make the loans while most declining, Summer had another idea. Although the museum was to house works of antiquity, there was no reason that it could not employ new technology. In addition to the exhibits on the main floor, the lower level should be devoted to educational and technology projects. It would have a film screening theatre. It would have a room of interactive terminals that would allow patrons to select an area of interest and delve into it more deeply. It would have photo exhibits of those items that, realistically, the museum could not hope to acquire or display. It would have a lounge available for lectures and discussions.

Invigorated by her ideas, they went about the work of making them a reality. Hans Bueller, having become interested in the proper education of children, designed an interactive activity for young patrons that guided them through the wonders of archeological discovery. Cinzia and Summer together were to make a film marking the life and work of Marija Gimbutas. At Summer's urging the Anglican priest, James Stroud, agreed to put together a photo exhibit of the Black Madonnas of Europe along with narratives from some of the many pilgrims who come to see them. Stroud wrote an amazing essay linking the Black Madonna and Gitane Marie as material manifestations of the Sophia and the true feminine. Gitane Marie, he argued, is the Sophia's earthly embodiment.

Both had been notoriously hidden away and obscured from our understanding. In spite of that suppression, the Black Madonnas, who are venerated across Europe and elsewhere, kept the flame of her spirit alive and in his view, hidden in plain sight.

The most popular exhibit, second only to Gitane Marie herself, was designed and coordinated by Barry. He documented their quest for discovery in photos, drawings, and narratives, beginning with a photo provided by Omar Shabaka of the monastery where the Gitane Marie was found. He outlined the process that led to discovering her identity, highlighting Brother Thomas' invaluable clue, and included a photo of Prudence along with a proper interpretation of her symbology as written by Madame Conti. Yvette agreed to write a short history of what is known about Magdalenian culture. Using artistic renderings, Barry compared the markings found on Gitane Marie with the runic symbols in the Magdalenian caves and explained the insights that arose from the comparisons. He recounted Dr. Espezi's revelation that the stone the statue was carved from is full of nanodiamonds and commissioned an artist's rendering of the comet strike that created them. The display included a rare photo of Brother Thomas that James Stroud was able to supply along with a photo of Narbonne Cathedral's acoustic chamber and an explanation of how it works. Pictures of them all of were exhibited as well, even Stuart's photo, with descriptions of the contributions each made to the unearthing of the true feminine that for so long had been buried along with the statue in a remote desert in Egypt. What was missing from the account, besides details of how Barry and Stuart spirited her back to Europe, was the kidnapping, murder, and mayhem brought on by the secret cult intent on burying her once again.

Barry had decided not to mention it for two reasons. First, he thought it best to let sleeping dogs lie; and second, he did not know what group the assailants belonged to. He did not even know their names. Eventually the deceased was buried in a potter's field outside Saintes-Maries-de-la-Mer since without an address or identity his body could not be returned to Rome. His partners refused to deny their guilt or cooperate with French authorities in any way and were serving time in a French prison. Barry feared that if he published an account of their deeds without being able to identify them, all kinds of unwarranted

354

conspiracy theories would emerge. Besides, threats against him and her had ceased for a time; and although Stuart was convinced that this could be the lull before a greater storm, Barry hoped otherwise. If the mysterious cult gave him any trouble again, he was prepared to reveal the whole story but not until then.

Madame Conti's contribution was fascinating. After having many a lively discussion with Hans Bueller who had become her bosom companion, she suggested that the goal of the museum should be not only to inform but also to stretch the imagination. She prepared an interactive dialog that would ask her audiences to envision what the world would be like if women had been cast in the business of creation as Sophia and not Eve. "Not only would men and women think very differently about themselves and each other," she argued, "the whole conflict between us might have been avoided. Our talent for art, healing, insight, and prophetic wisdom would not have been stifled and turned on us as something to be feared. Alas, our failure to know ourselves for who we really are condemned us all to lives as half a man," she opined, using that odd expression Cinzia had once used. With great passion and conviction she said, "We must start anew!"

Summer asked her later what she meant by half a man instead of half a woman or half a human. Madame Conti looked shocked that she had not understood. "My dear," she said, "our lack of understanding of the true female character made it impossible for us to be even half a woman let alone blossom into our fullness. And without the true feminine, it is impossible for any of us to be fully human or for men to be fully men. That is all that I meant."

"Oh, that's all!" Summer replied as she considered the enormous ramifications of what Madame Conti had just said.

***

Twelve months from the day of the attempted theft and arrest at Saint Sulpice, the bare bones of Le Musée de la Femme de la Mythologie opened to great fanfare. The event drew praise and headlines in newspapers from France to New York: "L'âme des Femmes Révélée," "Le Mystère Enfin Dévoilé," "Exhibit Puts Women at the Heart of the

Matter."

Etienne stood with his grandmother at the unveiling, his eyes riveted onto Summer who grew more beautiful to him with each day.

Cinzia stood by the piano and watched as the passionate young pianist played his own composition. She watched his fingers race across the keyboard from the low deep tones at one end to the soft high notes at the other, his fingers artfully controlling the pressure he applied to each key. He pressed hard against the low keys, extracting all of their weight then lithely struck the high keys producing achingly pure sounds. The effect was the opposite of what one would expect. The pure notes were not lost or drowned out. Ironically, the very drama of the piece arose through the delicate high notes made more exquisite by the contrast.

She drew back next to a vase of Madonna lilies in the rear of the large rotunda room, joining Barry and the museum patrons who stood watching and listening as the winter solstice sun poured down through the oculus high above the pianist and the Gitane Marie, who stood unveiled on a pedestal in the center of the large marble gallery, her eyes glistening, her feather-like hair seeming to lift her in flight, her copper crown batting about the light in utter joy.

Shadows filled the room when fast moving clouds passed overhead. It was in one of those shadowy moments that Rosalind detected images taking shape on the rotunda's marble walls. Was she hallucinating, she wondered? She blinked her eyes twice, then three times. Instead of disappearing like some half imagined mirage, the scene grew decidedly more distinct. She made out horns, course hair that jutted out around a head and a neck, and mysterious runes that appeared within the curves of the bison's body. Taken aback, she grabbed Summer's hand, seeking confirmation.

"I don't see anything," Summer whispered.

"Try harder!"

Summer stared forcefully then squinted her eyes as lines and shapes began to emerge out of the brightness that flashed out through the oculus against the rotunda walls. "The animals are with us!" she cried excitedly.

For one long moment the whole circle of the room became a pageant of bison, deer, horses, and the ibex standing peacefully together as if they too had come to celebrate.

Rosalind looked about for a hidden projector of some kind. There was none; nor did the others in the room seem to have noticed the spectacle that had miraculously appeared.

"That must be how she does it," Rosalind whispered into Summer's ear, realizing she and her sister were the only two in the room to bear witness.

"This is creation," Rosalind whispered.

"Out of light and shadow," Summer said. "Is this how the future happens?"

Author Biography

Linda Oxley Milligan was born in Grandview Heights, in Columbus, Ohio. She is the granddaughter of Italian immigrants whose successful restaurant made the American dream very real for themselves, their children and grandchildren. Her real Columbus home however became The Ohio State University where she earned three degrees culminating in a Ph.D. in English and American Literature with a specialty in folklore. For many years she has taught a variety of composition courses and folklore as an adjunct professor in the English department. Linda is married to John and has a wonderful daughter Stephanie. All three have a passion for travel and the exploration of cultures, which mixed with a love of adventure, serves as the inspiration for her writing.

Made in the USA
San Bernardino, CA
25 October 2018